His passion is forbidden.

His love is eternal . . .

The sway of her hair . . .

. . . the graceful curve of her spine and firm set of her shoulders, the inquisitive lean of her head as she looked about . . . so familiar. Painfully familiar.

His shoulder blade itched as his tattoo grew warm. *Turn, turn toward the camera.*

Her head moved slightly, tilted as if she might have heard him. *Turn, turn to me.* A sizzling sensation started on the tail of his tattoo, then burned a path along the dragon's body, over his shoulder to his chest, till it erupted in the fiery breath etched in crimson over his heart.

A strange way to have heartburn, he thought, gritting his teeth against the surprising burst of pain. Why was the tattoo tormenting him now, when it had been quiet since 1746?

By Kerrelyn Sparks

THE VAMPIRE WITH THE DRAGON TATTOO
WILD ABOUT YOU
WANTED: UNDEAD OR ALIVE
SEXIEST VAMPIRE ALIVE
VAMPIRE MINE
EAT PREY LOVE
THE VAMPIRE AND THE VIRGIN
FORBIDDEN NIGHTS WITH A VAMPIRE
SECRET LIFE OF A VAMPIRE
ALL I WANT FOR CHRISTMAS IS A VAMPIRE
THE UNDEAD NEXT DOOR
BE STILL MY VAMPIRE HEART
VAMPS AND THE CITY
HOW TO MARRY A MILLIONAIRE VAMPIRE

Also Available
LESS THAN A GENTLEMAN
THE FORBIDDEN LADY

KERRELYN SPARKS

THE VAMPIRE WITH THE DRAGON TATTOO

AVON

An Imprint of HarperCollinsPublishers

AVON BOOKS
An Imprint of HarperCollins*Publishers*
10 East 53rd Street
New York, New York 10022-5299

Copyright © 2013 by Kerrelyn Sparks
ISBN 978-0-06-210773-2
www.avonromance.com

First Avon Books mass market printing: September 2013

Avon Trademark Reg. U.S. Pat. Off. and in Other Countries, Marca Registrada, Hecho en U.S.A.
HarperCollins® is a registered trademark of HarperCollins Publishers.

Printed in the U.S.A.

10 9 8 7 6 5 4 3 2 1

To the angels,
both heavenly and worldly,
who watch over us.

Acknowledgments

I can't believe this is book fourteen of the Love at Stake series! I would have never dreamed back in 2005, when I was first getting to know Roman Draganesti, that the series would last this long. There are numerous people to thank. First, my husband and children for their love and encouragement. Then, my critique partners, MJ, Sandy, and Vicky. Each book represents such a long journey, and it helps immensely to know I'm not alone on that road as I plod steadily into the unknown.

On the business side, I am blessed by the fabulous support of my agent, Michelle Grajkowski; my editor, Erika Tsang; and her assistant, Chelsey. My thanks to all the professionals at HarperCollins, especially Pam, Caroline, and Jessie from the Publicity Department, and Tom from the Art Department, who has outdone himself with this latest cover.

My personal thanks to Susan Chao, who taught me how to say, "Gun bei!" My thanks also to hairstylist Wilson at the Etheria Salon and Spa in Houston, who was the inspiration for the vampire stylist at the Digital Vampire Network.

And finally, my heartfelt gratitude to all the readers and booksellers who have helped the Love at Stake series continue for fourteen books. Thank you for giving my vamps and shifters such long and happy lives!

THE
VAMPIRE
WITH THE
DRAGON TATTOO

Chapter One

*D*ougal Kincaid was not in a partying mood.

As he entered the ballroom at Romatech Industries, his stomach churned. Too many people. The jarring noise of all their voices grated on his ears, and he dreaded the thought of participating in meaningless chatter. For centuries, he'd avoided these situations by playing the pipes, but those days were gone. That left him with one option for surviving the night.

Blissky.

Hopefully the mixture of synthetic blood and whisky would deaden his undead senses before he was confronted with the same questions he'd been hearing for the past four years. *How's your new prosthesis? Can you still wield a sword? Will you be able to play the pipes again?*

He had a better question: how fast could he get drunk? He headed for the refreshment tables.

They mean well, he reminded himself. It was the only way they knew how to show their concern. It was better than having no one who cared. But damn, he'd lost a hand, not his pride. A man was more than his hands. *More than his music?* His chest clenched with the familiar pang of grief. Without music, his soul felt half empty. And the half that remained was a sad melody of regret.

The first refreshment table was covered with mortal snack food. He kept walking.

"Hey, man, what's up?" Phineas slapped him on the back. "Say hello to my little dudette."

Dougal glanced at the bairn Phineas was holding. Phin's wife, Brynley, had given birth to twins six months ago. This had to be the girl, judging by her frilly pink dress.

"Hello." Dougal became aware of an awkward pause. Was he supposed to say more? He racked his brain, trying to remember the little girl's name. Gwyneth, that was it. And Benjamin was the boy. For short, they were called Gwyn and Ben, which rhymed with their parents' nicknames, Phin and Bryn.

His stomach churned. "Hello, Gwyn."

The little girl squealed so loud that Dougal winced.

"She likes you." Phineas beamed proudly at her. "Isn't she beautiful?"

"Yes." After a pause, Dougal suspected more flattery was in order. "Nice . . . dress."

"Yeah, her mom loves shopping for her." Phineas smiled at him. "So, dude, how's your hand?"

He gritted his teeth. "Which one?"

Phineas laughed. "Good one, bro. Well, I gotta go see how Bryn's doing. Ben just had a bomb go off in his diaper."

Thanks for sharing. Dougal strode toward the next refreshment table. It was surrounded by mortals and shifters, mostly women and children, gawking at the giant five-tier cake. Where the hell was the Blissky?

"Hey, Dougal. Have ye met my Tara Jean?"

It was Ian MacPhie, carrying another little girl. This time Dougal knew what to say. "She's beautiful. Nice dress."

"Thanks." Ian regarded him sadly. "I remember how ye played the pipes at my bachelor party. I really miss that."

Dougal winced inwardly. *They mean well.*

"How's the fancy new hand treating you?" Ian asked.

Here we go again. "Well, since ye asked, it is made of pure titanium alloy, strong enough for spacecraft and the deepest-diving submarines. In three seconds, I could pierce yer chest cavity and rip yer bleedin' heart out."

Ian's eyes widened. "Och, man. Get a grip."

"That's about all I can do." Dougal lifted his right hand, and, using his vampire mind control, he curled the fingers into a tight fist. The movement was smooth but caused a series of clicking sounds. The superstrong grip was great for wielding a sword, but the lack of manual dexterity made it very difficult to play the pipes. In other words, he was now more suited for killing than making music.

He swallowed down his frustration. "Have ye seen the Blissky?"

Ian snorted. "This is a birthday party for a bunch of bairns. There is no Blissky."

No Blissky?

"Tara turned one last month in September," Ian continued. "Austin's little girl will be one in a few days and Robby's boy in November. With three birthdays so close together, we thought we should have a big party. I'm glad ye could make it."

As if he'd had any choice. The Echarpe family had come, and as their bodyguard, Dougal had accompanied them. "There has to be Blissky here somewhere. The damned stuff is manufactured here."

Ian shook his head. "Try to relax and enjoy the party."

"Is there any Bleer?"

Ian arched a brow. "What ye need is a good woman."

I had one. And lost her. "I need a drink." Dougal wandered toward the last refreshment table. How much had he lost over the centuries? His first and only love. His freedom. His family. His mortality. His hand. His music. Did so much loss make him a loser?

He instantly shoved that thought aside. He would never have lasted this long if he had succumbed to that sort of negativity. He was a survivor. He kept fighting no matter what.

I will find you. No matter what. If it takes a thousand years, I will find you.

The old promise reverberated inside his skull, reminding him that he'd failed the one person who had meant the most to him. His gaze wandered over the ballroom, taking note of all the happily married couples. They were chatting, laughing, admiring their babies.

His heart clenched in his chest. The loss he'd suffered almost three hundred years ago struck him anew, as if it had happened a few moments ago.

He wrenched a bottle of Bubbly Blood out of an ice

bucket and poured the mixture of synthetic blood and champagne into a flute glass.

"For those special vampire occasions," he muttered, then guzzled down half the glass.

Someone tapped on his arm. It was Bethany, the eldest of the Echarpe children. Jean-Luc had adopted her a few years back when Heather had been pregnant with the twins.

The nine-year-old girl gave him a shy, embarrassed look. "I forgot where the restroom is. Can you show me?"

He glanced around, searching for Heather. "Yer mum canna take you?"

"She's busy with the twins, and Papa's in an important meeting with Uncle Angus and Roman."

Dougal tilted up his glass, finishing off the contents. No one had told him about an important meeting.

"Dougal!" Bethany's eyes grew desperate. "I need to go!"

"I'll take you." He grabbed the bottle of Bubbly Blood. "This way."

He led her out the double doors into the foyer of Romatech, then headed down the west hallway. Halfway to the MacKay security office, they reached the restrooms. Bethany went inside, while he leaned against the wall, drinking Bubbly Blood and wondering what was going on. Angus MacKay, head of MacKay Security and Investigation, sent a monthly report to all his employees to keep them informed, but there had been no mention of a meeting tonight.

According to the reports, after the deaths of Malcontent leaders Casimir and Corky, most of their followers had fled back to Russia and Eastern

Europe. Angus sent security teams there whenever the bad vampires got out of hand.

Master Han, another evil vampire, was still growing an army in China and acquiring more territory. There had been three vampire lords assisting Master Han, but MacKay S&I employee Major Russell Hankelburg had managed to kill one before ripping out his tracking chip and going AWOL. About three times a year, Angus sent guys to hunt for Russell, but as far as Dougal knew, the ex-Marine had never been found.

Dougal's last mission had been over a year ago when he'd helped a were-bear in Alaska. And he'd only landed that job because all the other guys had been busy in the field elsewhere.

With another gulp of Bubbly Blood he chided himself mentally. While the other lads were battling evil, he was waiting for a little girl to finish using the restroom. *Face the facts. They doona think ye're suited for being more than a babysitter.*

After that disastrous battle four years ago when he'd lost his hand, he'd been grateful just to stay employed at MacKay S&I. Angus had arranged for him to be transferred to Jean-Luc Echarpe's house in Texas, where he had replaced Robby MacKay as head of security. It was a cushy job, since Jean-Luc was the best swordsman in the vampire world and could easily take care of himself. But when it came to keeping his family safe, Jean-Luc wasn't going to turn down the extra help, even if it was one-handed.

Dougal had been grateful to Jean-Luc, too. In spite of his busy schedule, Jean-Luc had taken the time to teach Dougal how to fence with his left hand.

And then two years ago, when he had received his first prosthetic hand, Jean-Luc had trained him once again.

Now Dougal could fence equally well with both hands—a rare talent amongst the employees of MacKay S&I. So why was he still working as a glorified babysitter? Why wasn't he being sent on field work? The boredom was becoming increasingly hard to bear. Maybe he should just retire.

And do what? Sit in his cottage on the Isle of Skye and stare at the sea all night? There would be no one there, no sound other than the plaintive cry of birds and the rhythmic beating of waves against the cold rocky shore. One night would follow another, a hollow, desolate refrain stretching into eternity.

His friends here might pester him with painful questions, but at least they cared. He wasn't left alone with a half-empty soul.

He lifted the bottle for another drink.

"Dougal?" Angus's voice boomed down the hallway. "What are ye doing out here?"

He swallowed so fast that his eyes watered. Angus and his wife, Emma, approached him, their gazes shifting from him to the bottle of Bubbly Blood in his hand. Damn, they were going to think he was drinking on the job. Well, technically, he was.

"We've been looking for you," Emma said with an amused twinkle in her eyes.

"Aye," Angus agreed. "We need to talk." He motioned to the security office.

"I'll be there in a moment." Dougal glanced at the restroom door, his face growing warm. "I-I'm waiting for Bethany so I can escort her back to the party."

Emma smiled. "I'll take her. You two go on."

Dougal nodded and accompanied Angus to the office.

Inside, Phineas's younger brother, Freemont, was seated behind the desk, munching on a donut. He jumped to his feet and saluted with the donut still in his hand, leaving behind flakes of sugar on his brow. "Everything's cool in the building, sir. Robby did a perimeter check ten minutes ago. The grounds are clear."

"Good." Angus strode across the office, his kilt swishing about his knees. "And our guest downstairs?"

"The weird psycho dude?" Freemont gestured at the wall of security monitors opposite the desk. "He's still in stasis."

A weird psycho dude? Dougal studied the screens. The party in the ballroom was in full swing. In the hallway outside, Emma was leading Bethany back to the ballroom. The foyer was empty. Same with the cafeteria and Roman's laboratory. Laszlo was in one of the labs. He appeared to be cleaning and organizing. No activity in the parking lot and front entrance.

On the bottom row, Dougal spotted an interesting scene, and he leaned over for a better look. It was the silver room in the basement, a room designed for imprisoning vampires. A man was laid out on a stretcher, unconscious, with his arms and legs buckled down with restraints. "Who is he?"

"A more likely question is *what* is he?" Angus replied.

Dougal straightened. "He's no' a vampire?"

Angus shook his head. "No' exactly human, either. We have him in the silver room so none of his vampire friends can teleport in to rescue him. He has superstrength, as strong as we are. And since he's normally awake during the day, I was worried he would overpower our mortal guards. The only safe way to hold him was to put him in stasis."

"You should have seen it!" Freemont's eyes sparkled with excitement. "The psycho dude is so strong, it took three Vamps to hold him down while Abby gave him the injection."

Dougal searched his memory. He'd been out of the loop for too long, stuck in Texas. "Abby is Gregori's wife?"

"Aye. President Tucker's daughter. Luckily for us, she's a biochemist who earned her Ph.D. on stasis research." Angus patted Freemont on the back. "Ye can go to the party now."

"Cool!" Freemont headed for the door, stuffing the last of the donut in his mouth. "I think they're about to cut the cake."

When the door shut, Angus took a seat behind the desk. "I just came from a meeting with Jean-Luc and Roman."

"Aye." Dougal sat in one of the chairs facing the desk and set the bottle of Bubbly Blood on the floor next to him.

"Phineas and Austin have been in charge of security here at Romatech," Angus began. "Austin wants to continue when he's no' needed on missions, but Phineas wants to take an extended leave of absence. He's verra busy with the twins and his ranch in Wyoming. And I think he prefers the country now that he has to shift every month."

Dougal nodded. It must have been difficult for Phineas to make the transition to his new hybrid status of half vampire, half werewolf. He was fortunate to have a werewolf wife to help him adapt.

Angus leaned back in his chair. "So that leaves a position open here. I asked Robby if he was interested, but he wants to be transferred to Texas. His wife, Olivia, has family there. She wants her grandmother to help her with the bairn."

Dougal wasn't surprised. It had to be tiring for the mortal wives when their vampire husbands were dead all day and unable to help with the children. "So Robby is going to do security at the Texas Romatech?"

"He'll oversee that, but he'll also be in charge of Jean-Luc's security." Angus sat forward, his elbows on the desk. "He's taking his old job back."

Dougal blinked. "Ye mean—"

"Aye. That leaves you without a job."

I'm being let go. Dougal rose to his feet. "I understand. I was thinking of retiring—"

"The hell ye are. I need you." Angus motioned for him to sit, but Dougal was too tense to comply. "Jean-Luc tells me ye can fence equally well with both hands."

"Aye."

"He thinks yer talents are being wasted. Roman and I agree. So how would ye like to be head of security here?"

Stunned, Dougal sat. "Here?"

"Aye, and I'd like to put you back on the mission roster." Angus's gaze shifted to the prosthetic hand, then back to Dougal's face. "Can ye do it?"

"Aye." When Angus continued to stare at him, Dougal figured he needed to sound more convincing. "I can do it. I want to do it."

Angus smiled. "Good." He motioned to the bottle on the floor. "How about a drink to celebrate?"

"Aye." Dougal grabbed the bottle and poured Bubbly Blood into the two coffee cups Angus retrieved from the sideboard. "When do ye want me to start?"

"Right away." Angus drank from his cup.

Dougal glanced at the monitor showing the silver room. "I need to know more about the . . . guest. Who is he?"

"We doona know his name. He's refused to say anything other than curse at us in Chinese. J.L. and Rajiv brought him back two weeks ago. I'd sent them to China again to hunt for Russell."

"Did they find him?" Dougal asked.

"Nay. But they think he found them." Angus took another sip from his cup. "A group of Master Han's soldiers ambushed them. They were in serious trouble, when a barrage of arrows took out half the enemy."

"Russell?"

Angus nodded. "It must have been him, but when the battle was over, they searched the vicinity and couldna find him."

Dougal motioned to the monitor. "So this is one of Master Han's soldiers?"

"Aye. He's mortal, or started out that way, but he now has some of the superpowers that we possess. We're no' sure how Han is transforming the mortals, but it has something to do with the demon Darafer and some drugs he made."

Dougal frowned. They'd defeated villainous vampires before, but never one who had teamed up with a demon.

"The problem with hunting for Russell is that he's hoping to kill Master Han," Angus continued. "So in order to find him, we also have to search for Master Han."

"What's wrong with that?" Dougal asked. "Should we no' be trying to kill the bastard?"

"We need to, aye, but 'tis verra hard to actually find him. He's taken over a large portion of southern China, Tibet, and the northern portions of Thailand and Myanmar. 'Tis a huge area to canvas. J.L. and Rajiv have spent months there, and they've discovered thirty outposts, each one heavily guarded. As far as they can tell, Master Han teleports from one fort to another, and they never know where he'll pop up next."

Dougal winced. "Like playing whack the mole."

"Aye. Master Han has nearly a thousand soldiers now, spread over the thirty outposts. J.L. and Rajiv are so outnumbered that they try their best to avoid any confrontations." Angus sighed. "I was discussing this with Roman and Jean-Luc. We find ourselves in a moral dilemma."

"How so?"

"They may be the enemy, but they're mortal." Angus extended his cup toward Dougal so he could refill it with Bubbly Blood. "We never felt guilty about killing Malcontents. They're a bunch of rotten bastards who've spent centuries killing mortals and enjoying it."

"Aye," Dougal muttered. "And they're already Undead. They simply turn to dust after ye skewer them." Just like his hand, once it had been sliced off in battle.

Angus nodded. "But when we kill Master Han's

soldiers, they doona disappear. Their bodies remain. And so does our guilt. As far as we know, their souls go straight to hell."

Dougal winced. "I dinna know that."

"Our guys learned about it on their first mission to China. The mortals enjoy their superpowers as a gift from Darafer, but when they die, their souls belong to him forever." Angus dragged a hand through his hair. "We doona know if the mortals agree to the bargain, or if they are coerced through vampire mind control. Roman and I have discussed it at length, and we're reluctant to engage in battle with these mortals. We doona want to kill them."

And dispatch their souls to hell. Dougal finished his Bubbly Blood and refilled his cup. "While we wait, Master Han is making more of them. Dooming more souls."

"I know." Angus drank. "That's why J.L. and Rajiv brought back one of the soldiers. We have some good scientists here: Roman, Laszlo, and Abby. We hoped they could figure out how the mortal was changed and how to change him back."

"Then we could save them instead of killing them," Dougal concluded.

"Aye." Angus finished his cup and set it on the table. "Abby has been studying blood and tissue samples from our guest, and she claims he's been altered genetically. 'Tis beyond her area of expertise, so she suggested we find an expert to help us out."

Dougal nodded. "Did ye find someone?"

"Dr. Lee did." Angus referred to the vampire doctor from Houston. "He's been looking for an assistant, since he has an increasing number of Vamps and shifters and wee bairns to take care of. He found a physician who also has a Ph.D. in genetics. A young mortal. And a genius, according to Dr. Lee. He's bringing her here tonight."

"*Her*?"

"Aye." Angus stood and paced across the room. "He hired her a week ago, but he had some trouble breaking the news to her about vampires and shifters."

Dougal finished his cup of Bubbly Blood. Was it right to drag an innocent, mortal woman into this mess? "She dinna take it well?"

"Nay. She became so upset that she wanted to quit, and he ended up erasing her memory in order to keep her employed. We doona want to lose her."

Dougal winced. "And he's bringing her here? The place is swarming with supernatural creatures."

"We thought it best. As a scientist, she has great admiration for Roman and his invention of synthetic blood. She also knew about Abigail's achievements and was eager to meet her." Angus motioned to the monitor showing the ballroom. "And there's a blasted party going on for a bunch of bairns. How frightening can we seem when we dote on our children?"

Dougal snorted. "So we'll convince her that we're as meek as lambs?"

Angus smiled. "That's the plan."

"What of the moral dilemma of exposing an innocent woman to a dangerous world? What if she wants nothing to do with us?"

Angus's smile faded. "We need her. And since ye'll be working here, I expect you to do yer part to convince her to help us." He held up a hand when Dougal started to object. "Ye may think it's wrong to involve her, but what if she can free the soldiers who've been enslaved by Master Han? There could be over a thousand souls she saves."

So the needs of the many outweighed the needs of one? There was a ruthless logic to it, but it still didn't sit well with Dougal. How often in the past had he ranted against a cruel fate thrust upon him without his consent? The same thing could happen to this woman.

He took a deep breath. The die was cast, and he couldn't fight it. All he could do was protect her to the best of his ability. "Hopefully she will react well tonight."

"Like ye said, we'll be as meek as lambs." Angus stepped closer to the wall of monitors. "They're here."

Dougal glanced at the screen that showed a black Town Car pulling into the parking lot. "Who's with her?"

"Abby picked her up this afternoon at LaGuardia and took her to Roman's townhouse. After the sun set, Dr. Lee and Gregori joined them. That's Gregori's car. He's driving."

"They plan on telling her the truth soon?" Dougal asked.

"Aye," Angus replied. "Abby will take her to the lab first. Laszlo's been getting things ready."

Dougal glanced at the monitor, where Laszlo could be seen straightening a stack of papers. No wonder the chemist had cleaned the room. He'd even combed his unruly hair and put on a fresh white lab coat with a full array of buttons.

Dougal's gaze shifted back to the dimly lit parking lot, where the Town Car had come to a stop by the front entrance. His nerves tensed as a heavy feeling swept over him. Something was wrong. The air was suddenly too thick to breathe. He grabbed the bottle of Bubbly Blood and swallowed down a gulp. It didn't help.

Gregori and Dr. Lee exited the front seats and opened the rear car doors. Two women emerged. One was short with curly auburn hair. Abigail Tucker Holstein: renowned scientist, daughter of the American president, and Gregori's wife. The other . . . Dougal glimpsed a slim young woman, who turned away from the camera, her long black hair swinging about her shoulders.

His prosthetic hand tightened around the bottle of Bubbly Blood.

Gregori punched in the security code at the entrance, then opened the doors so they could enter the foyer.

"Dr. Lee made the mistake of simply blurting out the truth," Angus said, watching the monitors. "Abby thinks we should pique her scientific curiosity first. Then we'll have a better chance at reeling her in."

They paused in the well-lit foyer, and Dougal had a clearer view of her from behind. The graceful curve of her spine and firm set of her shoulders, the inquisitive lean of her head as she looked about . . . so familiar. Painfully familiar.

His shoulder blade itched as his tattoo grew warm. *Turn, turn toward the camera.*

Her head moved slightly as if she might have heard him. *Turn, turn to me.* A sizzling sensation started on the tail of his tattoo, then burned a path along the dragon's body, over his shoulder to his chest, till it erupted in the fiery breath etched in crimson over his heart.

He gritted his teeth against the surprising burst of pain. Why was the tattoo tormenting him now, when it had been quiet since 1746? It took a great effort just to whisper. "What's her name?"

"Dr. Chin. Leah Chin," Angus replied.

Li Lei. Dougal's heart thudded in his ears, a pounding rhythm for the sad melody that had haunted him for so long. *I will find you. No matter what. If it takes a thousand years, I will find you.*

It had taken almost three hundred years, but he'd found her. *Turn, Li Lei, turn to me.*

She swiveled, looking around the foyer, then glanced straight up at the camera.

It wasn't her.

His heart seized with an abrupt pain. Of course it wasn't her. How could it be? He'd buried her himself in a grassy mound overlooking the Yangtze River that had claimed her life. She was lost to him forever.

His fist clenched, and the bottle of Bubbly Blood shattered in his prosthetic hand.

Chapter Two

Leah Chin was not in a partying mood. After one glance at the large room where a party was in full swing, her nerves tensed. So many people, laughing and chatting, happy and comfortable with each other. She'd witnessed similar events numerous times in college, med school, and grad school. And she'd never fit in.

She'd grown up without the benefit of friends or classmates, so she'd been ill prepared for the social aspects of college. And starting at the age of fourteen hadn't helped. She found people fascinating, but only from a distance. She could watch the lively antics of brightly colored fish in a giant aquarium but never dive in and play. Jump in and you risk drowning. Or being eaten by sharks.

She glanced again at the security camera in the corner by the front door. Someone was staring at her, she could feel it. *Stop being so paranoid!* Still, her skin prickled with a strange sensation. Instead of being the scientist observing a specimen under a microscope, tonight she had an odd feeling that she was the specimen.

"Would you like to drop in and say hello?" Dr. Lee motioned to the large, noisy room.

"I-I don't want to interrupt." After all, she'd come here believing she would tour Romatech Industries and meet its owner, the renowned scientist Roman Draganesti. No one had said anything about a party. "I wasn't invited."

"Everyone's invited," Dr. Lee told her. "It's a birthday party for three kids. Very friendly people. You'll like them."

"They won't bite," Gregori Holstein added, his eyes twinkling when his wife shot him a disapproving look.

"You can meet them later." Abby Holstein gave her a reassuring pat on the arm. "How about we go to my lab first?"

"Yes." Leah jumped at the lifeline. "Please."

"Wonderful." Abby smiled at her. "I can't wait to show you what I've been working on."

"I'll see if I can find Roman for you." Gregori winked at his wife, then strode down a corridor on the left.

Leah noted the tender look in Abby's eyes as she watched her husband walk away. *Must be nice to love someone that much.*

"I'll join you in a few minutes after I see how the birthday kids are doing." Dr. Lee paused at the entrance to the large, noisy room. "I delivered them, you know."

Leah blinked. "You mean these people are your patients?" A week ago, when Dr. Lee had hired her, he'd mentioned he was the personal physician for a select group of clients. She would be expected to help him whenever he needed her, but she'd been hired mainly for her expertise in genetics.

He smiled. "You're their doctor now, too. They'll want to meet you sometime tonight. When you're ready."

She swallowed hard as Dr. Lee sauntered into the noisy room. There were so many of them. It would take her awhile to be comfortable with them all. Her gaze flitted quickly over the crowd. Bouncy, happy children. Only a few adults looked over the age of forty. In fact, most of them appeared to be in their peak years of fitness.

"They're really nice people," Abby said softly.

"They seem very healthy." Leah retreated into the foyer when a few partiers cast curious glances her way. "Why do they need two doctors at their beck and call?"

Abby hesitated before replying, "They have . . . special needs." With a quick smile, she motioned toward the double doors at the back of the foyer. "My lab's this way."

After one last worried glance at the party, Leah headed toward the double doors.

"Not much of a people person?" Abby asked as she held open a door.

Leah entered the next corridor. "I've always wanted to help people. That's why I became a doctor. But I discovered I was better suited for lab work." And being alone.

"I recognized the deer-in-the-headlights look on your face." Abby gave her a sympathetic smile. "I felt the same way when my father wanted me to attend campaign rallies or state dinners. It was all I could do not to throw up."

"Really?" Leah stared at her, stunned. "But you seem so . . . confident."

Abby snorted. "I learned to mask it, but I always felt terribly awkward at social events. Once I left the lab, I never knew what to say. Is it like that for you, too?"

"Yes. I've always found science much more reliable than people."

With a nod, Abby smiled. "I felt the same way . . . but then I met my husband." She turned left into the corridor. "Come on, this way."

Leah glanced about as she walked. The left wall was interspersed with doors; the right wall was made entirely of glass and overlooked a basketball court and a well-lit patio furnished with tables and chairs. She spotted a gazebo covered with white twinkling lights in the distance. So pretty. "This looks like a nice place to work."

Abby nodded. "I'm very happy here. I have a fabulous lab."

Leah slanted a curious look at Abigail Holstein. Could she actually become a friend? There'd been plenty of students eager to befriend Leah in college and med school, but they'd only sought her out in hopes of free tutoring from the infamous freak who had started college at the age of fourteen and med school at the age of seventeen. Dr. Freakazoid, they had called her behind her back. And when they'd no longer needed her to pass a course, they'd quickly disappeared.

She'd started off so naïve and trusting. It had been a cruel lesson, realizing that people were often undependable and unpredictable. Mercenary and combustible. You never knew when a seemingly harmless fish would turn out to be a shark. The only way to remain safe was to remain alone.

Science, on the other hand, she could trust. Unlike people, chemicals bonded in a consistent, reliable manner. They could break apart or combust only if *she* introduced a new variable. In her lab, she was in control, queen of a universe where all her constituents obeyed the rules.

She took a deep breath. "When Dr. Lee hired me, he said I would spend most of my time in a lab. It was my genetics research that interested him the most."

"Yes, we're very excited about that." Abby slowed to a stop. "Don't let the number of patients alarm you. You were right about them being very healthy. They won't need your services unless one of them is injured. Or expecting a child."

Leah noticed that Abby's hand had moved to her stomach. "Are you . . . ?"

With a grin, Abby nodded. "We found out last night."

"Wow. Congratulations."

Her face beaming, Abby leaned toward Leah. "Don't tell anyone, okay? We're going to announce it at the party."

Leah nodded. Would Abby be shocked to know she'd never had a friend confide a secret to her before? "I won't say a word."

Abby clasped her hands together. "Gregori is so excited. And his mother—she'll be ecstatic!"

"I imagine your parents will be thrilled," Leah added.

Abby's smile faded a bit. "I hope so."

Was there a problem there? A chill skittered down Leah's spine, and she peered over her shoulder. Another camera, its red light blinking. "Are we being watched?"

Abby glanced at the camera. "Maybe. We have excellent security."

"Can they hear us?"

"I suppose, if they turn up the volume." Abby shrugged. "I wouldn't worry about it. There hasn't been an incident here since the bombing years ago." She winced. "It wasn't a big deal. No one was seriously hurt."

Leah's mouth dropped open. "This place was bombed?"

"I know it's hard to believe someone would do that when synthetic blood saves so many lives, but I'm afraid there are some strange . . . people out there." Abby patted her on the arm. "I didn't mean to frighten you. I'm sorry."

"It's okay." Leah glanced again at the camera. Were they listening? "I know the world is full of weirdos."

Abby gave her a worried look. "As you say." She walked forward a few steps, then stopped next to a door. "Welcome to my lab."

"**W**hoa. Are you partying without me?" Gregori asked as he sauntered into the security office. "It smells like Bubbly Blood in here."

"There was a wee accident." Angus motioned to where Dougal was partially hidden beside the desk, picking up shards of glass that were once a bottle and tossing them into the litter bin.

"Hey, dude, long time no see," Gregori greeted him. "How's the bionic hand?"

"Fine." Dougal straightened. "I . . . miscalculated my grip for a second." No way was he going to admit he'd lost control. Angus might reconsider putting him in charge here. Or refuse to let him go on missions.

Fortunately, Angus seemed more interested in watching the monitors than speculating on his *wee accident*.

"Where's Roman?" Gregori scanned the monitors, searching for his boss.

Angus pointed at a hallway where Roman was walking with Jean-Luc. "They're on their way to the party."

"I'll give him a call." Gregori punched a number on his cell phone, then asked Roman to head toward Abby's lab in ten minutes.

Meanwhile, Dougal located a broom and dustpan in the small closet. If this was going to be his office, he'd start taking care of it now. He swept up the last of the broken glass and dumped it into the litter bin.

"I wonder what they're talking about." Angus turned up the volume on the monitor showing Abby and Leah.

"*We found out last night,*" Abby said, smiling and patting her stomach.

"*Wow,*" Leah replied. "*Congratulations.*"

"Och, man." Angus turned to Gregori. "Ye're going to be a father?"

Gregori grinned. "Yep. You bet your little plaid skirt."

Angus rolled his eyes. "The puir bairn."

With a laugh, Gregori punched Angus on the shoulder. "I knew Abby wouldn't be able to keep it a secret. She's so excited."

"Congratulations," Dougal told him. His gaze shifted back to the monitor just as Leah glanced over her shoulder straight at the camera. His hand flinched, the fist tightening around the handle of the dustpan.

"Are we being watched?" Leah asked.

Hell, yes. He winced at the dents he'd left in the metal handle. Why was he reacting so strongly? She wasn't Li Lei.

"Maybe," Abby replied. *"We have excellent security."*

"Can they hear us?" Leah asked.

He turned away, feeling a twinge of guilt for eavesdropping. As he returned the broom and dustpan to the closet, he spotted a half-empty bottle of Blissky on the top shelf. Just what he needed. He set the bottle on the desk, then fetched three paper cups from the sideboard.

When Abby explained about the bombing a few years back, he glanced at the monitor just in time to see Leah's wide-eyed reaction. Damn, they had no right to drag her into this world. She looked so young. Early twenties, perhaps. There was a fragile innocence to her features, an innocence about to be crushed.

He poured Blissky into the three cups. "How about a wee dram?"

"Great idea!" Gregori lifted his cup in the air. "To our beautiful wives!"

"I'll drink to that." Angus grabbed a cup and downed the contents.

Gregori shot Dougal an amused look. "Or in your case, a future beautiful wife."

Dougal snorted, then looked at the monitor and found Leah staring at the camera as if she could see him. His heart stilled. Another itch skittered along the length of his tattoo, and he shrugged his right shoulder.

"I know the world is full of weirdos," she said softly.

Och, lass, ye have no idea. But she would be finding out soon. He had a sudden urge to teleport straight to her and take her away, far away from a world of vampires and shifters and demons. But how could he protect her from the *weirdos* when he was one of them?

"Cheers." He tossed back the Blissky and let it burn down his throat. He deserved the burn.

"Welcome to my lab." Abby opened the door and ushered Leah inside.

Angus moved to the monitor that showed the lab and turned up the volume.

"Must we listen in on them?" Dougal asked.

Angus sighed. "I know it isna normal procedure, but I'm worried about how Dr. Chin will take the news."

"This is a colleague of mine." Abby motioned to Laszlo as he rushed forward. "Laszlo Veszto. He's the most brilliant chemist I've ever met."

Laszlo blushed and extended a hand toward Abby. "I'm delighted to meet you." When she placed her hand in his, he pumped her arm. "We're very excited to have you here. I've been busy all evening getting the lab ready."

"Really?" Leah eased her hand from his grip.

"Yes!" Laszlo's hand gravitated straight to his lab coat, where he grabbed onto a button. "We have some interesting case studies to show you."

"Sounds good." Leah glanced around the lab. "This is very nice."

"Yes." Laszlo smiled at her while he fiddled with his buttons.

Leah's eyes narrowed as she spotted the camera in the corner. Dougal poured more Blissky into his paper cup and downed it.

Abby strode toward the long stainless steel table that was topped with several microscopes and stacks of paper. "Everything is ready?"

"Yes," Laszlo answered, still smiling at Leah.

"Ha!" Gregori pointed at the monitor. "Look at that silly grin on Laszlo's face. He's in love!"

Dougal's fist snapped shut, crushing the paper cup in his hand. What the hell? Before anyone could see the mangled cup, he tossed it into the litterbin. Or attempted to. His fist refused to open. *Release,* he ordered his hand. It remained locked around the crushed paper cup.

Angus shook his head. "Smitten, perhaps. I'll have a talk with Laszlo. We canna let anyone's personal feelings jeopardize our plans."

Release, dammit! Open! Finally Dougal's fist relaxed, and the cup fell into the litterbin.

Meanwhile, Leah had moved to the table and was peering into the first microscope. "Interesting," she murmured, then picked up the stack of papers beside it.

"Let's hope she takes the bait," Angus said.

Dougal moved closer to the monitors.

Leah scanned the first page, then the second. Abby watched, chewing on her lip. Laszlo twisted a button on his lab coat.

"Definite mutations in the DNA sequencing." Leah moved on to the third page. "Some rather drastic changes. Is this man still alive?"

Abby hesitated. "At the moment, yes."

Gregori snorted.

Leah set the papers down. "I've never seen anything like this. Some of these mutations might possibly strengthen a person, but others . . ." She shook her head. "I'm not sure a human can survive this. Is he exhibiting any bizarre symptoms?"

Abby's mouth twitched. "Other than a strange desire to disco dance, no."

Gregori stiffened. "What's so strange about that?"

Angus hushed him.

Leah shook her head, confused. "Where is the patient? Can I see him?"

"You've already seen him," Abby replied. "It's Gregori."

Leah gasped. "What?" She thumbed through the papers once more. "I don't understand. Your husband seems so healthy."

"He is," Abby agreed. "When he's . . . awake."

Dougal winced. The shit was about to hit the fan.

Angus frowned. "I have a bad feeling about this. Gregori, call Dr. Lee. Tell him to get to the lab right away."

While Gregori made the call, Leah tapped her hand on the stack of paper. "Your husband could be in serious trouble. He should be hospitalized immediately for observation." Her eyes widened. "Oh my God, you're pregnant with his child?"

"I'm fine, really. And so is Gregori." Abby exchanged a worried look with Laszlo.

He nodded, furiously twirling a button. "There is a perfectly reasonable explanation for this, I assure you."

"Really?" Leah gave them an incredulous look. "How do you explain it?"

Abby took a deep breath. "My husband is a vampire."

Chapter Three

*L*eah's heart leaped into a fast, pounding rhythm. She stepped back, resisting an urge to run for the door. Her gaze shifted from the president's daughter to the so-called brilliant chemist, then back. Did the president know his daughter was insane?

Holy crapoly, the whole building might be full of crazy people. Even the creepy people watching her through the camera—her breath caught. Of course, she was being punked! The camera was recording this, and it was going to end up on the Internet somewhere. It wasn't the first time people had tried to make her look like an idiot.

In college, her young age and genius label had rendered her a target for silly pranks. One time a bunch of frat boys had circled the girls' dormitory dressed as the Living Dead, while the girls had begged her to use her superior intellect to save them from the zombie apocalypse.

So this time it was the Undead. She crossed her arms and acted nonchalant. "You're married to a vampire?"

"Yes." Abby nodded with a hopeful expression as if she expected her to believe this nonsense.

Leah shot the camera a wry look, then turned back to Abby. "How did you reach that conclusion? Did he turn into a bat and fly around the bedroom?"

Abby's eager expression faded into disappointment. "You think I'm kidding."

"Did you expect me to take this seriously?" Leah asked.

Laszlo motioned to the stack of papers on the table. "But we showed you the lab work. And the data—"

"Which can be manipulated," Leah interrupted. "Or in this case, manufactured." She glowered at the camera. "The game is over. I'm not playing." She headed toward the door, but halfway there, it opened.

Dr. Lee rushed inside. "Is there a problem?"

"Yes," Leah replied in the affirmative, at the same time as Abby and Laszlo. She aimed a frown at them. "They're playing a dumb joke on me."

"It's not a joke," Abby insisted. "Vampires are real."

Leah snorted. "Why would you believe that? Did your husband bite you?"

"Well, yes, he has. And he can—"

"What? Leap from one tree to another like a monkey?" Leah lifted a hand to stop Abby. The poor woman was suffering from delusions. "You should lie down and get some rest. Given your condition, you could be experiencing some hormonal fluctuations—"

"I'm not imagining this," Abby grumbled.

"Or it could be a case of being overworked," Leah continued. "I know how it is. When I get really involved in a project, I can forget to eat or sleep. Just this last week, I was so busy, I can hardly remember it."

Dr. Lee winced. "Perhaps a demonstration is in order."

"Good idea." Abby turned to Laszlo. "How about you levitate to the ceiling?"

Laszlo frowned, tugging hard at a button. "If you wish, but it might cause her to panic."

"Go ahead," Dr. Lee told him. "She needs physical evidence."

Leah scoffed. "So the chemist is a vampire, too?"

Laszlo's button popped off and landed on the stainless steel table with a *ping*. He gave her an apologetic look. "It's not really a bad thing. Just think of it as a . . . an unusual medical condition."

Leah shook her head. These people were certifiable. "You're a vampire?"

"Yes," Laszlo admitted but hastened to add, "but a very friendly one, I assure you."

"Well, that is . . . comforting," Leah muttered. A friendly bloodsucker. That made as much sense as a friendly serial killer. She glanced at Abby. "And you? Are you Casper, the friendly ghost?"

Abby gave her a sympathetic look. "I'm mortal like you. I know you must be shocked. I was shocked, too, when I found out. I even fainted."

"I don't faint." Leah waved a dismissive hand. "And I'm not shocked. I'm . . . saddened that you've deluded yourselves into believing such a ridiculous—" She halted when Laszlo's body floated up to the ceiling.

Okay, that wasn't normal. It had to be wires. A spark of anger flared inside her. These people were really taking the joke too far. "That's enough! I don't believe anyone here is a vampire!"

"But I am." Laszlo winced as his head bumped into the ceiling.

"Me, too," Dr. Lee added.

Leah spun to face him. Her boss was a vampire?

"I am as well." Another man sauntered into the lab. He was tall, dark, and handsome.

And Undead? Leah stared at him. "Who are you?"

He bowed his head. "Roman Draganesti, at your service. I'm delighted to meet you, Dr. Chin."

This was the scientific genius who had invented synthetic blood? Leah swallowed hard. He was either as crazy as the other guys in the room, or they were actually . . .

Vampires.

Her skin chilled with instant goose bumps. *No, this isn't possible.* There had to be a reasonable, scientific explanation for this. *Why bother to explain it? Just get the hell out of here!*

She stepped toward the door, but Dr. Lee and Mr. Draganesti were blocking the exit. A quick look around confirmed it was the only way out.

"Her heart is racing," Mr. Draganesti murmured.

She turned toward him, her eyes narrowed.

"Superior hearing," he explained.

"Why should I believe you? Given the situation, anyone could guess that my heart rate would be elevated." A thudding sound startled her, and she whirled about to find that Laszlo had landed on the tile floor.

She rushed toward him, and standing on her tiptoes, she swept her hand through the air over his head. No wires. "How did you do it? Are you wearing special shoes that will lift you in the air? Or maybe it's magnets?"

"It's levitation." Laszlo regarded her sadly. "Do you need me to do it again?"

"No." She grabbed his wrist and pressed her fingers against his vein. "You see?" She dropped his arm. "You have a pulse. You're alive. So stop this crap *now*!"

"Leah, calm down." Dr. Lee moved toward her.

"I will not!" She stepped back. "And I'm not working for you anymore. This is a cruel joke, and I won't put up with it!"

"Leah, for God's sake." Dr. Lee gave her a beseeching look. "We're not trying to be cruel. Just honest."

"*No!*" She shook her head. "I won't listen! Vampires aren't real. You're lying to me! You're lying—"

"Dammit, don't make me erase your memory again!" Dr. Lee winced and lifted his hands. "I didn't mean it like that. We would never hurt you. You have to believe us."

A chill swept over Leah, and she shivered. "You . . . what did you do?"

Dr. Lee dragged a hand through his short gray hair. "This is so damned frustrating. I tried to tell you the truth a few days ago, but you didn't take it well."

"You—you erased my memory?"

"You were having a panic attack. It seemed like the best way to calm you down."

Leah struggled to breathe. Oh God, was that why the past few days were a blur? He'd . . . tampered with her mind?

"My dear child," Roman said softly. "Perhaps you should sit down?"

"You look very pale," Abby added.

"I don't faint." Leah stumbled toward the far wall, where a countertop and sink were located. She didn't know whether to be angry or . . . scared to death. Her mind had been tampered with? Dr. Lee had that kind of power?

She glanced at herself in the mirror over the sink and grimaced at her pale, stricken look. Damn them all. She would not allow anyone to alter her memory. She would remember this.

But did that mean she had to accept a new reality, one that was occupied with *vampires*? With trembling fingers, she turned on the cold water.

"Let me help." Abby joined her at the sink and pulled some paper towels from the nearby dispenser.

She eased away a few inches.

"Leah, please," Abby whispered. "I'm mortal. And a scientist like you. I had trouble accepting it, too." She folded the towels into a pad and moistened it under the cold running water. "Here, press this against the back of your neck."

Leah accepted the damp pad and looked in the mirror over the sink. She and Abby were reflected there, and the stainless steel table in the background. No Laszlo.

She glanced back, and with a gasp, she dropped the damp pad to the floor. Roman Draganesti was standing right behind her. "What? How did you—?" She turned back to the mirror.

He wasn't there.

"Do you believe us now?" his voice spoke softly behind her.

The room swirled, and she gripped the edge of the counter. *Vampires are real?* It wasn't scientifically possible. She squeezed her eyes shut. Had her world just turned upside down? Had she stumbled into an alternate reality? Was she hallucinating?

"Take deep breaths," Abby whispered. "You'll be okay."

Leah shook her head. No, it would never be okay. Her safe and scientific world had crumbled around her. What was left to rely on? How could she even trust her instincts, when they were telling her she'd lost her mind?

A cold sweat broke out on her skin. She cupped her hands in the cold running water, and her eyes burned at the sight of her shaky hands. Was this really happening to her?

She splashed water on her face, then straightened to watch the rivulets running down her face in the mirror. It was real. Was the vampire still behind her? She cupped more water in her hands and tossed it over her shoulder.

A wincing sound. She turned and found Mr. Draganesti standing behind her, wiping droplets of water off his shirt and tie.

He gave her a wry look. "My wife didn't take the news well either."

"Your *wife*?" Leah scoffed. "Apparently she got over it."

He nodded. "Shanna's looking forward to meeting you. Our children are at the party, too. Sofia is four, and Constantine's six."

"Already?" Dr. Lee strolled toward them, smiling. "It seems like just yesterday I delivered them."

"I know." Mr. Draganesti grinned. "They grow so fast."

Leah grimaced at the pointed canine teeth on display. Did they have fangs that shot out like the ones in movies? How many carotid arteries had they punctured with those?

When Mr. Draganesti noticed the apparent horror on her face, his smile faded. "Dr. Chin, there is no need to fear us. I invented synthetic blood to free us from the need to use mortals for our survival."

So Romatech Industries was their equivalent to a grocery store. Leah moved to the side beyond their reach. "Before synthetic blood, you fed off people?"

Mr. Draganesti nodded. "Unfortunately, yes. We would take what we needed, then erase the mortal's memory."

"I never liked hurting people," Laszlo grumbled as he stuffed the loose button into his pocket. "It was a blessing to us when we could rely on synthetic blood."

"We try not to hurt mortals, but there are some bad vampires who do," Dr. Lee warned her. "We call them Malcontents. They enjoy tormenting and killing mortals."

"We've been fighting them for centuries," Mr. Draganesti added.

"These are the good guys." Abby motioned to the men. "I would never have fallen in love with Gregori if he hadn't been one of the good guys."

How could a vampire be good? Their very nature was parasitic. Leah crossed her arms. "How old are you?"

"I'm just over a hundred." Dr. Lee gave Mr. Draganesti an amused look. "You're the old one here."

He shrugged. "I was born in 1461, transformed in 1492."

"You knew Columbus?" Leah winced. She was too frazzled. Now she was asking stupid questions.

Mr. Draganesti smiled. "My son asked me that,

too. Would you like to go the party now? You might feel better if you have something to eat."

"You have real food there?" Leah asked.

"There's a bunch of food," Dr. Lee answered. "And a giant birthday cake. Five layers, each one a different flavor. According to Tino, the chocolate one is the best."

Mr. Draganesti snorted. "I'm sure he tasted each layer."

"Of course." Dr. Lee grinned. "When I saw him, he had a smear of chocolate icing on his nose."

Leah took a deep breath. In spite of the seemingly normal cake conversation, she was still having trouble wrapping her mind around this. Vampires. Vampires with wives and children. How could that be possible? The chocolate cake sounded good, though.

She shook her head. "Mr. Draganesti—"

"Call me Roman."

She gave him a wary look. *Just don't call me dinner.* "Why am I here? What do you want from me?"

His eyebrows lifted. "Straight to the point. I like that. The truth is we find ourselves in a moral dilemma. We've always tried to protect mortals from bad vampires, but there's one in China who's giving us major grief. He goes by the name Master Han."

"He's mutating mortals and using them to fight his battles," Dr. Lee added. "We need to defeat Master Han, but we don't want to kill the mortals."

"That's big of you," Leah muttered. "Where do I come in?"

"The mortals have been transformed at a genetic level," Abby explained. "Since you're an expert in that field, we were hoping you could find a way to change them back."

Leah swallowed a pang of disappointment. She knew she was here on business, but for a few minutes, she had hoped that Abby wanted to be her friend. Her eyes burned. Here she was, surrounded by vampires, possibly in danger, and she was fretting over hurt feelings? How silly of her. But everyone always approached her with an agenda. They wanted her brain, her expertise, her learned opinion. No one ever saw her as a normal person to hang out with.

"I was looking forward to working with you." Abby regarded her sadly. "And I hoped we could get to know each other."

Did she really mean that? Leah stared at her. Did she know the loneliness of never fitting in?

"We'll understand if you refuse," Roman said. "But please give it some thought before you decide. If you can help us, you could possibly be saving the lives of over a thousand men."

Over a thousand lives? That was not something she could turn away from easily. "I'll think about it. But I need some time."

"Of course." Roman nodded. "You've had a lot thrown at you this evening."

"But you're doing great." Dr. Lee smiled. "We can relax and enjoy the party now, okay?"

Relax with vampires? Leah glanced at the camera. Those watchful eyes she felt—did they belong to a vampire? Had he observed her like a lab mouse trying to find its way through a maze? Unfortunately, the evening wasn't over, and she was still in the maze. One step away from a nervous breakdown. "I'd rather be alone with Abby right now."

"We understand." Roman stepped back to let her pass.

"Come on." Abby headed for the door. "Let's get some of that chocolate cake."

"**D**amn, this is good." Freemont forked a bite of cake into his mouth as he sauntered into the security office. "You guys don't know what you're missing."

"About five thousand calories," Gregori muttered.

Dougal eyed Freemont's plate, loaded down with five slices of cake. So he was doing like Tino and trying all the flavors.

Grinning, Freemont set the plate on the desk. "I'm gonna make this cake my bitch."

Angus snorted. "While ye're doing that, keep an eye on the monitors. I'll leave in a few minutes to update Emma on what's happening. I think everything's going verra well."

Dougal wasn't so sure about that. As he watched Leah walk down the corridor, he had a bad feeling she was one step away from full-fledged panic. Still, her head was held high and her back was straight. She was a courageous lass, showing fortitude as her safe world crumbled around her. She'd stood up to everyone in the lab, refusing to let them intimidate her. Her strength of character was impressive.

"Gregori, ye should go to the party," Angus continued. "Flirt with yer wife and show Dr. Chin how charming ye can be."

Gregori scoffed. "Is that an order?"

"Is it too much for ye to handle?" Angus asked.

"No." Gregori gave him a wry look. "I'm always charming."

"Good. Show the doctor how harmless we are.

Meek as lambs, as Dougal puts it." Angus's eyes narrowed on Dougal. "Ye should go with him. She might feel better knowing who was behind the camera."

Dougal winced. Each time she'd glanced at the camera with that defiant, reproachful look, his heart had squeezed in his chest. He knew in his soul that she had resented being observed while everything she held safe and secure had been stripped away from her.

He'd been torn the entire time. Part of him had wanted to turn away and give her the privacy she deserved. But a larger part had kept him glued to the screen, hoping somehow that his presence would lend her strength, that he could lessen her pain by sharing it. He knew too well the pain of losing everything.

He watched on the monitor as she crossed the foyer with Abby. He was still torn. His heart was thudding wildly at the thought of meeting her in person. She was the most intriguing woman he'd seen in centuries. But his mind was telling him to wait. She was hanging on by a thread. If it snapped, she would run and never come back. "I'm no' sure she wants to meet any more Vamps for a while."

"I'll call Abby and see what she thinks." Gregori opened the office door. "Come on, Dougal. Let's party."

"Remember," Angus said, "we're as meek as lambs."

"And randy as goats," Gregori added with a laugh. He slapped Dougal on the back. "Let's go."

Chapter Four

Leah was greatly relieved to see that all the adult partygoers had gravitated to the far side of the room. They were so focused on opening presents and watching the children that they barely gave her and Abby any notice.

At the first refreshment table, she loaded cheese, crackers, and fruit onto a small plate while Abby poured two cups of punch. Popping a pineapple chunk into her mouth, she glanced warily at the crowd across the room. How many of them were vampires? And how on earth did vampires have babies? Did those pretty little children shoot fangs out on occasion and transform into bloodthirsty monsters?

Mommy, I just killed the nanny. Can I have a cookie?

With a shudder, her gaze shifted to the foyer. Maybe she should say she needed to go to the restroom, then she could sneak out the front door and call a cab. But it would take time for a cab to arrive. Could she slip past the guarded front gate, or would she have to climb the wall?

Would they let her leave? She knew their big secret. And they claimed to need her help.

"Here." Abby passed her a cup of fruit punch.

Leah took a sip. "Is it true? If I help you, I could save over a thousand lives?"

Abby nodded. "We think so." She drank some punch. "If you recall, there were three microscopes in the lab. The first one, the one you looked at, showed a blood sample from Gregori. The second one is from Roman's son, Tino. And the third is from one of Master Han's soldiers. You're welcome to look at them whenever you're ready."

Leah sighed. "I'm afraid I'm not taking this very well."

"You're doing fine." Abby patted her shoulder, then headed toward the second table. "Come on, let's check out the desserts."

Leah followed her, but instead of admiring the giant cake, her gaze drifted back to the crowd across the room. What on earth? There were two men in kilts? The last man she'd seen in a kilt had been her Irish grandfather. A wave of grief swept over her with the vague memory of a haunting melody. How she missed him.

No one had enjoyed life as much as Grandpa, so it seemed like sacrilege for the Undead to dress the same way. Each of the kilted men held a young child in his arms. "Are all the children half vampire?"

"The kids like Tino are. Did you want to go back to the lab and see his blood work?"

Leah gave her a wry look. "Was that the plan all along? Appeal to my curiosity to lure me in?"

Abby winced. "Well, you have to admit it's all fascinating. Right?"

"I admit nothing. To even consider vampires as real—I'm either crazy or dreaming." Leah ate a cube of cheese. Cheddar, sharp and creamy. Would it taste this real if she were dreaming? But the alternative was she was crazy. And that conclusion put her one step closer to utter panic.

She glanced at the third refreshment table. It was covered with bottles and empty flutes and wineglasses. "Is that synthetic blood?"

"Yes." Abby bit into a chocolate-covered strawberry. "The bottles on ice are Bubbly Blood, a combination of synthetic blood and champagne. Roman's invented a whole menu of Vampire Fusion Cuisine. Bleer that's half beer. Blissky that's half whisky. You get the idea."

"Vampires like to get drunk?"

Abby chuckled. "I've seen Gregori overindulge." A humming noise emanated from her pants pocket, and she retrieved her cell phone. "Oh, that's him now." Smiling, she put the phone to her ear. "Hi, sweetie."

Leah shuddered. Sweetie bloodsucker?

After a pause, Abby frowned. "Not now. Give us some time, okay?" She hung up. "I didn't think you wanted to visit with any more Vamps for a while."

"I don't." Leah glanced again at the vampires across the room. They were smiling and chatting like normal people. But they weren't normal. Nothing was normal anymore. "Why are some guys wearing kilts?"

"They're Scottish." Abby scanned the crowd. "That's Robby MacKay and Ian MacPhie. They're security guys."

Leah pivoted around till she spotted the camera with its red blinking light. Was she still being watched? If she dashed out the front door, would she be chased down by a vampire in a kilt? "If I don't accept this, they're going to erase my memory again, aren't they?"

When Abby was silent, Leah turned toward her. "Are they?"

Abby winced. "Is it that hard to accept?"

Leah's heart raced. What was hard to accept was the way she felt trapped. Coerced. It was like they were holding her brain hostage. Play along or have it tampered with. With trembling hands she set her cup and plate on the table.

"Leah, no one will hurt you," Abby assured her, her voice sounding muffled and far away.

A wave of dizziness blurred Leah's vision, but she shook it away. She'd rather make a run for it than faint. Better to show strength than weakness. She turned toward the entrance, desperately gathering her energy and courage for the mad dash to the foyer and front door . . . and froze.

Gregori paused in the entrance, spotted her and Abby, and waved. Another man joined him. A short man in a lab coat. Laszlo. He raised a hand in greeting, giving her a hopeful smile.

Leah's heart thundered in her ears. No escape. The lab mouse was thoroughly caught in the maze. The guppy had been tossed into an aquarium with sharks. *Welcome to your new world.*

A third man moved into view, and her breath caught. He was large, his shoulders easily taking up half the entrance. A kilt. Another security guy? Why was he blocking the door? Did he know she was about to make a break for it?

Her gaze lifted past his wide chest and impossibly broad shoulders to his face. His eyes. He was looking straight at her. Straight through her as if he could see her soul. He shrugged his right shoulder.

She turned away.

Who was he? Her back tingled as if she could feel his green eyes boring right through her, sharp emeralds slicing through her defenses till she was laid completely bare. The thundering in her ears grew quiet. A strange sense of calm stole over her, a sense of inevitability, as if her entire life had ticked away slowly for the sole purpose of arriving at this one moment in time. She knew without a doubt who he was. She'd felt him watching her all evening.

He was the man behind the camera.

Dougal winced inwardly. Leah Chin had taken one look at him and turned away. He rolled his shoulder once again where the damned tattoo continued to sizzle with warmth.

"Dr. Lee and Roman think it's going well," Laszlo said.

Wishful thinking. She was ready to bolt. Dougal could see the tension in her stance, feel the aura of desperation radiating from her. She was a brave lass, but her courage was being taxed to its limit. It made him want to pull her into his arms, though he doubted she'd accept comfort from a Vamp. "Ye doona think it is wrong to drag her into our world?"

Laszlo twisted a button. "We need her help. She's absolutely brilliant in her field of expertise."

"She speaks Mandarin, too," Gregori added. "In case we need to go back to China."

Dougal stiffened. "Ye would take her on a mission? She shouldna be put into a dangerous situation because of our problems."

"Relax, dude," Gregori told him. "As long as we've got the prisoner in the silver room, she'll be able to work here."

Laszlo nodded. "I'm looking forward to working with her."

With a grin, Gregori elbowed the short chemist. "Admit it, bro. You're crushing on her big time."

Laszlo blushed. "Well, she is a genius. Very pretty, too."

Dougal's prosthetic hand fisted, and he hid it behind his back. *Release, dammit*! Unfortunately, Leah chose that precise moment to glance at him. She looked away quickly before he could wipe the angry scowl off his face. *Bloody hell.* She would think he hated her, when in truth—what was the truth? He desperately wanted her to be the girl he'd lost almost three hundreds years ago? It was impossible. And an insult to this lass who was brave, bright, and beautiful in her own right.

"I could give you a few pointers," Gregori offered.

Laszlo tugged harder at the button. "I—I'm not sure if she would welcome any attention from me."

"Dude." Gregori frowned at him. "If you want her, you gotta go for her."

The button popped off and clattered onto the marble floor. When Laszlo bent over to retrieve it, his unruly hair flopped over his eyes. He pushed his hair back and stuffed the button in his pocket.

Gregori patted him on the back. "Don't worry, bro. I'll get you ready for her."

The hell you will. Dougal tensed, his hand still fisted. Should he declare his intentions? What intentions? If it were up to him, he'd let the poor girl escape.

"What you need, dude, is a makeover," Gregori announced. "I'll set you up with Wilson over at the Digital Vampire Network. He's the one who makes regular Vamps look like TV stars."

"H-he can make me look good?" Laszlo asked.

"He does my hair." Gregori smoothed a hand over his perfect hair. "He'll update your wardrobe, too. No offense, bro, but you're looking . . . well, like a nerd."

Laszlo glanced down at his plaid shirt, plastic pocket protector, and khaki pants belted high at the waist. "Something's wrong with my clothes?"

Gregori heaved a sigh. "You need help, bro." He glanced over at Dougal. "It wouldn't hurt you to update, too, you know. How long have you been wearing that kilt? A couple of hundred years?"

Dougal scoffed. "'Tis new." He'd ordered it in Glasgow a few years back. Well, ten years. He finally managed to relax his prosthetic hand.

"And the poufy shirt?" Gregori eyed it askance. "Did you steal that off a pirate?"

"Nay." Dougal had had his share of scuffles with pirates, but never over a shirt.

Gregori's mouth twitched. "We should trade your bionic hand in for a hook and get you an eye patch. Then you'd really look like a pirate. You already have the long, wild hair."

"'Tis no' wild," Dougal grumbled. He'd tied it back with a strip of leather. He glanced over at Leah and discovered her looking at him. She turned away. For the first time in centuries, he wondered what a woman saw when she looked at him. Did he actually look like a bloody pirate?

"What am I going to do with you guys?" Gregori sighed. "Laszlo looks like a dork, and you—Dougal, you gotta lose the skirt, the poufy shirt, and the hairy handbag. That thing is scary."

Dougal glanced down at his sporran, made of black muskrat fur. " 'Tis verra practical. Where else would I keep my coin?"

"Pockets!" Gregori gave him an incredulous look. "Have you heard of those? Sheesh, dude, you're medieval."

He stiffened. "I'm no' medieval."

"Dougal, you're accessorizing with a dead animal."

"I'm no' medieval. I was transformed after the Battle of Culloden in 1746. 'Twas called the Age of Enlightenment, in case ye dinna know."

Gregori snorted. "You fought for Bonnie Prince Charlie? How enlightened was that?"

Dougal gritted his teeth. "I fought for freedom from English tyranny. As a bloody Yank, ye should understand that."

Gregori shrugged. "Fine. But I'm telling you, man, if you want to find a woman, you need to upgrade." His eyes lit up. "I bet you need some practice, too. Don't go anywhere." He took off across the foyer and down the hallway.

Laszlo fiddled with another button. "What is he up to?"

"No good, most likely." Dougal looked at Leah. She was nibbling on a strawberry and casting curious glances at the crowd of Vamps across the room. "Are ye serious about her?"

"I-I'm not sure," Laszlo answered quietly. "She may be in shock, so I should probably leave her be for a while and give her some time to adjust . . ."

As Laszlo continued to reason with himself, Dougal studied her. She was a natural beauty, and he would wager a year's earnings that she was unaware of it. Her hair was long, thick, and black, her face small and delicate, her neck slim and graceful. So much like Li Lei. Same creamy, porcelain skin. Same tilt of her head. Same little nose and exquisitely shaped mouth. He nearly moaned when she bit into a strawberry, then licked the juice from her lips.

Her eyes were different. They were a lighter, more golden brown, and their shape was a little rounder. And there was another difference. A huge one. Leah Chin was alive. This was no ghost shrouded with regret but a vibrant, lovely woman.

Li Lei's hair had always been pulled tightly back, but Leah's hair was loose. A glorious, shimmering curtain that swayed gently with her every move. He couldn't wait to touch it, feel its silky texture, and run his hands through it.

His gaze drifted lower. Her knit shirt covered her shoulders, but he had no doubt they were beautiful. The clingy material outlined her breasts nicely, allowing him to envision the—

" . . . mounds," Laszlo said. "More like mountains."

"What?" Dougal gave him a wary look.

"Paperwork," he clarified. "Mounds of it. I doubt I have time to court Dr. Chin."

"Right." Dougal glanced once again at Leah and discovered her staring at him. Her eyes widened, and she turned her back. Damn, was he that scary to look at? Her abrupt movement had caused her hair to swing back and forth. It was cut bluntly across, the ends right below her shoulder blades.

A vision popped in his mind with him flat on his back and her sitting astride him, riding him, with her hair swaying wildly. And when she leaned forward to kiss him, her hair fell forward to sweep gently across his face. He would be immersed in her softness, her sweet fragrance. Just imagining it made his groin grow—

" . . . tight," Laszlo continued. "Very tight schedule. So much to do and so little time."

"Aye," Dougal muttered. So much he would do. He would caress her all over, explore every inch of her creamy skin, make her moan and writhe and scream with pleasure. He adjusted his sporran to conceal his hard—

" . . . staff," Laszlo said. "We have staff meetings every night."

"Every night, aye," Dougal mumbled. He would pleasure her every night.

"Oh God, no," Laszlo whispered.

Dougal followed the chemist's line of vision and spotted Gregori coming toward them. He was carrying VANNA in his arms. Who would bring a life-sized sex toy to a birthday party for bairns? Obviously, she wasn't intended to be a present for the children. That meant . . .

"Bloody hell," Dougal growled.

Chapter Five

*H*ow many times had she caught him staring at her from across the room? About as many times as he'd caught her doing the same. Leah's face grew warm. What was it about him that kept her eyes gravitating toward him?

First of all, he was probably a vampire, so it was crazy to look at him at all. But she was. Over and over again. And that, unfortunately, provided more proof that she was no longer firing on all her synapses. Just one step away from going completely bonkers.

He was handsome, but then, so were most of the men in the room. Because of her Irish grandfather, she'd always had a fondness for men in kilts, but there were other kilted men in the room, and she wasn't gawking at them. And it wasn't as if he made her feel safe. Quite the contrary. Laszlo looked a lot safer. So did the cheerful men holding babies.

Was that the difference? Everyone looked happy except the guy in the doorway. Was it her own frazzled nerves that caused her to be drawn to the one person who appeared as agitated as she did?

She could feel his stare, the heat of it prickling her

back. The last few times she'd glanced at him he'd seemed grim and angry. Intense. As if a roiling fire inside him was threatening to erupt like a volcano.

She glanced at him again and froze. So much hunger in his eyes. And pain. It shook her, grabbing onto her heart.

There'd always been a strong need inside her to fix people who were suffering. As if that could somehow erase all the pain she'd suffered in silence. It was why she'd insisted on going to medical school in spite of the awkwardness she felt around others.

But this was no ordinary man. She couldn't let herself get drawn in. Not with him. Deep in her heart she knew he had the power to devastate her more than any other man on the planet.

She turned her back to him. "Who is he—the man next to Laszlo?"

Abby narrowed her eyes. "That must be Dougal. Dougal Kincaid. Haven't seen him around much lately. He's been guarding the Echarpes in Texas."

"He's security?" Leah sipped some punch and swallowed hard when Abby nodded her head. Of course he was security. He'd been watching her all evening. Even now she could feel his sharp emerald eyes burning into her back. "A vampire?"

"Yes."

Single? Leah stopped herself from asking. She had to be out of her mind.

"He's always struck me as a bit shy," Abby continued. "A quiet kind of guy."

Quiet until the volcano erupts. Leah wondered if she was the only one who sensed he was about to blow.

"He's a musician." Abby stepped closer, smiling. "You want to hear a funny story? Lara told me about it. One of the Vamps, Jack, was throwing a bachelor party for Ian in a hotel room at the Plaza. Dougal was playing the bagpipes, and they were all drunk on Blissky and trying to dance a jig. They were so loud that the hotel called the police, and Jack had a hell of a time trying to explain it all."

Leah glanced over at the happy crowd. Apparently vampires liked to party. "So what happened? Were they arrested?"

Abby chuckled. "No, but Jack ended up married to the police officer. Lara's over there somewhere." She motioned toward the crowd. "She's expecting a baby, too."

Leah gulped. She was sensing an alarming pattern here. "Do the Undead always take mortal women for their wives?"

"Well, not always." Abby picked up the cake knife. "Which flavor cake would you like?"

Not always? Did that mean some of the women here were vampires? Or something else?

Her heart started racing again. What if vampires were just the tip of the iceberg? What if the normal world around her was actually abnormal?

"I think I'll try the pink layer." Abby put a slice on a small plate. "I'm not sure if it's cherry or strawberry. What would you like?"

My sanity back. Leah studied the different layers. White, lemon yellow, pink, red velvet, and devil's food.

"You should get the chocolate," a young voice said beside her.

Leah jumped. The little boy had curly blond hair, blue eyes, and a dab of chocolate icing on his nose. "You—you're Roman's son?"

He nodded, smiling. "I'm Tino."

Half vampire? Leah eased a bit to the side.

"What's your name?" Tino asked.

"I'm . . . Dr. Chin."

"Oh." Tino took a chocolate chip cookie off the table and munched on it. "The chocolate cake is the best."

"You eat regular food?" Leah asked.

Tino nodded, his mouth full. "My mom says I'm surprisingly normal." He wrinkled his nose. "I'm not sure if that's a good thing." He pointed up to the ceiling. "Would you like a balloon?"

Leah glanced up. Helium-filled balloons covered the ceiling.

"What color would you like?" Tino asked.

"I don't kn—" Leah halted when the little boy rose through the air. "Oh God. Oh my God." *Half vampire.*

"He's really very normal," Abby assured her quietly. "He can just do a few tricks that—"

"Do you know what you've done here?" Leah pressed a hand to her chest, struggling to breathe. "You've created a new species."

"The children are basically human. You'll see that when you study Tino's blood work."

"*Basically* human?" Leah wondered if she could still make a run for it. Unfortunately, the big, volcanically inclined Dougal would stop her.

Or maybe not. Gregori had returned with a woman, and the other men had retreated into the foyer, completely focused on her. She was dressed in a sparkly red dress that barely covered her rump and clung to a body that was downright voluptuous. Gregori had an arm around her waist and was grinning at her.

"Oh, no," Abby whispered. "It's Vanna. I thought he'd gotten rid of her."

Leah winced. Poor Abby was pregnant, and her husband was seeing another woman?

Gregori pushed the woman into Dougal's arms. Scowling, he tried to hand her back, but Gregori simply laughed. Dougal glanced at Leah, and his scowl grew even more menacing. He stalked away, taking the woman with him.

Leah shuddered. "Will that woman be safe?"

"She's not—"

"Here's your balloon." Tino interrupted Abby as he landed beside them, holding a pink balloon. "I thought you might like pink cause you're a girl."

"Thank you." Leah automatically took hold of the pink ribbon. She glanced back at the foyer, but Dougal and the woman were no longer in sight.

"Don't let Coco touch it," Tino warned her. "Her claws are too sharp, and she might pop it."

"Claws?"

"Let me get you a piece of cake." Abby rushed back to the cake and plopped a slice onto a plate. "Tino, you want another piece?"

"No, thanks. I'm full." He smiled at Leah. "Coco wanted to help with the balloons, but her nails are too sharp. All the were-panther kids are like that."

Leah gasped, and the balloon escaped her hand. "Were-*what*?"

The second Gregori shoved VANNA at Dougal, he objected and pushed her back. Unfortunately, his prosthetic hand had locked onto her forearm and refused to let go.

"Bloody hell," he whispered. He didn't want anyone to witness his lack of control. Why tonight, of all nights? He was just getting back into the game. If Angus saw that he couldn't control his own freaking hand, he might never get another chance.

As he stalked down the hall to find a vacant conference room, he heard Gregori chuckling behind him. *Dammit.* Everyone would wonder why he wanted to be alone with a rubber doll, and by the sound of Gregori's sniggering, he knew what their conclusions would be.

He entered the first conference room and kicked the door shut. The room was empty, dimly lit from the window that overlooked the front parking lot.

Release! he ordered his hand. Nothing.

"Let go!" He shook his right arm, trying to fling VANNA across the room. She flopped wildly, still in the grip of his traitorous hand. One of her stiletto heels flew off and clattered onto the conference table. Her blond wig stayed on, but the hair stuck out like she'd been plugged into an electric socket.

Damn. He rammed her against the wall, pinning her across the chest with his left arm as he attempted to tug his right hand free. With each tug, her arm lifted higher and higher. Her stiff fingers caught in his hair, pulling his hair loose from its tie.

"Dammit. *Let go!*" He tried jerking his hand to the side. Her whole body moved with him, but her dress didn't. Clasped in his left fist, the flimsy material tore completely off her shoulders.

"Bollocks," he growled and let the dress fall.

He hesitated a second, surprised by how real her breasts looked. The nipples were even beaded, as if she was aroused. Her glassy eyes stared at him through strands of messy hair. Her mouth was permanently set in a dopey grin. There was even a tongue in her mouth. And teeth.

Bloody hell, of all the stupid situations to be in. He took a deep breath and closed his eyes. He just needed to relax, and then his prosthetic hand would let go. He would toss VANNA back into Gregori's office and forget this had ever happened.

Gregori and Laszlo had invented VANNA years ago as an alternative to biting real women. As good Vamps, they had all switched to drinking synthetic blood out of bottles, but some had missed the thrill of sinking their fangs into a lovely neck. To solve that dilemma, Gregori had come up with VANNA, the Vampire Artificial Nutritional Needs Appliance.

He had bought two lifelike human sex toys, VANNA White and VANNA Black, and Laszlo had installed a pump and rubber tubing inside each of them. The pump sounded like a real heart, and it made synthetic blood flow through the tubing, which ran up the sides of VANNA's neck to simulate carotid arteries. Gregori must have filled her up, for Dougal could smell the blood coursing inside her.

VANNA had seemed like a good idea at the time, but it hadn't worked. Her rubberlike skin had proven difficult to bite, and Roman had lost one of his fangs giving her a trial run.

Dougal was more in danger of losing his sanity than his fangs. He could also lose his job if he didn't get his damned hand under control.

Release, he calmly ordered the prosthesis. Nothing.

He took a deep breath and tried again. No response.

Gritting his teeth, he glared at his hand. *You will obey me! Release!* Still nothing.

"Dammit!" He sat VANNA on the table, forcing her legs to bend at a ninety-degree angle at the hips. Her legs jutted out, spread wide.

He stepped between them. "I'm not losing my job over this. *Release!*"

His hand remained locked on her forearm.

Rage burst inside him, and he roared. With his left hand, he shoved her back on the table. As her legs flew up, feet toward the ceiling, her one remaining stiletto caught the hem of his kilt and pulled it up.

"Ye bloody witch from hell!"

"**W**ere-*what*?" Leah repeated when Abby hesitated.

"Were-panthers." Tino watched her balloon float back to the ceiling. "Do you want me to get it back?"

A chill skittered down Leah's spine. "Panthers? As in big killer cats?"

Tino frowned. "They're nice. My aunt is a werepanther. You want to meet her?"

The room swirled, and Leah grabbed onto the table edge.

"Take it easy." Abby approached her slowly. "We were going to tell you as soon as we thought you could handle it."

Tino winced. "Did I mess up?"

"It's okay," Abby assured him.

"It's not okay." Leah struggled to breathe. "There are some big killer cats in the room with us?"

"Were-cats," Abby said. "Or were-panthers, to be precise. I'm not sure if Rajiv is here. He's a were-tiger."

"What does that mean?" Leah pressed a hand against her chest. Her heart was thudding wildly. "They're half cat?"

"They're fully human right now." Abby touched her arm. "We call them shifters. Werewolves, were-cats, were-bears. I even met a were-dolphin in Hawaii. They shift once or twice a month when the moon is full. I can get you some blood work from one of them if you'd like to study—"

"I don't want to study them!" Leah stepped back, raising her hands. "I want my world back, my safe world where humans stay human!"

"I'm sorry." Abby gave her a sympathetic look. "I know it's a lot to take in. But once you get to know everyone, you'll see how nice—"

"I don't want to know everyone!" Leah yelled. She winced when the crowd across the room looked her way. Oh God, the vampires and shifters were staring at her now.

She stepped back. *Great move, Leah. Make the pack of supernatural creatures angry.*

"Relax," Abby whispered softly. "No one is going to hurt you."

Tino gazed at her sadly. "I didn't mean to scare you. I thought you already knew everything. My dad said you were going to join us."

Join them? Leah gulped down some air. "I-I need to . . ." *Escape.* But she could hardly say that out loud. "Is there a ladies' room nearby?"

"In the hallway across the foyer." Abby pointed toward the entrance. "I could go with you."

"I-I'm fine. I just need to be alone for a few minutes." Leah ran for the foyer. Breathing heavily, she glanced back. No one had followed her. Thank God.

But they were watching her. Her skin crawled with gooseflesh. She looked up at the camera by the front door. The red blinking light mocked her. *No escape*. Her gaze lowered to the front double doors. Locked, most probably.

How about a window? Maybe she could sneak out from a vacant room. She crossed the foyer calmly so it would look like she was simply on her way to the restroom. She sauntered into the hallway and tried the first door on the left. Locked.

The second doorknob moved with a tiny click. Bingo. She pushed the door open and froze.

"Ye bloody witch from hell!"

The room was dark, but she could see enough to recognize the man in the kilt. The volcano had erupted.

Dougal had pinned a woman down on the table. His back was to Leah, but she could see his hair flying wild, his kilt lifted in front. The woman's legs were spread wide and jolted each time he shoved against her.

"Let go, dammit!" He pushed at her so hard that her head banged against the table.

Leah gasped.

He looked over his shoulder and stiffened.

"Oh God," she breathed, stepping back.

"Wait!" With a jerk, he pivoted toward her, and the woman's arm ripped from her body.

Leah screamed.

Blood spurted from the woman's shoulder, spraying drops across Dougal's white shirt and face.

She stumbled back. The room swirled, along with his stricken, bloodstained face.

" 'Tis no' what ye think." He stepped toward her, the woman's arm dangling from a blood-smeared metallic hand.

Red, bloodlike dots flickered before her eyes, then Leah did something she'd never done before.

She fainted.

Chapter Six

"The devil take it, man, what the hell happened?" Angus shouted in the security office.

Dougal squared his shoulders. "'Twas my fault. I'll explain it to Dr. Chin—"

"The hell ye will!" Angus interrupted him. "Ye've terrorized her enough for one evening."

Dougal glanced at the monitors but couldn't spot her anywhere. Seeing the pale, horror-stricken look on Leah's face had caused his grip on VANNA's arm to finally relax. The arm had hit the floor just seconds before Leah had crumpled, and his heart had plummeted along with them. How would she ever see him as anything but a hideous monster?

Her scream and collapse had caused all the party-goers to come running. And there he'd stood in the dark conference room, his kilt askew, his hair wild, his face and clothes splattered with blood, while half-naked VANNA reclined on the table, looking thoroughly ravished and dismembered. Leave it to Gregori to comment she was still smiling.

"Where is Dr. Chin?" Dougal asked.

"Gregori carried her down to a bedroom in the

basement. Ye willna see her on a monitor. Emma told me she insisted they turn the camera off."

So she was awake. "How is she?"

"She's demanding we call the police and turn you in for sexual assault and battery." Angus grimaced. "It looked like ye were—"

"I wasna tupping a rubber wench!" Dougal's heart plummeted even farther. Did Leah think he was a rapist?

"Well, we can be grateful for that," Angus muttered. "But ye still ripped her bloody arm off. Is that what ye call meek as a lamb?"

Dougal sighed. He could look like either an incompetent fool or a violent sex offender. "My prosthesis locked onto VANNA's arm and wouldna let go. I dinna want anyone to see, so I took her to the nearest conference room—"

"Yer hand is malfunctioning?" Angus interrupted.

"'Twas no' responding to my mind control." Dougal closed his fist and opened it. "'Tis working now, but I've been having trouble on and off all evening."

Angus gave him an exasperated look. "Ye should have said something. Roman and Abby can examine the hand to see what's wrong with it. If it's broken, they can fit you with a new one."

Dougal sat heavily in a chair. "I doona think it is the hand's fault. I know I should have told you, but I dinna want to look incompetent."

Angus leaned against the desk, studying the prosthesis. "Yer fist locks and doesna release?"

"Aye. So when I turned toward the door, VANNA's arm came with me."

Angus snorted. "Then ye would have an excellent grip on a sword. I think ye can still do security here."

Dougal exhaled with relief. "Thank you."

"In fact, 'tis best for you to remain here, where Roman and Abby can work with you to get the problem fixed." Angus sighed. "But until then, we'll have to remove you from the mission roster."

Dougal groaned inwardly. "I understand."

Angus grabbed a new MacKay S&I polo shirt off a bookcase shelf and tossed it to him. "Put this on and clean yerself up. I'll tell Emma what happened so she can explain it to Dr. Chin. Hopefully, she'll still agree to help us with our guest in the basement."

Dougal glanced at the monitor that showed the silver room and the captive soldier still in stasis. Would Leah want to help? Or had he frightened her so badly that she would wish only for escape?

As he strode to the restroom, his old vow reverberated inside his head. *I will find you. No matter what. If it takes a thousand years, I will find you.*

Another sizzle skittered along the length of his tattoo, and he rolled his right shoulder to relieve the itch. Why was it bothering him after all this time? The last time he'd felt it had been after the battle of Culloden when he had crawled beneath a bush to die. As his lifeblood had seeped from his wound, he'd imagined Li Lei sitting next to him, promising him that someday they would be together again. He had murmured yes as comforting heat had spread along his tattoo, lulling him into the deep sleep of the dead.

He knew now that it was Connor who had sat beside him and his "yes" had been interpreted as an agreement to join the ranks of the Undead. He'd awakened a vampire, and for centuries the tattoo had remained as cold as his Undead heart.

Had Leah awakened the dragon? Could she bring his half-dead soul back to life? Unfortunately, after waiting close to three hundred years, he was in danger of losing her before he could even talk to her. If she demanded to leave, they would teleport her back home and erase her memory.

He had to see her tonight. Before he lost his chance.

Leah stiffened when Gregori walked into the room carrying a woman in his arms like a sack of potatoes.

"Don't worry." Abby perched beside her on the bed. "I asked him to bring her here so you could see she's not real. This is VANNA Black, the sister to the doll you saw with Dougal."

Leah watched as Gregori set the lifelike woman in an easy chair. "Why is she dressed like a cheerleader?"

Abby gave her husband a wry look. "Good question."

"I didn't do it," Gregori mumbled. "Phineas must have dressed her like this before he got married."

Leah shook her head. A few minutes earlier, Abby had explained that VANNA was a failed experiment the guys kept around as a joke, but it all sounded a bit crazy to her. "And this doll is supposed to keep vampires from attacking us?"

"You don't need to worry about being attacked."

Emma sat in the other easy chair, facing the bed. "The Vamps are morally opposed to it."

Leah scoffed. "They're vampires. How moral can they be?"

Emma smiled slightly. "Well, I can speak on the matter with some knowledge, since I've become a Vamp myself."

"Oh." Leah winced. "I . . . didn't mean to offend."

Emma's smile widened. "You haven't. There was a time when I hated vampires. But then I got to know them better. You see, the Malcontents imprisoned me with Angus and let him go hungry so he'd have no choice but to bite me. For several nights he restrained himself. He was starving to death, biting himself, and I even caught him climbing on a table where the sunlight would hit him."

Abby gasped. "He was going to commit suicide?"

Emma nodded. "Yes. He was ready to die rather than harm me. I had to beg him to bite me so he could survive."

"So vampires retain a sense of right and wrong?" Leah asked.

"Death cannot change a person's character," Emma explained. "Bad people become evil vampires, and good guys like Angus—well, he's my hero."

Leah hated to admit it, but Emma's story sounded a bit romantic. "And you're married to him now?"

"Yes. We're very happy." Emma's smile grew wistful. "He reminds me of a historical hero—Braveheart or Rob Roy. And the way he talks—it still melts my heart."

Abby nodded in agreement. "There's something about a guy in a kilt. I've been trying to talk Gregori into getting one."

He snorted. "I'm not wearing a damned skirt."

A vision of Dougal flitted through Leah's mind. She'd thought he was wonderfully attractive until she'd caught him assaulting a woman. Or a doll. "I still don't understand why Dougal was attacking a rubber doll." She shuddered, remembering the shock of seeing the arm rip off and the blood squirt out.

The room grew silent. Emma and Gregori exchanged a worried look.

"I-I'm sure he had a reason," Abby mumbled.

"Like he's a violent pervert?" Leah asked.

Abby winced. "He never struck me that way. I always thought he was shy."

"Actually," Gregori said, "I don't think he approved of us bringing you here. He questioned if we had the right to drag you into our world."

Leah sat up. Was that why he'd looked so tense and agitated when everyone else had been cheerful? Was he actually on her side? She shook that thought away. He was a violent, wild person. She didn't dare trust him.

Emma's cell phone rang. "It's Angus. I'll take this in the hall." She hurried from the room.

Gregori picked VANNA up and headed for the door. "I'll get rid of this."

"Permanently, I hope," Abby muttered, then shifted on the bed to look at Leah. "So you're okay now?"

"I guess." Leah shrugged. "Did you have a hard time accepting all this supernatural stuff?"

"Not too hard. I was desperate to find some plants in China that I thought would help my sick mother, but it seemed impossible. That's when my father arranged for the vampires to teleport me there."

"So you were well motivated to accept them."

"Exactly." Abby smiled. "The Vamps and shifters took me there and protected me." Her smile faded. "At one point, we were captured by Master Han, and while we were escaping, one of the bad guys came at me with a sword. Gregori jumped in front of me and was stabbed in the back. I almost lost him." She blinked away some tears and smiled. "I cry way too easily these days. Must be the hormones."

Leah slid off the bed and paced across the room. Abby and Emma made their husbands sound like heroes. Undead heroes fighting against the supernatural forces of evil. It sounded as fanciful as the stories her grandfather used to tell her.

Grandpa had always said there was a world beyond science, a magical world that could not be explained with logic. Her mother had warned her to pay no attention to his silly tales. Grandpa could never stroll along a rocky shore without looking for a selkie, or roam the green fields without searching for the fae. He had claimed his Uilleann pipes could entice the leprechauns to come out of hiding.

Mom had rejected her father and Ireland. She'd moved to the States to study at MIT, and there she'd fallen in love with a brilliant physics professor, Dr. Kai Ling Chin.

Leah had been raised on a strict, home-school regimen of science and rationalism. Her mind had thrived on it. But her heart had loved the one magical summer she'd spent with Grandpa. Her parents had been invited to speak at several prestigious conferences, and her two teenage brothers were already in college. After realizing that a nine-year-old girl was too young to fend for herself all summer, her parents had shipped her off to Ireland.

Grandpa had made her feel loved instead of abandoned. And wonderfully free. She'd danced barefoot in the meadow while he'd serenaded her with the pipes. She'd gathered flowers without learning their names in Latin. And she'd reveled in Grandpa's stories where nothing was what it seemed. If he were still alive, he would laugh and drink a toast to this bizarre, new world she'd stumbled into.

So what should she do? Run back to her safe, secure world that made sense and followed the rules? Where dead people remained dead without waking up and craving blood, and humans remained human without shifting into killer cats? Her parents would say run. It was the logical choice.

But Grandpa would lean close to her ear and whisper, "Life is an adventure, lass. Live it to the fullest, and never look back."

If she were fanciful like Grandpa, she would suspect that somehow his spirit had guided her here. She recalled the odd feeling that had swept over her earlier. As if her whole life had been a series of small steps leading her to this one moment in time. *Fate*.

She shook her head. She was too logical to believe in fate. Her decisions had been her own. She was master of her own destiny. She'd accepted the perfect job, one that required a physician and geneticist. And Dr. Lee had offered great benefits and an outstanding salary. *Because the Vamps wanted you.*

She'd been drawn into this world on purpose. *Fate*. And she'd felt it the first time she saw *him*. Dougal. The Undead pervert who ripped arms off lifelike sex toys. She could almost hear her grandfather's cackling laughter.

"Dougal!" Emma's voice yelled in the hallway. "You shouldn't go in there."

Leah spun toward the door, her heart thudding.

"Angus told me about your prosthesis malfunctioning," Emma continued. "I'll explain it to Leah."

Prosthesis? Leah's thoughts raced as she searched her memory. The room had been dark, but she'd clearly seen the blood splatter across Dougal's pale face and white shirt, the shocked expression on his face, and the bloody arm clutched in his hand. A metallic, bloodstained hand. A vampire with a prosthetic hand? And, apparently, a malfunctioning one. Did that mean the bloody assault had been nothing more than an accident?

When a deep voice responded, she stepped closer to the doorway.

" . . . my fault. I should apologize. I frightened her out of her wits."

She smiled to herself. He had pronounced *out* like "oot." And his lilting accent sounded like sweet, soothing music. She slapped herself mentally. What was she thinking? That a vampire was attractive? His voice and handsome looks hardly made up for the fact that he was a bloodsucker. And why was she so eager to excuse the assault as a simple accident? He had looked like a wild man, his hair flying and his voice roaring in anger.

Her heart jolted when his large frame filled the open doorway, and his gaze immediately fixed on her. Green, expressive eyes that studied her intently.

He was even bigger close up. His navy polo shirt clung to every muscled contour of his chest and shoulders. He still wore his bright and colorful kilt, made of a green, black, and red plaid. Green knee socks hugged his muscular calves.

He stood with his feet wide apart and his hands at his sides. His right hand was gray and metallic. A series of tiny clicking noises emanated from it as he curled it into a fist. Was it strong enough to tear a real person's arm off?

She eased back a step, then lifted her gaze to his face. To the injured look in his eyes.

"I doona blame you for being afraid of me," he said softly. "But I willna harm you."

She squared her shoulders. "I'm not afraid."

His eyes softened. His skin was pale, a stark contrast to the dark whiskers lining his chiseled jaw and the long black hair brushed neatly back and tied in a ponytail at the base of his neck.

A wide brow, high cheekbones, strong chin, and an abundance of lean muscle in all the right places. He was the type of man who could actually be called beautiful and still be wonderfully masculine.

A shame he was dead.

A bigger shame that she found him so appealing. *Vampire*, she reminded herself. Strong and wild enough to rip a woman's arm off.

She lifted her chin. "You were watching me on the cameras, weren't you? Did you enjoy the show? Was my performance amusing?"

His eyebrows drew together in a frown. "Nay. I dinna enjoy it." He stepped into the room. "But I thought ye were verra brave and strong."

Her heart squeezed in her chest.

Emma walked into the room, pocketing her cell

phone. "Well? Are you going to explain, or shall I?" she asked Dougal.

"I will." He turned to Leah and lifted his right hand. "My hand locked on VANNA's arm. The prosthesis wouldna obey my command to release. I dinna mean to tear her arm off. 'Twas an accident."

That was a relief. Sorta. He had still reacted like a wild man. The volcano might be sleeping now, but who knew when he would erupt again? Leah's eyes narrowed on his hand. "How do you command it to do things?"

He hesitated. "Mind control."

She suppressed a shudder. He probably had the power to tamper with her mind like Dr. Lee had done. "Then what was malfunctioning—the hand or your mind?"

Dougal winced. "My mind, I think." He rolled his right shoulder. "I'm no' crazy. I just lost control. I'm no' sure why."

Well, at least he seemed honest. It would have been so much easier for him to claim mechanical failure. "How did you lose your hand?"

"In battle." He shifted his weight. "I'm no' a bad swordsman. I was outnumbered. Five to one."

"You were fighting with swords?"

"Aye. I lunged at one, and another one sliced my hand off. It turned to dust."

Leah grimaced. "That had to be awful to see."

"It dinna feel verra good, either."

"You can . . . feel pain?"

He gave her a wry look. "Ye think my feelings are dead?"

"I don't know what to think."

He lifted one brow. "I can feel anything ye can."

One look at his expressive eyes and she knew that was true.

He stepped closer and lowered his voice. "May I have a word with you, lass?"

Her heart fluttered. She hadn't been called a lass since the last time she'd seen her grandfather. Odd, but this man was probably older than her grandfather, even though he looked fairly young, only a few years older than herself.

"In private," he added.

"Not a good idea," Emma said. "We can't have you scaring her away."

He cast an annoyed look at her. "Verra well." He turned back to Leah, and his dark brows quirked slightly with a questioning expression. "Do ye wish to leave?"

Her breath caught. "Leave?"

"Aye. If ye want to go home, I can take you."

He *was* on her side. A burst of warm hope spread through her chest. She could go home. Dougal would help her.

"Dougal," Emma warned him.

"Aye, I ken." He shot her an irritated look. "Ye want to drag the puir lass into our world and our problems. But has anyone asked her what she wants?" He shifted his gaze back to Leah. "We have no right to keep you here. If ye want to go, I can teleport you home right away."

Leah blinked. "Teleport?"

"Dougal," Emma spoke more sharply. "We need her."

"She doesna need us."

Emma sighed. "We can't simply let her go, not

when she knows about us. There's protocol to follow—"

"You mean erasing my memory?" Leah asked.

"I willna do that," Dougal said.

"What?" Emma stiffened. "That's against regulations, and you know it."

"To hell with yer regulations," Dougal growled. "If ye trust her enough to expect her to help us, then ye can trust her to keep our secret." He turned back to Leah. "Am I right? Do ye plan to make us public?"

She shook her head. "Everyone would think I was crazy. And then I'd have a really hard time getting another job."

The corner of his mouth tilted up. "Aye, there is that." He moved closer. "Shall we go?"

She stepped back. Her prior reluctance to remain had stemmed from feeling forced, but now that she actually had a choice, she wasn't sure she wanted to leave. Any other job would seem boring compared to what she could do here. Still, it wouldn't hurt to get away for a few days to think it over. "How does this teleportation work?"

"I hold onto you and read yer mind to see where ye want to go. Then we go."

The prospect of him holding onto her was intriguing, but she had serious doubts about the mind reading or going part. If he read her mind, he might see how attractive she thought he was. And the going part simply sounded impossible. "You mean we disappear and rematerialize?"

"Aye."

"That can't be safe. What if our bodies get accidentally fused together?"

He leaned forward and whispered, "Lass, if our bodies fuse together, 'twould no' be by accident."

Her mouth dropped open, and she stepped back. Was he referring to sex? The gall of the man. He certainly wasn't as shy as everyone thought. "How could I rely on you to take me home? You might take me to . . . to your underground lair." Wasn't that what vampires did?

His mouth twitched. "I'm fresh out of underground lairs."

He'd said "oot" again, but she ignored the way it made her heart flutter. "I don't trust you."

"I understand. Ye doona know me."

No, she didn't. And if she refused to stay at this job, she might never get to know him. And that suddenly seemed like a terrible shame. How old was he? When and where had he been transformed? Why did he look at her like he was starving, and not just for blood?

Would it hurt to stay in New York while she made her decision? Would it hurt to even try the job for a few days? It might be the most interesting work she'd ever find. What if she could actually help these people and save lives? Maybe her own life would seem more like an adventure. Maybe, for the first time, she would find a place where she could actually make friends. These people would never consider her a freak, not when they were abnormal.

She took a deep breath. "I think I'll stay here and give the job a try."

Emma clapped her hands together. "That's wonderful! Thank you!"

Abby rushed forward, grinning. "I'm so excited! It's going to be great working with you."

Leah smiled. "It should be interesting." She cast a nervous glance at Dougal, who was watching her with a fierce gleam in his green eyes. Was he excited or angry? She couldn't tell. "Are you going to be here?"

"Aye." He shrugged his shoulder, and his gaze grew more intense. "I'm in charge of security here. I'll be keeping you safe."

A shiver pebbled her skin with gooseflesh. *He* would be keeping her safe? He presented a bigger danger than anyone else.

To be honest with herself, she knew that she'd based part of her decision to stay on him, so in an alarming sense, she was flirting with danger. And even more alarming, she was looking forward to it.

Chapter Seven

*L*eah woke with a jolt, sitting up in bed. For a second she felt disoriented, then she remembered where she was—a guest bedroom in Roman Draganesti's townhouse in the Upper East Side of Manhattan. More memories from the night before flooded back. Vampires, shifters, hybrid children, and *him*. Dougal.

With a shudder, she pulled the blanket up to her chin. He had given her a chance to escape, but then he'd also become a major reason to stay.

She shook her head, not comfortable with that thought. In truth, she had many reasons to stay. She was intrigued by this new supernatural world, challenged by the work, and honored to have a chance to save lives. Those were legitimate reasons that made her decision sound much more noble than the way her heart pounded whenever he looked at her.

Even so, he was the one who dominated her thoughts. When would she see him again? Where was he now? Light filtered in around the curtains, so it was daylight outside. He would be sleeping or whatever happened to vampires during the day.

To her surprise, the bedside clock read a few minutes past noon. She jumped out of bed and headed to the shower. As she washed her hair with her favorite jasmine-scented shampoo, she let her mind wander back to the night before. After her decision to stay, she'd gone back to the lab with Abby to study the two remaining blood samples.

Abby was right. Tino was basically human. But the third sample, taken from a soldier for Master Han, had shown an alarming number of mutations. Changing him back to a normal mortal would not be easy, but it was a challenge she was looking forward to.

By two in the morning, she'd been exhausted, so Gregori and Abby had driven her back to the townhouse before going on to their own place. Abby had promised to pick her up at 3:30 p.m. so they could return to Romatech and get what she called an early start. Leah supposed these strange hours would become the norm for her now that she was working with vampires.

She was too hungry to mess with her wet hair, so she towel-dried it, threw on some jeans and a T-shirt, and headed downstairs to the kitchen. To her surprise, she heard voices inside. And smelled coffee brewing.

She peeked inside the swinging door. There were two women and three children. Two of the kids looked like twins, and they were sitting in high chairs.

The younger woman, a pretty redhead, glanced her way and smiled. "Hi, Leah. Come and have breakfast with us."

She eased inside. "Good morning. I mean, afternoon." She'd been introduced to the party crowd the

night before, but there had been so many of them
that she couldn't recall any names.

"*Buenos dias,*" the older woman said. "I'm Fidelia."
She placed pieces of toast and jelly onto two plastic
plates. "The little ones are Jillian and Jean-Pierre."

"We call him John for short," added a young girl.
"I'm Bethany."

"And I'm Heather." The mother poured milk into
two cups and snapped spouted lids on top before
passing them to the toddlers.

"Papa's still asleep," Bethany added.

Fidelia snorted. "That's a nice way to put it. Dead
as a rock is more—" She paused when Heather
cleared her throat.

Dead? The older woman must be exaggerating. "So
you're married to a vampire?" Leah asked Heather
as she eyed the children. They were probably hy-
brids like Tino.

Heather nodded, smiling. "Yes. I'm married to
Jean-Luc Echarpe. You met us briefly last night."

Leah blinked. "The famous fashion designer?" He
was a vampire?

"That's Papa!" Bethany sat up in her seat, grinning.

"We came for the party last night, but we'll be
staying a while, getting ready for fashion week."
Heather motioned toward the counter. "We bought
some groceries yesterday. Please help yourself to
whatever you like."

"Thank you." Facing the counter, Leah twisted a
bagel in half and dropped the pieces into a toaster.
She located a saucer, a knife, and some cream cheese.
"So I guess you live in Paris?"

Fidelia scoffed. "I wish."

"We're in Texas." Heather sipped some coffee. "Jean-Luc went into hiding there when the media started wondering why he wasn't aging."

"And then he fell in love with my mom," Bethany added.

Heather smiled at her daughter.

They seemed like a happy family, Leah thought wistfully as she poured herself a cup of coffee.

"Those Vamps, they're very macho." Fidelia bit into a bagel, and her eyes narrowed on Leah. "You're a pretty young thing. I bet they'll go after you next."

"Fidelia," Heather whispered. "You might frighten her."

"She should be frightened," Fidelia insisted, then twisted her square frame in the chair to face Leah. "If one of those Vamps sets his sights on you, he'll be like a dog with a bone. A rabid dog. With a boner."

"Fidelia!" Heather gave her a warning look.

The older woman shrugged. "Okay. They're more like those heat-detecting missiles. If they think you're hot, they'll zoom right after you till they catch you. And then, *bam*!" She clapped her hands together. "It's an explosion of love!"

Bethany giggled.

Leah swallowed hard. Was that why Dougal had watched her with such an intense, hungry look in his eyes? Had he set his sights on her?

"They're *muy macho*, very sexy." Fidelia patted her hair, which was black with two inches of gray roots. "I had my eye on Robby, but he found a girl a few years younger than me."

"More than a few years," Heather muttered.

"I like the Scottish ones the best." Fidelia's eyes

twinkled. "And I like what they're wearing underneath their kilts. *Nada*!"

Bethany grinned. "Aunt Fee, you should marry Dougal. He's still single."

Leah's breath caught. She turned her back, pretending to wait on the toaster.

"Ah, Dougal," Fidelia murmured. "He's a handsome *hombre*. Never says much, but I suspect he's more a man of action."

"He's real good with a sword," Bethany said.

Fidelia chuckled. "Those Scotsmen have some really long swords. And I bet they know just how to use them."

Heather cleared her throat. "I'm afraid Dougal won't be our guard anymore. He's going to be in charge of night security at Romatech."

Where I'll see him every night. Leah started when the bagels popped up in the toaster.

"I'm going to miss Dougal," Bethany whined. "Who's going to guard us then?"

"Don't worry, honey," Fidelia replied. "Mr. Glock and Senor Beretta will keep us safe."

"Oh God, no," Heather whispered. "You brought them with you?"

"Of course," Fidelia said. "That's why I love teleporting with the Vamps. They never take my guns away."

Leah glanced back and saw the older woman patting her large handbag.

Heather sighed. "You didn't need to bring them."

"How else do we stay safe during the day?" Fidelia asked. "We left Billy in Texas to guard the house, and Dougal's dead as a doornail right now."

Dead? That was the second time Fidelia had said

the Vamps were dead. How could that be possible? Wasn't being Undead different from being dead? Leah spread some cream cheese on her bagel. "Where is Dougal?"

"In the basement, most probably." Heather sipped some more coffee. "That's where the guards stay when they sleep here."

Leah brought her bagel and coffee to the table. The basement. Maybe she could sneak down there when no one was looking.

"Guess what?" Bethany asked her. "Mom and I are going to a show this afternoon. *Mary Poppins*!"

"Oh, that's nice." Leah sat.

"Don't worry about me," Fidelia muttered. "I'll just stay here with the twins."

"John and Jillian?" Bethany asked.

"No." Fidelia patted her handbag, her eyes twinkling. "Smith and Wesson."

Leah shot a wary look at the handbag. How many guns were in there?

"We'd better hurry." Heather stood, stuffing the last of her bagel in her mouth.

While Leah ate, they bustled about, putting things away and cleaning up the happy toddlers, who had grape jelly smeared all over their faces. Then they went upstairs to a playroom Heather mentioned. She and Bethany would be leaving soon for their Broadway matinee.

With it quiet in the kitchen, Leah's thoughts kept returning to Fidelia's insistence that Dougal was dead. It didn't make sense. A body couldn't remain dead for hours and then magically revive itself. He had to be in a deep sleep or something like a coma.

The more she thought about it, the more she had to know the truth. She set her dirty dishes on the rack in the dishwasher, then left the kitchen in search of the basement. She didn't have to go far. The first door she tried opened onto a staircase.

At the base of the stairs, she found a washer and dryer. Then she entered a large, well-lit room with a billiard table in the middle. Sofas and chairs lined the walls. A small fridge held bottles of something called Bleer. Synthetic blood and beer. Racks lined the upper walls, where an assortment of weapons were stashed—swords, knives, guns and rifles. Interspersed between the racks were four coats of arms belonging to four clans. The MacKay, Mac-Phie, Buchanan, and Kincaid. The plaid background on the Kincaid coat of arms matched Dougal's kilt. *Dougal Kincaid.*

So where was he? She spotted a closed door and opened it. The creak made her wince. If he was sleeping, the noise might wake him up.

The room was dark, so she left the door open to allow light to filter in from the billiards room. Two rows of twin beds lined the walls. All were empty except the first one on the left.

"Hello?" she whispered.

No answer.

She approached the bed slowly. It was him. Dougal. "I don't mean to interrupt your sleep," Well, that wasn't exactly true. She fully expected him to wake up any second. After all, he was a security guard. Weren't they trained to be light sleepers?

His large frame filled the bed to the point that his feet practically hung off the bottom edge and his shoulders took up the entire width. He was flat on his back, his hands folded at his waist, his left hand resting on top of the prosthetic right hand.

She eased closer. "Hello?" Her gaze drifted down his body. What on earth was he wearing? Some kind of nightgown? It looked like the sort of thing Ebenezer Scrooge would wear. It was white, baggy, and ended at midcalf. His feet were covered with white tube socks. The gown had long sleeves buttoned at the wrist, and another row of buttons marched up his chest to the high collar.

She smiled. The collar even had a ruffle at the top. How old-fashioned could he get? At least he wasn't wearing one of those silly nightcaps on his head.

"Are you awake?"

No answer. She leaned over to see his face, prepared to jump back whenever his eyes opened. His hair was loose about his shoulders. His jaw and mouth were outlined with dark whiskers. His mouth was closed. How could a man have such a pretty mouth?

She glanced back at his eyes. Still shut. "You know I'm here, don't you? You're only pretending to sleep?"

His face remained completely still. Not a twitch from those dark eyebrows. She'd never seen eyebrows or a forehead that could be so expressive. Her mother's emotions showed in her eyes and her voice. Her father either smiled slightly or more often, his lips thinned in disapproval.

But Dougal—she'd recognized anger, fear, pain, hunger, curiosity, approval, and inquisitiveness all from the way he'd moved his brow and eyebrows. Without thinking, she reached out to touch his forehead. It was smooth and cool.

She lifted her hand quickly and checked his eyes. Still closed.

"You're breathing, aren't you?" She held a hand an inch below his nostrils.

No air.

She rested her hand on his chest. Hard as a rock. *Dead as a rock?*

"Come on, wake up." She shoved at his chest. "You can't be dead. It's not possible."

She touched his cheek. Cool. The dark whiskers prickled her fingertips. "You're just too pretty, you know that?"

She glanced at his eyes again. "Sexy rascal. Shall I have my way with you?"

No response. Wouldn't a normal guy stop faking it and make a grab for her?

But he wasn't normal. She pressed her fingers against his carotid artery, but his high, ruffled neckline was in the way.

"Well, this should wake you up." She unbuttoned the top three buttons of his nightshirt, then slid her hand to his neck to feel his pulse.

Nothing.

"This can't be." She felt the other side. *Damn.* He didn't have a pulse.

With her own pulse racing and fingers trembling, she unfastened more buttons. She peeled back his shirt and froze. This was the last thing she expected. A green and purple dragon curled over his right shoulder and down toward his chest. The mouth was wide open, breathing red and orange flames. An Oriental-style dragon, colorful and fierce. She placed her hand on the fire etched over his heart.

Nothing. She lay her head on his chest to listen. His skin was cool against her cheek.

No heartbeat.

"Oh God," she whispered, straightening. Should she attempt CPR? Would that even work on a vampire? It was almost two in the afternoon. He could have been dead since sunrise that morning.

"Dougal." She pulled the edges of his nightshirt together and looked at his handsome face. He couldn't be gone for good. He had to come back at sunset, right? Wasn't that what vampires did?

Her eyes burned with tears. "You will come back, won't you?"

Why was she feeling so drawn to this man? He couldn't be doing some sort of hocus-pocus glamour on her, not when he was dead. So that could only mean her attraction was real.

"Really crazy," she muttered, blinking away the tears. If she had any sense, she would avoid this man like the plague.

She rushed from the room, closing the door behind her and not looking back.

Dougal jolted back to life right after sunset. His vision adjusted quickly to the dark room. This wasn't the opulent basement of Jean-Luc's house in Texas but the old, familiar basement in Roman's townhouse. And tonight, he started his new job. If he was lucky, he'd see Leah again. He might even get to teleport her to Romatech.

He still felt bad about eavesdropping on her the

night before, but his guilt was overshadowed now by his admiration for her. She'd remained so strong and brave while her safe world had crumbled around her. And then she'd shown even more courage with her decision to stay. Even though she was wary of Vamps, she was still willing to work with them in order to save lives.

She had a good, honorable heart. And she was bright, beautiful, and brave. Just thinking about her made him smile. He hadn't felt this excited in years. Centuries. He wanted to know more about her. What made her happy? What were her dreams? Could she fall for someone like him?

As he sat up, he noticed his nightshirt was unbuttoned and gaping open. Who? He glanced around quickly, but the room was empty. He peered into the billiards room, but it was empty, too. Whoever had unbuttoned his shirt was gone.

He caught a slight whiff of perfume. Jasmine. His heart raced. Could it have been Leah? Was she curious enough about him that she'd examined him during his death-sleep?

He jumped in the shower as he considered other possible culprits. Heather Echarpe? No way. Fidelia? He shuddered at the thought. The woman was always trying to peek under his kilt whenever he levitated.

It had to have been Leah. He winced, imagining her reaction to his old-fashioned nightshirt. Maybe he should do as Gregori suggested and go to that fancy stylist over at DVN. The other guys always teased him about his old nightshirt. They had modernized to the point that most of them slept in underwear or less. He clung to the old shirt because it completely covered his tattoo, and he didn't want to answer any questions about it.

Leah must have seen it. He groaned at the thought. How could he explain it to her?

When he stepped out of the shower, he turned on the digital camera and monitor so he could see to shave. Normally, he didn't bother much with his appearance, but tonight he might see Leah again.

Would she confess to unbuttoning his shirt? If not, how could he ask if she had? *By the way, lass, did ye molest me during my death-sleep?*

Before dawn, he had teleported back to Jean-Luc's house to gather up his belongings: his clothes, tartan blanket, bagpipes, Uilleann pipes, and old tin whistle. So now he was able to dress in a fresh white shirt and kilt and tie his damp hair back with a new leather strip.

Upstairs, he found Jean-Luc in the kitchen, drinking a bottle of synthetic blood while his family ate dinner.

"*Félicitations, mon ami.*" Jean-Luc handed Dougal a bottle from the fridge. "You start tonight?"

"Aye." Dougal popped the bottle into the microwave.

Bethany gazed at him sadly, her bottom lip sticking out. "I'm going to miss you."

"Och, lass." He patted her shoulder. "Ye'll be fine."

"I'll miss you, too." Fidelia winked at him.

He stiffened. Had she been the one unbuttoning his clothes? He removed his bottle from the microwave and took a sip. "Where is Leah?"

"She left over an hour ago," Heather replied.

"I watched a movie with her when the twins were taking a nap," Fidelia added. "She had to go to work and couldn't finish it, but she said she's seen it a jillion times."

Heather stood and gave him a hug. "We'll miss you, but we're happy about your promotion. I know you'll do great!"

With a smile, Dougal nodded. "Thank you." He stepped back, his bottle in hand. "I should be going now."

He went back to the basement to slip his dagger into the sheath beneath his knee sock. So Leah had spent the afternoon watching something she'd seen many times before? What kind of movie would inspire such devotion?

Upstairs, he ventured into the parlor. It was empty, the television turned off. On top of the DVD player he found a plastic case. *An Affair to Remember.*

Curious, he read the synopsis on the back of the case. It sounded a bit sappy to him, but at least she wasn't watching a movie about slaying vampires.

He teleported to the side door at Romatech, then pressed his palm against the sensor to unlock the door. An alarm system had been installed years ago that detected anyone teleporting into the facility, so he and the other Vamps routinely teleported to one of the entrances.

He strode down the hall, drinking from his bottle. Outside the MacKay security office, he punched in the code to unlock the door. Inside, Austin was putting on his coat.

"Hey, Dougal." Austin slapped him on the shoulder. "It's good to have you back."

"'Tis good to be here." Dougal glanced at the monitors. Leah and Abby were in a lab, hunched over some papers on a table. The captive soldier was still in the silver room. Tino was on the basketball court, playing with his father, Angus, and Carlos.

Dougal's gaze shifted back to Leah, and his tattoo itched. She seemed even more beautiful tonight. "How's everything?"

"Good. Freemont's making the rounds right now." Austin grabbed his keys off the desk. "I gotta run. Matthew has soccer practice tonight."

"I understand."

"See ya tomorrow." With a smile, Austin left.

Dougal finished his bottle of breakfast blood while he watched the monitors. Austin was hurrying out the side door to his car in the parking lot. He lived nearby in White Plains with his wife and kids.

It seemed like everyone was having bairns these days. Dougal's gaze shifted back to the monitor showing Leah and Abby. Even Abby and Gregori were starting a family.

Laszlo entered the lab, sporting a fresh white lab coat, a striped shirt, and a bright red bowtie. His hair was neatly combed, and his round face gleamed a rosy pink, as if he'd scrubbed it too hard. The two women glanced up at him and smiled.

Dougal's prosthetic hand tightened around the bottle, and he glared at it. *Doona act up tonight.* He finished the bottle and tossed it into the recycling bin.

The office door opened, and Gregori sauntered inside. "Hey, dude. What's up?"

Dougal inclined his head. "Good evening."

Gregori peered at the monitor showing the lab and grinned. "Laszlo's looking less nerdy tonight, don't you think?"

Dougal shrugged.

"I made an appointment for him with Wilson," Gregori continued.

Dougal wondered if he should do the same.

"And I gave him some advice on how to charm the ladies," Gregori added. "The most obvious way to win a woman's heart."

It didn't seem so obvious to Dougal. He waited, but Gregori was entirely focused on the monitor.

"Isn't Abby beautiful?" he whispered. "She's practically glowing."

"What is the way?" Dougal asked. When Gregori gave him a blank look, he added, "The obvious way to win a woman's heart."

"Oh, that." Gregori waved a dismissive hand. "It just takes a sense of humor. You gotta make the lady laugh."

Dougal swallowed hard. "Laugh?"

"Yep. Let's see if Laszlo pulls it off." Gregori turned the volume up on the lab.

" . . . an alarming amount of genetic mutation," Leah was saying, pointing at a printout.

Laszlo sat next to her at the table. "I've always found genetics fascinating."

Leah nodded as she read.

Laszlo twisted a button on his lab coat. "Before I was transformed, I was a student at the University of Vienna. I was able to visit Gregor Mendel a few times in Moravia."

Leah turned to him, her eyes wide. "You knew Gregor Mendel?"

Laszlo blushed. "Yes. He was very kind. He would discuss his theories with me for hours."

"Holy crapoly," Leah whispered. "I can't believe you knew him."

"That is so cool!" Abby added.

"And he would invite me to sup with him." Laszlo fumbled with another button. "Of course, we always had pea soup."

Leah and Abby laughed.

Gregori punched his fist in the air. "Way to go, Laszlo!"

Dougal's prosthetic hand clenched.

Laszlo's blush deepened. "I-I was serious. Mendel had over twenty-nine thousand pea plants."

Abby and Leah chuckled.

The office door opened, and Freemont sauntered inside. "What's up, dudes?" He nodded at Dougal. "Finished my rounds. Everything's clear."

"Good." Dougal ordered his fist to relax and it slowly obeyed, making a few clicking sounds.

"Your robot hand is so awesome." Freemont grabbed a donut from the box on the sideboard. "You look like a Terminator."

Dougal winced inwardly. "Thank you."

"Oh, that reminds me," Gregori told him. "Abby is expecting you to see her tonight, so she can examine your hand. She wants to do an X-ray or a CAT scan, I think."

Dougal stifled a groan. " 'Tis fine now."

"Orders from Angus." Gregori gave him a wry look. "And you don't say no to big Mongo."

On the lab monitor, Abby rose to her feet. "All this talk about pea soup is making me hungry." She nudged Leah. "Why don't we head to the cafeteria for some supper?"

"Okay." Leah stood. "I could use a break."

Laszlo eased to his feet, a hopeful look on his face as he twisted a button.

"We'll be back in about thirty minutes," Abby told him as she strolled toward the door.

"Bye." Leah left with Abby.

Ping. Laszlo's button popped off.

"Damn, Laszlo," Gregori muttered. "You missed your chance." He adjusted his tie. "Well, I need to get to work. Though I might stop by the cafeteria for a few minutes." He grinned.

"I'll come with you," Dougal said. He wasn't going to miss his chance. When Gregori gave him a questioning look, he added, "I need to make the rounds."

"I just did that." Freemont stuffed half a donut in his mouth.

Dougal's jaw shifted. "I need to set up an appointment with Abby."

"Oh, right." Gregori slapped him on the back. "Well, let's go."

As Dougal marched toward the cafeteria, he resolved to impress Leah and win her heart. According to Gregori it was simple. He only had to be charming and make her laugh.

His prosthetic hand clenched. He was doomed.

Chapter Eight

Leah was drizzling more dressing onto her grilled chicken salad when Abby looked toward the cafeteria door and grinned.

"Gregori's here!" Abby set down her soup spoon and jumped to her feet.

"Hi, sweetheart." Gregori hugged her, then motioned to her bowl of potato soup. "Don't let me stop you. You're eating for two now."

Leah concentrated on her salad to give the two lovebirds some privacy.

"I missed you," Abby whispered.

"I missed you more." Gregori nuzzled her neck. "I woke up from my death-sleep, and you were gone."

So the Vamps called it death-sleep? Leah took a big bite of salad. Was Dougal awake now, too?

Abby swatted her husband's shoulder. "I told you I was coming to work early and bringing Leah."

Gregori seemed to notice her for the first time. "How are you today, Leah?"

"Fine," she mumbled, her mouth full of lettuce.

"Oh." Abby glanced toward the door. "I didn't see you there, Dougal."

Leah stiffened. He was alive! She gulped down her

food, then swallowed some water, her eyes watering. She peered over her shoulder and saw him coming toward them. Alive. And as handsome as ever.

She turned back, focusing on her salad.

"I think I need more food," Abby said. "I'm going through the line again."

"I'll go with you." Gregori accompanied her.

Leah pushed her salad around with her plastic fork. He was still behind her, staring at her, she could feel it. His presence seemed to engulf the room.

"Good evening," he said in a deep, lilting voice that caused a delicious little shiver to run down her back.

"Hi." She looked up as he moved to stand beside her.

He leaned forward, his nostrils flaring, then he straightened, his mouth curling into a slight smile. "How are you?"

"Fine." She paused. "How are you?"

"Well, thank you."

She fiddled with her plastic fork. If only she could come up with something brilliant to say. Would he want to hear about the research she did for her doctorate degree? Probably not. "Would you like something to eat?"

"I had a bottle when I wakened at sunset."

"Right." *He doesn't eat, dummy.* She slapped herself mentally. Her gaze drifted to the window, where she could see the basketball court outside and the game still in progress. "I recognize Angus, Roman, and Tino, but who is the man they're playing with?"

Dougal glanced at the window. "That's Carlos. He's a were-panther."

"Another killer cat?"

"We could give him a CAT scan to be sure."

She winced.

With a sigh, he shifted his weight. "I doona have the gift of blarney."

Did he feel socially awkward, too? "I was never good at meaningless chatter, either," she muttered.

Time stretched out as he eyed her intently. What on earth was he thinking? She filled the awkward pause by taking a bite of her salad.

"Then perhaps we should say something meaningful," he said softly.

She swallowed her salad without tasting it. "Meaningless is safe."

"If ye wanted safety, ye would have run away." He sat in the chair beside her. "Why did ye decide to stay?"

"Many reasons." *But mostly you.* She sipped some water. "I have an opportunity to save lives. It would be cowardly of me to refuse that, don't you think?"

"Ye're a brave lass, to be sure."

Her heart swelled. Not only did he compliment her but he also did it in a way that sounded like sweet music. She picked up her plastic knife to saw on one of the grilled chicken strips. "Another reason—as a scientist, I'm naturally curious about this new world I've stumbled into."

"Curious enough to venture into the basement while I was sleeping?"

Her plastic knife snapped in two.

"It was you, aye?" He leaned an elbow on the table as he twisted to face her. "Ye unbuttoned my shirt."

She shrugged, feigning indifference in spite of her pounding heart. "Any number of people could have gone downstairs."

"I recognize yer scent of jasmine. 'Tis verra nice."

Busted. Her cheeks grew warm. "Fine. I went to check on you. I was concerned. I am your doctor now, you know."

His mouth twitched. "So ye had a medical reason to see my chest?"

She huffed. "I wanted to see if you had a heartbeat. You didn't. I have no idea how you can be dead for hours and then magically resuscitate yourself just because the sun went down."

" 'Tis the way it is."

"It doesn't make sense."

His eyes softened and he leaned close to her. "Does everything have to make sense?"

Her skin chilled with goose bumps. No, it made no sense that she was so drawn to him.

"I'd like to spend some time with you so we can get to know each other."

He wanted to date? How could she date a vampire? It was impossible, even if a small part of her was thrilled. "I-I don't think it's wise to date anyone where I work."

He looked away, frowning, then turned back to her. " 'Tis business. Right now, ye're surrounded by vampires ye doona trust. And ye canna trust us until ye know us better. So getting to know me will help you work more efficiently."

Did he expect her to buy that leap in logic? Still, it was sweet that he was trying so hard.

His gaze lowered to her mouth, then returned to her eyes.

She swallowed hard. Was he thinking about kissing her?

"Will ye give me a chance?" he whispered. "I've waited so long for you."

Her heart lurched.

"We're back," Abby announced as she plunked down a plate filled with fried chicken strips and French fries.

Dougal straightened and looked out the window.

Leah took a deep breath. *I've waited so long for you.* Did that mean he thought they were somehow fated to be together? Her heart thundered in her ears. How could she have a future with him?

Abby sat at the table. "I don't usually eat like this, but I'm so hungry." She bit into a chicken strip.

Gregori sat beside her, his gaze focused on Leah and Dougal. "So what's up? You two were deep in conversation."

"It was nothing." Leah took a sip of water.

"She was explaining why she decided to stay," Dougal said.

"Ah." Gregori gave her a charming smile. "How could you resist us? We're so utterly fascinating."

Abby snorted. "And modest."

Leah smiled. "I guess it's not surprising that I would end up in a strange world. The other kids in college always said I was strange. 'Dr. Freakazoid' they called me."

Beside her, Dougal stiffened.

Abby winced. "That was mean."

Leah groaned inwardly. What had possessed her to confess that? It was all Dougal's fault. He'd completely unnerved her, and now she was babbling like a fool. "To be honest, I was kinda strange. I was fourteen when I started college."

Gregori leaned forward, his elbows on the table. "Since you were so young, they should have been nicer to you, not meaner."

"Aye," Dougal said quietly. "If ye give me their names, I'll track them down—"

"*Doon*?" Leah looked at him. Why did he have to sound so adorable?

"Aye, doon," Dougal muttered. "They deserve to have their heads knocked together. And as head of security here, it is my duty to protect you."

"Retroactively?"

His eyes flashed an intense green. "Anytime, anywhere."

Another wave of goose bumps prickled her arms as if he'd reached out to caress her. "It was a long time ago. I'm over it."

"Are you?"

No. For the entire twenty-three years of her life, she'd felt like she was alone in the world without any friends. Alone in a world where she didn't fit.

So how old was Dougal? Did he have centuries of pain that he carried around on those broad shoulders? *I've waited so long for you.* Did he crave a comforting touch as much as she did?

Her so-called friends in college had wanted her for the free tutoring. Her parents had wanted her as living proof of their own intellectual superiority. Even Dr. Lee and the other Vamps here wanted her for her expertise.

But Dougal was surprisingly different. He looked at her like she was the most desirable woman on the planet. And even more surprising, she reacted like a woman. Heart pounding, breathless, and nerve endings tingling all over. She wanted to know everything about him. And God help her, she wanted to touch him.

She shook herself mentally. He was a vampire, a volcanically inclined Vamp with a fiery dragon tattooed on his chest. She couldn't let herself get involved with him. Her carefully mapped-out life would go up in flames.

"I'm fine." She stood, pushing back her chair. "And I'm going back to work."

Dougal groaned inwardly. His one joke had been lame, and his attempt at being charming had chased her away. How could he manage to be alone with her? What would impress her? His thoughts returned to the movie she'd watched earlier. Of course. He knew exactly what to do.

He cleared his throat. "Gregori, instead of giving Leah a ride home from work, would ye mind if I teleport her?"

Gregori's eyes narrowed. "I suppose that's all right."

"And can ye give me the phone number for the guy at DVN?"

"Wilson?" Gregori stood. "Excuse me a minute, okay?" he said, patting his wife on the shoulder.

She nodded, her mouth full.

Gregori motioned for Dougal to join him over by the window. "You want a makeover? Why?"

Dougal shrugged. "Ye said I looked like a pirate."

"That never bothered you before." Gregori frowned at him. "You were staring at Leah like a half-starved animal."

Dougal winced. Was he that obvious?

"You don't deny it." Gregori sighed. "You realize Laszlo has a crush on her?"

"Aye."

"But you're still going to pursue her?"

"Aye." When Gregori continued to frown at him, Dougal added, "As far as I can tell, she's no' interested in either of us."

"Her heartbeat shot off like a rocket the minute you stepped into the room."

Dougal nodded. "I know. I frighten her."

"Maybe." Gregori gave him a speculative look. "But not the way you think." Without explaining further, he walked back to Abby. "Sweetheart, do you have time to examine Dougal's hand?"

"Sure." She dipped a French fry into a dollop of ketchup. "As soon as I'm done here."

An hour later Dougal sat in Abby's office as she studied the results of the ultrasound and X-ray of his hand. He'd asked Gregori to explain his cryptic remark, but Gregori had simply passed him Wilson's phone number and said, "Let the best man win."

Dougal frowned. The best man was most likely Laszlo. Intellectually, he was a better match for Leah. And he didn't have the checkered past that Dougal had. Most probably, Laszlo had never been kidnapped or forced to work as a slave or a pirate. He'd probably never failed someone he loved. Or buried her.

"Everything looks fine." Abby set the X-ray down and handed him a hand exerciser with black rubber grips. "The sensors in this will measure the strength of your grip. Give it a tiny squeeze."

He did, and on Abby's computer screen, a red light went up an inch on a bar graph.

"Okay, that was within the normal range for a mortal." She wrote it down in her notes. "Try again, a little harder."

He flexed his hand tighter, and the red light traveled halfway up the bar.

"It seems to be working perfectly." She gave him a curious look. "Why do you think it malfunctioned last night?"

"I think the fault was mine," Dougal confessed.

"I don't see how. Your mind is controlling it perfectly now. Why would it go awry all of a sudden?"

He recalled the moment his hand had shattered the bottle. He'd been watching Leah on the monitor. Was she the reason he'd lost control? His hand flinched, and the red light shot nearly to the top of the bar.

"Whoa, careful there." Abby cast him a worried look. "Did you do that on purpose?"

He hesitated, then shook his head.

Abby frowned. "So there is a problem. Can you remember when it first started?"

He shifted in his chair. "Last night."

"What happened last night?"

He shrugged. "I got promoted."

"That must have made you happy." Abby tapped her pen on the desk as she considered. "I wonder if your emotional state is influencing your mind control."

"It shouldna." He winced. "But I doona know how else to explain it."

"Did something upset you last night?" Abby's

eyes twinkled with amusement. "Could it be that you're so old you hate birthday parties?"

A knock on the door sounded.

"Abby?" Leah cracked the door open.

Dougal's hand clenched, snapping the metal spring in two. The red light shot to the top of the bar and beeped.

Abby gasped.

He dropped the hand exerciser, and the beeping stopped.

Abby stared at him, agape.

"Is something wrong?" Leah eased into the room, giving him a wary look.

"Nay." Dougal stood. "I'm done here."

Leah turned to Abby. "I don't mean to interrupt, but I wanted to get your opinion on something."

Abby was staring wide-eyed at the monitor, then her gaze shifted to the broken hand exerciser, then to Dougal. "Did you do that on purpose?"

"Sure," he lied. There was no way he was going to admit that he only lost control when Leah was in the vicinity. Especially when she was standing in the same room.

Abby's eyes narrowed with suspicion.

Damn. She was going to figure it out. "I should get back to work now." He headed toward the door, then paused close to Leah. "What time did ye want to quit working tonight?"

Leah shrugged. "About one thirty. Why?"

"I'll be taking you home then."

Her eyes widened. Before she could object, he rushed back to the security office.

He had plans to make. Leah didn't realize it, but she was taking a little trip with him tonight.

Chapter Nine

"*A*re ye ready to go?"

Leah's heart leaped in her chest at the sound of Dougal's voice. She looked up from her microscope and spotted him at the door, watching her intently with his emerald green eyes. Why was he holding a blanket?

" 'Tis one thirty in the morning," he added.

She glanced at the clock on the wall. She'd been so busy that she'd lost track of time. But her back and shoulders ached from sitting on a stool, hunched over her work.

She glanced at Abby, who sat beside her at the lab table. "Do you mind if I leave?"

"Of course not. I'll be leaving soon, too. Gregori should be here any minute now."

"Don't worry about me." Laszlo smiled at her from across the room. "I'm used to working all night long."

Leah stood, picking her handbag off the floor. Dougal had stepped into the room. For a large man, he could move very quietly. "Are you driving me back?"

"Nay."

Her heart stilled. "If you're planning on teleporting me, I'm not comfortable with that."

"I know, but it is something ye should accustom yerself to. Now that ye're working with us, there will be times when ye'll need to teleport with us."

"I can take a cab."

"Across the world? Ye need to learn how to travel with us. 'Tis a business matter."

She supposed he was making a valid point, but still . . . She leaned close to Abby and whispered, "Is it safe?"

"Yes," Abby whispered back. "And he can hear us."

She straightened with an annoyed huff. He didn't need to look so amused. "Why do you have a blanket with you?"

"'Tis no' a blanket, but my tartan." He draped it over one of his broad shoulders. The plaid design matched his kilt. "It could be a bit chilly where we're going."

"I thought we were going to the townhouse."

"Eventually. We'll make a short stop on the way."

Her eyes narrowed. "Did you find a new underground lair?"

"Nay." His mouth twitched. "We will definitely be aboveground." He extended a hand toward her. "Ready?"

She eased toward him, frowning. "You're not planning to invade my mind?"

"Nay. I know exactly where we're going. I did a test run a few minutes ago."

Now he was making her curious. She hitched her handbag onto her shoulder. "Where are we going?"

"'Tis a surprise." He took hold of her arm and drew her into the hallway.

Her heart lurched. Damn. With his superhearing, he could probably tell that her heart was racing.

"Ye need to hold on to me," Dougal said quietly.

Her gaze met his and froze. He was so close. She could see little specks of gold in his green eyes.

He gripped her around the waist and pulled her against him. "Hold me," he whispered. "Trust me."

Her heart thundered in her ears. Did she dare trust him? Tentatively, she rested her hands on his broad chest.

"Ready?"

To teleport? Panic shot through her, and she wrapped her arms around his neck.

Everything went black. Then in a flash, she was surrounded by color and light. She stumbled, looking about, and he steadied her.

Her eyes focused on the graffiti-covered metal wall close to her face. *For a good time, call Lorenzo?*

"We're in a bathroom stall?" She glanced at the toilet. "This is where you wanted to take me?"

Dougal smiled. "It was the safest place to arrive. I locked this door from the inside about five minutes ago." He opened the stall door and led her into the restroom.

A woman gasped as they walked by.

The ladies' room? Leah winced as they hurried to the exit.

"Where are we?" she whispered as Dougal led her through a glass door.

Immediately, a cold wind whipped at her.

She gasped, barely aware that he was wrapping the tartan around her shoulders. A starry sky was overhead, and before her, the bright lights of New York City stretched for miles in every direction.

"The Empire State Building?" She ran toward the barricade, then glanced back at Dougal, grinning. "This is so awesome!"

He smiled back. "Ye like it?"

"Yes!" It was cold and windy, but she didn't care. She huddled beneath his tartan and looked out at the city. "I've always wanted to do this."

"Ye've never been here before?"

"No." She skirted the wall, gazing out at the sea of lights. "How far up are we?"

"Eighty-six floors." He followed her.

She snorted. Definitely not an underground lair. "I didn't know they were open this late."

"Till two."

She spun around, grinning. "It's just like the movies. We practically have it to ourselves."

"Aye."

She continued to circle the observation deck, then stopped to look at the Chrysler Building. "This is great, Dougal. Thank you."

"You're welcome. Leah."

She couldn't recall him saying her first name before. It made her heart flutter, and she tightened the tartan shawl around her shoulders. The heat of a blush warmed her cheeks, but hopefully it would look like a result of the crisp wind. "I-I'm grateful. But I meant what I said earlier. We shouldn't date."

He nodded, gazing into the distance. "This is business. So ye'll learn to trust us."

"Right." She winced inwardly. Were they both in denial? But as long as she didn't confess to being attracted to him, she could pretend it wasn't true.

She glanced at him, quickly admiring his profile, before looking away. "How old are you?"

"I was born in 1721. Transformed at the Battle of Culloden in '46."

"So you became a vampire when you were twenty-five?"

"Aye."

"So young."

He turned to her, his eyes glittering with humor. "I havena been called young in a long time. How old are you?"

"Twenty-three."

"So young."

She lifted her chin. "Old enough."

"Aye." He brushed back a strand of hair that blew across her face.

She turned away and wandered over to one of the binoculars. Dougal retrieved a few quarters from his sporran and inserted them in the machine.

"Thank you." She peered through the binoculars, too tense to know what she was looking at. She could feel his presence close by. He made her heart race, and yet he was solid in a steady, comforting way. Dependable and exciting at the same time.

She moved closer to the barricade. "How does a person become a vampire?"

"A vampire drains you dry, then ye go into a coma until he feeds his blood back to you. Then ye wake up with a powerful hunger. For blood."

She shuddered. "I can't imagine having to live on nothing but blood."

"It can be verra tasty." He leaned close. "Can ye spare a pint?"

"No." She glared at him when he smiled. "Not funny."

He sighed. "According to Gregori, I'm supposed to make ye laugh."

"So I'll learn to trust you?"

"So I can win yer heart."

She swallowed hard. "We're not dating."

"Aye, I know."

The wind whipped her hair across her face, and she pushed it back. "Don't your knees get cold?"

"Nay."

The wind blew her hair in her face again, and she shoved it back.

"Here." He pulled the leather tie from his hair and stepped behind her.

"You don't need to—" She paused at the feel of his hands on her neck, gathering up her hair. When he finished tying the strip, she turned to face him.

The wind blew some strands of his long black hair across his face, and they caught on the whiskers along his jaw.

"Silly man. Now you're having trouble." She brushed his hair back, her fingertips lingering on his cheek. Her gaze met his, and the fierce yearning in his eyes took her breath away.

She spun to face the city lights. *We're not dating. I'm not falling for him.* "How did you know I wanted to see this place?"

He moved to stand beside her. "Fidelia mentioned ye were watching a movie. After I investigated it, I suspected ye would enjoy this."

"You investigated *An Affair to Remember*?"

"Aye. 'Tis what I do. I work for MacKay Security and Investigation." He glanced at her. "Tell me about yerself."

Her mouth twitched. "Are you investigating me now?"

He smiled. "Aye. I want to know all about you."

"Why?"

He tilted his head while he considered. "Because ye're you. From the moment I first saw you, I felt drawn to you."

She shivered under his tartan blanket. "You first saw me on a security camera."

"Aye." His brows drew together in a frown. "'Twas difficult to watch. I wanted to teleport you away from the pain. My offer still stands, ye ken. If at any time ye want to leave, just let me know."

She nodded slowly. "I appreciate that." Just knowing that he was on her side made her feel all squishy and warm. He would be absolutely perfect if he wasn't a vampire.

"What do ye like to do when ye're no' working?"

She shrugged. "I hardly know. It seems like I've spent my whole life studying. But I enjoy my work. I like helping people, even if I'm not very comfortable around them."

"It must have been hard for you to start college so young."

She nodded. "I was ready academically, but not socially. I was homeschooled by my parents. They're both professors. I have two brothers, but they're older than me. And they each started college at the age of thirteen, so I never got to know them very well."

"Ye were lonely."

Her eyes burned with resentment and unshed tears. How could her parents be so brilliant and never realize that sometimes a young child didn't

need another book or another assignment? Sometimes she just needed a damned hug.

Grandpa had understood. A wave of grief swept
over her. "I had a grandfather in Ireland. He used to
wear a kilt and play the pipes."

"He's gone now?"

She nodded, blinking away tears. "I miss him."

" 'Tis sorry I am that I dinna meet him."

"Abby told me you're a musician?"

He glanced down at his prosthetic hand. "I used
to be."

Did he lose his music when he lost his hand? That
had to hurt something awful. "I'm sorry."

He nodded. "Now I'm known throughout the
vampire world as the guy who lost a hand. My
friends try to make it sound swell by calling me the
Bionic Man or the Terminator."

She winced. After years of being called Dr. Freakazoid, she knew how it felt to be singled out for a
certain trait that made her different from others.

He sighed. "I shouldna have told you that. I doona
want to sound like I'm complaining."

"Why not? Maybe you should tell your friends—"

"Nay! I would sound like a whiny, wee bairn. I
should take it like a man."

She bit her lip to keep from smiling. Apparently
the male ego survived after death.

The wind blew the hem of his kilt up a few inches,
revealing strong, muscular thighs. Wincing, he
pushed it down.

She laughed. "Come on, take it like a man."

He smiled. "Och, so I made ye laugh after all."

She nodded. But did that mean he could win her
heart?

Fear swelled inside her to the point of near panic. What was she doing here? She'd told him so much about herself. And she was enjoying being with him.

A vampire. A gorgeous vampire who made her heart race.

She couldn't let this continue. "I'd like to leave now."

She was still afraid of him. Dougal strode into the security office at Romatech, wondering what he should do next to earn Leah's trust. When he'd teleported her to the townhouse, she'd barely looked at him. She'd thanked him before running upstairs to her room. He was reasonably sure she'd enjoyed the trip to the Empire State Building, and they had succeeded in getting to know each other a little better. That had to be progress.

"You're back," Freemont said from behind the desk.

"Aye. Thank you for manning the fort for me." Dougal scanned the monitors. Abby and Gregori had left. Laszlo was working alone in the lab. The captured soldier was still in the silver room.

"No problem. You were gone for only half of your lunch hour." Freemont stood. "I'll do a perimeter check." He headed out the door.

"Thanks." Dougal retrieved a bottle of blood from the small fridge and popped it into the microwave.

What should his next move with Leah be? Should he take her to another place tomorrow night? What did modern people do on dates? Dinner and a movie? Dinner would be awkward, since he couldn't eat. And Leah would object if it was too obvious that he was trying to date her.

He sipped from his bottle, recalling their conversation at the Empire State Building. She'd had a lonely life. He understood that all too well. After being kidnapped at the age of fourteen, he'd learned quickly that he was alone against the world.

She didn't have to be alone anymore. She could have someone who admired her courage, her brilliant mind, and her strength of character. Someone who ached to touch her beautiful face and explore every lovely inch of her.

She could have him.

Chapter Ten

*L*eah woke up the next day around noon. Immediately her thoughts fixated on her trip with Dougal to the Empire State Building. The date that wasn't a date. The attraction she didn't want to acknowledge. How could she keep from falling for a guy who was so sweet, so attentive, so gorgeous, strong, and dependable? So Undead?

With a groan, she shoved him out of her mind. She would think about work instead. On her first night on the job, she'd succeeded in isolating three genetic mutations. Thankfully, Abby and Laszlo were expert chemists who could devise a serum to reverse the mutations.

Unfortunately, she doubted one antidote would do the trick. Changing the mutated soldier would probably require numerous injections over a period of time. So how could they hope to change a thousand mutated soldiers?

She might have to work here for a long time. And that meant more Dougal. Even if she refused to date him, he would always be nearby. He was probably close now. Downstairs in the basement. She smiled to herself. He did have an underground lair. And she could go see him if she dared.

She pushed him from her mind once again as she climbed out of bed. By the time she showered, dressed, and went downstairs, the Echarpe family was preparing for an outing to Central Park. She declined their invitation to join them, citing dirty laundry as an excuse. Not that she didn't like them. She was just accustomed to quiet and solitude.

And she did need to do some laundry. She'd originally come with clothes for only three days, thinking it would be a short trip. But it made more sense for her to work alongside Abby and Laszlo, and to remain close to the test subject in the Romatech basement.

That made her think about Dougal again. Was he in the townhouse basement?

She started a load of laundry, then flipped on the lights in the billiards room. Empty. Her gaze drifted to the closed door.

With a groan, she paced back to the washer. How could she let this attraction continue? So what if he was incredibly handsome? And intriguing? Did it matter if his deep, lyrical voice made her bones melt? Or that her heart pounded when he looked at her like she was the only woman on the planet?

He was dead.

But he was close by. What was the harm in taking a little peek? This time, she would be careful not to leave any trace.

She opened the door wide to allow plenty of light inside, then moved quietly toward his bed. He was stretched out on his back, his face peaceful. His eyes were closed and fringed with thick black eyelashes. His beautifully shaped lips were relaxed, almost touching. Dark whiskers shaded his jaw. She smoothed her fingers across his cheek, intrigued by the transfer from soft skin to prickly.

Her gaze drifted down his body, the long, white nightshirt buttoned up to his neck, covering the fiery dragon. No wonder she found him so fascinating. Beneath his old-fashioned, staid surface, he concealed an unexpected, dangerous interior. A solid, quiet mountain of a man, hiding a volcano in his center. A beautiful man, but a vampire.

Her arms tingled with goose bumps. It was safe to be here now, admiring him while he was dead, but how exciting it might be to get caught up in one of his explosions. Or even to be the cause of his explosion.

She shook her head. What was she thinking? She would simply end up burned.

As she turned to leave, she spotted something odd. A piece of paper stuck out from his left hand. He must have fallen into his death-sleep holding it.

She leaned over for a closer look and froze at the sight of large, bold letters. *Leah*. He'd written her a note? A thrill of excitement shot through her, quickly followed by a jab of annoyance. How dare he assume that she would come downstairs to ogle him in his death-sleep? It wasn't as if she was obsessed with him.

She winced. She was here, wasn't she?

With a tug, she slipped the note from his hand, then opened it.

Dear Leah,

I doubt you'll come downstairs to see my dead carcass, but in case you do, I am leaving you this note. I'm not good at saying what I feel, so I thought I would write what was in my heart.

If I could dream, I would dream of you.

If I could see the sun, it could not shine brighter than you.

If I died a thousand deaths, I would come back to search for you.

Leah's eyes blurred with tears. She'd been told he was shy, but she hadn't realized he was so romantic. How cruel could fate be that she'd finally met the perfect man, but he was a vampire?

She folded the note and wedged it back beneath his left hand. It would be better if he didn't know that she'd read the note. She didn't dare let him know how deeply he affected her.

A tear ran down her cheek and landed on his hand. She wiped it dry and hurried from the room.

"**H**ow is everything?" Dougal asked that evening as he strode into the security office.

"The usual." Austin slipped on his coat. "Angus and Emma will be returning to London tonight, so it'll be just you and Freemont. Oh, and Abby wants you to come by her office tomorrow night at five thirty."

"All right." Dougal hoped she wasn't planning to

run more tests on his hand. He took a sip from his bottle of synthetic blood as he scanned the monitors. Plenty of mortals were still in the facility, but that tended to happen in the fall and winter months, when the sun set early. He spotted Freemont in the cafeteria, presumably making his rounds, although it looked more like he was flirting with the pretty young cashier.

His gaze shifted back to the lab. "When did Abby and Leah arrive?"

"About two hours ago." Austin pocketed his car keys. "They needed to see the guy in the silver room, so I took them down there. Leah wanted more blood and tissue samples, and Abby gave him another injection to keep him in stasis."

Dougal eyed the monitor showing the silver room. "There was no problem then?"

"Nope." Austin headed out the door. "See you tomorrow."

"Aye. Have a good evening." Dougal's gaze drifted back to the monitor showing Leah and Abby hard at work.

Had Leah come to see him during the day? Had she read his note? When he'd awakened, he'd thought there had been a slight whiff of jasmine in the air. But was it simply wishful thinking? He couldn't be sure.

The cell phone in his sporran dinged, so he took it out. There was a text message from Angus. He and Emma were teleporting back to their townhouse in London and wished him good luck with his new job. As soon as Abby reported that his hand was working perfectly, Angus would put him on the mission roster.

Dougal texted back his thanks, then finished his breakfast bottle while watching the monitors. A few minutes later, Laszlo arrived at the lab, this time sporting a purple polka-dot bowtie. Dougal's eyes narrowed, watching Leah carefully to see how she reacted to Laszlo. She seemed friendly, but there were no stolen glances, no blushes, nothing to indicate she returned his affections.

Thank God. Dougal exhaled with relief. He didn't want to feel like he was stealing Leah from anyone. He had another trip planned for her tonight. As soon as Freemont returned to the office, he would set his plan into action.

A little after seven, he spotted Abby and Leah on a monitor, deep in conversation as they wandered toward the cafeteria. He strode there quickly to meet them at the door. When Leah saw him, her heart rate sped up. Fear or excitement, he wasn't sure which.

"Good evening." He inclined his head. "May I speak with you alone?"

She glanced at Abby. "We were about to eat."

"You can catch up with me later." Abby shot him a suspicious look, then headed toward the cafeteria line.

"Is something wrong?" Leah asked, avoiding eye contact.

"Nay. I—" He wished he wasn't so awkward at this. "I'd like to take you out to dinner."

She turned to him with an exasperated look. "You don't eat."

"Ye do. And I think ye'll like the place we're going."

She winced. "I don't think I should go anywhere with you."

That hit him hard in the chest. "I thought ye enjoyed our trip last night."

A pained look flitted across her face. "I did."

"I enjoyed it, too. And I like talking to you."

"Dougal." She motioned for him to follow her to a quiet corner. "I don't want to get involved with anyone at work."

He frowned. "Do I frighten you?"

Her eyes glistened with moisture, and she looked away.

"I would never harm you, Leah."

"I-I believe you mean that, but I-I can't . . ."

His heart sank. "Ye canna date a vampire?"

She turned to him with a beseeching look. "Please try to understand. I only learned about vampires two nights ago. I'm still trying to adjust. I need time."

Was that reason to hope? If she had enough time to adjust, would she change her mind?

She sighed. "Where did you plan to take me?"

"Niagara Falls. I went earlier to check it out."

She closed her eyes briefly. "That would have been nice. I've always wanted to see it."

"We could still go. As friends. There's a place there where ye can eat. And then, there's a boat ride—"

"No!" She stepped back, turning pale. "I-I can't do that."

"I dinna mean to frighten you—"

"It's not you. I-I'm afraid of boats. I always think they're going to sink. I know it's silly."

He stiffened. A memory flashed through his mind. A storm on the Yangtze River almost three hundred years ago. A boat capsizing and his desperate attempt to keep Li Lei from drowning.

"I'm sorry." Leah gave him a sympathetic look. "I know you want to date me, and I-I'm really flattered. But I can't do it right now. I'm sorry." She rushed off to get in line with Abby.

Rejected. His heart squeezed in his chest. He would have to honor her feelings and leave her alone. But there was still hope. She might change her mind eventually.

He glanced over at her. Afraid of boats? That wasn't something he'd expected.

He trudged back to the office. The first time he saw Leah from behind, she had reminded him of Li Lei. Something about the way she moved and the tilt of her head. But he'd quickly realized that Leah was different. Vibrant and beautiful. He'd admired her strength and courage when her safe world had been stripped away. The pain and loneliness she'd endured over the years reminded him of his own suffering and made him long to comfort and protect her. He'd become so intrigued with Leah that Li Lei hadn't even crossed his mind since that first night. He'd completely forgotten about her.

But now he wondered—could Li Lei's soul have found a way to return to him? For almost three hundred years, he'd felt regret and shame for failing her. In his heart, he had begged for forgiveness. If Li Lei had come back, did that mean she wanted to forgive him?

His heart swelled at the thought. If it was true, it would mean he could finally put his painful past behind him. Lay the ghost of Li Lei to rest and move on with his life.

He could be with Leah. He wanted Leah. *This time,* he vowed, *this time I will not lose the woman I love. I will protect her no matter what.*

His tattoo itched, and he rubbed his shoulder where the scars remained from having a slave brand burned into his skin. It had been Li Lei's idea to cover his mark of shame with a symbol of power. She'd claimed the dragon would give him the strength to endure. And he had. For centuries.

Now it was time to move on. If only he could convince Leah to give him a chance.

Chapter Eleven

*T*he following night at five thirty, Dougal met Abby in her office.

"I started developing this drug six months ago," Abby said, showing him a vial containing an ominous green liquid. "It's designed to help the Vamps defeat bad vampires by simply taking over their minds. You wouldn't have to fight them if you could order them to lay down their weapons and surrender."

Dougal nodded. "A good idea." He wouldn't have lost his hand four years ago if he had been able to order those five Malcontents to stop.

"We're still working on it," Abby continued. "But it occurred to me that a diluted version might help you. If we boost your mind-control ability, then we could increase your control of the prosthesis. Do you want to try it?"

"Do I really need to? My hand worked perfectly well last night."

"But it malfunctioned for two nights before that." She held up the green vial. "This could help you. Are you willing to test it for us?"

He frowned. "Are ye saying it has never been tested?"

"No, afraid not." She gave him a wry look. "We don't keep any vampire lab mice here. But if it makes you ill, you'll recover during your death-sleep, right?"

"Ye're no' a verra good salesman, are ye?"

She smiled. "Just trying to be honest. And I honestly do think this will increase your mind control and help you control your hand."

He hesitated.

"If it works, I can approve you for fieldwork and have Angus put you on the mission roster," she added.

Now that was a better sales pitch. "Ye've diluted it?"

"Yes. We don't want you controlling all the Vamps in the vicinity, just your hand."

He still hesitated.

Abby propped her elbows on the desk and leaned toward him. "As far as I can tell, the prosthesis works fine. The problem is your control, and it's being affected by your emotional state. If you prefer, I could have you talk to our psychologist, Olivia—"

"I'll take the drug." There was no way he would discuss his emotions with Robby's wife. His feelings were personal. His past was private. He didn't share it with anyone.

"All right." Abby filled a syringe with the greenish liquid. "It will take some time before you'll feel the effect. Twenty or thirty minutes." She gave him a wry smile. "Do you want to roll up a sleeve or lift your kilt?"

He snorted, then unbuttoned his cuff and rolled up his sleeve. She wiped his arm with antiseptic, then plunged the needle in.

"That's it." She fixed a Band-Aid over the spot. "Just go about your normal routine and let me know how it works. Oh, and let me know if you have any strange side effects."

"Now ye tell me about strange side effects?"

She grinned. "I have to get back to work now. Good luck!" She hurried from the room.

He stepped into the hallway, rolling his sleeve back down. His normal routine. That was easy enough. He checked the office, and Freemont was there, manning the desk, so Dougal offered to do a perimeter check.

He exited the building through the side entrance and strode around the parking lot. In a few hours, once all the mortals were gone, he would zoom about at vampire speed, but for now, he kept a normal pace. The mortals were starting to get off work, and some were returning to their cars.

He headed into the woods. The crisp autumn air felt refreshing against his face. It wouldn't be long before the first snow, and he looked forward to it. He hadn't seen snow at all during the four years he'd spent in Texas.

Was the drug taking effect? He curled his prosthetic hand into a fist, then relaxed it. There was no difference that he could tell. The real test would be if he could control it with Leah in the vicinity.

He headed back toward the building, walking past the gazebo, which was glittering with white Christmas lights. A sharp pain shot through his skull, surprising him with its intensity. He shook his head, and it cleared.

As he crossed the basketball court, another pain pierced his head, shooting from his temple to the base of his skull. He halted, squeezing his eyes shut. *Damn.* Was this one of the blasted side effects? If so, he wouldn't be taking the drug again.

He took deep breaths, waiting for the pain to ease.

When he opened his eyes, he spotted a group of female employees in the cafeteria. Mortals. Ten of them. He watched them through the window. Apparently they had stayed after work to have a party. A birthday party, from the looks of the big cake skewered with candles. Another table was covered with brightly colored gift bags. The sound of the women's laughter and chatter was so loud that he could hear it outside. There were times when superior hearing was not a blessing.

One of the ladies lit the candles, and just as they started singing the happy birthday song, another pain screeched across his brain.

"Och." He squeezed his eyes shut. *Stop!*

The singing stopped.

He opened his eyes and saw that the ladies were all staring at each other with confused looks on their faces.

Had he done that? Was this another side effect? The women continued to stare at each other while the small candles burned down, the flames sputtering in the icing. *Blow them out!*

All ten women leaned over the cake, huffing and blowing.

He winced. Abby had certainly managed to increase his mind control. With the flames blown out, the women stood in a circle around the cake, staring at it. Were they awaiting further orders?

Ye can cut the cake now.

All ten women made a grab for the cake slicer, but when one claimed it, the others grabbed plastic knives, and they all chopped away at the cake, hacking it into pieces.

He grimaced. What a bloody mess. *Go on as ye normally would.*

They stopped and looked aghast at the slaughtered cake.

He slipped inside, and they gave him a suspicious look. "Excuse me. Just passing through." He hurried through the cafeteria doors.

Halfway down the hall, he wondered how powerful his mind control was. How far could it reach?

Crow like a rooster.

His superior hearing caught the sound of crowing all over the facility.

Damn. The crowing continued. *Stop it!* Silence.

He headed for the lab. Maybe Abby could give him an antidote.

He strode into the room. Leah was there, seated next to Abby and Laszlo. His heart squeezed at the sight of her, and he wondered once again if she had read his note.

"Yes," she replied, then winced.

She had. His prosthetic hand clenched. *Relax*, he ordered it, and it opened. Then he noticed that Leah and Abby had sprawled in their chairs. They had relaxed!

With a small shock, he realized he could control

Leah if he wanted to. He could order her to fling herself into his arms and kiss him.

When she jumped to her feet, he forced those thoughts to a screeching halt. *Doona move.* "Abby, there's something wrong."

"Tell me about it." Laszlo twisted a button. "Just a few seconds ago, they were both crowing like roosters. The whole building seemed to be crowing."

"That was my fault." Dougal looked at Abby. "Can I see you in private?"

She and Leah both walked toward the door.

"Nay, no' you." He looked at Leah, but both women stopped. They were obeying his speech, too? He supposed that made sense, since he had to think to talk.

"You. Abby." He pointed at her. "I need to talk to you in yer office." She headed out the door.

"And you." He pointed at Leah. *My God, ye're beautiful. I could kiss you all—*

Her eyes widened.

He wiped those thoughts clean. "Take a seat."

She sat on the floor.

"Nay! In yer chair. Ye can work now. If ye like."

She moved to her chair and went back to work.

Laszlo frowned. "How are you controlling them? And why?"

Dougal grimaced. " 'Tis a long story. I'll take care of it." He hurried to Abby's office and found her sitting at her desk, frowning at the vial of green liquid.

She looked up. "I guess we discovered one of the side effects."

He nodded. "It dinna affect Laszlo?"

"No." She gave him an annoyed look. "It was only

the mortals who were crowing. I'll ask Gregori to do damage control and erase the memories of those who were affected."

"Can ye stop what's happening to me?"

She sighed. "There's no antidote. But I gave you a small amount. It should wear off in a few hours. Most of the mortal employees will be leaving soon, so . . ."

"But you and Leah will still be here."

Abby nodded. "It might be better for you to keep some distance from us. And don't think about us. Occupy your mind with something else for a few hours."

He groaned. Telling him not to think about Leah was a sure way to make him think of her.

"Have you tried using your prosthesis?" Abby asked. "Maybe you could type a report or something. It would occupy your mind, and we could see if you have better control."

"I'll think of something." He left her office, trying not to think of Leah. What else could occupy his mind? And test his manual dexterity?

His pipes. He'd left his Uilleann pipes at the townhouse. In a matter of seconds, he had teleported to the basement, collected the pipes, and teleported back to the grounds at Romatech.

Doona think about Leah. He strode into the woods to where a bench was located underneath a large oak tree. There he sat and situated the bag beneath his elbow. By moving his arm, he would pump air into the bag. He'd start off with something slow so he'd have a better chance at moving his prosthetic fingers in time with the music.

Doona think about Leah.

The pipes filled the air, their wailing cry echoing through the woods. God, how he had missed that sound. And such a sad song. That was the problem with slow music. It was so forlorn that it could make your heart break with the sadness of it.

Leah, I've waited so long for you.

Chapter Twelve

*D*oona think about Leah.

Leah blinked as she peered into a microscope. That was Dougal's voice reverberating in her head. There was no mistaking the deep, musical lilt or the adorable way he pronounced *aboot*.

Abby had returned to the lab a few minutes earlier and explained the weird side effects Dougal was experiencing from a drug she'd given him. His boosted mind control was affecting all the mortals in the building.

Leah had only a vague memory of the crowing incident. Abby assured her that Gregori would make sure none of the other mortals remembered it. Luckily, Leah would be exempt from any mind tampering. She needed to remember the progress she'd made at work. And she wanted to remember Dougal's thoughts. *My God, ye're beautiful. I could kiss you all—*

He'd abruptly stopped that trail of thought, which was a shame, since now she was left wondering where he would kiss her. All over her face? Her body? Her skin tingled, and a warm, fuzzy feeling flooded her from head to toe.

Doona think about Leah. His voice echoed once again in her mind, and she found herself smiling. The poor guy was trying so hard but failing miserably. She was, too. She could barely concentrate on her work.

Leah, I've waited so long for you.

His voice was laced with pain, she could feel it. How long had he waited? A lifetime? Three lifetimes? Had he never loved before? Had he truly waited just for her? How badly had she hurt his feelings the night before? A yearning built inside her, a need to see him, comfort him, touch him. If she stayed here any longer, she would suffocate.

She pushed back her chair and stood. "I need a break."

"You want to grab something to eat?" Abby gave her a sheepish look. "I seem to be hungry all the time."

"I would be happy to join you," Laszlo said with a hopeful expression.

"Maybe later," Leah answered. "I just need some fresh air. To clear my mind."

Abby nodded. "The gazebo's nice. There's an exit close by."

"Okay." Her sweater in hand, Leah left the lab and spotted a red exit sign down the hall. It was above a glass door opening onto the patio.

She stepped outside and felt immediately refreshed by the cool, crisp air. On the other side of the patio, she could see the cafeteria and a party going on inside. A woman was opening presents, while others chatted and laughed.

A wailing sound echoed in the distance, and she turned her head toward it. It sounded familiar somehow, like a distant memory. A chill skittered down her back, and she pulled on her thick cardigan sweater.

She crossed the basketball court, headed for the gazebo. The sound grew louder, more confident.

More beautiful. She halted with a gasp. It was pipe music. Just like Grandpa had played that magical summer. She'd thought the pipes were the most beautiful sound in the world.

She closed her eyes to listen, and the plaintive melody enveloped her, seeped into her skin, and settled in her heart. So much emotion. She didn't know how the pipes could sound like they were crying, but they did.

Tears filled her eyes as flashes of memory returned from fourteen years ago. The green fields of Ireland. Her grandfather's lilting voice and warm hug. She'd never had to earn his hugs with straight As. He had loved her for simply being herself. He would have loved this music.

Was it Dougal? It had to be him. How could she resist such a man? His handsome face touched her heart, and his music lured her soul. As she followed the sound of the pipes, her skin pebbled with goosebumps. Was she following her destiny?

Leah, I've waited so long for you.

His voice whispered in her mind. He was still thinking about her, still wanting her. She passed the gazebo and headed for the woods. A white shirt came into view.

It was him. She didn't want to disturb his playing, so she remained halfway hidden behind a tree. He was seated on a bench, his head bowed and forehead furrowed as he concentrated on his hands. His left hand moved easily and gracefully, but the fingers of his prosthetic hand were jerky and slow.

Leah's heart ached for him. How it must hurt him to struggle with his music. He ended the plaintive melody and sighed.

"Enough of sadness," he whispered. "I need joy in my life." *I need Leah.*

Her breath caught. Should she tell him she was here? Did she dare? In a split second, she knew that if she approached him now, her life would be forever changed. She would fall for a vampire, and he would never let her go.

Her feet froze, unable to move.

He launched into a happy jig, but after a few bars, his prosthetic hand couldn't keep up. She grimaced as the music soured and declined into a jarring noise.

"Dammit!" He tossed the pipes onto the ground, and they let out a dying wail as leftover air fizzled from the bag. "Damn it to hell." He strode toward the building, his kilt swishing about his knees.

She stood still, watching him go, then her gaze shifted back to the pipes where they rested on a bed of dead leaves. A breeze stirred up more leaves, and they settled on the bag. In another hour, they might be completely covered with dead leaves. Buried.

A surge of anger shot through her. How dare he give up! He played from his soul. Without music, how would his soul survive?

She wouldn't let him quit. She strode toward the pipes and gathered them up in her arms. Her grip caused the remaining air in the bag to escape, and the pipes protested with a forlorn wail.

"What are ye doing?" he asked softly.

She whirled around. "I-I didn't think these should be left outside."

His brow furrowed with a deep scowl. "How long have ye been out here?"

"Long enough." She lifted her chin. "You came back awfully fast."

"I can move verra quickly." His mouth thinned. "At least my feet can."

"I know you were having trouble with the jig, but you shouldn't let that stop you from playing. The slow music was absolutely—"

"Sad," he interrupted her, his eyes flashing.

"I was going to say beautiful."

"Nay. It was melancholy. And pathetic. Should I spend the rest of my miserably long life with only sad music to fill my soul?"

"Better to have a sad soul than an empty one." She held the pipes out to him. "And you have to believe that it will get better. You can't give up on yourself."

"Are ye concerned for my soul then?" He snatched the pipes from her hands. "Do ye believe a vampire even has a soul?"

She winced. Apparently, she had hurt his feelings the night before. Somehow, in just a few days, he had ceased to be a monster, an Undead creature, and he'd become a tortured soul who intrigued her. She was hopelessly drawn to him and painfully aware of a yearning she didn't dare act upon.

"I'll take that as a no." He lifted the pipes. "What were ye planning to do with these?"

"I was going to return them to you. With a note of encouragement."

"Ye were going to bring them to my office?" When

she didn't answer, his eyes narrowed. "Ye were going to visit me again in the basement?"

She nodded. "Yes."

He dropped the pipes on the bench. "Why do ye seek me out when I'm in my death-sleep? I realize I'm no' a verra good conversationalist, but I can manage a wee bit better when I'm no' dead."

She swallowed hard. "I feel safer when you're asleep—"

"Dead," he corrected her with a wry look. "Am I so frightening when I'm awake?"

Yes. She crossed her arms. "Maybe."

"I would never hurt you."

Her eyes burned. He could break her heart. Already it was aching.

"How can I prove to you that I'm no' a soulless monster?"

"I know you have a soul. You played from your soul." She blinked away tears. "And it was beautiful."

He stepped toward her. "Then can ye stop seeing me as a vampire?"

Her heart pounded. She was teetering on a precipice, so close to falling, and God help her, she wanted to fall.

"Can ye see me as a man? I canna share a meal with you, nor a day in the sun. I canna sleep like a man. But I can feel. I can touch." With his left hand, he touched her face so gently that it squeezed her heart, and a tear escaped.

He caught the tear with his thumb. "I can love like a man." He leaned closer. "And I can kiss."

She drew in a shuddering breath just before his lips pressed gently against hers. Soft, but firm.

He pulled back and gave her a questioning look as if asking permission to continue. More tears threatened to fall. She didn't know what to say. She only knew she wanted more.

His hand moved to cup the back of her neck while his other hand, the prosthetic one, pressed against the small of her back, pulling her against his chest. She rested her hands on his shirt, feeling the hard rock of his chest beneath the soft white cotton.

"Leah," he whispered, and she lifted her eyes to meet his.

Desire flared hot in his emerald eyes, melting the last of her resistance. "Yes," she whispered back.

He kissed her again. A long, sensual kiss, his lips moving, nibbling, and tasting.

Warmth drizzled down her body, settling with a more heated sizzle between her legs. She moaned, and he deepened the kiss, invading her mouth with his tongue.

Her senses swirled, and a vague thought flitted through her mind. She'd never been kissed senseless before. She hadn't thought it was possible. But she was reeling now, free-falling, rapidly becoming a mass of nerve endings, all sizzling and hot.

Her hands slid up to his shoulders, then his neck, and she pulled him closer. Her fingers delved into his ponytail, tangling with his long, soft hair. A whimpering sound escaped her mouth, a sound of surrender, and he growled softly in response.

"Leah." He scattered kisses across her cheeks and brow. "I want you. I want you something fierce."

Her heart nearly burst with longing, and she pulled back to touch his face.

Red, glowing eyes!

With a small yelp, she jumped back.

He released her, lifting his hands. "Doona be alarmed."

She stepped back. "Your eyes are red!"

"Aye. I want you."

"For dinner?" She retreated another step.

"Nay. 'Tis my heart that hungers for you." With a grimace, he adjusted his sporran. "My body wants you as well."

She swallowed hard. What was she doing? It would be crazy enough to get involved with a mortal she'd known only four days, but here she was with a vampire? For a person who had always prided herself on her intelligence, she wasn't being very smart. What did she really know about this man? If she fell for him completely, would she be completely lost?

"I-I can't do this." She ran back to the building.

The next day she woke shortly before noon. With a groan, she rolled over to try to fall asleep again. After a night of tossing and turning, she was still tired.

Sleep had been nigh impossible, for every time she'd drifted off, memories of his kiss had flooded back, and she would experience it all over again. The sweetly possessive feel of his mouth moving on hers. The light touch of his lips caressing her cheeks and brow.

And then the yearning would return, the longing in her heart, and the empty ache between her thighs. And she would wonder if she'd made a mistake. Maybe she should talk to Abby or Heather. They were both happily married to vampires.

Groaning, she rubbed her hands down her face. Enough of this wishy-washy confusion. How could a sane woman even contemplate marriage with a vampire?

Leah, I've waited so long for you.

"No!" She sat up in bed. She wouldn't let those words continue to haunt her. How could he have been waiting for her when he'd only known her for four nights? Maybe he was waiting for someone to love, but that didn't mean it had to be her.

The man was interfering with her job. Last night, after the kiss, she'd tried to go back to the lab to work, but it had been a disaster. The kiss had kept creeping into her thoughts, refusing to let her concentrate. It had replayed in her mind, over and over, growing in importance till it seemed her whole life could be slotted into two categories. Life before the kiss, and life after the kiss. Her life before the kiss had moved step by step ever closer to the predestined event. Meeting Dougal. And kissing him.

She shook her head. She would not allow herself to be manipulated by theories as erroneous as fate or destiny. She would make her own decisions in life. Her own choices.

For example, she would choose not to venture into the basement today. Even if he had written a new note for her, she would not go near him. She would distance herself. She would do her job at Romatech, and then leave.

And never see Dougal again. For she was far too logical to fall in love with a vampire.

Chapter Thirteen

She hadn't read his note. Dougal was fairly certain of it.

He stood in the security office the next evening, drinking his bottle of breakfast blood while he watched the monitors. The captive soldier was still in stasis in the silver room. Leah was in the lab with Abby, concentrating hard on her work. Not once did she glance at the camera.

There had been no lingering scent of jasmine in the basement when he'd awakened from his death-sleep. The newly written note clasped in his left hand had appeared unopened.

He gulped down more synthetic blood. She'd rejected him. He'd poured all his longing into the kiss last night, hoping somehow he could touch her heart, and it hadn't worked.

She'd rejected him.

Had his red eyes frightened her? It wasn't something he could avoid. Whenever a Vamp became sexually aroused, his eyes automatically glowed red.

Was he pushing her too fast? He'd been waiting almost three hundred years, but for Leah, it was now only five nights. He needed to slow down. Give her a chance to adjust. Give her time to get to know him. And trust him.

It might help if he didn't look like a bloody pirate. After the fiasco last night, he'd called the number Gregori had given him. The stylist at DVN had agreed to see him after Laszlo's appointment two nights from now.

He finished his bottle while memories of the kiss flitted through his mind. He could have sworn she had enjoyed it. She'd wrapped her arms around his neck. She'd moaned and melted against him. It had taken just a few minutes for his eyes to turn red and his groin to grow stiff.

He pushed those thoughts from his mind and sat at the desk to e-mail a report to Angus. Freemont had the night off, so Dougal did the rounds himself. A few hours later, back in the office, he saw his chance. Leah and Abby were headed to the cafeteria for supper. It was the perfect time to do another round.

He zipped through the grounds, then slowed down as he approached the basketball court. At this time of night, she and Abby had the cafeteria to themselves. He let himself in through the patio door.

Leah glanced up. Her eyes widened before she refocused on her piece of apple pie.

"Oh hey, Dougal." Abby smiled at him. "What's up?"

"No' much." He approached their table.

Abby spooned some ice cream into her mouth. "I guess your increased mind control wore off. We didn't hear any crowing tonight."

"Nay." He watched as Leah pushed an apple slice

around her plate. "I appear to have no effect at all on any mortal."

She glanced up, and he heard her heartbeat pounding louder.

His mouth curled up. *Gotcha*.

A blush stained her cheeks, and she stabbed the apple slice with her plastic fork.

"I'm glad you stopped by." Abby finished her ice cream, licking the spoon. "We're very close to having a serum to test on the guy in the silver room. Can you come with us tomorrow night when we try it out?"

"Aye." He glanced at Leah. "Congratulations. Ye're making excellent progress."

She shrugged, refusing to look at him. "I'm concentrating on my work from now on."

"I'm sure that is the wise thing to do."

Her blush deepened.

He breathed deeply, letting her scent of rushing blood and jasmine fill his head.

Abby stood and motioned toward the hallway. "Can I talk to you for a second?"

"Aye." He followed Abby out the door.

"I had to send a report to Angus about your prosthesis," Abby whispered. "I told him your mind control was being affected temporarily by your emotional state." She slanted a glance toward Leah. "But I didn't elaborate on it."

So she suspected Leah was the cause of his distress. "Did ye tell anyone?"

"I mentioned it to Gregori, and he agreed." Abby frowned. "He said you wanted to pursue Leah. Is that true?"

Dougal crossed his arms. "Ye doona approve?"

"I'm not sure." Abby glanced at Leah. "She's brilliant, but at the same time, young and naïve. She seems completely oblivious to Laszlo's puppy dog looks. But you—I think she's very aware of you."

A surge of hope flared in his chest. "Ye think I have a chance?"

Abby grimaced. "I really like her, Dougal. I don't want her to get hurt."

"I would never hurt her."

Abby gave him a dubious look. "You guys always say that. Just be careful, okay?"

As Abby walked back to the table, he glanced again at Leah. Their eyes met, and a pained look crossed her face before she turned away.

Dammit. Abby was right. He was already hurting her. With an inward groan, he walked away.

The following night, Dougal glared at the monitors. How long would she continue to ignore him? He'd fallen into his death-sleep, clutching the same damned note, but Leah had not come to see him. Now she and Abby were busy in the lab, preparing the serum for the captured soldier.

He paced about the office. Then he zoomed around the grounds and the building.

Finally, Abby called and asked him to meet her in the silver room. He dashed down the stairs and punched in the code to unlock the silver room.

The elevator door opened, and Abby, Laszlo, Leah, and Gregori filed out. Laszlo was carrying a tray.

"Good evening." Dougal inclined his head at Leah, but she refused to look at him.

"Hey, dude." Gregori punched him on the shoulder. "I didn't want to miss out on the excitement." He shot a proud look at Abby. "My wife is quite the cook."

Abby snorted. "I can't guarantee the serum will work. And if it does, it will be only the first step in a long process."

"I believe we're off to a good start." Laszlo carried the tray into the room and set it on a table next to the stretcher.

Dougal strode to the other side of the stretcher so he could see the captive soldier up close. He was a young man, lean and muscular, with a shaved head.

Laszlo moved to the foot of the stretcher, while Leah and Abby stood across from Dougal.

Gregori circled the stretcher, testing the restraints. "You sure you want to wake him up?"

Dougal stiffened. "I wouldna recommend that."

Abby filled a syringe. "The serum won't work as well if he's in stasis. His bodily functions are so suppressed it would take forever to get any reaction. Besides, if he's awake, he should be able to give us some feedback—"

"Ye expect him to cooperate?" Dougal asked.

"I hope so, once we explain what we're doing," Abby replied.

Laszlo twisted a button on his lab coat while he gave Leah an admiring look. "We're very fortunate to have Leah with us. She can speak Mandarin."

Leah nodded. "I'll tell him that we're helping him get back to normal."

Gregori winced. "What if he doesn't want to be normal? I thought these guys made a deal with

Darafer. He gives them superpowers, and in return, they belong to him."

Leah looked confused. "I thought the soldier belonged to Master Han."

"He does." Abby turned to Gregori. "I think he *will* want to return to normal. Once we explain to him that Darafer owns his soul—"

"What?" Leah looked shocked.

Dougal gave Abby and Gregori an annoyed look. "Ye dinna tell her about Darafer?"

"I did," Abby insisted. "I said he was the one mutating the soldiers so they could fight for Master Han."

"Then why does he own their soul?" Leah asked. "How can anyone own someone's soul?"

Dougal snorted. "Apparently, they dinna tell you he's a demon. And when the soldiers die, he takes their souls to hell."

Leah's eyes widened. "Are you serious?"

Abby grimaced. "We should have explained it in more depth, but I didn't want to frighten you even more. You were already stressed out—"

Leah scoffed. "This could only frighten me if I believed it. There's no such thing as hell. Or demons. It's not logical." She glanced at the soldier. "And there's no way I'm telling him such nonsense."

Dougal tilted his head. "Ye doona believe in hell?"

Leah shrugged. "People make their own hell here on earth."

"There's some truth to that," Dougal conceded, "but there is more to life than what we see here. A few days ago, ye dinna believe in vampires or shifters."

He saw her wince. Did she regret being part of their world? Was she sorry she'd met him? Was their kiss nothing but a bad memory for her? "I know our existence defies logic. We shouldna exist at all, but that doesna mean that we are evil."

Her eyes met his, her gaze searching as if she hoped to see into his soul. He tried to show her his feelings. When tears glimmered in her eyes, he thought he might have succeeded.

She closed her eyes briefly and turned away.

Abby heaved a huge sigh. "There was a time when I would have agreed with you that demons don't exist. But Darafer is real. I met him. I saw him blast a guy off a cliff with just a flick of his hand."

"He's the one who made Abby's mom sick," Gregori added. "He admitted that he invented plagues. He gets his jollies out of watching people suffer."

Abby shuddered. "He's scary as hell. He was behind the assassination attempt on my father."

Leah blinked. "Someone tried to kill your father?"

Abby nodded. "You never heard about it because my father had it hushed up. He thought the killer wanted fame, so he made sure he didn't get it." She made a face. "Darafer knew about it. He bragged that he was the one who had twisted the killer's mind."

Leah's eyes widened. "So he's really a . . . ?"

"Demon," Gregori said. "Yes."

Her face paled.

Dougal stepped toward her, and she moved back. "I'm okay."

"Are you?" he asked softly.

She shook her head. "I always knew evil existed. But I always saw it as something vague and shadowy, floating here and there without purpose, randomly causing people to commit terrible acts. I never thought of it inhabiting a powerful being with an agenda." She shuddered. "The world keeps getting stranger. And more dangerous."

"Aye, lass," he murmured. "But ye doona have to face it alone."

Her eyes met his again, and he winced at the pain glimmering in their golden brown depths.

"That's right," Laszlo piped in. "We're here for you."

She sighed. "Just when I think I have it figured out, and that I've adjusted to everything, something new gets thrown at me."

"Try not to let it bother you," Gregori said. "There's no reason you should ever have to meet Darafer."

Leah shuddered, then took a deep breath. "Let's get on with this then."

"Brave lass," Dougal whispered.

She winced. "Not so brave." She moved closer to the stretcher.

Was she ignoring him out of fear then? Dougal tightened the restraints while Abby placed sensors over the soldier's heart and major pulse points, then connected them to a monitor.

"Here we go." Abby injected the soldier.

In a few minutes, the soldier's eyelids flickered. His fingers twitched. Suddenly, his eyes popped open and his hands fisted, straining at the belts that tied him down.

He growled something in Chinese, glaring at them all. He twisted on the stretcher, pulling hard against the restraints.

Leah spoke softly to him. His eyes narrowed on her, rage causing them to glimmer.

She continued to talk, then gave him an encouraging smile and pat on the shoulder.

"Why should I believe you, bitch?" he growled. "You stinking whore!"

"You damned fool." Dougal seized him by the neck, his prosthetic hand clenching tight. "She's trying to save your ass. Talk to her like that again, and I'll kill you."

"Dougal?" Leah stared at him, her eyes wide.

"Dougal!" Abby shouted. "Let go! You're killing him."

His hand tightened, and the soldier's face turned a mottled red.

"Dougal!" Gregori shoved at his shoulder. "What are you doing? We need him alive!"

He ordered the prosthesis to release, and it did. The soldier gasped for air, and the others exhaled with relief.

"Oh, dear." Laszlo tugged at a button. "Why did you attack him like that?"

Dougal stepped back. *Damn it to hell.* What had he done?

"You spoke to him in Chinese," Leah whispered.

"That was Chinese?" Gregori looked stunned. "I thought it must be Gaelic. Why would a Scotsman know Chinese?"

Dougal squeezed his eyes shut. *Dammit!* He hadn't realized what he was doing. He'd heard the soldier abusing Leah, and the next thing he knew, he was choking the bastard. "I-it was an accident."

"You accidentally spoke Chinese?" Abby asked dryly.

He winced. "I dinna mean to." He motioned to the soldier. "Can ye give him the injection? He's being verra still and cooperative now."

Gregori snorted. "Yeah, because he almost died. Why did you attack him all of a sudden?"

"He was cursing me," Leah explained, then gave Dougal a pointed look. "You understood it."

With a groan, he dragged a hand over his hair. The secret was out.

"How interesting." Laszlo twirled a button. "When did you learn Chinese?"

"I doona discuss it." Dougal headed for the door. "If ye need me, I'll be in my office."

Chapter Fourteen

*H*ow on earth did he know Chinese? Leah tensed with frustration. Once again, she was finding it impossible to concentrate. All she could think about was Dougal. Why had he never told his friends? Had he kept it a secret for hundreds of years? What other secrets did he have? What did he mean when he said he'd waited for her so long?

"Leah?" Abby touched her shoulder.

She started. "Yes?"

"I asked you to talk to him." Abby motioned to the soldier. "His blood pressure is spiking. See if you can calm him down. I don't want to give him a sedative."

"Of course." It might interfere with the serum they were testing. Leah leaned over the soldier and spoke in Chinese. "I'm Leah Chin. What's your name?"

"None of your damned business!"

"We're trying to help you."

"Bullshit." The soldier glared at her. "You plan to torture me."

"No. We're simply trying to reverse some of your genetic mutations." Although there was nothing simple about it. "Once we're done, you'll be able to return to a normal life."

He scoffed. "Like a billion other people? I don't want to be normal!" He tugged at the restraints. "Why am I so damned weak? What have you done to me?"

"You've been in stasis for a while, so your muscles haven't been used. Once we have you back to normal—"

"No! Damn you, you have no right to change me back. I want to be superstrong and powerful!"

"His pulse is dangerously high," Abby warned as she watched the monitor.

"He says he doesn't want to be changed back," Leah said in English.

"I was afraid that would happen," Gregori murmured.

Laszlo shook his head. "He's been brainwashed. Perhaps in time . . ."

"He won't have time if his heart gives out," Abby muttered.

"I'll try to reason with him." Leah switched to Chinese. "They tell me a demon changed you, and in exchange for giving you superpowers, he now owns your soul."

The soldier sneered at her. "So?"

"If you die—"

"I won't die, bitch! Even your torture can't kill me. I was made invincible!"

"No one is invincible."

"Darafer is! And he made us the same way. After Master Han takes over the world, we will be kings."

Leah groaned. Why did bad guys always want to take over the world? "I don't know much about

Master Han or demons, but it seems highly likely to me that they could be lying to you. And using you. Would you really expect a demon to be honest? And do you think this Master Han will want to share his worldwide power with you?"

A flicker of doubt glimmered in the soldier's eyes, then he blinked and glowered at her. "You're wrong. Master Han is loyal to his men. He'll come for me. He'll rescue me and destroy you."

"I've been told that vampires can't teleport into this room. It's made of silver."

The soldier hissed and pulled at his restraints. "They won't abandon me! You'll see! Master Han will rescue me." His face turned red as he screamed, *"Master Han!"*

"I'm giving him a sedative." Abby injected him.

Leah winced. "Sorry. I think I made it worse."

Laszlo twisted a button, gazing sadly at the soldier, who drifted off into sleep. "It's always hard to save someone who doesn't want to be saved."

Leah sighed. Was it right to change the mutated soldiers back against their will? But if they weren't changed back, they would help an evil vampire and demon take over the world.

If the Vamps didn't change Master Han's soldiers, they would be forced to fight them. And when they killed them, the soldiers' souls would go straight to hell. Leah wasn't sure she could believe in hell, but she could understand why the Vamps wouldn't want a bunch of doomed souls on their conscience. No wonder they had been so determined to get her help.

She'd heard from Abby that the Vamps were terribly outnumbered by Master Han's army. If she could reverse the mutations, then the Vamps could avoid a war where many of them would be killed.

Her heart squeezed.

For the first time, she understood just how heroic the Vamps were. They protected a mortal world that didn't even know vampires existed. They sacrificed themselves knowing there would be no gratitude, no glory in return. They did it for honor, because it was the right thing to do.

That left her with an important question that could affect the rest of her life: how could rejecting an honorable man like Dougal be the right thing to do?

"**W**hy did ye no' tell me ye speak Chinese?" Angus demanded over the phone.

Dougal glanced at the clock on the desk. It had taken only ten minutes for the news to reach Angus in London. While watching the monitor, Dougal had seen Gregori move out of camera range in the silver room. "Gregori called you?"

"Aye, and he said ye nearly pinched the soldier's head off. Why did ye do it? Was yer hand out of control again?"

"Nay."

There was a pause, then Angus grunted in frustration. "Are ye going to tell me why?"

"He insulted Leah."

"And that was reason to kill him?"

Dougal curled his hand into a fist. "It seemed appropriate at the time."

"Abby was right. Ye're letting yer emotions run amok."

"I'm in control," Dougal insisted. "I dinna kill him." He glanced at the monitor showing the silver room. "The captive is fine. Abby and Leah are watching him."

"So how come ye never told me ye speak Chinese? I checked yer job application from 1928. Ye dinna mention it there."

"It dinna seem important at the time. We were concentrating on the Malcontents in Eastern Europe and Russia."

"And when Master Han came along, ye dinna think to tell me? I've been sending J.L. and Rajiv there alone, thinking they were the only operatives we had who knew Chinese. I would have put you back on the mission roster a lot quicker. Ye should have told me!"

Dougal gritted his teeth. "It was personal."

Angus snorted. "I gather that, but whatever yer problem is, deal with it. Ye're back on the roster now."

"I've been approved for fieldwork?"

"I still have doubts about yer hand, but we need you. The next mission to China—"

"No," Dougal interrupted. This was why he'd kept it secret. "Anywhere but China. I canna go back there."

Angus paused, then lowered his voice. "What happened to you there?"

Dougal grimaced.

"When were ye there?" Angus asked. "I've known you since Culloden. It must have happened before ye were transformed."

Dougal clenched his hand, then released it. "I willna go back there."

"The devil take it, man. We may all end up in China, fighting Master Han. He's our worst threat. So whatever is bugging you, get over it. Fast." Angus rang off.

Dougal sighed as he returned the phone to its cradle on the desk. He'd been trying to get over it for three hundred years. He'd lost everything. His country, his home, his family, his freedom.

He rubbed the scar on his right shoulder, where he'd been branded a slave at the age of seventeen. When other young men were just starting out, he'd thought his life was over. How could he admit he'd been reduced to a commodity, stripped of his humanity, and whipped until he'd lost all hope?

Li Lei had saved him. He'd become human again in her eyes, and she'd risked her life to set him free.

But when she'd needed him, he'd failed her.

The dragon tattoo sizzled, then erupted in heat over the etched flames covering his heart. He winced with pain. What if Li Lei had found a way to save him once again? Had her soul returned to set him free from the pain that enslaved his heart?

He blinked away tears. Even if Li Lei's soul had come back, Leah was unaware of it. And she was ignoring him.

Perhaps that was the way it should be. If he was going to earn redemption, it was only fitting that he worked for it. He would have to earn her love and her trust all over again.

I will find you. No matter what. If it takes a thousand years, I will find you.

A second chance. The more he thought about it, the more he was convinced. After almost three hundred years, he'd been given a second chance.

And this time, when Leah needed him, he would not fail her.

Chapter Fifteen

The following evening, Dougal teleported to the lobby at DVN and asked the receptionist for directions to Wilson's salon.

"Down the main hall." She pointed behind her at the double doors. "Then turn left and you'll find it just past the dressing rooms."

"Thank you." He strode toward the doors.

"You're not really getting your hair cut, are you?" the girl asked.

He paused with the door half open. "I look like a pirate."

She sighed, a wistful look in her eyes. "I know."

Was that a good thing? He wandered down the hall, then turned left. As he passed a dressing room, his superior hearing caught the sound of Laszlo's voice.

"Two hundred dollars? For a haircut?"

"You think it was easy?" a man asked. "You came in looking like your hair had been groomed at a pet store."

"Only once," Laszlo mumbled.

The man snorted. "I knew it. Oh, and here's the bill for your new clothes."

"Five hundred dollars?" Laszlo squealed.

Dougal winced. Apparently a makeover was expensive.

"Relax, dude," Gregori told him. "You look great!"

"I-I'm not so sure," Laszlo mumbled.

Dougal reached the open door and peered inside. Laszlo was wearing expensive gray slacks, a red knit shirt of some strange modern design, and a black double-breasted jacket in a military style. The jacket boasted a ton of buttons, which seemed like a good match for Laszlo, but it was his hair that gave Dougal pause. The long, floppy bangs were gone. Laszlo's hair had been cut short.

Dougal swallowed hard.

"Trust me," Gregori said. "Leah will think you're hot."

"*What*?" The third man pressed a hand to his chest.

He has to be Wilson, Dougal thought. He was slim with a mop of blond curls and sharply assessing blue eyes.

"You're trying to impress a girl? Why didn't you say so?" Wilson grabbed a pair of scissors off the counter, snipped at the neck of Laszlo's red shirt, and ripped it halfway down. "There. Perfect!"

"What? You just destroyed a" —Laszlo glanced at the bill—"a hundred-dollar shirt!"

"And it looks fabulous!" Wilson peeled the shirt back to reveal Laszlo's pasty white chest. "Now you're saying, 'Let's get it on, hot mama. I can go all night long.'"

Laszlo gulped and grasped at a button on his new jacket.

"Stop that." Wilson slapped at his hand. "It ruins your aura of confidence."

"I don't have an aura of confidence."

Wilson groaned, then glared at Gregori. "Do you expect me to turn a kumquat into caviar?"

"You did great," Gregori assured him. "Laszlo has never looked so good."

"His name is *Laszlo?*" Wilson asked in a shocked voice. "Oh God, no. We're getting rid of that."

"What?" Laszlo sputtered. "But—but—"

"Stop that." Wilson swatted his shoulder, then stepped back, tapping a finger against his mouth. "Hmm, how about Lance?"

Gregori shook his head. "Not manly enough."

"You're right." Wilson waved a hand in the air. "I once knew a lovely man named Lance, but he fell for a werewolf. Can you believe he chose a fur ball when he could have had me?"

"Unbelievable," Gregori muttered.

"I've got it." Wilson snapped his fingers, then pointed at Laszlo. "Laser!"

"Where?" Laszlo looked over his shoulder.

"No, you! You're Laser." Wilson adjusted the lapels on his jacket. "And I'll give you some advice for free. Join an all-night gym and put on some muscle. The girls love a man with a strong chest."

"Oh. Okay." Laszlo tried to ease the ripped shirt back together.

"Stop that." Wilson slapped at his hands. "Don't you want to look sexy?"

"I-I thought she might like me for my intelligence."

Wilson snorted. "Are you kidding? Women want a guy with presence. Powerful, strong, and—" He glanced toward the door when Dougal stepped in. "Oh. My. God."

Gregori smiled. "This is Dougal. The other guy who needs a makeover."

"Oh yes." Wilson approached him slowly, his discerning eyes examining him carefully. "Yes."

Dougal inclined his head. "How do ye do?"

"Yes," Wilson repeated, tapping a finger against his mouth. "Yes."

Laszlo looked confused. "You're getting a haircut, too?"

Dougal shrugged. "I look like a pirate."

"Oh." Laszlo frowned, twisting a button on his jacket.

"Hmm." Wilson circled Dougal slowly, studying him, then reached out to touch his white shirt. "No." He eyed his kilt. "No." His eyes widened at the sight of his sporran. "No!" His gaze lifted to Dougal's hair. "Oh hell, no!"

"What happened to yes?" Dougal asked.

Wilson waved a dismissive hand. "You have great presence, but—" He grimaced. "What in God's name have you been doing to your hair?"

"I . . . wash it."

"With what?" Wilson wrinkled his nose. "Lye soap?"

"No' recently."

"When did you last use conditioner?"

Dougal paused, trying to remember.

"Oh God." Wilson shot an annoyed look at Gregori. "How many miracles do you expect me to perform in one night?"

Gregori chuckled. "If anyone can do it, it's you."

"Well, that's true." Wilson touched a strand of Dougal's hair and hissed. "Your split ends have split ends. What have you been cutting it with, a dull axe?"

Dougal snorted. "I'm no' a barbarian." He reached down to remove the *sgian dubh* from his knee sock. "I use a wee blade."

"Oh God." Wilson jumped back. "That's appalling." He tilted his head as Dougal leaned over to slide the knife back into its scabbard. "But kinda sexy. What is that on your hand? A metal glove?"

"A metal hand," Dougal muttered as he straightened. "I lost my hand in battle."

"Oh my. It looks so strong. And powerful." Wilson's eyes lit up. "I've got it! We'll redo your image based on the theme full metal jacket so we can highlight your metallic hand."

Dougal winced. "Must you?"

"Yes!" Wilson punched the air with his fist. "We'll dress you all in black and cover you with zippers and chains. And handcuffs!"

Dougal frowned. "I doona believe that chains and handcuffs will inspire a woman's trust."

"Are you kidding?" Wilson grinned. "She'll love it!"

Gregori chuckled. "Sounds kinky to me."

Laszlo twisted a button. "You're doing this for a woman? Which woman?"

"Stop that." Wilson swatted at him. "Now hush, I have to think." He walked back toward Dougal. "We'll get rid of the antique shirt and skirt."

" 'Tis called a kilt," Dougal muttered.

"And what is this strange thing?" Wilson leaned over for a closer look.

Dougal gritted his teeth. " 'Tis called a sporran—a fine, manly tradition amongst the Scots."

Wilson smirked. "A furry thing in the groin

area. Yeah, I'd call that manly." He reached out to stroke it.

Dougal stepped back. "Doona touch the muskrat."

Wilson straightened, his hand pressed to his chest. "Oh my God. I'm in muskrat love!"

Gregori grinned. "I remember that. Captain & Tennille."

Dougal glowered at them. "What captain?"

"Never mind, gorgeous. Let's get you started." Wilson motioned toward a row of sinks and reclining chairs against the wall.

"I need to get back to work," Laszlo mumbled.

"See you later, Laser." Wilson waved at him. "You can pay at the receptionist desk."

Gregori patted him on the back. "Good luck, dude. Tell Abby I'll be back soon."

Laszlo cast a worried look at Dougal, then hurried from the room.

Dougal sighed. He should have told Laszlo that he was pursuing Leah. But since he wasn't making any progress, it hadn't seemed necessary.

Wilson grabbed a smock off the counter. "Here, take off your shirt and put this on."

Dougal hesitated. "I canna put that on top?"

"The neckband on your shirt is too high." Wilson waved a hand. "Come on, strip."

Dougal winced inwardly, then unbuttoned his shirt. Maybe if he took it off with vampire speed—

"What is that?" Wilson yanked back his collar. "A tat?"

" 'Tis nothing." Dougal quickly pulled off his shirt and reached for the smock.

Wilson whisked the smock out of his reach. "Oh my God! It's magnificent!"

"Snap!" Gregori's eyes grew wide. "That's a huge, freaking dragon!"

Dougal turned to grab the smock and heard Gregori's gasp. *Damn!* He quickly pulled the smock around his shoulders. Gregori must have seen the scars on his back from being lashed. And being the snitch that he was, he would tell Angus about it. And his wife.

"Wh-what happened to you?" Gregori whispered.

"'Tis nothing." Dougal snapped the smock together.

"Dougal, your back . . . sheesh, man." Gregori grimaced. "I guess it must have happened before you were transformed?"

"Aye." Dougal strode toward one of the reclining chairs in front of a sink. "Can we get on with this?"

"What did I miss?" Wilson demanded. "Was it another tattoo?"

Gregori sighed. "I think it's personal."

"Ye're damned right," Dougal growled.

"Hmm." Wilson tapped his mouth with his finger. "Talking about personal, I think we'll put you in some incredibly tight black pants. So what have you got on now? Boxers or briefs?"

Dougal blinked. "Ye—ye mean underdrawers?"

Gregori snorted. "If he's a real Scotsman, he's going commando."

"Really?" With a grin, Wilson walked over to his workstation. "So tell me, are you a real Scotsman?" He grabbed a blow dryer. "'Cause I feel a breeze coming on."

Dougal groaned. It was going to be a long night.

* * *

Leah was in the lab, concentrating on a printout of a DNA strand, when Abby nudged her with her elbow.

"Look who's back! It's Laszlo!"

"Hi," Leah mumbled, not looking up.

Abby nudged her again harder.

"What?" Leah lifted her head and discovered Laszlo standing across the room with a hopeful expression on his face. For the first time she could see his forehead. "You got a haircut."

"Yes." Laszlo fiddled with a button.

"It looks great!" Abby said. "Don't you think it looks great, Leah?"

"Sure." *It looks short.* "I guess you'll be able to look in a microscope now without your hair falling in your eyes."

Laszlo nodded. "Yes."

"And that new jacket is fabulous," Abby said, nudging Leah with her foot.

What was going on? Leah aimed a questioning look at Abby, then glanced at Laszlo. "Yes, it looks wonderful on you."

"Really?" He gave her a hopeful smile.

"Did something happen to your shirt?" Leah asked.

His smile faded as he tried to push the torn edges together. "It was an accident."

"Oh, that's a shame." Leah gave him a sympathetic look.

"Did Gregori come back with you?" Abby asked.

"No, he's still at the salon." Laszlo tugged at a button on his jacket. "He's there with Dougal."

Leah stiffened. "Dougal's there? Why?"

Laszlo frowned, twisting the button. "He said he looked like a pirate."

Then he was going to get his hair cut off? Leah jumped to her feet, her heart pounding. "Do you have his phone number?"

"Dougal's?" Laszlo shook his head. "I don't believe so."

"Abby?" Leah turned to her.

She shrugged. "I don't have the number for his cell. I usually call the office."

"Then call Gregori!" Leah yelled. "Hurry!"

Abby pulled out her phone and pushed some buttons. "What's wrong, Leah? Oh, hi, sweetie," she said into the phone.

"What's happening to Dougal?" Leah demanded.

Abby paused to listen. "Gregori says he just sat down in the chair—"

Leah grabbed the phone. "Gregori, you have to stop him!"

"Leah?" Gregori asked. "What's wrong?"

"Don't cut his hair. Don't change anything about him. I like him just the way he is."

"*What*?" Laszlo's button popped off and hit the floor.

"I—" Leah's breath caught at the devastated look on Laszlo's face. *Oh no!* Had he gotten his makeover to impress her?

"Dougal, what are you doing?" Gregori said on the phone. "Aw, sheesh. Leah? He heard you."

She gulped. "What is he doing?"

"He tore off the smock and he's putting on his shirt. He just left some money on the counter," Gregori reported.

"Dougal!" a voice shouted over the phone. "Come back! You have to at least let me cut the split ends!"

"He vanished," Gregori said. "He's probably teleporting to Romatech."

Leah's heart lurched. *Holy crapoly!* What had she done? Dougal knew how she felt, and he was coming.

"Tell Abby I'll be there soon." Gregori hung up.

In a daze, Leah handed the phone to Abby.

"You like Dougal," Laszlo whispered.

His sad face tore at her heart. "I-I'm sorry. I didn't know how you . . . I'm sorry."

The lab door burst open, and Dougal zoomed inside. He stopped, his shirt unbuttoned, his hair wet, loose, and wild, and his eyes focused on her, gleaming like emeralds.

Her heart stuttered. "Dougal."

He strode toward her and grabbed her hand. "Come with me."

Chapter Sixteen

Leah struggled to keep up with his fast, long-legged stride. "Wait."

He swept her up in his arms and walked even faster.

"Where are we—" She grabbed his neck as the hallway zoomed by in a blur. Before she knew it, they were outside, speeding toward the gazebo.

He set her on her feet. "We'll have privacy here. No cameras."

She pivoted, looking around. The white Christmas lights were on, so it felt like they were in the middle of a jewelry box full of sparkling diamonds. It was magical, romantic . . . and dangerous. For she was tempted to throw herself into the arms of a vampire. Hunching her shoulders, she stuffed her hands into the pockets of her lab coat.

"We can go somewhere warmer if ye're too cold."

"I'm fine." She was wearing a pullover sweater beneath her lab coat.

Her gaze drifted to his unbuttoned shirt. The dragon was showing. It curved around his broad chest, its mouth spewing red and orange flames over his heart. She wanted to touch him. She wanted to know all his secrets. She wanted the volcano inside him to erupt with passion for her. But would she get burned if she followed her heart?

She retreated to the far side of the gazebo and pretended to be admiring the view, even though the forest in the distance was too dark to see well. "You didn't need to rush back so fast."

"I heard you on the phone," he said softly behind her. "Ye dinna want me to get my hair cut."

Her heart raced. "Of course not." She turned toward him, waving a dismissive hand. "Who could imagine you with short hair? It wouldn't suit you."

"Ye dinna want me to change."

"Don't read more into it than—"

"Ye said ye like me the way I am." He stepped toward her.

Her heart thudded louder in her ears. "I like a lot of things. Salad. And apple pie. And things that are logical and consistent."

"Och, then ye're in luck, for I'm verra consistent."

"Your pulse isn't. It stops at sunrise."

"Aye, but every sunrise. I'm more reliable than a clock. My feelings for you are consistent as well. No matter what happens, they willna change. And I'm verra logical, too."

Also very sweet and sexy, but she tried not to dwell on that. "What's logical about being Undead?"

"Allow me to explain." His eyes glimmered. "After centuries of searching, I found the most beautiful woman ever, and she's so brilliant and brave that I'm falling for her. Does that no' seem verra logical?"

It did. And even more, it touched her heart, although she didn't want to admit it. She crossed her arms. "You're pretty clever for someone who's brain dead all day."

His mouth twitched as he moved closer. "Ye like me."

She stepped back, bumping against a wooden post. "Just . . . *like*. Nothing more."

"Ah." He stopped in front of her. "Tell me then, does yer heart always pound this fast for things ye like?"

Damn his superior hearing. She lifted her chin. "I've been known to get very excited over chocolate."

The corner of his mouth curved up. "What else do ye like?" He skimmed his fingers down her cheek. "Do ye like this? Or this?" He stroked her neck.

God, yes. She bit her lip to keep from moaning.

"Do ye know what I like?" He ran his fingers along her jaw. "I like to touch yer sweet, soft skin." He wrapped an arm around her to pull her close. "I like the way ye feel in my arms. And the way ye react to me. Yer heart sounds like a thunderstorm about to break loose."

She clutched his shirt in her fists. How could she resist such a man?

"I like the way ye taste." He rubbed his thumb across her bottom lip. "Och, lass, I would like to kiss you."

Good God, she was about to melt into a puddle at his feet. She glanced up to his eyes.

They were red and glowing.

She jumped back, breaking his hold. Just when she'd felt ready to surrender her heart, reality had rushed back to slap her in the face. She was falling for a vampire.

"Doona let it frighten you." He watched her sadly.

"My eyes will always turn when I hunger for you. So ye'll be seeing it often."

She cleared her throat. "No offense, but would you mind clarifying that a bit? Am I to assume that you're not referring to physical hunger? That the sudden change in your eyes is merely an indication of sexual arousal?"

His mouth curled up. "Yes, Doctor. That is an accurate assessment."

She narrowed her eyes. "Are you making fun of me now?"

"Never." He gave her an injured look. The red in his eyes faded back to green.

"Oh, I guess I ruined the mood." She blinked innocently. "So sorry."

He smiled. "Doona fash. 'Twill come back soon enough."

She gave him a dubious look. "You think so?"

"Aye. And while we wait, allow me to give you the clarification ye requested." His gaze drifted down her body. "I was thinking of tupping you, no' supping from you."

"*Tupping* me?"

"Is that too old-fashioned? I'll try to modernize." He leaned closer, a smile tugging at his lips. "I want to boink you, no' bite you."

Boink? She bit her lip when she felt an odd urge to giggle. "And here I was, thinking you could be wonderfully poetic."

He narrowed his eyes. "Are ye making fun of me now?"

"Never." She mimicked his injured look.

With a chuckle, he pulled her into his arms, and

she went willingly. How could she fear him when he was so adorable? So sweet and honorable.

Seven days, she realized. In only seven days, she'd gone from fainting in his presence to snuggling against him.

She turned her head, her cheek pressed against his bare chest. She could hear his heart pounding, feel his chest moving with each breath. "You're warmer than I thought you'd be."

"I'm alive at the moment."

Very alive. She skimmed a hand up to his rib cage. "You have some amazing choco-abs."

"I do?" His breath stirred her hair. "What is that?"

"A six-pack that looks like a Hershey bar." She pressed a kiss against his chest. "And tastes like one."

"Och, lass." He rubbed his chin against her hair.

She skimmed her hand over his tattoo, tracing the dragon's head, then touching the flames. "I tried ignoring you 'cause I'm afraid of getting burned."

"I know. I'm a wee frightened myself."

"Why?"

"I've waited so long. I canna bear to lose you."

Her heart fluttered. "How long have you waited?"

"Almost three hundred years."

"You've aged well." She smoothed a hand over a well-developed pectoral muscle, then caressed his nipple.

His chest expanded as he inhaled sharply. "Och, lass. My eyes have turned again."

That hadn't taken long. She smiled, knowing that she had caused it.

He kissed her brow. "I should apologize for using

words like *tupping* and *boinking*. I said them in jest, but I dinna mean any disrespect."

Her smile widened. "I've heard a lot worse. During my residency, I worked in the E.R., and some of the patients called me some really nasty things."

"They did?" He leaned back, frowning. "If ye give me their names, I'll track them down and knock their heads together."

She laughed. She didn't know which she liked more—his protective nature or the funny way he said *doon*. "What am I going to do with you?"

He regarded her seriously. "Give me a chance to be with you." His arms tightened around her. "When I draw my dying breath at dawn, my last thought is of you. And when my heart jolts back to life, my first thought is of you. My mind is filled with you. And my heart longs for you something fierce."

Her eyes burned. He was poetic after all. She'd wondered earlier how she could resist him, but she hadn't been ready yet to admit the truth.

She couldn't. She was falling in love with him. So quickly. So completely.

"Dougal," she whispered.

He rested his forehead against hers. "Leah."

Their noses touched. Their mouths hovered close.

"Yes." She slid her arms around his neck.

His lips pressed against hers once. Twice, lingering a bit longer.

Then suddenly his arms tightened around her, crushing her against him as his mouth covered hers, hungrily devouring.

The volcano within him had erupted, and she was being swept along on the blast, melting in his heat.

His tongue invaded her mouth. His hands explored. His groan reverberated through her, sending little shock waves past her stomach to settle with a delicious hum between her legs.

She needed to be closer. Her hands tangled with his wet, wild hair.

"Leah." He scattered kisses across her face and down her throat.

Her breasts ached to be touched, and she rubbed against his rock-hard chest. It wasn't enough. The ache slid down to her core, and she moaned.

He pushed aside her lab coat and palmed her breast. "Leah." His thumb grazed over her nipple.

"Please." Her sweater was too thick.

As if he'd heard her, he dug his hand beneath the hem of her sweater and slid it up to her breast once again.

She gasped. This time there was only the thin silk of her bra in the way. She shuddered when his fingers coaxed her nipple into pebbling.

"Leah," he whispered in her ear, giving the hard tip of her breast a little squeeze.

Her legs quivered, moisture pooling between her thighs.

"I want you." He traced the curve of her ear with his tongue. "I want to—"

He stiffened suddenly, and his head turned toward the building.

"What's wrong?"

He swung her up in his arms and rushed toward the side door. "The alarm went off. Someone's teleported inside."

* * *

The security office was empty. Dougal dropped Leah onto her feet. "This is the safest place for you."

"What's going on?" she asked.

Good question. He punched the flashing button to turn off the alarm, then scanned the monitors, searching for the intruder. He spotted Freemont in the silver room standing next to the empty stretcher.

The captured soldier was gone.

Laszlo and Roman rushed into the office, followed by Gregori, carrying Abby. He set her down next to Leah.

"What triggered the alarm?" Roman demanded.

"I never heard it," Leah said.

Abby leaned close to her. "It's set at a pitch where only Vamps and shifters can hear it."

Dougal punched the intercom next to the monitor showing the silver room. "Freemont, what happened?"

Freemont winced, glancing at the camera. "I'm not sure. It all happened so fast. The alarm started flashing, and I thought I saw someone in here. But he vanished, taking the soldier with him."

"Oh no," Abby whispered.

"Do a thorough search of the basement, then the building," Dougal ordered Freemont.

"Yes, sir."

Dougal zoomed to the computer on the desk so he could rewind the video recording in the silver room. The monitor flickered, then cleared.

"This was two minutes ago." Dougal approached the monitor. The captured soldier was asleep on the stretcher, all the restraints in place.

The others gathered around the monitor, waiting for something to happen.

"There!" Roman pointed when a figure suddenly appeared in the room.

Abby gasped.

"Oh, shit," Gregori whispered.

"I don't understand," Leah said. "I thought a vampire couldn't teleport into that room."

Dougal's eyes narrowed. The intruder was male, tall, dressed entirely in black, with long, dark hair. With a flick of his hand, the restraints fell open all at once. With a wry look toward the camera, he grabbed the soldier, then vanished.

"Oh dear." Laszlo fumbled with a button. "I don't think that was a vampire."

"He's not," Gregori said, wrapping an arm around Abby, who was visibly shaken. "That was Darafer. The demon."

Chapter Seventeen

*E*verything was happening so quickly that Dougal hardly had time to think.

Roman immediately called Angus MacKay in London, and since it was still dark there, Angus and Emma teleported straight to Romatech.

"Are ye sure it was Darafer?" Angus asked as soon as he entered the security office.

"Aye," Dougal replied from behind the desk. "Gregori and Abby identified him."

Angus paced across the office. "We need to find a way to keep him from returning."

Abby snorted. "He's a demon. He can go anywhere he wants."

Angus halted with a jerk. "Do we know that for a certainty?"

"Why don't we ask Marielle?" Dougal suggested. As a former angel, she would know more than anyone else would about demons.

Angus nodded. "Call her. Emma can call Dragon Nest for reinforcements. I'll call the Coven House in San Francisco to get J.L. Wang here." He stepped into the hallway with Emma and Roman.

Dragon Nest Academy was where the shifter

and hybrid children lived and went to school, so a number of MacKay employees worked there. On the monitor that showed the side entrance, Dougal spotted Ian MacPhie arriving. He was bringing werewolf Phil Jones with him. Roman met them to update them on what was happening.

Next to arrive was J.L. Wang, head of security for the West Coast Coven in San Francisco. He had were-tiger Rajiv with him.

Darafer's invasion had changed everything. The mutated soldier was gone, and most likely he was with Master Han and the other soldiers in China. Would Angus decide to move the entire project there? Was that why he'd sent for J.L. and Rajiv? Dougal didn't want to consider the possibility that he would have to go. Or Leah. Just the thought made his prosthetic hand clench.

He forced his hand to relax and called his old friend, Connor Buchanan, in Scotland. Connor was semi-retired from MacKay S&I, only rarely accepting missions, for he hated to be parted from his wife and child. A few years back he'd met and married Marielle, a fallen angel.

When Connor answered, Dougal quickly explained what had happened. "We're sure it was Darafer. Gregori and Abby recognized him. They've run into him before."

"He's no' someone ye easily forget," Connor muttered. "I almost ended up in hell thanks to him."

"We need to know if there's any way to block him from entering Romatech," Dougal said.

"I doubt ye can, but I'll ask Marielle. Hang on a bit."

"Okay." Dougal set the receiver on the desk while Connor talked to his wife.

Gregori hunched down beside his wife, who was sitting in a chair in front of the desk. "Are you all right? Do you want me to take you home?"

"With all the reinforcements coming in, the women will be safer here with us," Dougal said, glancing at Leah, who also sat in front of the desk. She looked pale, staring at her clutched hands in her lap.

"How about something from the cafeteria then?" Gregori asked.

"I'm fine, really." Abby waved a hand. "Though some ice cream would be nice."

"You got it!" Gregori straightened. "Would you like something, Leah?"

"She likes apple pie," Dougal said. "And she gets verra excited over chocolate."

Leah glanced at him, their eyes meeting for the first time since the alarm had gone off. She blushed slightly. "Yes, something like that would be great, thank you."

"I'll get it." Laszlo hurried to the door. "You guys need to stay here to protect the ladies."

"Dougal?" Connor's voice called over the phone.

He picked up the receiver. "Aye."

"Do ye need my help?"

Dougal's heart swelled with gratitude. He knew if he said the word, Connor would be there in a second. He'd been the one to change Dougal, and he'd always taken his duty as sire seriously.

The night Dougal had lost his hand, Connor had stayed with him, clasping his forearm tighter than a tourniquet to stop the bleeding. He'd retained that grip for hours even though it must have pained him.

"I appreciate the offer," Dougal said. "What does Marielle say about Darafer?"

Connor sighed. "Bad news. At the moment, Darafer is free from the confines of hell. That means he can travel anywhere in the universe except Heaven. There's nothing ye can do to stop him."

Dougal swallowed hard. Romatech was no longer safe. "If we relocate, will he automatically know where we are?"

"Good question," Connor replied. "Let me see."

Dougal lowered the receiver. "Gregori, tell Angus the bad news."

Gregori opened the door. Angus, Roman, and Emma were in the hallway, talking to the newly arrived Vamps and shifters.

After Angus heard Marielle's dire warning, he strode inside the office. "If Darafer decides to stop our plans, he may target our scientists next." He glanced at Abby and Leah. "We need to move them somewhere safe."

Abby and Leah exchanged a worried glance.

Dougal's hand clenched, and he moved it behind the desk where no one would see. When he heard Connor's voice, he used his left hand to punch a button. "Connor, I'm putting you on speaker phone so Angus can hear."

"All right," Connor said. "According to Marielle, a demon isna omniscient. There are too many mortals in the world for him to handle all their thoughts and information at once. If ye change yer location, ye'll be safe for a week or so, depending on how motivated he is to find you."

Angus nodded. "Then we'll move. Emma, Roman, and I will figure it out. Gregori, take yer wife somewhere for a few nights."

"Doona go to Howard's cabin in the Adirondacks," Connor said on the phone. "Darafer knows about that place."

"I want to learn more about demons," Dougal said. "Do ye mind if I come to yer house?"

"Ye're always welcome here, lad," Connor replied.

"Thank you." Dougal glanced at Leah. "Would ye like to go to Scotland?"

Her eyes widened. "I've always wanted to go there."

"Good." Angus clapped his hands together. "Then it's settled. Laszlo can stay here and help us with the move."

Dougal glanced at the clock on the desk. Scotland was five hours ahead, so the sun would be rising there in a few hours. "I'll be there within an hour, Connor. And I'm bringing a guest."

"That's fine. We'll see you then." Connor rang off.

Angus took most of the Vamps and shifters to the conference room across the hall.

Dougal flexed his prosthetic hand. It was relaxed now that he knew Leah would be safe. "I'll teleport you to the townhouse soon so ye can pack."

She nodded. "Who is Connor?"

"He's my sire." When she gave him a questioning look, he explained, "He's the one who changed me."

"Oh." She frowned. "So he's a vampire."

"And he's married to an angel," Abby said. "Well, former angel."

Leah's mouth fell open. "Are you serious? An angel married to a vampire?"

"Maybe we're no' so bad after all." Dougal gave her a wry look.

She snorted. "Or it could be that an angel is too naïve and trusting."

"She's not an angel anymore," Abby said. "She's human now."

Dougal nodded, although he had serious doubts that Marielle was a hundred percent human. "I need to ask her about Darafer. There must be a way to defeat him."

Abby shuddered. "He's vicious. Don't even try to fight him."

Dougal shifted in his chair. They might not have any choice.

"I'm back." Laszlo sauntered into the room with a tray. He handed a bowl of ice cream to Abby, then a saucer of apple pie to Leah. "Did anything happen while I was gone?"

"Angus told Gregori and me to take a trip." Abby dug into her ice cream. "And Dougal's going to Scotland to see Connor and Marielle."

"I'm going, too." Leah ate a bite of apple pie.

"You're supposed to stay here, dude," Gregori told Laszlo. "Angus is planning to move the mission, and he'll need your help."

Laszlo twisted a button on his lab coat. "We're moving?"

"Aye." Dougal glanced at the clock. Angus might appear any second to announce the new location. "Leah, I need to have a word with you. In private."

Her eyes widened. "Now?"

"Aye."

She took a sudden interest in her pie. "I-I'm not ready to discuss . . . anything."

Meaning she wasn't ready to talk about their relationship. "'Tis about work."

"Oh." She looked relieved. "Then it doesn't need to be private."

"Aye, it does." He gave her a pointed look. "'Tis important."

"What's going on?" Gregori asked, his eyes twinkling. "Are you two having a lovers' quarrel?"

"No!" Leah exclaimed at the same time Dougal muttered, "Nay."

Abby gave her husband an amused look. "See how well they agree with each other? I think they must be dating."

"No!" Leah said at the same time Dougal said, "Aye." She glowered at him. "We're not dating."

"Ye have a date with me tonight."

She huffed. "That's business."

Dougal arched a brow. "And pleasure."

Gregori grinned. "So which is it? Business or pleasure?"

Leah scowled at Dougal. "Business, no pleasure."

He slowly smiled back. "But pleasure is my business."

Gregori snorted.

Abby snickered. "Definitely dating."

Dougal leaned forward, lowering his voice. "Leah, I need to talk to you before Angus returns."

She shrugged and ate some more pie. "Then go ahead."

Dougal sighed. He'd have to do this with an audience. "I wouldna be surprised if Angus moves this entire mission to China."

Leah stiffened. "Oh."

"You think we'll go to China?" Abby asked.

"You're not," Gregori muttered. "Not when you're expecting. It's too dangerous."

" 'Tis too dangerous for any mortal," Dougal growled. "Leah, if Angus asks you to go, I want you to refuse."

She frowned. "But I've made so much progress."

"Did ye hear what Angus said? Our enemy might target you next. And our enemy consists of a vicious vampire named Master Han, his two vampire lords, plus an army of mutated supersoldiers and a demon."

She grew pale. "I don't intend to fight them. I'll do all my work in a lab. You can keep me safe in a lab, can't you?"

"I'll do everything in my power to keep you safe, but Darafer can travel anywhere. The safest course for you is to retire from this mission before Darafer knows ye're involved."

Leah winced. "I told the soldier my name."

Dougal hissed in a breath. It was too late then. He circled the desk and squatted next to her chair. "I will protect you. No matter what."

"So who is the lass ye brought with you?" Connor asked an hour later.

Dougal ignored the question as he paced across the library.

Connor leaned against his desk, folding his arms across his chest. "She seemed to be holding you verra tight."

Dougal snorted. "Teleporting makes her nervous."

Right after their arrival, Marielle had hugged her,

and Leah's heart rate had immediately stabilized. Dougal suspected Marielle's touch had retained a healing quality. She'd certainly healed Connor. "Yer house looks much better than I remember."

Connor smiled. "Aye. We've been renovating it, making it more comfortable."

Dougal nodded. "'Tis verra nice." Connor had neglected the old manor house for over a century. After all, a Vamp had very few needs—a supply of synthetic blood and a safe place for his death-sleep. But now that he had a wife and child, Connor's cold shell of a house had been transformed into a warm and happy home.

After their arrival, Marielle had insisted on giving them a tour. Now she was upstairs in the nursery with Leah so they could admire the sleeping Gabriel.

Connor walked over to the sideboard and opened a bottle of Blissky. "So did Angus decide what to do?"

Dougal's prosthesis fisted tight, but he managed to relax it. "He told us right before we left."

Connor watched him closely. "Ye have to go to China then?"

"Aye. I'll be going with J.L. and Rajiv."

Connor poured two glasses of Blissky and handed him one. "I know ye never wanted to go back."

Dougal took a sip and relished the burn down his throat. He wasn't happy about going back, but since Leah had wanted to continue with her work, he was determined to help her however he could. "The mission will be headquartered in Japan. The Coven Master there, Kyo, is purchasing an old abandoned school building on a remote island. One classroom will be turned into a modern laboratory for Abby, Leah, and Laszlo. Then the other classrooms will be changed into dorm rooms, no' just for the people working there but for any captured soldiers we bring out of China."

"Ye plan to keep them prisoner at this old school?" Connor asked.

"Aye. We'll keep them sedated or in stasis. Apparently, it will take time to change the mutated soldiers back to normal. One injection is no' enough."

Connor frowned. "What will keep Darafer and Master Han from rescuing them?"

"They'll be guarded constantly. And we'll keep them knocked out so they canna attempt to contact Darafer mentally." Dougal sighed. "But it is the weakest link in the plan." He shrugged. "What else can we do? We canna set up the operation in China without being attacked by Master Han's army or being noticed by the government. And Romatech is no longer safe. Besides, it is too far away to teleport a large number of prisoners."

Connor nodded. " 'Tis a tricky situation to be sure." He sipped some Blissky. "This Leah ye brought with you is one of the scientists then?"

"Aye. She's a doctor. Dr. Lee hired her to be his standby, but she also has a Ph.D. in genetics, so she's the one figuring out how to undo the damage wrought by Darafer."

"Och, ye're proud of her." Connor's mouth twitched. "Though it sounds to me like she's too smart for you."

Dougal snorted and drank more Blissky.

"Is she the one?"

Dougal swallowed so fast his eyes watered. "I

doona—" He stopped. What was the point in feigning ignorance?

When Connor had drained his blood, drawing the last drop from his veins, he'd also sucked all of Dougal's memories into his mind. And then, when Connor had fed his vampire blood back to Dougal in order to complete the transformation, all of Connor's memories had been embedded in his blood. They knew each other's pasts. All the secrets, all the regrets, all the sins, and all the joys.

It didn't always happen that way. Dougal had learned since then that most vampires were strong enough to shield their minds when transforming a mortal. Connor had been strong enough, but after experiencing Dougal's painful past, he'd shared his own.

It had been an unspoken pact between the two of them never to tell anyone else what they knew. For almost three hundred years, they had protected each other's backs and each other's secrets.

"Did ye find forgiveness?" Dougal asked.

Connor's mouth curled up slightly. "Aye."

Dougal swallowed hard. "That's good. I'm glad for you."

"It is good. Ye should try it sometime."

Dougal sighed. Could he ever deserve forgiveness? Or deserve Leah's love?

"Is she the one ye've been searching for?" Connor asked quietly.

Dougal nodded. "I believe so."

"Good." Connor finished his Blissky and set his glass down. "Ye've suffered enough."

Dougal winced. He had a bad feeling there was more suffering in store for him. But hopefully not for Leah. Somehow, he would keep her safe. "I canna fail her like I did Li Lei."

Connor patted him on the back. "Ye'll be fine. 'Twill all work out in the end."

Dougal gave him a wry look. "Since when did ye become an optimist?"

He smiled. "I've learned to have faith. Come on." He strode toward the door. "I want to meet this lass who's too smart for you."

Chapter Eighteen

"*H*e's beautiful," Leah whispered as she watched the little boy sleeping in the crib, his pink cheeks and blond hair nestled against a blue pillow. "He looks like you."

"Thank you." Marielle smiled as she gazed at her son. "But when he's being stubborn, which is most of the time, I say that he takes after his father."

"Can I ask you a personal question?" When Marielle nodded, Leah continued, "How does it work—I mean, do you like being married to a vampire?"

Marielle's mouth twitched. "Are you contemplating a similar marriage?"

"No, no." Leah waved a dismissive hand. "I'm just curious."

"I see," Marielle said, although her eyes still glinted with humor. "Well, I know very little about other marriages, but I believe mine is very happy. Even our housekeeper says it works wonderfully well."

"She knows your husband is a vampire?"

"Yes. She even told me she'd like a vampire of her own. Do you know why?"

Because he might be gorgeous, sweet, and sexy like Dougal? Leah shook her head. "I have no idea."

"Because you never have to cook for them. And they never snore."

"Right." *'Cause they sleep like the dead.*

"I can't imagine being married to anyone but Connor. And Gabriel—" Marielle glanced down at the sleeping boy. "I am still in awe that I actually gave birth. To have life growing inside me, then to see him, and hold him in my arms. There is so much love in my heart, I feel like it could burst."

Leah gazed at the little boy, and a vision flashed across her mind of a little boy with black curly hair and green eyes. She pushed the thought aside. Dougal seemed to be constantly monopolizing her thoughts. "Is it true you were an angel?"

Marielle nodded and led her toward the nursery door. "Not a very good one, I'm afraid. I didn't always follow orders. When I was a Healer, I healed two children I wasn't supposed to."

"You saved their lives?" Leah stepped into the hall with her. "How could that be bad?"

"One grew up to be a serial killer."

Leah winced.

Marielle headed toward the staircase. "When I became a Deliverer, I disobeyed again. My wings were stripped off, and I was cast upon the earth. That's when Connor found me, and I fell in love."

"But surely, as an angel, you already knew about love."

"Yes." Marielle paused at the head of the stairs. "For millennia, I was one of the Heavenly Host, a part of the whole. We were connected to each other, always communicating with each other and singing praises to the Heavenly Father. We could always feel His presence, so we were surrounded by love, and filled with love for His children."

Leah's skin prickled with goose bumps. "It sounds . . . heavenly."

"It was." Marielle smiled with a wistful look. "It was a warm and peaceful sort of love, a love for everyone. But with Connor, it all changed. All of a sudden, love was personal and . . . fierce. There was a desperation to it, so powerful that I could not live without him."

"So you gave up Heaven for him?"

With a sigh, Marielle started down the stairs. "When I was cast out for disobedience, I was afraid that I was a fallen angel and that I was doomed for hell. But now I realize that my rebellious nature didn't mean I was evil. It only meant I was human." She shrugged. "So I'm convinced I'm where I'm supposed to be. Connor needed me more than Heaven did. And the Heavenly Father works in mysterious ways."

"I see."

Marielle smiled at her. "I'm probably talking your ears off. We don't get much company here. How long will you be able to stay?"

"A day or two, I suppose."

Marielle touched her arm. "We'll take good care of you here. Why, I could take you on a tour to-morrow." She smiled proudly. "I've learned how to drive."

"That sounds great, but I should check with Dougal."

Marielle waved a dismissive hand. "He'll be in his death-sleep. Come on. We'll go to Inverness and go shopping. You can get your own kilt! And I'll show you Loch Ness on the way, and Urquhart Castle."

Leah grinned. "I'd love to."

"Great!" Marielle hugged her. "Let's go to the kitchen and have some shortbread to celebrate. I've been learning how to cook, too!"

Leah followed her, smiling. Who would have known a week ago that she would acquire two new friends—Abby and Marielle. And a suitor who just happened to be a vampire.

"There ye are." Dougal smiled at Leah as he entered the kitchen with Connor. She smiled back, her hands curled around a large mug with a cartoonish Nessie pictured on it. She was seated across from Marielle at the long wooden table, where they were having hot tea and shortbread.

Connor took two bottles of Bleer from the fridge and brought them to the table. "Och, that shortbread looks good."

"It is," Leah agreed.

"Thank you." Marielle turned to her husband as he sat beside her. "Leah's going to spend the day with me and Gabriel tomorrow. We're going to Inverness!"

"Sounds great." Connor cast an amused look at Dougal. "Apparently, ye'll be staying here awhile."

"That's fine." Dougal sat beside Leah and twisted the top of his bottle of Bleer. "We have some time before we move the mission to Japan."

Leah nodded. "Angus said it would take at least two weeks to get the old school ready, and that's with a small army of workers going twenty-four/seven."

Marielle gave her a worried look. "Be careful."

"I should be fine," Leah insisted. "I'll be on some remote island in Japan, working in a lab."

Dougal frowned. Missions had a way of changing once you were forced to adjust to whatever the enemy threw your way.

Marielle frowned, too. "It would be a mistake to underestimate Darafer. The second he sees you, he will know all about you. He'll know which fears to manipulate, which wounds to pick at, and the most efficient way to tempt you."

"Aye." Connor patted his wife's hand. "We were fortunate to escape him unscathed."

Marielle nodded. "He's superstrong and fast. Extremely intelligent. He can appear and disappear anywhere at any time. And he can even control time if it suits his purpose."

Leah's eyes widened. "Really?"

Marielle sipped from her mug. "He can freeze everything on a local scale, and no one realizes that it's happened. Except for the Heavenly Host."

"Is there a way to defeat him?" Dougal asked.

Marielle sighed. "Only the Heavenly Father has that power, and I've never known Him to destroy an angel, even the fallen ones. The most likely way to handle Darafer is to banish him back to hell, but only the Father or a God Warrior has the power to do that."

"A what?" Leah asked.

"A God Warrior. An angelic soldier," Marielle explained. "You see, there are five kinds of angels: Messengers, Guardians, Healers, Deliverers, and then, the God Warriors. They are the strongest and fiercest of the Heavenly Host. They fly in chariots of fire, and if they wish, their swords can turn into blades of fire."

"Holy crapoly," Leah whispered.

Dougal leaned forward. "Then there's nothing a mortal or a Vamp can do against a demon?"

Marielle winced. "The best you can hope for is to survive."

Leah shuddered.

Underneath the table, where no one could see, Dougal took hold of her hand. "Is there a way we can get these God Warriors to help us?"

Marielle tilted her head, considering. "There is a way, but only if the demon in question has broken the rule of free will. You see, the Heavenly Father has decreed that all his children must have free will. From the viewpoint of mortals, it's a wonderful thing, but for the angels, it's a frustrating rule that severely limits their power. If a mortal decides to follow a demon, they cannot interfere. The mortal has the right to his decision."

Leah groaned. "The soldier we had was a willing participant."

Marielle nodded sadly. "If Master Han's soldiers are willing to let Darafer transform them, then there is nothing the God Warriors can do."

"Even if Master Han's army takes over the world?" Leah asked. "They would just sit by and let it happen?"

Marielle sighed. "As long as mortals choose to do evil, then evil will triumph. And Lucifer will laugh when people blame it on the Heavenly Father. But even with all the suffering in the world, the Heavenly Father will not take away your free will. He wants you to choose good or evil. He will not force us to choose good."

"Because forcing us would be . . . evil?" Leah asked.

Marielle nodded. "Exactly. Of course, demons like Darafer are evil incarnate, so occasionally, they will force someone, destroying that person's free will. When that happens, the demon has broken the decree, and the God Warriors have the right to step in."

"How would they know if that happened?" Dougal asked. "Maybe it already has happened, and they doona know."

"They would know." Marielle's gaze drifted to the corner of the room. "That person's Guardian would let them know."

"Guardian?" Dougal glanced at the corner, but there was nothing there. "Ye mean guardian angel?"

"Yes." Marielle smiled at the corner. "All mortals have at least one Guardian, and they are in constant communication with the Heavenly Host."

Leah glanced over her shoulder. "I have a Guardian?"

"Yes. Josephine." Marielle turned to her husband with a sad smile. "I'm afraid you lost yours when you died."

"That's all right." Connor wrapped an arm around her shoulders. "I have you."

Leah peered around the room. "Are you serious? I have an angel named Josephine?"

"Yes, and she loves you dearly." Marielle gave Dougal a sympathetic look. "None of the Vamps have any."

He shrugged. That was hardly surprising.

Leah glanced at him, then blushed. "Does my Guardian see everything that I do?"

Marielle smiled. "Angels don't have bodies, unless they need to take one for a specific purpose, so they don't normally relate to the physical aspects of human life. They simply turn away and rejoin the Host whenever you . . . I mean, if you do . . . anything." Her gaze shifted to Dougal and back to Leah.

Dougal smiled at the heated blush on Leah's face and squeezed her hand underneath the table.

She cleared her throat. "If people have Guardians, then why do they get hurt?"

"The Guardians protect you as best as they are able," Marielle replied. "But when free will comes into play, and a person decides to drink and drive, or chooses to take a drug, then there is very little they can do. It is painful to watch a soul we love destroy itself. And even more tragic when other innocent souls are destroyed in its wake."

Dougal took a long drink of his Bleer while Leah and Marielle continued to philosophize. As long as Darafer was finding humans who were willing, there would be no help from the God Warriors.

He figured the Vamps and shifters could handle Master Han and the two vampire lords. The army would be difficult because the Vamps were so outnumbered. Difficult, but possible. However, when it came to Darafer, as far as he could tell, they were screwed.

Chapter Nineteen

"*O*w!" Leah stumbled on the uneven pavement.

"Are you all right?" Marielle stopped pushing the stroller.

Leah put some weight on her left foot and winced. "I twisted my ankle."

"Let me see." Marielle leaned down to touch her ankle, and Leah felt an instant surge of relief.

"I think it's better." She tried walking, then winced. "But not much."

Marielle sighed. "I'm afraid my healing powers are not as strong as they used to be, at least not for physical ailments. We need Bunny."

"A rabbit?"

Marielle smiled. "Buniel. He's a Healer. Let's stop in that pub for a while so you can rest."

Leah limped toward the street corner where the pub was located. Her arms were so full of purchases that she hadn't seen the small pothole. But how could she have resisted buying herself a kilt? And then she'd needed the matching plaid shawl, a red beret, knee socks, and white Jabot blouse. She'd even splurged and bought herself a small sporran made of faux fur.

Marielle had bought plenty, too, and every storage space on the baby stroller was stuffed. She wheeled it into the pub and up to a table.

Leah set her purchases down on the nearby bench, then took a seat.

"I tell you what." Marielle leaned over to rummage through the large diaper bag. "After we've rested a bit, I'll run back to get the car. Then I can just pick you up, and you won't have to walk."

"Sounds good." Leah propped her foot up on the bench. Already the ankle was starting to swell. She glanced around. The place was mostly empty, except for a few older men close to the fireplace, drinking pints and playing chess.

"Here you go." Marielle handed Gabriel a stuffed tiger. He smiled, flailing the tiger about as she hunted for more toys in the diaper bag.

"May I be of service?" a deep voice asked, and Leah glanced up and blinked.

The waiter was tall, blond, and stunningly handsome.

"I'll have a lemonade," Leah said.

His mouth curled in amusement. "As you wish. And perhaps some warm milk for Gabriel?"

Marielle straightened. "Bunny! You came."

Leah's mouth fell open. He was rather heavenly to look at, even though she didn't think anyone, even an angel, could be as gorgeous as a certain dark-haired vampire in a kilt.

He gave Marielle a hug, then placed a hand on Gabriel's head. "God bless you, dear soul."

Gabriel gazed up at him and blew bubbles of spittle.

The angel laughed, then turned to Leah. "I hear you twisted your ankle."

"You did? How?"

He motioned to a space behind her. "Josephine told me, and Marielle wished for me." He turned back to Marielle. "Did you want something to drink?"

She chuckled. "Are you taking orders? I'll have a lemonade, too."

"Very well." He inclined his head. "Bless you all." With a last smile aimed at Leah, he turned and walked toward the kitchen.

"He forgot to—" Leah paused when she realized she was no longer in pain. "Oh my gosh." She leaned over to examine her ankle. The swelling was gone.

"Is it better?" Marielle sat down across from her.

"It's completely better." Leah set her foot on the floor. "How did he do that? He didn't even touch it."

"A twisted ankle isn't much of a challenge for Bunny."

A dark-haired waiter came toward them with a tray. He set two glasses of lemonade on the table, plus a glass of warm milk. Marielle poured the milk into a plastic glass and snapped a spouted lid on top.

"Where's Buniel?" Leah asked. When the waiter gave her a blank look, she continued, "The other waiter? The blond one?"

The waiter frowned, shaking his head. "I'm the only one here right now. Let me know if ye need anything else." He turned and strode back to the kitchen.

Leah's skin prickled with goose bumps. "That was weird. Where did Bunny go?"

Marielle shrugged. "His work was done."

"But I didn't get to thank him."

Marielle smiled as she handed the cup of milk to her son. "You just did. He'll know."

Leah glanced over her shoulder. Was Josephine there? It was strange to think that all those years when she'd thought she'd been alone, she'd had a guardian angel. Heck, a week ago she hadn't even believed in angels or demons. And she'd thought vampires were nonsense.

Now she was falling for a vampire in a kilt. She smiled to herself. She couldn't wait to see his face this evening when he saw what she'd bought.

"The sun has set in New York." Dougal slipped his cell phone back into his sporran after calling Freemont. "I need to go back to work tonight."

"Marielle said they'd be down soon. Apparently they have a surprise for us." Connor strode to the sideboard in his library and poured two glasses of Blissky. "Thank you for coming. Marielle had a great time today with Leah."

Dougal nodded. "Thank you for loaning me a clean shirt and some socks."

"Ye're welcome." Connor handed him a glass. "Come back any time ye like."

Dougal sipped some Blissky. "Is it hard being married to a mortal? I mean, we can only be a husband or father at night."

Connor frowned at his glass. "Sometimes I feel guilty for no' being able to do more, but she claims I shouldna, that she's verra happy." He shrugged.

"What is the alternative? To no' be with her at all? Then we would both be miserable."

Dougal winced. He would certainly be miserable if he had to give up Leah.

"I'll take fifty percent of her life rather than have none of it." Connor took a sip. "I have only the night-time with her and Gabriel, but those nights are filled with joy."

"We're ready!" Marielle's voice called out.

Dougal and Connor strode into the foyer and looked at the top of the stairs.

Dougal's heart stilled.

Connor chuckled. "What a bonny lass ye are."

Marielle started down the stairs. She was wearing a formal ankle-length kilt in the Buchanan plaid, al-though Dougal hardly noticed. His gaze remained focused on Leah as she descended the stairs, smiling.

If imitation was the greatest form of flattery, then she was flattering him something fierce. The style of her kilt, shirt, knee socks, and sporran all closely resembled his own. But whereas he considered his clothes to be merely functional, on her they looked adorable. Sexy. He wondered if she was mimicking him to the point that she was bare beneath the kilt. Just the thought made his groin tighten.

She reached the bottom step, and he moved close so their eyes were level.

She smiled, her cheeks blushing. "What do you think?"

"I think ye're lovely. The most lovely lass I've ever seen." He took hold of her shoulders and gazed down at her kilt. "So ye're part of the Stewart clan now?"

"They didn't have any Kincaid kilts on the rack. Those have to be ordered, and it would take a few weeks." She glanced down. "But it's the same basic colors."

After dying for Bonnie Prince Charlie, the Stewart plaid was not one of his favorites, but he wasn't about to ruin Leah's fun. He made a mental note to order her a kilt in the Kincaid tartan as soon as possible. "I like yer red bonnet."

"The beret?" She grinned. "I bought one for you, too, so we could match."

"Och." He moved closer and whispered, "Do ye think we're a good match now?"

She nodded, her blush deepening.

He kissed her brow. She lifted her chin, so their lips were a fraction apart.

"And we have matching sporrans," Marielle announced. "See? Oh, excuse me."

Dougal glanced their way and discovered Marielle and Connor watching him and Leah with big smiles on their faces. He stepped back and pretended to admire Leah's sporran. It was too small for his taste, but perfect for her. Thankfully, his own sporran was large enough to hide the growing problem under his kilt.

"What kind of skin is it?" Connor stroked his wife's sporran.

"It's supposed to look like beaver," Marielle explained, "but they're faux fur. Leah and I couldn't bear the thought of any animals being harmed."

Connor chuckled. "Ye have kind hearts."

"I'm afraid we need to be going," Dougal announced.

While he said his good-byes to Connor and Marielle, Leah ran back upstairs to her room to collect the tote bag she'd brought the night before.

"I bought more stuff than I could fit in my bag," she said as she came downstairs with her bulging tote bag and more belongings bundled in a plaid shawl that matched her kilt. After saying good-bye to Connor and hugging Marielle and promising to return, she stepped outside with Dougal.

"This way." He took her bag and led her up a hill. "Watch yer step." The moon was shining brightly, but her night vision wasn't nearly as good as his.

She gave him a wry look. "Are we walking all the way back?"

"I want to show you something."

"You found a new underground lair?"

He chuckled. "Nay." At the top of the hill, he stopped.

"Holy crapoly," she breathed.

At the base of the hill, on a flat stretch of land, a stone circle gleamed in the moonlight.

"It's beautiful." Leah scampered down the hill, her bundled shawl clutched against her chest. "I love it!" She ran into the center of the stone henge.

As Dougal came down the hillside, he gathered up a small bundle of heather. "Here." He handed it to her. "To remember yer first trip to Scotland."

"Thank you." She fumbled with her sporran to drop the heather inside. "I'll always remember this."

Still holding her tote bag, he pulled her into his arms. "Perhaps the next time we come to Scotland, ye'd like to see my house on the Isle of Skye?"

"I'd like that."

"'Tis a date then."

She grinned. "I guess we are dating."

"Aye." He kissed her brow. "Are ye ready to go back now?"

"Yes." She went up on tiptoe to wrap her arms around his neck, leaving her bundle of clothes squashed between them. "Don't drop me."

"Never." He kissed her, then teleported them to the back porch of the townhouse.

She heaved a sigh of relief. "We made it." Grabbing her bundle, she stepped back and stumbled.

He steadied her. " 'Tis common to feel a bit dizzy." When he turned to unlock the door, she fell forward. "Och, I think we're attached."

"We're fused together?" she squealed. "Oh my God! I was afraid—"

"Relax! 'Tis only our sporrans."

"Huh?" She stepped back and his sporran lifted, hooked onto hers. "How did this happen?"

"The chain on yers is caught on one of my tassels." He tugged at the chain, but it was stuck. "Apparently, my muskrat is verra attracted to yer beaver."

She snorted.

"Stay close to me." He unlocked the door, and they sidestepped into the kitchen, waddling like penguins.

"It's so dark in here." She fumbled along the wall, hunting in vain for the light switch while he shut the door.

"I can see." He dropped her tote bag on the floor, then tried to unhook her chain from his tassel. "Och, my right hand is too clumsy. I doona want to damage yer beaver."

She scoffed. "Don't worry. It's fake beaver."

"Then when can I see the real one?"

"Ha!" She shoved at his shoulder, and he pulled her tight against him.

Her bundle of clothes fell to the floor, and she splayed her hands against his chest. "This isn't going to get us untangled."

"I like it this way." He nuzzled her neck as his hands slipped around her hips to her rump, then moved about.

"Are you looking for something?"

"I was wondering how authentic ye were. A real Scotsman would never wear drawers. Ah." He traced the line of her underwear. "What a shame."

"Well, I hate to disappoint." She smoothed a hand up his neck to his face. "I can always take them off."

His heart lurched. "Ye want to . . . ?" His eyes turned red, and she gasped.

"Are ye afraid?" he whispered, aware that his glowing red eyes might be all that she could see in the dark.

She skimmed her fingers over his cheek to his lips. "I'm falling for you."

His heart swelled. "Leah." Pulling her close, he kissed her thoroughly, hungrily. Her beret tumbled to the floor when he dug his hands into her hair. Her scent of jasmine filled his senses as he deepened the kiss.

He explored her mouth while his hands roamed her body. Her rounded hips, her narrow waist, her sweet breasts. She moaned, arching her back as he caressed a breast. It was plump enough to fill his left hand and sexy enough to make him hard. He tweaked the nipple, and she responded with a small gasp.

"Lass." He unhooked her sporran at the small of her back, then unhooked his own and tossed the two onto the floor. This time when he pulled her close he was rewarded with a bigger gasp. His erection pressed against her.

She tugged at his shoulders, pulling him down for another kiss. Her tongue danced with his, her moans mixed with his. He gathered up her kilt till he could slide his hands underneath. Her soft, silky skin was heaven, the curve of her rump paradise.

He slipped his hands beneath her tiny silk panties, grasping her bare bottom and pulling her hard against him. His erection strained. All he had to do was lift his kilt and—the light came on beneath the swinging door.

Footsteps sounded in the foyer as they came toward the kitchen.

"We're no' alone," he whispered, hitting the light switch.

Leah blinked at the sudden light. "What?"

She looked beautifully disheveled, her lips plump and red from kissing.

"Who's there?" Angus called from the foyer.

Dougal winced. He should have remembered that Angus and Emma would be staying at the townhouse. He tugged the hem of Leah's kilt into place, then grabbed the beret off the floor and plopped it onto her head.

The door swung open, and Angus peered inside. "Och, ye're back." He stepped inside.

"Aye, just now," Dougal replied.

Angus's gaze swept over them, then drifted to their sporrans on the floor.

"Who is it?" Emma asked as she peered through the door. Her eyes widened. "Oh, I like your kilt, Leah."

"Thanks." Leah leaned over to grab her bundle off

the floor. The shawl's knot came loose, and all her dirty clothes tumbled onto the floor.

"Let me help." Dougal reached over to grab an item, then realized it was a pair of red underwear.

Leah snatched it from his hand, and he straightened to find Angus and Emma watching with amused expressions.

He cleared his throat. "I interviewed Marielle about the demon, Darafer."

Angus nodded. "I'll hear what ye have to say in a moment. We've been working with Laszlo, setting up a temporary lab in the basement. Everyone will be staying here until we're ready to move to the new base in Japan."

"How many guards do we have here?" Dougal asked.

"Emma and myself. Robby, J.L., and Ian will remain here until we move. And Howard, Phil, and Rajiv will guard during the day. We have an alarm system here as good as the one at Romatech, so if anyone invades the property, we'll know instantly."

Dougal took a deep breath. If Master Han or his vampire lords tried to invade the townhouse, they could do it only at night. The bad vampires spent their day in death-sleep, the same as the Vamps.

But Darafer wasn't limited by the sun. Would Howard, Phil, and Rajiv be able to stop him if he invaded during the day? That would be an interesting fight, Dougal thought. He'd like to see the demon handle a three-pronged attack from a were-bear, werewolf, and were-tiger. But not if it meant Leah was in danger.

Chapter Twenty

The next week was frustrating for Dougal. With so many people living at the townhouse, he could hardly find any time alone with Leah. She was working hard with Roman and Laszlo, mass-producing serums to repair the genetic damage wrought by Darafer.

After a few nights, Gregori and Abby returned. They were also staying at the townhouse, and Abby was busy making her drug that would put the captured soldiers into stasis.

The shifters, Howard, Phil, and Rajiv, were all rooming on the same floor as Leah, and they set up a security office nearby with monitors connected to all the security cameras. Dougal was still doing his death-sleep in the basement, but now he shared the room with J.L., Ian, Robby, and Laszlo. The married couples, Angus and Emma and Abby and Gregori, took rooms on the third floor. Each night, shortly before dawn, Roman teleported back to his home near Dragon Nest so he could be with his family.

Dinner was about the only time Dougal managed to be alone with Leah. He teleported to the cafeteria at Romatech to pick up the meal of her choice, then he had a bottle of blood with her while she ate in the kitchen. But they were never really alone, not with so many people nearby.

"Angus has asked me to teach you, Abby, and Laszlo some self-defense before we leave on the mission," he told her as she finished a piece of apple pie.

"Why? Won't we be safe with you guys guarding us?"

"'Tis a precautionary measure. The first session begins in an hour. In the basement at Romatech."

Her eyes widened. "I thought it wasn't safe there."

"Freemont and Austin are still working there as guards, and they say it's been quiet. We'll teleport in just for the practice sessions. We need to use the gym and shooting range there."

"Shooting range?"

"Aye. If one of the bad guys shows up, we'll use him for target practice."

She made a face. "I have to learn how to shoot?"

"Aye. And wield a knife."

"I don't like violence."

"Ye'll be glad to know how to defend yerself when yer life is in danger."

She took her dirty dishes to the kitchen sink. "I don't believe in killing. I'm a doctor. I'm supposed to save lives, not end them. That's why I'm doing all this, so I can save those mutated soldiers, and you won't have to kill them."

"Leah, if ye're under attack, I expect you to defend yerself."

"I thought you were supposed to protect me."

"I will! But are ye saying 'tis all right for me to kill, and no' you? Do ye think I enjoy it?"

She winced. "I didn't mean to sound hypocritical. I-I'm just not sure I can do it."

"Ye're verra brave. Ye can do it."

With a groan, she rinsed off her plates, then stacked them in the dishwasher.

" 'Twill be November by the time we go to Japan," Dougal continued. "I doona know how well insulated this old school building will be. Ye may need to go shopping for some winter clothes."

She gave him an amused look as she dried her hands on a dishtowel. "First you're worried about my safety. Now you're worried about me getting cold?"

"Aye. I spend a lot of time thinking about you."

She returned to the table and sat next to him. "I actually have some winter clothes back at my apartment in Houston. They're left over from my years of college and med school in Boston."

"I could teleport you to yer apartment." *And we could be alone.*

She nodded. "That would be good. I need more clothes." She smiled ruefully. "I've been wearing the same three outfits forever. When I first came here, I thought it was just for a weekend."

"And here we are two weeks later."

She placed her hand on his shirt, covering his heart. "Sometimes, when I think about it, I'm shocked that I could fall for you so fast. But then, other times, when it feels so right, I feel like I've been waiting for you forever." She gave him a bemused look. "Does that seem strange?"

"Nay." He rested his hand on top of hers. "We've waited almost three hundred years."

She gave him a playful shove. "Maybe I knew you in another life."

His chest expanded with a sudden gasp for air.

She rose to her feet. "I'd better get back to work. I need to finish something before you drag me off to the firing range."

As she strode from the kitchen, he sat still, his heart pounding. Was she remembering Li Lei? He wasn't sure he wanted her to. Then she might remember how badly he'd failed her.

"**H**ow did I do?" Leah asked an hour later in the basement shooting range at Romatech. She studied the paper man across the room but couldn't see any holes in him.

Dougal moved one of her ear muffs aside and leaned close so she could hear him. "Ye hit the ceiling. I think ye'd do better if ye dinna squeeze yer eyes shut."

She gave him an annoyed look. "I can't help it. These things scare me." She flinched when Laszlo's gun shot off in the cubicle to their left. He hit his paper man in the chest.

Freemont, who was tutoring Laszlo, punched the air with his fist.

In the cubicle to the right of them, Abby was practicing with Gregori. She was managing to hit her target, too.

Leah frowned. "I'm not any good at this."

Dougal leaned close to her ear. "Ye will be if ye practice every night."

"How can I possibly shoot a vampire or demon when they can vanish at will?"

" 'Tis possible to shoot a vampire if ye catch him by surprise. And the silver bullets will hurt like hell. I'm no' sure about demons, but this will definitely help you defend yerself against Master Han's soldiers."

"But—"

"No buts." He moved behind her and lifted her arms, covering her hands with his. "Widen yer stance."

She did, painfully aware that his groin was pressed against her rump. He'd surprised her when it had been time to teleport to Romatech. His kilt and old-fashioned shirt had been replaced by a tight black T-shirt and black pants with a dagger strapped to his leg. He looked modern, dangerous, and sexy as hell. She was sorely tempted to wiggle her hips against him.

"Again." He moved her ear muff back into place, then grasped her wrists to keep her steady.

This time she hit the paper, wincing at the hole ripped through the abdominal area. A patient would need surgery to survive that, and he'd probably lose part of his intestines.

With the next shot, she obliterated his right lung. But when Dougal stopped helping her, she missed the paper again. Disgusted, she set the pistol down.

"We'll do some more tomorrow." Dougal escorted her from the room, leaving the ear muffs in the entryway shelving unit.

Abby, Gregori, Freemont, and Laszlo followed them to the gym, complete with punching bags, dummies, a table filled with knives, and thick pads on the floor.

With everyone lined up behind him, Dougal drew the dagger from the sheath strapped to his leg and threw it at the dummy across the room. The knife whirled through the air, then stuck into the dummy's chest with a loud *thunk*.

Leah winced.

Dougal turned to face them. "Ye may be wondering why ye need to know how to shoot or throw a knife, but I canna stress enough the importance of killing or wounding the enemy before he can get close to you. Ye doona want to fight any of Master Han's soldiers, no' when they're superstrong. And it is imperative no' to let Master Han or one of the vampire lords get near you. If they grab you and teleport away with you, we would have a verra hard time ever finding you."

"I have a tracking device in my arm." Laszlo glanced at the two mortal women. "Perhaps we should do the same for the ladies?"

"It might be a good idea." Gregori wrapped an arm around Abby's shoulders. "If you're okay with it."

"But Leah and I should be safe in Japan," Abby said.

"Not entirely," Gregori grumbled. "That's why I'm going with you and sticking by your side like glue."

"Doona forget that Darafer came here," Dougal said. "Either he or Master Han could teleport to Japan to grab you. That's why we're teaching you self-defense."

Leah glanced at the dummy with a knife imbedded in his chest. Could she kill if she had to? She wasn't sure, so it might be best to have a chip in her arm. Just to be safe. "I'll take a tracking device. Until the mission is over."

Dougal nodded, looking relieved.

"All right," Abby agreed. "I'll do it, too."

Three nights later, Leah stood outside the security office at the townhouse. She'd arranged for Dougal to teleport her to her apartment at midnight. She hesitated before knocking, trying to remember how messy the place had been when she'd left over two weeks ago. Would Dougal be offended by a few dirty dishes lying about? She'd been in such a hurry to get to the airport. Never in a million years would she have believed that she would be teleporting back with a vampire boyfriend.

The door opened and Dougal invited her in, looking as handsome as ever in his kilt and old-fashioned shirt. "Ye're ready?"

"Yes." She stepped inside and smiled at Howard and Rajiv, who were both munching on donuts. "Thank you for filling in for Dougal."

"Not a problem." Howard cast an amused glance at Dougal. "Take your time."

"Pooh Bear and I will be fine." Rajiv laughed when Howard's nudge nearly knocked him over.

"Come on." Dougal led her back into the hallway and shut the door.

"They don't seem very scary for a grizzly bear and a tiger," she said as he walked beside her.

"They can be plenty scary if ye're a bad guy."

"You won't be offended if my apartment is a bit—" She hesitated when he held the door open to her bedroom.

"No camera inside." He gave her a gentle push.

"Oh. Okay. Privacy is good." She stepped inside and retrieved a folded piece of paper from her lab coat pocket. "Here."

"What is it?" He took the paper. "A love letter?"

She snorted. "You wish."

"I do wish." He gave her an injured look. "I had one for you weeks ago, but ye never came down to the basement to read it."

She winced. "I-I was avoiding you."

"I noticed."

She punched his arm. "I'm not avoiding you anymore. I'm very . . . fond of you."

"*Fond*? Is this a bloody fondness letter?"

"No. It's my address. So we can teleport to my apartment."

"Yer address?" His mouth twitched as he opened the note. "Do ye think I'm a GPS system?"

She blinked. She didn't want him reading her mind. "Is there another way to get there?"

"I need a sensory beacon. Or I could slip inside yer brilliant brain for a second to see where to go." He stepped closer, his eyes twinkling. "And while I'm there, I might see just how fond ye really are."

She stepped back. "You wouldn't dare."

"I do dare." He moved closer, a slow smile curling his mouth. "Of course, I wouldna have to if ye simply told me how ye felt."

She huffed. "I won't be coerced into a confession of love—"

"Love?"

She winced. "And I won't have you invading my mind."

"Doona fash." He gathered her into his arms. "Lately, I've been much more interested in invading yer body."

She bit her lip to keep from laughing. That was the main reason she didn't want him in her mind. He might see all the naughty thoughts and dreams she'd been having. "So what do you mean by a sensory beacon?"

"I can teleport somewhere if I can see it or hear it. If there was someone there to answer the telephone—"

"An answering machine?"

"Aye." He gave her a rueful look. "That would work."

"Excellent." She pulled her cell phone from her pocket and punched in her home number. "Okay, it should come on soon." She held the phone up to his ear.

"Grab on to me." He pulled her tight and bowed his head to gaze into her eyes. "Love?"

She grinned. "You wish."

"I do wish."

She went up on tiptoe to wrap an arm around his neck and give him a quick kiss.

"Och, lass." His eyes darkened.

The answering machine kicked on, and everything went black.

Chapter Twenty-one

*A*s soon as they arrived, Leah glanced about. Not too shabby. There were some dirty dishes, but at least they were in the sink. "It might be a little dusty."

"It canna be worse than my house on the Isle of Skye. I havena been there in six months."

She realized he was still holding her. "Are you going to let me go, or did we accidentally fuse together?"

His mouth curled up. "Any fusion 'twould no' be by accident."

She snorted, her hands resting on his chest. "You told me that the first night we met."

"Aye, and I've been wanting you ever since." He heaved a forlorn sigh. "Eighteen days I've been waiting."

"You're such a player."

His eyebrows rose. "A what?"

"A player. How did you win me over in only eighteen days? Especially when you're dead half the time."

He gave her an injured look. "Can I help that? I was

laying there in my death-sleep, innocent as a lamb, when ye molested me. Perhaps ye're the player?"

"What?"

"Ye unbuttoned my shirt and felt my chest."

"I was checking for a heartbeat. That's all."

His eyes twinkled with humor. "Ye were no' admiring my manly physique?"

"You wish."

"I do wish." He started unbuttoning his shirt. "My heart is beating something fierce. Would ye like to check it now?"

She swatted his chest. "Player. I need to pack." She headed for the bedroom.

"I'm packing something for you," he mumbled.

She stifled a laugh as she glanced around the bedroom. She grabbed some discarded pajamas off the bed and smoothed some wrinkles in the comforter.

"Need any help?" He sauntered into the room.

"I'm fine." She tossed the dirty clothes into the hamper, then pulled a large suitcase from her closet. "Are you going to be able to teleport this back with me?"

"Aye." He sat on the bed and gave her a hopeful look. "Can I make myself comfortable?"

"Sure." She grabbed several pairs of jeans and some T-shirts from her closet. While she was folding them into the suitcase, she heard two thuds and glanced up. He'd taken his shoes off and was rolling down his socks. Her pulse sped up. How far was he planning to strip?

He dropped his sporran on the floor, then propped up some pillows and sat with his back against the headboard. "This is verra comfy. Would ye like to try it?"

She bit her lip to keep from smiling. "I've tried it before." She selected several sweaters from the shelving unit in her closet and dropped them into her suitcase.

As she continued to pack, she became more and more aware that he was watching her every move. She could feel his desire, so strong it seemed to reach across the room to caress her. Her skin began to tingle. Her breasts felt heavy. When she leaned over to grab a pair of boots off the closet floor, he groaned.

She glanced back, and sure enough, he was focused on her rump. Without thinking, she squeezed her thighs together. The thought of getting caught up in one of his volcanic explosions made her heart race. And made her womanly core feel agonizingly empty.

She quickly zipped the boots into the front section of her suitcase, then moved to her chest of drawers. She tossed some underwear and bras into the suitcase, along with some thermal underwear.

In a flash, he was there beside her, picking up one of her panties. " 'Tis so tiny." He examined the small triangle of silk. "It must barely cover yer honey pot."

With a snort, she snatched it from his hand. Honey pot? Stifling another laugh, she stuffed all her underwear in a zippered compartment. Then she opened another dresser drawer to retrieve her warmest flannel pajamas.

"Och, now this is nice." He pulled a long red nightgown from the drawer. "Ye should bring this."

She tossed it back. "It's not warm enough."

"Ye wouldna keep it on long enough to notice."

She shook her head, smiling. The man had a one-track mind. "This is a business trip, remember?"

She went into the bathroom to gather some toiletries. When she returned to pack them, she discovered the red nightgown had been neatly folded and slipped between two sweaters.

"Is this yer family?" He lifted a framed photo off the top of her dresser.

"Yes." She moved closer so she could point out each person. "That's my mom and dad. Kathleen and Kai Ling. They're both physics professors."

"Ye told me about yer Irish grandfather. So yer mother is Irish?"

"Yes. When I was about five years old, I asked her why my eyes couldn't be green like hers, and ever since then, I've been fascinated with genetics."

"Ye like green eyes?" He gave her a wide-eyed look.

She smiled. "Yes. And I love the pipes, too. My grandfather used to play." She sighed. "The summer I spent with him was one of the happiest times in my life."

"We'll make more happy times for you." He pointed at her in the photo. "Ye were a bonny lass."

She snorted. The photo didn't capture how gawky and shy she'd been at the time. "I was eleven. An unplanned late addition to the family, or as my father called it, an accident of cosmic proportions."

Dougal winced. "I would have called you a miracle. Ye are to me."

Her heart swelled. How many times would she have loved to hear that while growing up? Instead, she'd been constantly pressured to live up to the high standards her brothers had set. Homeschooled, devoid of any friends until she'd gone off to college to swim among the sharks.

"And these are yer brothers?" Dougal asked.

"Yes, this one is Albert. He was eighteen at the time. And the one in the graduation robe is Isaac. He was sixteen and graduating college."

"That young?"

Leah nodded. "Albert and Isaac both started college at thirteen. And they both had their Ph.D.'s by the time they were nineteen. I left for college when I was fourteen, but I didn't become a doctor till I was twenty-one." She made a face. "I took some flak for that. They thought I should be a doctor of some kind before the age of twenty."

Dougal frowned. "Are ye serious?"

She shrugged. "My parents weren't happy with my decision to go to med school. And they think genetics is a waste of time. I was supposed to be like Albert and Isaac and get my doctorate in quantum physics. Why study lowly humans when I could take on the entire universe?"

Dougal gave her an incredulous look. "Do they no' realize how brilliant ye are?"

"I was slower than my brothers."

He huffed. "Give me yer parents' address, and I'll track them down and knock their heads together."

Leah grinned. "That would get you off to a great start with the future—" She stopped herself from saying *in-laws*. Dougal hadn't even confessed to loving her, so she was getting way ahead of herself. "It's not like I was abused. They paid for all my education, and I'm very grateful for that."

"They shouldna have made ye feel like a failure," he grumbled. "Ye're the smartest person I've ever met, and I've been around a few centuries."

Her heart squeezed. How could she not love this man? "Thank you."

He slanted her a worried look. "Connor thinks ye're too smart for me."

"Well, I'll have to track him *doon* and knock him in the head."

Dougal chuckled. "So yer brothers—are they named after Isaac Newton and . . ."

"Albert Einstein, yes." She put the framed photo back on the dresser. "Leah is just a nickname. My parents named me after Galileo, so my name is actually Galileah."

He flinched.

"I know. It's weird."

"Ga-li-leah?" he asked slowly.

"Yes." She wondered why he looked so shocked. "You don't like it?"

"I-I dinna realize how . . ."

"What?"

"Ka-li-lei," he whispered as he wandered back to the bed and sat on the edge. Staring at the floor, he shrugged his right shoulder.

"Is something wrong?" She approached him.

"Nay, it all seems verra . . . right." He rolled his shoulder again. "Sometimes my tattoo itches and burns."

"Is it infected?" She reached out to unbutton his shirt. "Let me see."

He frowned but didn't stop her. "Can ye accept me as I am? I'm far from perfect."

"You mean the vampire thing?" She finished unbuttoning his shirt. "I don't understand it, but I'm okay with it." She skimmed a hand over his tattoo. It didn't look infected.

"I left home when I was fourteen, too."

"You went to college? Or a boarding school?"

"Nay." His chest expanded as he took a deep breath. "I was kidnapped. Taken aboard a British merchant ship as forced labor."

"Oh, my gosh!" She sat on the bed beside him. "Are you kidding me? That's terrible!"

"I tried to escape. The first time, because I was young and ignorant, they gave me only ten lashes. But the second time, they gave me twenty-five." He took off his shirt and tossed it on the floor. "Ye should know what ye're getting with me."

She gasped when he twisted to the side. His back was crisscrossed with welts. "Oh, my God. Dougal." The poor man had carried these scars for almost three centuries.

Tears burned her eyes as she traced a scar with her fingertip. "This was so cruel." A fourteen-year-old boy, taken from his family and treated like this. "How did you survive?"

"There was a cook on board, an old Irishman, who took pity on me. He told me the best way to survive was to be valued by the crew. He did that by cooking for them and entertaining them with his bagpipes. First he taught me how to play the tin whistle. When I caught on quickly, he taught me to play the pipes."

"The Uilleann pipes?" She smoothed her fingers over each scar.

"Aye. After a few years, I had adjusted to my new life, but one time, when we were leaving India, we were attacked by some Indonesian pirates. I was captured and taken to Shanghai, where I was sold."

She flinched. "Sold?"

"Aye. A few years later, after I regained my freedom, I took on the dragon as a symbol of power and to hide my mark of shame." He turned toward her to show her his right shoulder. "This is where I was branded when I was seventeen. As a slave."

Wincing, she touched the raised skin. Whoever had done the tattoo had made the welts look like scales on the dragon. "I'm so sorry."

"Eventually I made it back to Scotland, but my family had died."

"And then you died at the Battle of Culloden," she finished, her eyes welling with tears. "Oh, Dougal." She placed her hands on his cheeks. "I'm so sorry."

"Doona fash. 'Twas long ago." He took her hands in his own. "I only told you about the scars 'cause I dinna want you to be alarmed or to think I was a criminal."

"How could I think poorly of you?" A tear ran down her face.

"Och." He swept it aside with his thumb. "I shouldna have told you. The last thing I want is yer pity."

"What do you want?"

"Ye doona know?" He gave her an exasperated look. "Lass, I've taken everything off but my kilt. And I can be rid of it in about three seconds."

She smiled, even though her face was growing hot. "You want me to desire you?"

"Aye."

Her skin tingled, and she wondered how quickly she could make his eyes turn red. With her fingertips, she traced the dragon where it curled around his chest. "Should I feel uncontrollable lust for you?"

"Aye."

His eyes were still green. She rubbed his nipple. "Should I have wild and crazy sex with you?"

"Aye. Please."

Still no change in his eyes. She smoothed her hand up to his face. "Should I confess to being madly in love with you?"

His eyes glowed red.

Bingo. Another tear rolled down her face. "Were ye waiting to hear the word *love*?"

"Aye." He cradled her face with his hands. "I've been praying ye could love me. For I love you with all my heart and soul."

"Oh, Dougal." More tears escaped, and he wiped them away.

"Leah." He kissed her gently, then sat back and grasped the lapels of her lab coat. "May I?"

"Yes." In two seconds, her lab coat was on the floor.

He kissed her again, then his fingers trailed down the front of her T-shirt, lingering over her breasts, then moving down to grab the hem. "May I?"

She smiled. "Yes." She lifted her arms as he whisked the T-shirt over her head, then tossed it on the floor.

Again he kissed her and smoothed his hands down to her bra. Under the thin silk, her nipples pebbled.

"Look at that," he whispered, rubbing his thumb over the hardened tip.

She sucked in shuddering breath. Moisture pooled between her legs.

His hands moved to the bra clasp on her back. "May I?"

"God, yes! Please!"

He unhooked her bra and flung it across the room. "Och, so lovely." He cupped her breasts, stroking the nipples with his thumbs. His eyes glowed a brighter red.

She squeezed her thighs together. "I can't take it anymore." She unfastened her jeans and pulled down the zipper.

"I was going to do that."

"You're too slow!" She wiggled, pushing the jeans over her hips.

"Ye're complaining already? We've barely gotten started." He stood and grasped the hem of her jeans. With a hard tug, he pulled them off so fast that she fell onto her back. "Ye realize now that ye've insulted my manhood."

She rose up onto her elbows. "I haven't even seen your manhood. 'Cause you're too slow!"

His mouth twitching, he grasped her ankles and lifted them up to his face. "As the injured party, I have the right to demand compensation." He nipped at her big toe.

More moisture seeped from her core. "What would you like?"

"To do as I please." He tickled her instep with his tongue, and her leg jerked in response.

"You wish."

"I do wish." He smoothed his hands down her legs to her hips, where he grabbed her underwear. In a few seconds he had them tossed aside, and he grasped her ankles again.

Her heart raced, and her breathing grew erratic.

Slowly he spread her legs and looked at her.

She shuddered.

"Och, lass. Ye've been shorn like a sheep." He rested her ankles on his shoulders while he touched her smooth waxed skin, then stroked the narrow strip of hair.

"Dougal." She pressed her heels into his shoulders, lifting her hips. "Please. Hurry."

"If ye're going to keep complaining, I'll have to make you scream."

She hissed in a breath when his fingers slid between her folds. "I—I'm complaining."

"Och, ye're so slippery and wet. I can see it. And smell it. 'Tis like rich, sweet honey."

"I'm complaining!"

"Are ye now?" He pinched her clitoris, and her heart stuttered. "Did ye want to scream, lass?"

"Yes," she squeaked.

He kneeled beside the bed and pulled her core to his face.

She squirmed under the onslaught of his mouth and tongue. He tickled, sipped, and nibbled till she was panting for air and whimpering. It was too much, too glorious, too exquisite.

A keening cry escaped when he latched onto her clitoris and suckled hard. Tension coiled, then shattered with a climax that made her scream.

With her eyes shut, she drifted in a sensual sea of aftershocks, her body sated and throbbing, and her heart pounding. As her breathing returned to normal, she opened her eyes and found him standing naked by the side of the bed.

"Oh my gosh," she breathed. He was huge. Totally erect and magnificent. She scooted back. "Holy crapoly."

He frowned. "Are ye complaining again?"

A smile tugged at her mouth. "Yes. Definitely. You're way too big."

"Am I?" He climbed onto the bed on all fours.

"Yes. And much too gorgeous."

He pushed her onto her back and moved between her legs. "Then I'll have to demand compensation."

Thank God. "I never knew you could be so demanding. That was another complaint, you know."

His mouth twitched. "All I want, lass, is to give you all the pleasure ye can bear."

"I can take it." She reached down to stroke his erection. "How much can you bear?"

He sucked in a breath. "No' much. I'm about to explode." He moved her hand to his chest. "Ye'll have to molest me later."

"You wish."

"I do wish." He fitted himself at the entrance to her core. "Are ye ready?"

"Yes." She wrapped her legs around his waist and her arms around his neck.

"Leah." He eased inside a few inches, and his eyes glowed a deep red. "I'll never lose you again."

Again? She started to question him, but gasped when he plunged inside. He was so big, she was grateful when he stayed still for a moment so she could adjust.

"Are ye all right?" he whispered, his breath feathering her ear.

"Yes." She smoothed her hands over his back, feeling the welts that crisscrossed his skin.

"I love you." He kissed a path down her neck.

"I love you, too."

"Leah." He nuzzled her breasts, then drew a nipple into his mouth to suckle.

With a moan she dug her heels into his back and rocked against him.

He responded, withdrawing almost completely before plunging back in.

"Dougal." She gripped him tighter.

He kissed her while he withdrew once again at an agonizingly slow pace.

"Oh, God, faster. Please."

"Are ye complaining?" He kissed her brow. "Shall I make ye scream?"

"Yes!" She gasped when he plunged inside, then continued to thrust at a faster and faster pace. Deeper and deeper.

Her climax hit suddenly with a force that stole her breath and left her dazed, with stars spinning around her head. With a groan, he pumped into her, then collapsed, half sprawled, on top of her.

"Holy crapoly," she whispered. She'd never known sex could be this good. But then, she'd never been in love like this before.

A kernel of fear lodged in her heart. The more she loved, the more vulnerable she was. The more her heart would break if anything—she pushed those thoughts away. She was always thinking too fast and getting ahead of herself.

She tightened her grip around Dougal's neck. He loved her. She loved him. And they were perfect for each other. That was all she needed to think. This was a time to feel. And she had never felt so loved and cherished.

He eased himself off her and gathered her in his arms. "Are ye all right?"

"Mmm." She smoothed a hand over his choco-abs and looked at his face. His eyes were glittering green, and his hair was wild about his shoulders. "That was the best."

"The best is yet to come." He lifted his head to kiss her. "Do ye have any food here?"

"Some chips. Frozen pizza." She propped herself on an elbow to look at him. "Why do you ask? You don't eat real food."

"I have a bottle in my sporran." He brushed her hair back from her brow. "I was worried about you keeping yer strength up. I'll be ready to go again in a few minutes."

"Really?"

"Aye. I've waited almost three hundred years for you. Ye think once is going to be enough?"

She smiled. Forever would be long enough.

"Beside, ye're with a Vamp now." He fondled her breast. "And we can go all night long."

"Hmm." She slid her hand down to his groin. "As a scientist, I may have to put your theory to the test."

He hissed in a breath as she stroked him. "I willna let you down." He hardened in her hand.

"Wow. You passed."

His eyes turned red. "I'm just barely getting started."

Chapter Twenty-two

$\mathcal{D}$ougal grew increasingly frustrated over the next few nights. With all the busy preparations going on and lack of privacy at the townhouse, he couldn't find another opportunity to be alone with Leah.

One night had not been enough. He couldn't see her on the monitor without longing to touch her. He couldn't sit with her in the kitchen without hungering for her.

After a long night of lovemaking, he knew every inch of her body. How she felt and tasted. The softness of her breasts tipped with hardened nipples and the sweet taste of her core when its folds grew swollen and slick for want of him.

He knew how to make her moan and incite her to scream. He knew how to drive her over the edge, and he'd watched all the expressions that flitted over her beautiful face as she journeyed from pleasant arousal to a frantic, desperate climax. But even knowing all that, it still wasn't enough. He needed more.

Three more nights had passed, and he was sitting with her in the kitchen while she ate a grilled chicken salad he'd teleported in from the Romatech cafeteria.

"We've produced enough serum to treat fifty soldiers," she said as she cut a chicken strip in two. "I just wish we'd been able to test it better."

"Ye'll get the chance soon enough."

"I'd like to try it on two or three soldiers first to see how well it works. Then we can make any necessary adjustments before tackling a larger group." With a sigh, she set down her plastic knife. "The chicken is a little tough tonight."

He leaned closer and whispered, "Are ye complaining?"

She glanced up, her cheeks turning pink. "I wish. You have an excellent way of handling complaints."

He squeezed her leg under the table. "My main concern right now is keeping you safe on this mission. It worries me that I canna stay with you all the time." The plan had her working on the small Japanese island with Abby and Laszlo, while he and J.L. went to China to snatch a few of Master Han's soldiers.

"We should be fine." She patted his hand, then picked up her fork to continue eating. "Gregori, Angus, and the shifters will be staying with us."

Dougal nodded. "Kyo will be there, too, with some of his employees."

Leah took a bite of salad. "Who is Kyo exactly? He's a vampire, right?"

"Aye. He has a huge estate outside Tokyo, and he's covering all the expenses of renovating the old school building."

"Why is he being so helpful?"

"If Master Han succeeds in taking over China, he

might turn to Japan next. Kyo is Coven Master of Japan, so it is his duty to protect his territory and followers."

Leah sipped some water. "The Vamps seem to do a good job of looking out for each other."

"We protect those we care about."

Her eyes met his, and he nearly groaned for wanting her so much.

"Och, lass. I'm going to miss you."

"You have to leave soon?"

"Aye, we're moving out as soon as the sun sets in San Francisco. Ye have yer luggage and laboratory supplies ready for us?"

She nodded. "Who all is going?"

"J.L., Angus, Gregori, and myself. Rajiv is hitching a ride with us, and we'll leave him on the island to guard the supplies."

"So you just keep teleporting west until you reach Japan?"

"Aye. We'll wait in San Francisco for the sun to set in Hawaii, and then we wait in Hawaii to go to Japan. After we have everything stashed away in the new facility, we'll keep moving west till we finally return here. We call it chasing the moon."

"So I'll see you again tomorrow night?"

"Aye. We'll start teleporting you, Abby, Phil, and Howard tomorrow night. Be ready to go."

She squeezed his hand. "Be careful."

He lifted her hand and kissed it. She was the one in a lot more danger. After a week of self-defense training, she was still at a beginner's level. Her reluctance to hurt anyone was causing him grave concern. He could only pray that Gregori, Angus, and the shifters would be enough to keep her safe.

*　*　*

Twelve hours later, Dougal was in Hawaii with Angus, Gregori, J.L., and Rajiv. They'd already spent several hours at a were-dolphin's beach house, waiting for the sun to set in Japan. Finally, the call came from Kyo.

"I'm putting him on speaker phone," Angus said. "Kyo, are ye ready for us?"

"Yes," Kyo replied and kept talking so they could focus on his voice.

After slinging his duffel bag over his shoulder, Dougal grabbed Leah's suitcase and another case containing supplies she wanted for the lab. Angus and Gregori grabbed more suitcases and supplies, and J.L. took hold of Rajiv. In a few seconds they arrived on the small Japanese island.

Dougal gritted his teeth at the bitterly cold wind that welcomed them. He glanced around, his eyes adjusting quickly to the dark. No wonder the school had been abandoned. It was a desolate, dreary place, all rocks, dirt, and gravel covered with patches of icy snow, so everything was black with shades of gray to silver. The wind blew in from the rocky beach to the east. A large silver moon hung low in the sky, causing glimmers of light to ripple on the dark sea. Waves crashed with a constant rhythm on the pebbly shore.

The icy ground crunched under his feet as he turned to look west. The school was situated on a bluff in a one-story building elevated above the ground in case the sea surged during a storm.

Creaking sounds emanated from an old neglected playground, where the wind toyed with a rusty swing set and whistled across a drooping metal slide.

"Greetings!" Kyo bowed to them.

Angus slapped him on the back. "It looks great, Kyo. Verra well isolated."

"That is exactly what we needed, right? The village nearby is almost gone. Only a few old people left. Young people want to live in cities." Kyo smiled at them all, then gave Dougal a curious look. "You are the Scotsman who knows Chinese?"

"Yes. I'm Dougal Kincaid." He bowed.

"Welcome." Kyo motioned toward the school. "Let's go in now."

They followed him up a steep path to the top of the bluff, then crossed the snow-covered schoolyard to the stone steps leading up to the front door.

"My friend, Yoshi," Kyo introduced the square-built man who was standing guard at the top of the stairs.

Yoshi bowed, then held the door open for them to enter the foyer.

"It's warm in here." Rajiv was the last one to enter.

"Yes, we had a new furnace put in." Kyo motioned to the walls. "And new paint. Let me take you to the lab first so you can set down your supplies."

Dougal and the other guys followed him down the hall to the right.

"This side of the school has the security office, lab, and large clinic for holding prisoners. Yuki!"

A man stepped out of the security office and bowed. "I'm putting in cameras now, and monitors."

"Excellent," Angus told him. "Thank you."

Yuki bowed again and went back inside the office.

"The next room is the lab." Kyo strode inside.

Dougal and the guys set down the supplies. The lab was small. Black-topped tables were covered with microscopes and other equipment. Desks with computers lined the two side walls. The wall facing the ocean had bookcases on the bottom half and windows on the top.

Kyo motioned to the large room across the hall. "This is the clinic for holding the prisoners."

Dougal peered inside and saw a row of stretchers with restraints. IV poles and monitors were interspersed among the beds. It looked like Kyo had spared no expense.

Kyo led them back down the hall, crossing the foyer into the hallway on the left. "Here we have dormitories and restrooms for men and women."

"What about us Vamps?" J.L. asked.

"We fixed a room in the basement, boarded up the windows." Kyo opened a door to show them the staircase to the basement.

"Something is cooking." Rajiv lifted his chin to sniff. "Smells good."

"Oh, our daytime guard is making herself dinner. Gu Mina. Shifter from Korea." Kyo opened the double doors at the end of the hall. "This is the cafeteria and kitchen."

Dougal and the others filed inside. The cafeteria was small, with only six square tables with plastic chairs, and a row of windows overlooking the ocean. The kitchen was half-hidden behind a tall counter. A microwave sat on a small table next to a refrigerator.

"This is stocked with blood." Kyo opened the fridge and handed some bottles to the Vamps. They unscrewed the tops and stuffed all the bottles into the microwave.

Rajiv sniffed. "Smells like beef."

Kyo smiled. "You must be hungry. I will ask Gu Mina to share her food with you. Mina!" He yelled something in Japanese, and a female voice answered back.

Rajiv's eyes widened. "A girl shifter? Is she a tiger like me?"

"No, but she's an excellent fighter," Kyo told them in English. "She has worked for me for one year."

A young woman appeared in the window above the tall counter. Dougal figured she was short, since only her head could be seen. She smiled and set a tray on the counter, containing a bowl of steaming beef and noodles and a set of chopsticks and long spoon.

Rajiv smiled back and took the tray. "Thank you." He hurried over to a table, his eyes twinkling. "She's pretty," he whispered.

Angus chuckled as he removed warm bottles of blood from the microwave. "What kind of shifter is she?"

"A fox." Kyo took a sip from a bottle. "With nine tails."

Rajiv gasped and dropped his tray on the table with a clatter. "A nine-tailed fox?"

"That's a lot of tail," Gregori muttered.

Rajiv shook his head in horror. "Nine-tailed foxes are very bad. Evil!"

"She's fine," Kyo insisted. "She's very good at martial arts. Excellent with swords and knives."

"Right! So she can cut out your liver." Rajiv shuddered. "Nine-tailed foxes hate men! They eat our livers!" He backed away from his bowl of food. "She cooked a man's liver?"

"It's beef," Kyo said with an annoyed look. "I teleported it here myself. Very expensive, but it is her favorite."

"You don't believe me?" Rajiv turned to J.L. "You know the story of Korean Gumiho, right?"

J.L. shrugged. "Supposedly, the female fox shifter likes to seduce men so she can eat their livers. But it's just a fairy tale."

The female shifter sauntered from the kitchen carrying a tray. She was short and slim, with long black hair and silvery gray eyes. She set her tray on the table next to Rajiv and gave him an amused look. "Scaredy-cat."

He jumped back and hissed.

"Oh, I forgot to say," Kyo chuckled. "Gu Mina speaks very good English."

Rajiv grabbed his tray and scurried across the room. "How soon can Pooh Bear and Phil get here?"

"Tomorrow night." J.L. sat beside him. "Don't worry, bro, it could be worse."

"How?" Rajiv frowned at Mina, who was ignoring them and eating her food.

"She could have a taste for tiger meat," J.L. said, grinning.

Kyo and Angus sat down with Mina to keep her company.

While Dougal drank his bottle, he took Leah's suitcase to the female dorm room.

Gregori joined him, depositing Abby's suitcase on one of the twin-sized beds. "I guess I won't be able to sleep with my wife for a while," he grumbled.

"Yeah." Dougal eyed the bed he'd picked out for Leah. How would he ever find any time alone with her? With a sigh, he grabbed his duffel bag, then headed down the stairs to the Vamp room in the basement.

Eventually the rest of the Vamp guys joined him, dropping their duffel bags on one of the eight cots. Kyo pointed out the three cots that he, Yoshi, and Yuki were using.

Angus stretched out on his cot. "We have a few hours before we can move on to Mikhail's place in Russia."

Rajiv clambered down the stairs to their room. "You guys can't leave me alone with the fox!"

"She's not dangerous," Kyo muttered.

Rajiv sidled over to J.L. and Angus. "Let me go to Tiger Town so I can see my grandfather."

"Tiger Town?" Gregori asked.

"It's a village on the Mekong River in China where the were-tigers live," J.L. explained. "It has a name in Chinese, but you guys would have a hard time pronouncing it, so Rajiv and I call it Tiger Town."

"Dougal would be able to say it." Angus slanted him a curious look. "Ye never did tell us how ye know Chinese."

Dougal shrugged.

"Can I go to Tiger Town?" Rajiv asked again. "I want to see my grandfather. And you can bring me back tomorrow night."

Angus sighed. "I suppose so. There willna be anything happening until we return."

Rajiv grinned. "Thank you!" He grabbed onto J.L. "Let's go."

J.L. vanished, taking Rajiv with him.

Dougal rummaged through his duffel bag till he found the small box containing the chain and pendant he'd bought in San Francisco's Chinatown.

"What's that?" Gregori peered over his shoulder when he opened the box.

Dougal groaned inwardly. There would be no privacy for the rest of this mission. "I bought it for Leah."

"You're serious about her then?" Gregori asked.

"Aye." He'd wanted to buy an engagement ring, but he was worried that he was pushing her too fast. Marriage to a vampire was a commitment that could last for centuries if she was willing to become Undead.

He ran a finger over the jade dragon and rolled his shoulder when his tattoo sizzled. If she wore the dragon, then they would each have one. Hopefully, hers would protect her from harm.

Chapter Twenty-three

*W*as he sleeping? Leah leaned over to peer at Dougal. He was sprawled on the couch at the beach house in Hawaii. He had to be exhausted. After circumnavigating the globe, he and the other Vamps had arrived at the townhouse in New York City almost twelve hours ago.

When the time had come to teleport to San Francisco, Angus had taken Howard the were-bear, J.L. had given werewolf Phil a lift, Gregori had taken his wife, and Leah had traveled with Dougal. As a Vamp, Laszlo had been able to teleport himself, along with some additional supplies and luggage. Angus's wife, Emma, was staying behind to run MacKay S&I.

After their arrival, Dougal had taken Leah to Chinatown, where she'd enjoyed a nice meal while he sneaked sips of blood from the bottle in his sporran. A few hours later, they'd arrived in Hawaii at Finn Grayson's beach house. He'd arranged a luau on the beach for them, although only the shifters and mortals had been able to enjoy the roasted pig, rice, and fruit. The Vamps had looked so tired by then that they'd excused themselves to find places in the house to rest.

Leah perched on the edge of the coffee table to look at Dougal. The luau had wound down an hour ago. Finn, Phil, Laszlo, and Howard were lounging outside on the patio. Abby had run off to a bedroom with Gregori.

Leah's gaze started at Dougal's scruffed-up shoes, then wandered up his muscular calves, encased in knee socks, to his bare knees. In his relaxed state, his kilt was a bit askew, revealing a glimpse of his strong thighs. How easy it would be to reach underneath his kilt and give him a squeeze. That would probably wake him up. She smiled to herself.

"Are ye planning to molest me?" he asked softly.

She started. "I thought you were asleep."

"Just resting." He gazed at her with drowsy green eyes. "I think ye were about to get under my kilt."

She scoffed. "You wish."

"I do wish." He reached down to his sporran. "I have something for you."

"I know you do. It's quite a doozy."

He chuckled. "No' that." He rose to his feet and extended a hand to her. "How about a walk on the beach?"

"Okay." She held hands with him as they sauntered out the patio doors and past the pool.

"Way to go, Dougal," Howard called from a lounge chair.

Phil howled like a wolf, and the guys chuckled.

"Bugger off," Dougal muttered, and they laughed some more.

Leah smiled, relieved that even Laszlo looked amused.

They wandered down the beach, and she admired the way the moon glinted on the water. The breeze was gentle, and the scent of flowers filled the air.

"I wish ye could see it during the day." Dougal stopped to face her.

"It's still lovely."

"I have a present for you." He reached inside his sporran and pulled out a small box.

Her heart lurched. Was it a ring? Was he proposing? Her mind raced. What would she say? Everything had happened so quickly. Three weeks? Was that enough time to know how to answer something that would affect the rest of her life?

He opened the box, and she froze as she stared at the contents. Not a ring. Not a proposal.

She inhaled sharply. What a relief. Definitely a relief, she told herself. Then why was she feeling this strange little jab of disappointment? "It's a necklace?"

"Aye, there's a chain underneath." He gave her a worried look. "Ye doona like it?"

"It's beautiful." She ran a finger over the jade dragon. It was intricately carved and stunning in its detail. "I love it."

He exhaled in relief. "Good."

She lifted it out of the box and looped it around her neck. The dragon nestled between her breasts.

"Now we each have a dragon to protect us."

She glanced up at him. "You're still worried about me."

"Aye." He dropped the empty box back into his sporran. "I doona want to fail you."

"I'm not helpless, you know." She touched his face. "And I love you."

"Och, lass. I love you, too." He pulled her into his arms. "I was sorely tempted to buy you a ring. But I dinna know if ye were ready for that."

Her pang of disappointment melted away, and she glanced up at him. "You mean an engagement ring?"

He gave her a wary look. "Aye."

Her heart raced. "Are you proposing?"

"Only if ye're ready. If ye're no' ready, then pretend this dinna happen."

Her mouth twitched. "You don't want to be rejected?"

"Nay." His arms tightened around her. " 'Twould break my heart."

"Ah." She nestled her cheek against his chest. "We can't have your heart breaking. That would break my heart."

He was silent a moment, then whispered, "Was that a yes?"

Was it? "I-I need a little more time. I'm about ninety percent there." Somehow she would have to explain an Undead fiancé to her family. They would probably think she'd lost her mind.

"Ninety is good."

She glanced up at him, and her heart swelled. He was so sweet, honorable, loyal, and handsome. How could she ever reject him? "More like ninety-two percent."

"Mmm, I like that." He leaned down and kissed her so deeply that her knees trembled.

She drew in a shaky breath. "Make that ninety-five percent."

He chuckled, then squeezed her bottom. "If I get in yer pants, will it improve my odds?"

She grinned. "I never thought I'd say this to a guy, but I'd like to get in your skirt."

"That could be arranged." His cell phone dinged, and with a groan, he removed it from his sporran. "Aye, we're coming." He hung up. "That was Angus. The sun has set in Japan. 'Tis time to go."

The difference was startling. In just a few seconds, Leah had gone from a warm, cozy beach with golden sand and green vegetation to a frigid, bleak shore with a bitterly cold wind. Dougal had warned her, and she'd put on a sweater and insulated jacket, but the abrupt change still came as a shock.

Dougal wrapped an arm around her. "Let's get you inside."

The icy ground crunched beneath their feet.

"Brr—" Abby shuddered. Gregori swept her up in his arms and dashed up the bluff to the school.

"I could teleport you inside if ye like," Dougal offered.

"I'm fine." Leah pivoted around. This was her first trip to Japan, so she was eager to look about. Maybe tomorrow in daylight she could do a little exploring.

A phone dinged.

"That's mine." J.L. checked his phone. "A text from Rajiv. He says the sun's still up in Tiger Town. And stay away from the fox."

"Fox?" Phil asked. "What fox?"

"The shifter I told you about," Angus said. "Gu Mina. She works for Kyo."

Another phone dinged.

"That's mine." Howard looked at his phone. "Rajiv's busy. He just sent me a warning to stay away from the fox."

J.L. laughed. "He thinks she wants to eat our livers."

"Our *livers*?" Laszlo asked, his eyes wide.

J.L. shrugged. "Don't worry about it. It's a fairy tale."

Phil exchanged a look with Howard. "I know at least one fairy tale that turned out to be real."

Howard grinned. "That doesn't mean this one will. Besides, we could eat a fox for breakfast."

Phil nodded. "True."

With a sigh, Angus started up the bluff to the school. "Be polite to Mina. She works for Kyo, and we need his support."

Once they were all inside, Kyo greeted them and proudly gave them a tour of the small building. His employees, Yoshi and Yuki, were finishing the installment of security cameras inside and outside the school.

Dougal showed Leah where he'd put her suitcase at the foot of a bed in the female dorm. "Will ye be all right here?"

"Sure. I've been in dorms a lot smaller than this." It still looked like a classroom, with a bookcase beneath the window overlooking the beach. Curtains had been installed for privacy. Three twin beds lined the back wall, interspersed with bedside tables topped with lamps. She supposed the third roommate was the lady fox that had Rajiv freaked out.

On the front wall, she spotted a message written in chalk on the old blackboard. *Welcome!* Had the fox shifter left that for them? If so, she seemed friendly enough.

"The restrooms and showers are across the hall," Dougal told her. "And the cafeteria is at the end. Did ye want something to eat?"

"No." Leah tossed her coat, hat, and mittens on the bed. "I'm eager to get started in the lab."

Dougal nodded. "J.L. and I will leave as soon as the sun sets in Tiger Town. Before we go, we'll drop by the lab for the sedatives."

"We brought some tranquilizer darts so you wouldn't have to fool with needles." The captured soldiers needed to remain unconscious during their entire stay at the school so they couldn't call out to Darafer for help.

"That's good." Dougal headed for the door. "I need to get ready to go."

"Wait a second." She ran toward him. For the moment they were alone, and she doubted that would happen often over the next few weeks. She wrapped her arms around his neck. "Be careful."

"I will." He pulled her close. "I'll miss you."

She pressed a hand against her jade pendant. "Thank you for the dragon."

"Ye're welcome. Am I still at ninety-five percent?"

"Yes. I-I've been wondering about something."

"When can we make love again?"

She smiled. He still had a one-track mind. "You said there was a letter you wrote that I never saw?"

"Aye, because ye were avoiding me." He heaved a forlorn sigh. "I may have been such a devastated lovesick fool that I burned it."

"You did?"

"Nay." His mouth twitched. "Were ye wanting to see it?"

She swatted his shoulder. "Yes."

Chuckling, he retrieved a folded piece of paper from his sporran. "Maybe this will bring me up to ninety-seven percent." He kissed her brow and handed it to her. "See you later."

She hurried back to her bed, turned on the lamp, and opened the note.

Dear Leah,

I know I frighten you, but I pray you will give me a chance. I know my chance is small, for you are so clever and beautiful. How could I ever be worthy of you?

You are a treasure to behold, a sweet melody to my ears.

You shine light into my dark nights and bring warmth to my cold heart.

You fill me with hope that all things are possible, even an eternity of love.

Dougal

She blinked back tears as she folded the note. He'd been wrong about the effect. He was up to ninety-nine percent.

With a sigh, she looked around for a safe place to keep his note. She might have to share the bedside table, since it was between her bed and Abby's, so she tucked the note underneath her mattress.

Wiping her eyes, she left the room, then hurried down the hall to the lab. Abby was already at work, telling her husband where to stash supplies. As far as Leah knew, there had been no business reason for Gregori to come on the trip. He simply refused to leave Abby's side.

Leah smiled to herself. It wasn't so bad being married to a Vamp. Maybe she should raise Dougal's status to ninety-nine point five percent.

Laszlo was also hard at work, making sure all the computers and equipment were ready to go.

Leah found the box containing the tranquilizing darts, and she bagged a dozen for Dougal and J.L. Master Han's soldiers were so strong that it might take several to knock one of them out.

The door opened and a short, young woman came in, carrying a huge box that nearly covered her face.

She peered to the side and smiled at Abby and Leah. "Hello. These are supplies. Kyo wanted you to have them."

"Let me help you." Gregori rushed forward to take the box. He set it on a table, then he and Abby started unloading it.

"This is great," Abby said as she removed test tubes and beakers. "Thank you."

The young woman bowed. "I am Gu Mina, but please call me Mina." She smiled at them, then turned and saw Laszlo, who was totally focused on calibrating a sensitive piece of equipment. Her mouth fell open, and her eyes widened.

Leah stepped forward. "Pleased to meet you. I'm Leah."

"I'm Abby, and this is my husband, Gregori."

No response. Leah exchanged a look with Abby. The young woman seemed to have forgotten they were in the room.

Mina eased slowly toward Laszlo. "Hello."

He glanced her way, then did a double take and jumped to his feet. Leah heard his gulp across the room.

"Are . . . are you a scientist?" Mina asked.

Laszlo nodded, and grabbed a button on his lab coat.

Mina licked her lips. "I think intelligent men are the most attractive."

"You do?" Laszlo twisted the button.

Mina stepped closer. "I like shorter men, too. Cause I'm so short."

"Y-you're not too short."

Mina blushed. "Thank you." She shoved her long black hair over her shoulder, and Laszlo gulped again. "I like your haircut. It's very stylish."

"Thank you." He plucked at the button. "I have to be honest with you. I'm a vampire."

She smiled. "I love honest men. And I like vampires. I know several back in Korea. One's a prosecutor."

Laszlo frowned. "Is he your boyfriend?"

She waved a hand. "*An-ni-o*! I don't have a boyfriend."

"You don't? But you're so . . . pretty." His face reddened.

She inched closer. "What's your name?"

"I-I'm Laser."

"I like that."

Leah exchanged an amused look with Abby and Gregori.

Laszlo tugged at the button. "What's your name?"

"Gu Mina. But you can call me—"

"You're the fox?" He jumped back.

Her shoulders drooped. "You don't like foxes?"

"Well, I—normally I think they're cute." He yanked at the button. "I like their tails."

She grinned. "I have nine tails!"

His button popped off. "*Nine*?"

She reached down to grab the button.

"I'll do it." He leaned over to snatch the button and bonked heads with her on the way up. "Oh, sorry."

"I could sew it on for you," she offered, rubbing her head.

"I-I don't know." He eased away from her.

She sighed. "Has that silly tiger been talking about me? I don't attack men and eat their livers."

"You . . . you don't?"

"No! I gave it up a while ago."

Laszlo turned even paler than usual. "I-I have to check on something." He ran from the room.

With a groan, Mina slumped onto the stool Laszlo had been using.

Leah winced. Was she supposed to share the dorm room with a cannibalistic shifter?

"Excuse me." Gregori waved to get Mina's attention, and she looked up. "When you say 'a while ago,' how long ago was that? I mean, you weren't chowing down on somebody's liver a month ago, right?"

Mina tilted her head, considering. "It's been three hundred years."

There was a collective sigh of relief from Leah, Abby, and Gregori.

Mina frowned. "No, make that two hundred and fifty years. I slipped up once."

Chapter Twenty-four

*A*fter swearing he would never return, Dougal was back in China. He took a deep breath, waiting for the tension to ease from his body. His clenched prosthetic hand slowly relaxed. *I can do this*, he told himself. There was no one here waiting to sear his flesh with a red-hot branding iron or whip him into submission.

He frowned at the thought of Li Lei, buried along the Yangtze River, a few hundred miles northeast of his current position. Thank God Leah had come into his life and given him a second chance at love.

He pivoted as he looked around Tiger Town. Three hundred years ago he never would have believed that a village of were-tigers existed in the Yunnan province. But then, he wouldn't have believed in vampires, either.

The village consisted of about fifty huts. Most of them were on the edge of the Mekong River, elevated on stilts, with small boats tied off on ladders. Apparently, a great deal of the were-tigers liked to fish. Higher up the riverbank, long racks held fish that had been left to dry.

Not many people were about. Since it was dark,

Dougal assumed they were inside their homes having their evening meal. Lights glowed inside the huts, and smoke curled from metal pipe chimneys.

Up on a bluff, there was an impressive building made of stone and wood in the Chinese style. The large columns and underside of the tile roof were painted in shades of green, gold, and red. The steps leading up to the building were flanked by two tiger statues. Smaller buildings of stone, wood, and stucco rested on each side of the main building.

In front of the main building, a stone-paved court-yard stretched to the edge of the bluff, where three stone staircases led down to the riverbank.

"There's Rajiv." J.L. pointed at him as he hurried down the center stairs to the riverbank.

"What is the big building?" Dougal asked as they walked toward him.

"Their palace," J.L. said. "Rajiv's grandfather is their leader, the top cat. They call him the Grand Tiger."

Dougal's mouth twitched. "He gets the biggest bowl of cream?"

J.L. chuckled. "They're very proud of their race. You will be expected to bow." He lowered his voice. "They're our best allies in the region. Whenever you need a safe place, you can teleport here. It'll be our home away from home."

Dougal nodded. That would explain why J.L. had insisted they bring two ice chests full of bottled blood and two backpacks filled with extra knives and ammo. Not knowing the way to Tiger Town, Dougal had grabbed onto J.L. for the journey, but now that the location was embedded in his psychic memory, he could come whenever he wished.

Rajiv reached them and bowed. Instead of his usual T-shirt and jeans, he was wearing an embroidered silk robe and cap. Around his waist, he wore an ornate belt of gold and jade with a golden sheath containing a small dagger.

"Welcome." He grinned at Dougal. "I told Grandfather about you. That you're a Scotsman who knows Chinese. He wants to meet you."

Dougal nodded. "It would be an honor."

"Let me take you to your rooms." Rajiv led them up the stairs. As they crossed the courtyard, he motioned with his hand. "We have our ceremonies here."

They followed him down a narrow alleyway of stone between two buildings.

"This is our guesthouse." Rajiv stopped in front of a building with steps leading up to a wooden porch. On each side of the porch was a small room. Papercovered lanterns hung beside each room's entrance and cast a golden glow.

Rajiv pointed to the room on the left. "That is where Jin Long always stays," he said, referring to J.L., then motioned to the one on the right. "And that one is for you, Dougal. The windows are boarded shut, so it is safe for your death-sleep."

"Thanks, Rajiv." J.L. climbed the steps.

"You are welcome. I will return for you in a few minutes so you can see my grandfather."

Dougal smiled as he watched Rajiv scamper off. He hadn't realized the young man was the weretiger equivalent of a prince.

He entered his room, leaving the door open to let in some light from the lantern. A small dresser was pushed up against one wall, and on top, a silk coverlet and thick mattress were folded. In the middle of the far wall, there was a square cushion on the floor next to a small table with short legs. Next to the table, a tall candlestick sat. He glanced around. No electricity. He'd be drinking his bottles cold.

He set the ice chest and his backpack against the wall, then swung the claymore off his back. It would be disrespectful to meet the mayor of Tiger Town fully armed. Before leaving the school, he'd changed into black cargo pants, black T-shirt, and black jacket. In addition to the sword on his back, he'd strapped a knife to each calf and holstered an automatic around his hips. The pockets of his cargo pants held extra ammunition and the tranquilizer darts Leah had given him.

It had been hard to say good-bye to her, even though he would be returning in a few hours if everything went according to plan. He'd left his *sgian dubh* on her worktable after she'd promised to use the dagger if she needed to defend herself.

She would be safe, he assured himself. Angus knew how dangerous this mission was. That was why he had insisted on coming himself, along with Howard, Phil, and Gregori. Kyo had his best security guys there, too—Yoshi, Yuki, and the fox shifter.

"Ready?" J.L. asked at the door.

"Aye." Dougal set his automatic and knives on the table.

J.L. nodded approvingly. "Let's go. Rajiv's outside."

They followed Rajiv to the palace, passing by the tiger statues to ascend the stairs.

Rajiv paused by the double doors. "My grandfather likes to be called Your Eminence," he said in Chinese. "And you must let him talk first."

"I understand," Dougal responded.

Rajiv grinned. "You really do speak Chinese."

"His Eminence is actually a fun guy once you get to know him," J.L. said, also switching to Chinese.

Rajiv laughed. "I have the Blissky ready. Come on." He led them inside past two guards holding long curved swords. The room was deep with columns set in two rows leading toward a dais. On the dais, a gray-haired man sat on a throne made of carved wood, inlaid with golden tigers.

Rajiv and J.L. both bowed from the waist, so Dougal copied them. He followed them to where three cushions rested on the floor. When Rajiv and J.L. dropped to their knees on the cushions, he did the same. Then they all bowed forward, their elbows and noses on the floor.

"Welcome, esteemed guests," the Grand Tiger said. "You may be at ease."

"You are most gracious, Your Eminence." J.L. sat cross-legged on the pillow.

Dougal crossed his legs, too, venturing a quick glance at the throne, where the Grand Tiger was glaring down at them imperiously. This was the guy J.L. said was fun?

His Eminence was dressed in red silk robes embroidered with golden tigers. His long gray hair was pulled tightly into a knot on top of his head, where it was held in place by a ring of gold and a long golden pin with a jeweled tiger on one end. He sported a long gray beard that was gathered together into a small ring of gold.

He scowled at J.L. "It is a pleasure to see you again, Jin Long."

"The pleasure is mine, Your Eminence." J.L. inclined his head.

The Grand Tiger narrowed his eyes. "You are Dou Gal, the Scotsman who speaks Chinese?"

"Yes, Your Eminence."

A disappointed look crossed the Grand Tiger's face. "I thought you would be wearing a skirt. I wanted to see your skirt."

Dougal bowed his head. "My apologies, Your Eminence. I will wear it the next time I come, if you will allow my intrusion."

The Grand Tiger grunted. "You are well spoken. How do you know Chinese?"

Dougal hesitated. He'd never intended to tell his story to anyone other than Leah, but it would be rude to ignore the Grand Tiger's request. He glanced over at Rajiv and J.L., who were watching him curiously. No doubt they would repeat his story, and then everyone would know his shameful secret.

The Grand Tiger cleared his throat, indicating that he was growing impatient.

"I lived in Shanghai for a few years," Dougal finally answered.

"When?" His Eminence demanded. "How did you come to be there?"

"It is a long story."

The Grand Tiger snorted. "Do you have somewhere else to go?"

Dougal took a deep breath. "It began in 1735, when I was fourteen years old. I was kidnapped from the town of Glasgow in Scotland and taken aboard a British merchant ship."

"Kidnapped?" The Grand Tiger's eyes lit up. "Tell me more."

"I tried to escape. Twice." He didn't want to mention the lashings he'd received. Or the hopeless humiliation that he'd felt when he'd finally accepted his new life.

"Good!" The Grand Tiger sat on the edge of his throne. "But you were recaptured? Did they punish you? Is that when you lost your hand?" He motioned toward Dougal's prosthesis.

"No. I lost my hand four years ago in battle."

"But you still fight?"

"Yes, Your Eminence."

"Excellent. Now tell me more of your story. Were you abused on the ship?"

"At first, but then I learned how to play the pipes, and that kept the crew happy with me."

"Very good." The Grand Tiger nodded. "I want to hear you play."

Dougal bowed his head. "I will bring them with me next time."

"Excellent! Now tell me what happened next."

"Our ship was departing from India when we were attacked by pirates."

"Pirates?" The Grand Tiger jumped to his feet, grabbing a cushion off his throne. He stepped off the dais, tossed the cushion on the floor, then sat across from Dougal. "What happened then?"

Dougal winced inwardly. His shameful secret would become public knowledge. Everyone would know he'd been whipped into submission, his spirit crushed with despair. "I was sold into slavery."

J.L. flinched. Rajiv hissed.

The Grand Tiger looked appalled. "Rajiv! Bring drinks for us."

"Yes, Your Eminence." Rajiv jumped up and helped a servant carry in a round table with short legs. They set it on the floor between Dougal and the Grand Tiger.

Another servant rushed forward with a tray. She set two bottles and four small cups on the table, then bowed and retreated from the room.

"Come." The Grand Tiger motioned for the four of them to gather around the table. "We must console Dou Gal for his sufferings."

"Yes, Your Eminence." Rajiv poured a clear liquid with a strong alcoholic smell into a cup for his grandfather and then for himself. "This is Blissky for our guests." He poured some into J.L.'s and Dougal's cups.

"To Dou Gal." The Grand Tiger lifted his cup, and the others followed suit. "*Gun bei!*" He tapped his cup on theirs and knocked back his drink.

"*Gun bei,*" Rajiv and J.L. responded, then tossed back their drinks.

Dougal took a sip, reluctant to drink too much before a mission. To his surprise, the Blissky had been watered down. He gave Rajiv a grateful look, then finished his cup.

Rajiv grinned, then refilled all the cups.

"I regret that I didn't know of your plight," the Grand Tiger said. "I would have come to Shanghai to rescue you."

"You are most kind, Your Eminence," Dougal said, uncomfortable with the sympathetic looks he was receiving. He'd rather be seen as a secretive grouch than be pitied.

"What are friends for? You are my good friend now, right?" The Grand Tiger lifted his cup. "A toast to friendship! *Gun bei!*"

"*Gun bei.*" They all drank, and Rajiv refilled their cups.

"Does that mean that Your Eminence was alive in the 1700s?" J.L. asked.

"Yes. I am four hundred and sixty-two years old." The Grand Tiger waved his cup proudly. "To having nine lives! *Gun bei!*"

"*Gun bei.*" They drank, and Rajiv filled their cups.

The Grand Tiger scooted around the table to be closer to Dougal. "So how did you escape?"

"Did you run your master through with a sword?" Rajiv asked.

Dougal shook his head. How many times in his life had music saved him? And now, because of his prosthesis, he could only play a sad tune. "I had a tin whistle with me, and I would play it at night to comfort myself."

The Grand Tiger patted his shoulder. "I want to hear you play."

"Yes, Your Eminence. The music drew the attention of my master's daughter. She would come every night to listen, and then we started talking."

"And you fell in love?" The Grand Tiger's eyes lit up.

"Yes." Dougal nodded. "She helped me escape."

The Grand Tiger grabbed his cup. "A toast to true love! *Gun bei!*"

"*Gun bei!*" J.L. and Rajiv shouted and downed their cups.

Dougal took a sip. He didn't want to talk anymore about Li Lei. It was shameful enough to admit he'd been enslaved, but he didn't want to confess how he had failed the girl who had saved him. "I would be honored to hear your story, Your Eminence."

"Of course." The Grand Tiger looped an arm around Dougal's shoulders. "I'm on my ninth life, you know. The next time I die, it's curtains for me, old friend."

Dougal lifted his cup. "May you live another four hundred and sixty-two years."

"I'll drink to that." The Grand Tiger tapped his cup against Dougal's. "*Gun bei!*"

"*Gun bei.*" They all drank.

"I had six beautiful daughters and twelve magnificent sons." The Grand Tiger waved a hand in the air. "Two of my sons were killed by hunters, may their souls be damned forever. Three more sons were killed by Master Han and his vampire lords."

"May they rot in hell!" Rajiv growled as he poured more liquor into all the cups.

The Grand Tiger nodded at him, then turned to Dougal. "Son number six went down the Mekong River and founded a tiger colony in Thailand. He was doing very well, and I was most proud of him. But then that nasty vampire, Lord Qing, slaughtered him, cutting him into pieces so he could not advance to another life. His oldest son, Raghu, became the leader of their village. Rajiv is the second son."

Rajiv placed a hand over his heart. "I will not rest until our family has been avenged, Your Eminence."

Dougal shifted on his cushion. He hadn't realized that Rajiv had a personal reason for helping the Vamps.

The Grand Tiger gazed fondly at Rajiv. "He is my youngest grandson. And the only one to learn

English and find us a worthy ally to help us defeat Master Han. He's a smart boy."

Rajiv bowed his head. "Your kindness is beyond measure, Your Eminence."

"We are honored to be your ally," J.L. said.

"To friendship!" The Grand Tiger lifted his cup. *"Gun bei!"*

"Gun bei." They drank, and Rajiv filled the cups with the last of the liquor.

The Grand Tiger slumped to the side, leaning on Dougal. "I'm so very proud of my grandson."

Rajiv's eyes glimmered with tears. "Thank you, Grandfather."

"We will help him and keep him safe," Dougal added.

The Grand Tiger patted his arm. "You are a good friend, Dou Gal. You must play for me. And I will sing for you. And dance the Tiger Dance."

"I would like to see that, Your Eminence."

"Then I will dance now!" The Grand Tiger attempted to get up but fell over.

"Your Eminence?" Dougal jumped up. "Are you all right?"

The Grand Tiger let out a loud snore.

Rajiv ran to his grandfather's side, then glanced up at the Vamps, smiling. "He's asleep. But he'll be talking about tonight for months to come. Thank you."

J.L. rose to his feet. "We need to be going now. The sun will have set on most of Master Han's bases."

Rajiv straightened. "Do you want me to come with you?"

J.L. shook his head. "We have to teleport some

captives back. We won't be able to teleport you at the same time. But we'll come back for you later."

Rajiv nodded with a resigned look. "All right. But call me if you need any help."

For the next few hours, Dougal teleported with J.L. to one enemy camp after another so he could embed all thirty of Master Han's bases in his psychic memory. The camps were quiet, with only a few lights burning along their palisade walls. According to J.L., the soldiers tended to do their military exercises during the day and rest at night, with a small contingent of guards on duty. In the last few years, they had become lax in security, since no local person dared approach a place that might harbor a hungry vampire inside. Only those who wanted to join the army ventured close.

They were in northern Myanmar when Dougal climbed onto a flat rock on top of a hill that overlooked the last camp. "See anyone ye know?"

"No." J.L. lowered his binoculars. "Sometimes I can spot Wu Shen. He's one of their top military officers, so it's a good bet that if we see him, then that's the camp where Master Han and the lords are hiding."

"There's a guard." Dougal pointed at a lone soldier venturing away from the camp, heading into the ravine below them.

"Probably needs to take a piss," J.L. muttered. "Want to nab him?"

"Sure." Dougal removed some tranquilizer darts

from his pocket. They had decided earlier to take only two captives, and to make sure they were from two different bases. That way, when the soldiers never returned to camp, they would probably be labeled deserters. Master Han wouldn't be alarmed over the desertion of two soldiers when he had an army of a thousand.

They teleported down to the ravine and crept up behind the soldier. When the soldier was zipping up his pants, they zoomed forward. J.L. grabbed him, slapping a hand over his mouth, while Dougal jabbed a dart into his neck. The soldier struggled, and Dougal inserted a second dart.

When the soldier slumped over, unconscious, J.L. tossed him over his shoulder. "Let's go."

Dougal grabbed the soldier's fallen rifle and teleported back to the Japanese island. After J.L. materialized with the soldier, they rushed inside the school and placed the soldier on a stretcher in the room for prisoners.

While they fastened the restraints, Gregori peered inside. "Yoshi told us you were back. You got one?"

"Yep," J.L. responded. "We need to get him into stasis."

Abby, Leah, and Laszlo ran into the room, followed by the fox shifter. Dougal exhaled with relief to see Leah looking well.

"Are you all right?" She glanced over him quickly before inserting an IV in the captive's arm.

"Aye. Did anything happen while we were gone?"

"No, it's been quiet."

"Don't worry," the fox shifter said. "I will not let any harm come to the scientists." She smiled at Laszlo, who smiled shyly back.

Dougal's mouth twitched when he realized Laszlo was wearing the red shirt Wilson had torn to reveal his chest. "We need to go so we can bring you another soldier."

Leah nodded. "Be careful."

Thirty minutes later, Dougal and J.L. returned with a second captive. While the scientists were busy, Dougal went to the cafeteria to report to Angus. J.L. teleported to Tiger Town to bring back Rajiv.

"We're off to a good start," Angus said as J.L. and Rajiv entered the cafeteria.

Rajiv sat at the table with Angus and Dougal. "If there's anything the were-tigers can do to help, just let me know."

J.L. grabbed a bottle of Bleer from the fridge. "We shouldn't take any more captives right now, or it will look suspicious."

"Aye," Angus agreed. "Let's wait and see if our scientists are successful with the two we have. Once we know that it works, we can step up our game."

Dougal took a sip from his bottle of Bleer. "I'm no' sure if this strategy is enough. Even if we change a hundred soldiers back to normal, willna Darafer just make a hundred more? Or two hundred? We would be stuck here forever, waging an endless battle."

J.L. sat beside him. "I doubt it would be endless. Once Darafer and Master Han figure out what we're doing, they'll attack."

Angus rubbed his chin. "They have a total of three vampires: Master Han, Lord Qing, and Lord Liao. That means they could only teleport three soldiers here at a time."

"We canna be sure how powerful Darafer is," Dougal said. "He might be able to teleport a huge number of soldiers. And even if he came alone, I'm no' sure we can defeat him, no' without the God Warriors."

The table grew silent as they all considered.

Dougal drank more Bleer. "If we can change the soldiers back to normal, then we need to keep Darafer from making any more." He turned to J.L. "Do ye know how he's doing it?"

J.L. shrugged. "Some kind of hocus-pocus, I think, but he needs a specific plant to pull it off. The demon herb."

"Oh, I remember that!" Rajiv sat up. "They were growing it at the zombie village."

"Zombies?" Dougal asked.

"Not real zombies," J.L. assured him.

"They move around like zombies," Rajiv insisted. "Their brains aren't working."

J.L. nodded. "Darafer's using them as slaves."

Dougal's prosthetic hand clenched, and he slipped his hand under the table. *Slaves.* "Are they being whipped?"

"No," J.L. replied. "Darafer's got them under some kind of mind control. They're unconscious all day, then get up at night to work in the field. When we saw them, they were gathering the demon herb, and some of Master Han's soldiers came to pick it up."

Angus drank some Bleer. "I wonder if our scientists can break the mental hold Darafer has on them?"

Rajiv nodded. "Maybe they can turn the zombies back to normal!"

Dougal's hand relaxed. "That's exactly what we

need to do. Change the zombies back, then burn the field of demon herb so Darafer canna make more mutated soldiers."

J.L. whistled. "He'll be really pissed. If he thinks the villagers have betrayed him, he might kill them."

"We'll evacuate them." Dougal turned to Rajiv. "Can the tigers help with that?"

Rajiv nodded. "Yes."

"And when Master Han's soldiers come to collect the demon herb, we'll attack and keep them from reporting it," Dougal added. "It should buy us some time so the villagers can escape."

Angus leaned forward. "How many villagers are we talking about?"

"About thirty," J.L. said. "They were all elderly or young women and children. All the young males are gone, probably serving in Master Han's army."

Angus shook his head. "I'm no' sure we can make this work. If we swoop in at night to teleport the villagers here so we can treat them, the soldiers will be there and try to stop us. If one of them reports to Darafer, then all our plans could fall apart."

"Then we have to do it during the day," J.L. concluded. "There won't be any soldiers. And the zombies will be unconscious. Our scientists could go there and work on them for hours, and no one would know."

Dougal sat back. When he'd started this train of thought, he hadn't realized it would end up with Leah being sent to China. "Laszlo canna do it during the day, and I doubt Gregori will let Abby go." Leah would be on her own. His hand clenched again. "We canna do it during the day."

"We have to," J.L. insisted. "It's the only way to

keep Darafer from being alerted. The shifters could go along to keep them safe."

Angus glanced at his watch. "The sun will be up here soon. You have forty minutes to bring back one of the zombies. We'll see if our scientists can make him normal. If they can, we'll move forward with the new plan."

Dougal swallowed hard. He'd hoped Leah could remain safe if she stayed on this remote island. But now she would have to venture into enemy territory. And she'd be there during the day, when he would be powerless to protect her.

Chapter Twenty-five

"*D*r. Chin, wake up."

Someone patted Leah's shoulder, and she jerked awake. For a second she thought she was back at the hospital in Boston doing her residency, but then she saw Abby sleeping in the bed next to her and Howard, the were-bear, leaning over her.

"I'm sorry to wake you," Howard whispered. "But the zombie girl is coming to."

"Oh. Okay." She sat up in bed. She was still wearing her clothes from last night.

"I woke up Rajiv," Howard said. "He's trying to talk to her in Chinese."

"I'll be right there." Leah ran across the hall to use the restroom. While she was washing her hands, she glanced at her watch. Eleven fifteen. So she'd gotten almost five hours of sleep.

Shortly before dawn, J.L. and Dougal had brought a girl to the clinic where the prisoners were being kept. They'd called her the zombie girl, explaining that she came from a village where the entire population was under Darafer's control. As far as J.L. knew, their only sustenance was some sort of drug Darafer made out of the herb the villagers grew.

It hadn't taken long for Leah to determine that the zombie girl was suffering from severe malnutrition in addition to whatever drug she'd been given. She had stared blankly, not saying a word, while Leah had cleaned her up, slipped her into a hospital gown, and hooked up an IV. Abby had come up with the idea of using a milder version of her drug that boosted a person's mind control—the same drug she'd used on Dougal—to see if it could help the girl break free from the zombielike haze that had been suppressing her mental faculties.

By then, the sun had come up, and the Vamps had all retired to the basement for their death-sleep. Howard and Phil, who had slept during the night, had woken up to take their shift in the security office. Leah and Abby, both exhausted from working all night, had finally gone to bed. Howard had promised to wake them if anything happened to the captured soldiers or the zombie girl.

Now Leah rushed to the lab to grab her stethoscope and blood pressure cuff. Then she dashed across the hall to the clinic. A quick glance at the two captured soldiers assured her they were still in stasis. The girl had wakened, and the panicked look on her face made it clear that she was no longer in a zombie state.

Rajiv was sitting next to her, talking to her gently in Chinese. "It's all right." He tried to pat her hand, but she jerked away from him, eying him with suspicion.

"Don't be afraid." Leah approached the girl slowly. "I'm a doctor. I'm here to help you."

The girl gave her a wary look.

"Thank God you're here." Rajiv stood. "I wasn't getting anywhere."

Leah looked the girl over. There was color in her cheeks now, but her lips were dry and cracked. "Bring her a bottle of water."

"Yes, Doctor." Rajiv ran out the door.

Leah set her equipment on the nearby table. "It's all right. We're here to help you." She reached for the girl's hand. "I want to check your pulse. Will that be all right?"

The girl frowned, then nodded.

Leah looked at her watch while taking the girl's pulse. It was a little fast, but that was to be expected when the patient was upset. At least it was strong now, and not weak like before.

Rajiv ran back in. "Here's the water." He unscrewed the top and handed the bottle to the girl.

She grabbed it and guzzled down some water.

Leah smiled at her. "This is Rajiv. And I'm Leah. What's your name?"

"Yu Jie." She drank more water. "Where am I? Where's my family?"

"Your family is back at the village, and you're in a clinic. We're trying to make you healthy again."

"I want to see my family. And I-I'm very hungry."

"I'm sure you are." Leah glanced at Rajiv. "Can you bring some food from the cafeteria? Something mild."

"Yes, Doctor." He hurried down the hall.

Leah hooked her stethoscope around her neck. "I'm going to check your blood pressure, okay?" When the girl nodded, Leah completed the procedure, then wrote the results on the chart she'd started six hours earlier. "You're making wonderful progress. I'd like to remove your IV now. And we'll take you back home as soon as you're well. Do you remember what happened to your village?"

Yu Jie drank more water. "My older brother wanted to join Master Han's army. All the young men in the village were doing it, 'cause they could earn good wages and send some money home for the rest of us. Master Han said he would employ them all if we would grow the demon herb for his friend, Darafer. The village elders agreed." She frowned at the bottle she held. "I haven't seen my brother since then. I think it's been a few months."

Leah smoothed a Band-Aid over the small puncture where the IV needle had been inserted. "Do you remember when your brother left?"

Yu Jie tilted her head, considering. "It was March. 2011."

Leah winced. The girl had lost about twenty months of her life. "This is November, 2012."

Yu Jie's mouth dropped open. "What? What happened?"

"You were drugged. I believe your whole village is drugged." Leah touched her shoulder. "I'm sorry."

Tears glistened in Yu Jie's eyes. "I-I'm sixteen now? I don't remember anything. How could this happen?"

"I think we can safely say that Darafer tricked you. You thought you were helping your brother, but Darafer turned you and all the village into his mindless slaves—"

"No!" The water bottle crackled as Yu Jie's hands tightened around it. "I have to go back! I have to save my family."

"Calm down." Leah patted her arm. "We're going to help you, okay? We succeeded in making you normal again, so that means we know how to save your village."

A tear ran down Yu Jie's face. "You can save my people?"

"Yes." Leah squeezed her arm. "I'll save them. What you need to do now is rest and get your strength back so you can help me. Okay?"

Yu Jie nodded, more tears spilling down her face.

Rajiv strode into the room, carrying a tray with a bowl of hot noodles and a cup of hot tea.

"Perfect. Thank you." Leah set the tray on a table that swiveled over Yu Jie's bed.

Yu Jie grabbed the chopsticks and pinched a huge hunk of noodles.

"Not so fast," Leah warned her. "Your system isn't used to food anymore. Take it slow and easy so you won't get sick."

Yu Jie nodded, then ate only a few noodles at a time.

"That's good." Leah smiled at her. "I'll check on you in about thirty minutes, okay?"

Yu Jie nodded and continued to eat.

"Can you hang around in case she needs something?" Leah asked Rajiv.

"Sure." He sat next to the bed and watched the girl eat. "I'm twenty-two. How old are you?"

Leah strode back to her dorm room to gather up some fresh clothes. Then she showered and dressed. After a quick breakfast in the cafeteria, she was feeling good.

She was on her way back to the clinic when Rajiv left the room, carrying the tray.

He stopped next to her in the hall. "Yu Jie fell back asleep."

"That's good."

"You could sleep, too," Rajiv suggested.

Leah smiled. "I'm wide awake now, so I'll get some work done. Thank you."

She took some blood samples from the captives to see if any progress was being made. While she waited for the results, she wandered down the hall to the security office.

"How's it going?" she asked the guys. Howard was sitting in front of the security monitors, and Rajiv was at a table, studying a map.

"Great," Howard replied as he munched on a donut.

Rajiv grinned. "Pooh Bear is happy 'cause Kyo brought him donuts from Tokyo."

"Phil's outside looking around." Howard motioned to a camera that showed the beach. "Congrats on curing the zombie girl."

Rajiv nodded. "We are eager to save the whole village."

"When do you think we'll go?" Leah asked.

"Probably tomorrow." Howard wiped his hands on a paper napkin. "The Vamps can teleport us and the supplies there tonight. As soon as the zombies go into their daytime trance, we'll move into the village."

Leah nodded. "Okay. I'll start figuring out what I need. Oh, we'll need to feed the villagers. They'll be starving when they wake up from their trance."

"We'll pack some food." Howard grabbed another donut. "Rajiv's got some good news about the evacuation."

"I do!" Rajiv pointed at the map. "The zombie village is only a mile from the Mekong River. Grandfather will send some men and their fishing boats down the river to pick up the villagers."

"Oh, that's wonderful! I'd better get back to work." Leah hurried back to the lab to box up supplies.

By late afternoon, her lack of sleep caught up with her. Abby was just waking, and she agreed to watch over their patients in the clinic and help Yu Jie get ready for the mission.

Leah slipped on her flannel pajamas and fell fast asleep.

"**L**eah, wake up." Dougal sat on the edge of her bed and patted her shoulder.

"Mmm," she moaned. "What is it, Howard?"

"Howard? Are ye dreaming of Howard?"

Her eyes flickered open. "Dougal?"

"Aye, 'tis me, yer true love, Dougal."

She smiled drowsily at him. "Yes, that's true."

"Good." He shifted on the bed to face her. "Now that we have that straightened out, let me tell you—"

"What time is it?" She scooted into a sitting position against the headboard.

"Just past midnight. Leah, I doona want you to do this mission at the zombie village. 'Tis too dangerous to send you into enemy territory."

She rubbed her eyes. "I have to go. I promised Yu Jie that I would save her people. They can't survive much longer at that level of malnutrition. Darafer is slowly killing them."

"I appreciate your wanting to help them. But we

have a total of eight Vamps here. We could teleport all the villagers here in just a few trips."

Leah shook her head. "They're awake at night and might resist. It'll be much easier to treat them during the day when they're unconscious. Besides, Master Han's soldiers would be there at night to stop you. This way is really the best."

With a sigh, Dougal ran a hand through his hair. He knew the daytime plan was the best way, but he hated the thought of not being there to protect Leah.

She leaned forward to touch his shoulder. "Howard, Phil, and Rajiv will be with me. That's a grizzly bear, a wolf, and a tiger. Who's going to mess with them?"

Dougal groaned. There was no stopping this. Angus had given the go-ahead, and already he and J.L. had teleported close to the village to find a good spot for hiding the supplies. "All right. I'll go along with it."

"You're the one who will be in more danger," Leah continued. "I'll be safe in Tiger Town by the time the sun sets. You'll be facing Master Han's soldiers when they show up at the village."

"I'll be fine." Dougal took her hand in his. "We'll take you and the shifters there shortly before dawn. Ye'll only have to wait about thirty minutes before going into the village."

"Won't the sun be up here? How will you get back?"

"We willna come back here. There's a camp nearby. J.L. has stayed there several times. 'Tis less than a mile from the village." He would be close to Leah, but unable to help her during the day.

She squeezed his hand. "You still look worried."

"Am I still at ninety-five percent?"

She smiled. "You're up to ninety-nine."

"Och, that's excellent." He pulled her into his arms. "How can I gain that last point?"

She wrapped her arms around his neck. "I'll think of something."

"Like making love?"

She snorted. "You wish."

"I do wish." He kissed her forehead, then her nose. With his lips a fraction away from hers, a knock sounded at the door.

J.L. called out, "Dougal? Are you in there? We're moving out."

He groaned.

Leah kissed his cheek. "Time to go save the world."

For the next few hours, Dougal teleported supplies with J.L. There were medical supplies, including ten IV poles, that Leah had packed, and an ice chest and several boxes of food that Rajiv had packed. Angus had found a shallow cave on the rocky ridge overlooking the village, and he remained there, standing guard, as they stashed away the supplies.

With that job completed, J.L. teleported Dougal to the nearby cave where the Vamps would do their death-sleep. It was a good defensive location, Dougal noted, for it was on a small island in the middle of a lake. They spent another hour teleporting supplies to the cave.

Then they returned to Angus and ventured close to the village to see what was happening there. Torches were set up around the field, and soldiers marched about while the villagers cut off stems of demon herb and dropped them into burlap sacks.

"I count ten guards," Dougal whispered, "and twenty-nine villagers."

"That's a few less than last time," J.L. said, half hidden behind a bush.

"There might be some in the village, too sick to work, or they may have died. Leah said they're all slowly dying."

J.L. sighed. "We should have done this months ago. The last time we were here, there were chickens and a cow. Now, there's nothing. And their homes are falling apart."

They hurried back to Angus, who had covered the entrance to the shallow cave with leafy branches.

He glanced at his watch. "Time for you to bring the others. I'll call in five minutes."

Dougal and J.L. teleported back to the school. Leah was ready, dressed warmly in a sweater and coat, and she had Yu Jie scrubbed clean and dressed in borrowed clothing. Kyo and his friends and all the shifters were ready and well armed. Abby and Laszlo would be left behind with Gregori and Gu Mina as their guards.

Angus called, and Dougal put his voice on the speaker phone so the Japanese Vamps could use it as a beacon. They grabbed the shifters and Yu Jie and teleported.

"Ready?" Dougal took Leah in his arms.

"Yes." She slipped her hands around his neck.

He kissed her, then teleported her to the ridge where the others had already materialized.

Angus showed the shifters where the supplies

were hidden. "Good luck. We'll see you tomorrow night in Tiger Town."

Dougal touched Leah's cheek. "Be careful."

She nodded. "You, too."

He teleported with the other Vamps to the island. The minute they stepped inside the cave, he spotted a figure moving about in the dark. He seemed to be holding a burlap sack and filling it with their supplies.

"Who goes there?" Angus clicked on a flashlight.

The figure glanced toward them.

"Russell," J.L. whispered.

He backed up, his hand going to the sword on his hip.

Angus lifted his hands to show they were bare. "Russell, we're no' here to capture you."

So this was the Marine major who had gone AWOL over a year ago. Dougal noted he was a large man, dressed like a peasant, although he had a sword and rifle half hidden beneath his shabby coat. His hair had grown long enough that he now tied it back in a ponytail. He clutched the burlap sack with one hand, while his other hand rested on the hilt of his sword.

"I'm not going back until I've killed Master Han," he said in a voice that sounded stilted and rusty, as if he hadn't talked to another person in months.

"Ye doona have to come back with us." Angus inched forward. "But we could use yer help tomorrow night."

"We're rescuing the people in the zombie village," J.L. explained. "Tomorrow night, we take on the guards. There could be ten of them, so we're a little outnumbered."

Russell frowned. "You're doing your death-sleep here?"

"Aye," Angus replied. "Ye can stay here with us, if ye like. We'd like to hear what ye've been up to."

Russell looked them over, his gaze lingering on their weapons. "I might return. Or not." He vanished.

Chapter Twenty-six

*A*s the following day progressed, Leah felt an odd mixture of satisfaction and disgust. Satisfaction that the plan was working so well, but disgust at how the villagers had been forced to live. In their drugged state, they had done nothing but sleep all day and work in the field all night, so the village itself had become a filthy pigsty.

Vegetables and fruit lay in rotten heaps. The lack of sanitation had rendered the place uninhabitable and dangerous. Poor Yu Jie had burst into tears when she'd seen the shambles that had once been her home, and her family lying on the dirty floor, unconscious. Leah had hugged her and reminded her that her family's slavery was coming to an end that day.

Instilled with new hope, Yu Jie proved to be an excellent assistant. As soon as the shifters brought down the medical supplies from the top of the ridge, she helped Leah go from one hut to another until everyone in the village was hooked up with an IV and had been injected with Abby's mental power boosting drug.

Leah estimated it would take about five hours for

the healthiest of the villagers to wake up from their zombielike state. There were two elderly women she found who were in serious decline and would have to be carried to the fishing boats. She hoped the two women could be driven to a hospital once they arrived in Tiger Town.

Meanwhile, the shifters brought down the food supplies and two big stockpots. They set up an outdoor kitchen with the pots set on grates over a fire. According to Rajiv, the menu would be chicken noodle soup and rice. Once they had the food cooking, Rajiv was left to watch over it, while Howard and Phil attacked the field of demon herb. They whacked down the plants with machetes and piled them in the center.

By noon, half the village, the youngest and healthiest half, was awake and eating. Leah unhooked their IVs while Yu Jie explained what had happened. By one in the afternoon, the elderly and weaker half had wakened, and some of the healthier villagers helped wash and feed the two women who were in serious trouble.

With their minds alert and their stomachs full, the villagers gathered in the central meeting area close to the cooking fire. The women, disgusted at the filth, were drawing water from the well and insisting everyone wash up. The elderly men started arguing.

"How dare you interfere with our village!" One of the elderly men pointed a gnarly finger at Leah.

Before Leah could respond, Yu Jie yelled back, "How dare you agree to turn us all into slaves!"

Most villagers shouted their approval, shaking

their fists at the elderly man. He yelled back, joined by another old man. Leah figured they were the village elders.

"Calm down!" she shouted in Chinese, but no one listened.

Rajiv let out a piercing whistle that silenced everyone. He motioned to Leah. "You should listen to the doctor who saved your lives."

"She has destroyed our village." The first elder motioned to the field where Howard and Phil were cutting down plants. "When Darafer finds out you've destroyed his field, he will kill us all!"

Several women screamed and grabbed their children.

Howard and Phil came running.

"Listen to me!" Leah shouted. "Darafer enslaved you with a drug that was slowly killing you. Two of your women are close to death. In another year's time, you would have all died."

Murmurs went through the small crowd. Most nodded in agreement.

"Twenty months have gone by," Leah continued. "That's almost two years stolen from your lives."

The women started crying and hugging their children.

"Darafer will come back to kill us!" the second elder shouted.

"That's why we're leaving." Rajiv pointed to a group of five men who were approaching the village. "Those are fishermen from my village who will take you all to safety."

"You can't force us to leave our home!" the first elder yelled.

"Look at your home," Leah replied. "Living in this filth without proper nutrition is killing you. If you want to live, you have to leave."

"You have no right to tell us what to do," the second elder insisted.

"Oh, shut up, old men!" An elderly woman shook a fist at them. "You're the ones who agreed to have us work for Darafer. Look what it's done to us! Look at our children!"

"They didn't even pay us the money they promised," another woman added.

"We should kill Darafer for what he's done to us!" a third woman shouted.

"If you want to hurt Darafer," Rajiv said, "the best way is to destroy his crop."

With a cry of revenge, half the villagers grabbed broken planks off doors and fences, then lit them in the cooking fire. Howard and Phil ran with them to the field to make sure the fire didn't get out of control.

While the field was burning, Rajiv's were-tiger friends made two stretchers for carrying the ill women. Leah and Yu Jie elicited help from the remaining villagers, and soon all the medical and cooking supplies had been safely stashed back into the cave on the ridge. Howard and Phil made a quick run through of the village to make sure no clues had been left behind as to who had interfered with the zombies.

It took about thirty minutes to walk to the Mekong River where five more were-tigers were standing guard over the ten fishing boats. Once everyone was aboard, they headed upriver to Tiger Town.

Leah waved at Yu Jie, who was in a neighboring

boat with her family. She grinned and waved back.

In two hours they arrived at Tiger Town. The were-tigers had prepared tubs filled with hot water so the villagers could bathe, then they offered them fresh clothes.

"That's very kind of your people," Leah told Rajiv in English.

He grinned. "They're doing it for themselves, too. Tigers have a very strong sense of smell and can't stand stinky people."

Howard wrinkled his nose. "It's been rough on me and Phil, too."

Tiger Town had several jeeps, and they offered to take the villagers to a nearby town the next day. Most of the villagers had relatives in other towns, so they were eager to reunite with their families.

Rajiv led Leah and the shifters up the stairs to the courtyard. "I have arranged for you to have private rooms and baths."

"Oh, thank you." Leah would be relieved to wash off the stench of the zombie village.

"I'll have a servant wash your clothes, too," Rajiv added. "We'll give you something clean to wear."

"Thanks," Phil said as he looked around the court-yard. "This place is awesome."

Leah nodded, admiring the palace. "Absolutely beautiful."

"You tigers are living good," Howard said.

Rajiv grinned. "Wait till tonight. It'll be so much fun!"

"What's tonight?" Leah asked.

"We celebrate! There will be a feast and music and dancing." Rajiv punched the air with his fist. "It'll be great!"

Phil chuckled. "You sound like Tony the Tiger saying it'll be great."

"I don't know Tony," Rajiv said.

Howard snorted. "I'll drink and eat, but don't expect me to dance."

"Oh, come on." Rajiv nudged him. "I want to see Pooh Bear do the Tiger Dance."

Leah smiled, although inside she was feeling an increasing amount of fear. The daytime part of the plan had succeeded without a hitch, but as soon as the sun set, the Vamps would have to handle the fallout when Master Han's soldiers discovered an empty village and a field of demon herb burned to the ground. Dougal might end up fighting for his life.

Dougal crouched, hidden behind some bushes with Angus and J.L. on one side of the burned field, while Kyo and his friends positioned themselves on the other side. Smoke curled up into the night sky from the smoldering ashes of demon herb.

Angus had passed out tranquilizer darts to everyone with the instructions to capture the soldiers if possible. Then they would teleport them back to the school.

Earlier, J.L. had received a text from Rajiv that they had safely transported the villagers to Tiger Town, so Dougal was looking forward to seeing Leah soon.

"Darafer's going to be pissed," a voice said quietly behind them, and Dougal glanced over his shoulder to find Russell standing about ten feet away.

"Glad ye could join us." Angus stood and extended a hand, which Russell ignored, keeping his distance.

"You shouldn't anger Darafer," he muttered. "He's more powerful than us, and he will retaliate."

"That's why we're here." J.L. motioned for Russell to hunch down. "We're going to stop the soldiers from reporting in."

Russell squatted. "That will only buy you one night at the most."

Angus hunched down. "We've developed a process that will turn Master Han's soldiers back to normal. We've established a clinic on a remote Japanese island so we can treat them."

Russell snorted. "They're the enemy. Just kill them."

"Their souls will go to hell," Dougal said.

"We're in hell," Russell muttered. "Besides, it was their choice."

"Shh." J.L. lifted a hand. "I hear a motor."

"Take them alive if possible," Angus whispered.

Two jeeps pulled up at the end of the field, and armed guards jumped out. After their initial shock, they divided into two groups. One group examined the field while the others ran to the village.

Angus motioned for his men to follow him toward the village. They remained hidden behind bushes and trees till they were just above the village, then they moved downhill and divided up.

The soldiers were ducking in and out of huts. Dougal positioned himself next to a door, and when a soldier exited, he slapped a tranquilizer in his neck, then another one for good measure. When the soldier slumped over, Dougal hefted him over his shoulder and carried him into the central meeting area. Angus was there with another unconscious soldier, and J.L. was bringing in a third.

"Where's Russell?" Angus asked as they deposited the soldiers in a heap.

A cry of pain sounded close by, and they ran to investigate. Two dead soldiers lay at Russell's feet, and blood dripped off his sword.

"The devil take it." Angus glared at him. "I told you we wanted them alive."

"You asked for my help." Russell wiped his sword on a soldier's uniform. "You got it." He vanished.

With a muttered curse, Angus headed back to the three tranquilized soldiers.

J.L. sighed. "Russell's been living among the enemy for too long."

Dougal nodded as he trudged back with J.L. He understood how harsh a person could get when just trying to survive. During his four years of slavery, he'd seen so many other slaves whipped and tortured that he'd grown cold and unfeeling inside. Only his music had kept his soul alive. And his music had brought Li Lei into his life. If she hadn't saved him, he probably would have died a slave. But it had been Li Lei who had died young.

Forgive me. He would earn her forgiveness by keeping Leah safe and happy for centuries to come.

Kyo dashed over at vampire speed. "We had to kill one, but we have three knocked out."

"Let's get them back to the school," Angus said.

In a few minutes they were dropping the captive soldiers on stretchers in the clinic. Abby and Laszlo quickly put them into stasis, while Gregori reported that all had remained quiet at the school.

Dougal was eager to see Leah, but first they had

to teleport back all the supplies left hidden on the ridge. They didn't want to leave any clues as to what had happened. Even the three dead soldiers were teleported to the island, where they would be given a proper burial.

Finally done with the mission, Dougal showered and changed into a kilt and white shirt. Then he grabbed his Uilleann pipes. He'd keep his promise to the Grand Tiger, then spend the rest of the night with Leah.

Chapter Twenty-seven

Leah clapped along with the pounding drums while Howard and Phil attempted the Tiger Dance. They'd resisted for the first hour of the celebration, but after a few cups of Tiger Town's homemade liquor, they were raring to go.

Most all of Tiger Town and the guests from the zombie village were in the courtyard celebrating. Torches lined the perimeter, and a half-full moon glowed in the starry sky. Each end of the courtyard was lined with tables bearing grilled fish, rice, fruit, and what Rajiv called Tiger Juice.

In front of the palace, large drums were being pounded in a compelling rhythm that was almost hypnotic. It certainly made everyone want to dance. That and the homemade liquor. After drinking half a cup, Leah was feeling much less nervous about Dougal. Then when she heard the news from Rajiv that the Vamps had safely completed their part of the mission, she jumped for joy and tried the Tiger Dance, too.

It was simple enough to do. Face a partner, pound your right foot four times, crouch and leap with a half spin in the air, then repeat facing another partner. Then link elbows and spin, ending with a hiss and fake showing of claws. Of course, the were-tiger men were trying to outdo each other by leaping the highest. Other men donned giant tiger masks and were leaping so high that they sailed over people's heads. Every now and then there was a drunken collision, but everyone laughed it off and went back to the table for more Tiger Juice.

"Is that Howard dancing?" J.L. yelled over the noise. "And Phil?"

Leah looked up to see that J.L. and Angus had arrived. Her heart lurched but quickly settled down when she didn't see Dougal with them.

J.L. set down an ice chest. "Whoa, they just hissed at me."

With a grin, Angus handed J.L. a Bleer from the ice chest. "Ye did a great job," he told her.

"Thank you. I heard everything went well for you guys, too."

Angus nodded and helped himself to a Bleer. "We have six more prisoners in stasis."

Leah couldn't wait any longer. "Where is Dougal?"

"He had to keep a promise to the Grand Tiger." J.L. took a sip of Bleer. "He promised to wear a skirt and play the pipes for him. You'll find him in the palace."

"Okay, thanks." Leah dashed up the steps to the palace.

Once she closed the thick double doors behind her, the pounding noise outside quieted to a dull throb. Instead, the air was filled with the plaintive, lyrical sound of pipes.

The guard nodded at her, allowing her to enter the throne room. She eased forward, keeping to the side, behind the columns. And then she saw them. Dougal was sitting on the edge of the dais, his head bowed as he concentrated on a slow, sad melody. Rajiv's grandfather was sitting on his throne, his eyes closed, his body swaying to the music.

Tears filled her eyes. How could she not spend the rest of her life with Dougal?

When the music ended, she stepped out from behind a column.

Dougal set his pipes down and stood. "Leah."

Her heart squeezed at the expression on his face. So much tenderness and love.

"Ah." The Grand Tiger watched them closely. "Have you found love again, Dou Gal?"

"Yes, Your Eminence," he said, never taking his eyes off Leah.

She glanced at Rajiv's grandfather, wondering what he meant by *again*.

"True love," the Grand Tiger whispered, his eyes glistening with tears.

Dougal bowed. "I apologize, Your Eminence. I did not mean to make you sad. I can play only slow music now."

"It was beautiful." The Grand Tiger waved toward the door. "You may go now. I wish to be alone with the memories of my wife, who passed before me."

"Yes, Your Eminence." Dougal grabbed Leah's hand and led her toward the double door.

She glanced back to see a tear running down the Grand Tiger's face. He must have loved his wife dearly.

Dougal pushed open the doors, and immediately the pounding drums filled her ears. The courtyard was teeming with life, people laughing and dancing. Tears crowded her eyes as she realized how blessed she was.

"Life is an adventure, lass," her grandfather had told her. "Live it to the fullest, and never look back."

I will, Grandpa. She blinked back her tears and smiled at Dougal. "Did you want to dance?"

He pulled her to the edge of the courtyard. "I have another activity in mind."

She followed him down an alleyway between two buildings. "Where are we going?"

"I have a room in the guesthouse."

"Wait." She dug in her heels.

He pressed her up against a stone wall. "Why should I wait? I've hungered for you every night."

"I have something to say."

He nuzzled her neck. "Then say it before I rip this pretty robe off you."

"It is pretty, isn't it? Rajiv's cousin, Jia, lent it to me. She's a lovely girl."

Dougal leaned back to give her an impatient look. "Is that what ye wanted to say?"

"No." The pounding noise from the courtyard grew louder, and her heart thundered along with it. "I was really worried about you."

"I was worried about you, too." He grabbed her hand to take her toward his room.

"Wait." She halted. "I was so worried that it made me realize something really important."

"What? That ye worry too much?"

"No. That I don't want to live without you." She touched his cheek. "I'm all yours, Dougal. One hundred percent."

His eyes glowed red. In a matter of seconds, he had swept her up in his arms and carried her to his room. In a few more seconds, he had lit the candle from the lantern hanging outside the door. She took the bedding off the dresser and spread it on the floor.

His shoes, socks, and sporran hit the floor.

"Wait," she said as he flung off his shirt.

"What now?"

"There's something I've been wanting to do. Actually a few things."

"Aye, me, too." He unfastened his kilt.

"No, wait!" She motioned to the bedding. "Lie down."

With an impatient huff, he sprawled on the bedding. "What now?"

She kicked off her shoes. "Enjoy the show." She slowly untied the ribbons that held her robe in place. The floor vibrated beneath her bare feet from the pounding drums in the nearby courtyard. She was naked underneath the silk, and it made her feel deliciously decadent. Her nipples hardened as she slipped the robe off her shoulders. She let the robe fall in a puddle at her feet so she stood naked before him with only the jade dragon around her neck.

He inhaled sharply, his eyes glowing a deeper red. "Ye're so beautiful." He made a grab for her. "Come here."

With a smile, she stepped out of his reach. "I'm not done. There's something else I've been wanting to do."

"What?"

She knelt at his feet. "This." She grasped the hem of his kilt and tossed it up to his chest.

His mouth twitched. "Ye wanted under my kilt?"

"Yes." Just the sight of him made moisture pool between her legs. He was gloriously hard and full, but she dragged her gaze away from his erection and skimmed her fingers up his muscular calves to his thighs.

"Lass, if ye want to molest me, ye're a bit south of the target area."

She smiled. "Are you complaining?"

He smiled back. "Aye, ye're too slow."

"Where have I heard that before?" She cupped his balls, and he hissed in a breath. "I demand compensation."

"Take whatever ye like," he growled. "But get on with it."

She circled a hand around his erection and squeezed. "I'll take this."

A drop of moisture seeped from the crown, and she leaned over to lick it, then take him into her mouth. She closed her eyes, concentrating on the feel and taste of him while the drums from the courtyard continued to pound faster and faster. She'd never felt so primal, so free.

"Enough!" He tossed her onto her back and dove between her legs.

The feel of his tongue and lips drove her wild. She thrashed, and he clasped her hips, lifting her to deepen the torture. A fierce orgasm struck, making her jolt from the power of it. As shudders racked her body, he plunged into her, and she came again. She was in a whirlwind of pounding drums and throbbing muscles as he pumped into her faster and faster. With a shout, he climaxed, then fell beside her, holding her tight.

She clung to him, rubbing a hand over the dragon

tattoo. His heart was pounding as fiercely as the drums in the courtyard.

"Leah." He stroked her hair. "Ye're mine. Forever."

She smiled. Her life was so beautifully perfect. With a contented sigh, she closed her eyes.

But how long can it last? a small voice in her head warned her, and her eyes opened. They'd burned down Darafer's precious field of demon herb. It was the same as declaring war on the demon. And no doubt, he would retaliate.

The next afternoon, Leah was back at work in the lab. The Vamps had teleported her and the shifters back to the school shortly before dawn, then they'd headed down to the basement for their death-sleep.

Leah was exhausted, too, from a night of love-making, so she'd grabbed some sleep before waking around one thirty. After taking some blood samples from the newly captured soldiers, she went to the lab to process them. Abby had the results from the first two prisoners, and it looked like they were making progress.

"What can you tell me about Laser?" Gu Mina asked, sitting on Laszlo's empty stool.

"He's a sweet man," Leah replied as she prepared a slide.

Mina waved a hand. "I already know that. But what else do you know?"

"He's Hungarian, I believe," Abby said, peering through a microscope.

"I know that, too." Mina swiveled impatiently on the stool. "But why is he so nervous around me? I keep telling him how cute he is, and that I would never hurt him, but he keeps fiddling with his buttons."

Leah smiled. "He always does that."

"Why?"

Leah shrugged. "I guess he's nervous."

"Why?"

Leah sighed. It was hard to get any work done with a curious fox in the room. "I don't know. I guess you'll have to ask him."

"I did, and one of his buttons popped off."

Smiling, Leah looked into a microscope.

The sudden screech of a sword being yanked from a sheath made her look up. Mina had her sword pointed at a strange man. He was dressed all in black, with shoulder-length black hair and sparkling green eyes. The same characteristics as Dougal, Leah thought, but he'd always looked wonderfully handsome. The way this man glared at her was cold and mean.

Abby gasped and scrambled to her feet. "Darafer."

He gave her an annoyed look. "I haven't come for you." His gaze refocused on Leah, and he stepped toward her. "You're the fool who's pestering me, aren't you?"

"Stop!" Mina charged toward him, but with a flick of his hand, Darafer sent her flying backward with so much force that the plaster cracked when she hit the wall.

She crumbled onto the floor, unconscious.

"Mina!" Leah started toward her, then hesitated. Her gaze fell to the dagger on her table. She would have to defend herself.

Abby pulled a gun out of a drawer just as Howard

and Phil ran into the room, leveling their pistols at the demon. Rajiv followed them, wielding a sword. With a bored look, Darafer waved his hand, and they all froze.

It took a second for Leah to realize what he'd done. Marielle had warned her that he could stop time. He'd frozen everyone in the room but her.

She grabbed the knife and threw it hard. It froze in midair.

"Dr. Galileah Chin. The brilliant disappointment of her family." Darafer strolled toward her and plucked the dagger from its frozen state. "They never appreciated you like I will." He tested the sharpness of the blade. "I wonder if your parents will grieve for you like they would your brothers?"

She swallowed hard. Marielle had warned her that the second Darafer saw her, he would know which wounds to pick at and which fears to manipulate. She looked frantically about for another weapon. A scalpel? She eased toward it.

"I wouldn't do that if I were you." In less than a second, Darafer had zoomed over to Abby. He pointed the dagger at her belly. "It would be a shame to slice her up when she's pregnant, don't you think?"

Leah clenched her fists. "What do you want?"

"Revenge, of course." He tossed the dagger on the ground. "And you're going to give it to me."

He zoomed toward her, morphing into a black cloud. She ran, but within seconds she was engulfed in darkness, choking for air. Panic seized her, freezing her with fear just before everything went black.

Chapter Twenty-eight

*T*he second Dougal woke from his death-sleep, he knew something was wrong. Howard and Phil were in the basement, watching him, their faces grim.

Rajiv hurried down the stairs, carrying a sack. "I warmed up some bottles for them."

"What's wrong?" Angus demanded.

"Leah," Dougal whispered. When the shifters grimaced, his heart stuttered.

He dashed up the stairs to Leah's dorm room. Her bed was empty. Abby was sitting on her bed, sniffling, while Gu Mina tried to comfort her.

Abby glanced up at Dougal and burst into tears. "I'm so sorry. We tried to protect—"

"Abby!" Gregori zoomed to a halt in front of her. "Are you all right?"

"Darafer came." She threw herself into Gregori's arms. "He took Leah."

Dougal stumbled back a step. Leah . . . gone? He ran down to the lab. It was empty. Mina's sword lay on the floor next to a cracked wall. The *sgian dubh* he'd given Leah was on the floor behind Abby's worktable.

"We tried to protect her," Howard said quietly

behind him. "We came in, prepared to fire our weapons, but the next thing we knew, he was gone and Leah was missing."

"He froze us," Phil added. "We've been watching the tape to see what happened."

"I want to see it," Angus said as he entered the room.

Dougal wandered to Leah's table and empty stool. There was a microscope loaded with a slide. She'd been working.

And now she was gone.

A searing pain slammed into him, jolting him out of his shock. Leah was gone. Taken by Darafer. And he'd failed to protect her.

His prosthetic hand clenched. There was hope left. "Her tracking device." He turned to Howard. "Did ye track her?"

Howard winced. "It's not working. We've been trying for three hours."

A cold chill swept down Dougal's spine. How would he ever find her? He'd failed her.

"I contacted everyone as soon as night fell wherever they live," Howard continued. "Mikhail in Moscow. Zoltan in Budapest. Jack in Venice, and Connor in Scotland. They all started teleporting west. Emma picked up a few of the older werewolf boys. Ian, Carlos, Robby, Jean-Luc, Phineas, Nate, and Finn all volunteered, so we now have a total of fifteen in Hawaii, waiting for our call."

"Call them," Angus ordered. "And call the three guys in Australia. We need all the manpower we can get."

"Here." Rajiv pulled a bottle of blood from his

sack and passed it to Angus. "You guys need to stay strong."

Dougal strode from the room, ignoring the bottle that Rajiv tried to give him. How could he have failed her? From the moment he'd met Leah, he'd sworn he would protect her.

The hallway was lined with Vamps, drinking their breakfast bottles and giving him sympathetic looks.

Dammit. Save yer sympathy for someone who deserves it. He rushed out the front door and down the steps. He was halfway to the beach when he realized his socks were wet from walking on snowy ground. He stumbled to a stop, gazing out at the black water while freezing pain seared his feet.

He deserved it. The cold wind whipped at his shirt and kilt, freezing his bones. He deserved that, too. All the pain in the world could not compare to the ache in his heart. He'd failed her.

Where was she? Was she still alive? Hopefully, Darafer would keep her alive, but only if he could use her. Was he torturing her? Whipping her into submission so she would be his slave?

Another pain shot through him, wrenching his gut and doubling him over. Guilt and hunger. But the guilt was the worst. He deserved the pain of hunger.

"There ye are," Connor said behind him. The pebbly shore crunched beneath his shoes as he approached. "Here." He offered Dougal a bottle of blood.

Dougal ignored him.

Connor sighed. "I know ye're suffering—"

"Leave me be."

"Nay."

Another hunger pain shuddered through Dougal's body.

"Take it." Connor jabbed the bottle at his chest.

Dougal stepped back.

"Bugger." Connor ripped the top off the bottle. "Yer suffering willna help Leah."

Dougal turned to gaze at the black waves crashing on the shore. "I failed her." Tears burned his eyes. "Again."

Connor paused, then said, "Ye can only fail her if ye give up."

Dougal didn't respond. If Leah was being harmed in any way, then he had failed her.

Connor sighed. "All right. Ye're allowed three more seconds of self-pity, and then I'll be bashing yer head in."

"Self-pity?" Dougal whirled to face him. "Ye think I'm thinking of myself? Leah could be facing torture right now!"

"Aye." Connor glowered at him. "So what are ye going to do about it?"

Dougal's prosthetic hand clenched. "I have to rescue her."

"Good." Connor motioned to the school. "Luckily for you, ye have a lot of friends, and they're all here to help."

Dougal blinked away tears and grabbed the bottle to guzzle down the blood.

"That's more like it." Connor shoved him toward the school. "Let's get back inside before ye freeze yer bloody feet off. Did ye want prosthetic feet, too?"

* * *

Five hours later in Tiger Town, Dougal was ready to rip something apart. Everyone kept telling him they were making progress. Keep your hopes up, they said with forced smiles. *Bollocks.*

They hadn't found her.

Ten units had been formed out of the twenty-six available Vamps and shifters. Laszlo, Gregori, Emma, and Gu Mina had remained on the Japanese island to protect Abby. Dougal and J.L. had teleported to all thirty of Master Han's campsites, calling back on their sat phones so the others could use their voices as a beacon. Within an hour, all the Vamps knew where the camps were located, and the ten most likely sites had been chosen. A unit was assigned to each site, and a Vamp from each unit teleported into his assigned camp to look for signs that Leah was there.

Now they had all returned to Tiger Town for a quick meeting. Everyone had managed to remain undetected by the enemy, and they congratulated themselves on their excellent work.

Bollocks. Dougal scowled at them. No one had any news about Leah.

Angus narrowed the search down to the five most likely sites. Shifters Howard, Phil, Rajiv, Carlos, and Finn were each given a location, and the remaining three werewolf boys were paired with Rajiv, Phil, and Finn. They would watch their assigned sites during the day. For now, they were told to get some sleep.

The Vamps teleported back to their sites to search for Leah. Shortly before dawn, they returned to

Tiger Town. No good news. The shifters were wakened and teleported to their daytime assignments.

As the sun neared the horizon, Dougal trudged to the room where he'd made love to Leah the night before. Her jasmine scent still lingered on her pillow, and he pulled it to his chest as he struggled against the pull of death-sleep. How could he rest when Leah was still a prisoner? Was she in pain? *Doona be afraid, Leah. I will find you.*

But no matter how hard he fought, death-sleep crept up on him, dragging him into darkness while his old vow swirled around in his mind. *I will find you. No matter what. If it takes a thousand years, I will find you.*

Leah came to with a gasp. More darkness. She breathed deeply, cautioning herself to remain calm while memories washed over her. The dark cloud. The icy-cold feel of Darafer grasping her. The terror that had escalated until she'd lost consciousness.

She was alive, she reminded herself. There was always hope as long as she stayed alive.

So where was she now? She looked about, trying not to move a muscle. If someone was watching, she didn't want them to know she was awake. She was lying on her side with something rough prickling her face. She slowly opened a hand to feel the surface. Straw or hay on top of stone.

It wasn't completely dark. In the distance, a torch burned, its flickering light casting shadows that danced ominously around her. She narrowed her eyes. Bars. Wooden bars like a grid. She was in a cage? Her gaze lifted up to the high ceiling. No, it was more like a jail cell.

Footsteps caused the ceiling above her to creak. There was a floor above her. She moved her head slightly, looking around. No windows. One stone wall in the back, and wooden bars on three sides. No windows anywhere. Was she underground?

Her hand slipped up to her chest to grasp the jade dragon. If it was nighttime, Dougal would be looking for her. They would all be looking for her. And she had the tracking device in her forearm.

She heaved a sigh of relief. No doubt a rescue team was on its way.

"I know you're awake, bitch," a voice snarled in Chinese. "You're not fooling anyone."

Her heart lurched. Was that a guard? She eased to a sitting position, looking around. A figure slipped out of the shadows and approached the wooden grid to her right. A prisoner in the cell next to her. As he moved into the light, she recognized him. The soldier from the basement at Romatech.

But he had remained loyal to Master Han. Why was he in jail? "Why are you here?"

He snorted. "So you remember me. It's all your fault, bitch." He motioned toward the front of her cell. "Did you want your supper? If not, I'll take it."

She rose slowly to her feet. "Are we alone?"

"For the time being." He motioned again. "Your food?"

She wandered toward the front of her cell. The cell to her left appeared empty. A narrow corridor ran in front of the three cells, ending with a stone wall to her right and a narrow staircase to her left. "Are we underground?"

The other prisoner scoffed. "Are you planning an escape? There's only one way out of Darafer's dungeon. Well, make that two."

She turned toward him. "How?"

"You join him. Or you die." He motioned to her food. "Come on, bitch. I'm hungry."

She spotted a folded blanket near the locked door. And next to that a tray holding a bowl and spoon and a tin cup filled with water. She dipped the spoon into the bowl. It was some sort of rice porridge, cold and runny. She lifted the cup of water and sniffed. A tiny sip. No strange aftertaste. After seeing what had happened at the zombie village, she was suspicious of any food or drink from Darafer.

On the other hand, she wouldn't last long without food or water. And she had to keep her strength up. She drank half the cup and took one bite of porridge before sliding the tray close to the next cell. She'd let her foul-mouthed neighbor eat the rest of the porridge and see if he exhibited any signs of being drugged.

Instead of reaching for the food, the prisoner made a grab at her, and she jumped back.

He sneered. "I'm trying to do you a favor, bitch. Wouldn't you rather die by my hands before Darafer starts on you?"

"Why would you want to kill me? I was trying to help you."

"Help me?" He spit through the bars at her. "I lost my superstrength, and now Darafer says I'm damaged! You destroyed me, bitch, and you'll pay for it!"

"Enough, Guang," a voice came from the stairs. "It's my turn to welcome our guest."

Leah suppressed a shudder at the sound of that cold voice. Darafer had come for his revenge.

He reached the base of the stairs, moving into the torchlight. She stepped back, steeling her nerves.

Her neighbor, Guang, fell to his knees. "Have mercy on me, Master. Return me to my former glory, I beg of you, so I can serve you."

Darafer cast an annoyed look at Guang. "How can I change you back when Dr. Chin and her friends have burned my supply of demon herb?"

"Then let me kill her for you!"

Darafer snorted. "And take away my fun? I think not." He crossed his arms, regarding Leah with an amused twist to his mouth. "It would be a shame to kill someone as smart as you. I'd much rather use you."

Leah kept her mouth shut. He'd have a harder time playing cat and mouse with her if she refused to play.

Darafer approached the bars and leaned his forearms on a horizontal beam. "How do you like your new home?"

She remained quiet.

"You could live in luxury and have everything you ever wanted." He shrugged. "All you would have to do is join me. Why don't you show your parents how smart you really are? If you join me, you could rule the world. You would be superior to your brothers. And all the jerks who bullied you in school—you could make them squirm."

She stayed quiet.

"Do you really think your side has a chance? You saw what happened. Your shifter friends couldn't stop me. Your vampire friends can't stop me, either. Why don't you join the winning team?"

She crossed her arms. *Join the evil team? Never.*

"You're going to resist, aren't you?" Darafer smiled slowly. "I was hoping you would. I do love a challenge."

She swallowed hard, and her hand moved to the jade dragon on her chest. *Stay strong. Dougal will be here soon.*

Darafer chuckled. "Perhaps I should tell you. After all, it would be a shame for you to get your hopes up." His face turned harsh. "There is no hope for you. That stupid device in your arm has been removed and destroyed. There will be no rescue."

A chill skittered down her back, and her hand clenched the dragon tighter. How would Dougal find her?

Darafer tilted his head, studying her. "You still think your lover will charge to the rescue? How will he find you?"

Her eyes burned. She couldn't give up. Dougal would come. He loved her.

Darafer snorted. "You think he'll stay true to you? Don't you know you're just a replacement?"

She flinched. She wouldn't listen. Marielle had warned her that he'd know the best way to manipulate her.

"Dougal is his name, right?" Darafer sneered. "He had his first and only love almost three hundred years ago. You're a cheap copy. Easy to find, and easy to replace. Come on, be honest. He got you into his bed easily, didn't he?"

She stepped back. She couldn't listen to this. It was too crude, too cruel, too . . . true? She shook her head. No, Dougal loved her.

"I'll give you some time to think about it." Darafer

ascended the stairs. "By the way, Lord Qing has come to visit. I might bring him downstairs to meet you. If he gets hungry."

With a chuckle, Darafer passed out of her view. A door slammed, and the grate of a key echoed down the stairs.

Guang laughed as he reached through the bars to grab her bowl of gruel. "You're going to be lunch, bitch."

Chapter Twenty-nine

*N*o rescue? And she would be fed to a vampire? Leah sank to the floor, shivering as she hugged her knees.

Get a grip, she told herself. *Don't panic. Darafer wants you to panic.*

She took deep breaths to calm herself. She would think about this logically. Rationally. Darafer wasn't going to kill her. He wanted her alive so he could use her. And he wanted her to panic so she would be easy to manipulate. *Be smart about this. Stay focused.*

She rose to her feet and strode toward the front of her cell. Starting on the left, she tried each horizontal and vertical bar.

Snickering came from the cell to her right. "You think you can escape, bitch?"

Maybe not, but she would be prepared for all possibilities. She tested the lock on the door. It was firm. She didn't dare get close to her neighbor, so she checked the wooden grid on the left by the empty cell.

Marielle had been right. Darafer knew which wounds to pick at and which fears to manipulate. Surprisingly enough, his digs about her family and so-called college friends hadn't bothered her at all. It was a good sign if those wounds were healed. She'd grown stronger and more confident since she'd started her new job with the Vamps.

She halted, recalling Darafer's claim that her tracking device had been removed. Why should she believe a demon? She pushed her sweater up to her elbow to examine her forearm. It was hard to see well in the dim light, but she couldn't spot any recent incisions. She smoothed her fingers over the spot where the device had been inserted just below the skin. Smooth. The slight bump was gone.

Her heart sank. Darafer had told the truth. What other truths had he thrown at her? *You're just a re-placement.*

With a shake of her head, she shoved that thought aside. Darafer was simply trying to mess her up, make her give up hope, so she would join him.

She strode to the back wall to examine it. A flimsy screen woven of straw sectioned off a small space that contained a chamber pot. *Lovely.* She wrinkled her nose. At least she wouldn't have to relieve her-self in full view of her surly neighbor.

Guang had wrapped himself in his blanket to go to sleep. Was he naturally tired, or had the porridge been drugged? She sighed. There was no way to be sure.

She resumed her examination of the back wall, pushing at each stone. *A replacement. A cheap copy. Easy to find and easy to replace.* She shook her head. *Don't think about it.* But she had fallen into bed with Dougal easily. She'd known him less than a month when they'd first made love at her apartment.

Her hands stilled. What had Dougal said that

night? *I'll never lose you again.* And just last night in the palace at Tiger Town, Rajiv's grandfather had asked him if he'd found love *again.* Dougal had said yes.

She paced across the cell. Dougal was centuries old. Of course he'd had other girlfriends. Did she really expect to be his first?

He had his first and only love almost three hundred years ago, Darafer's words came back to her. His first and only?

I've waited so long for you. How many times had Dougal told her that? He'd even admitted that he'd waited almost three hundred years.

A replacement. A cheap copy.

She grasped the jade dragon. Dougal loved her. She had to believe in him. This was nothing more than Darafer's preferred method of torture. How could she believe anything a demon told her?

Her eyes burned. Then why did Dougal's own words condemn him? *I'll never lose you again.*

She hunched down, hugging her knees. *Don't panic. Darafer wants you to panic.*

Her mind raced, trying to remember everything Marielle had told her. She had free will, so Darafer couldn't force her. Of course that didn't mean he wouldn't torture her or feed her to vampires.

She took deep breaths. *Don't give up hope.* There had to be a way.

With a start, she recalled something Marielle had said. She jumped to her feet and looked around. "Josephine?"

No response.

She narrowed her eyes, trying to see her guardian

angel. "Josephine? You're there, aren't you? Can you help me?"

"Who the hell are you talking to?" Guang muttered in Chinese.

She slumped. There was no sign of an angel.

"Shut up, bitch. I'm trying to sleep."

"**M**iss. Wake up, miss."

Leah blinked, coming fully awake. She wasn't sure how much time had passed, but eventually she'd grown tired enough to lie down on her blanket. Even then, she'd been too tense to fall into a deep sleep.

"Miss." The insistent whispering continued in Chinese.

She sat up, her hand automatically going to the jade necklace. Guang was snoring in his cell. A dark figure was crouched in front of her cell.

She scrambled closer, but not too close in case he tried to grab her through the bars like Guang had tried earlier.

"Are you Doctor Chin?" the figure whispered. He had a male voice and was dressed in black with a hood covering the upper half his face.

"Yes. I'm Leah Chin."

"You saved the people at the demon herb village."

It seemed more like a statement than a question, but Leah responded, "Yes."

"My sister and her family live there. Yu Jie says they would have died if you hadn't saved them."

"You know Yu Jie?"

"She's my niece." The figure backed away.

"Wait." Leah moved forward. "Can you help me? Can you get me out of here?"

The man dashed up the stairs.

"Wait," Leah called louder.

The door creaked shut.

"I need help!"

"Shut up, bitch," Guang snarled. "I'm trying to sleep."

At sunset, Dougal woke with a jolt. He breathed deeply, and Leah's scent of jasmine filled his senses.

I'll find you, Leah. I willna fail you.

After a quick breakfast bottle, the Vamps teleported to their assigned sites. Dougal crept around the camp, listening in on conversations. No mention of a lady prisoner or Darafer. She wasn't here.

He left the rest of his unit behind and teleported to more sites, one after another. No sign of her. Angus called to fuss at him for not following orders. Dougal hung up on him and continued to check all the camps.

Two hours later, he called Angus on his sat phone. "She's no' at any of these camps!"

"They may be keeping her hidden," Angus replied.

"I'm telling you she's somewhere else! Some place we doona know about. I say we gather our forces and attack one of the camps. Take the commander hostage and make him tell us where they're hiding her."

"I'd rather no' attack a camp," Angus grumbled.

"We would end up killing the soldiers, and the whole purpose of this mission was to avoid killing them."

"Ye think I care!"

Angus materialized beside him and took hold of his shoulder. "Get a grip, Dougal."

His eyes burned. "I canna fail her. Do ye understand?"

"Aye. I know how ye feel. I was ready to die to save Emma. We'll get through this. Ye must have faith."

Dougal snorted, punching the off button on his sat phone. "I'd rather use my sword right now."

"I understand."

Dougal took a deep breath. "They have camps we doona know about." They needed more information. Intelligence. "We need spies."

Angus tilted his head, considering. "They would have to be local. Maybe some of the were-tigers could infiltrate?"

"Or some of the people we saved from the zombie village," Dougal suggested.

Angus nodded. "Let's go back to Tiger Town to make plans."

The creaking sound of the door woke Leah. She sat up, grasping her jade necklace. Her heart pounded as she waited for the dark figures on the stairs to venture into the torchlight.

They were women. Servants, she guessed by the way they remained bent over, their heads down. Each one carried a tray, which they slipped between the bars of the two occupied cells.

"Thank you," Leah said in Chinese. She smiled at her servant, but the woman refused to look at her.

"Can you tell me what time it is?" Leah asked. "Is it nighttime yet?"

No answer. The women scurried up the stairs, and the door creaked shut.

Leah tasted the water, then gulped some down. The porridge was hot, so she ate a few bites. In the cell next to her, Guang was wolfing down his porridge. Darafer had claimed he couldn't fix Guang, since he was out of demon herb. If that was true, then the porridge was probably safe. At any rate, she was hungry, so she ate.

Was it nighttime? She had no idea how many hours had passed. If the sun had set, then Dougal would be looking for her. All the Vamps would be awake and searching for her. But then Lord Qing would be awake, too.

She shoved that thought aside. There was no sense in frightening herself. Things were scary enough—

The door creaked open.

She moved back, taking the spoon with her. Her search of the cell earlier had yielded no weapons, unless she knocked someone out with the chamber pot.

Two figures descended the stairs. One was dressed all in black. Darafer. The other: he wore a robe of embroidered red silk. His long black hair was braided down his back, and his long yellowish fingernails curled like claws.

Darafer reached the base of the stairs and turned toward her, his mouth twisting with a smirk. "Suppertime!"

Guang snickered.

"Allow me to introduce your dinner partner." Darafer motioned to the man beside him. "Lord Qing."

The vampire looked her over and smiled, revealing yellow pointed teeth.

Leah stepped back, sliding the spoon up the sleeve of her sweater. Maybe if she struck with enough force, she could stake the vampire with the spoon handle.

Lord Qing teleported into her cell and advanced toward her slowly.

"I could stop him, you know." Darafer leaned his forearms on some horizontal bars. "All you have to do is join me."

Leah steeled her nerves, preparing herself for the impending attack. Dougal would be so disappointed if she didn't do a kickass job of defending herself.

Lord Qing zoomed forward, and she whipped out the spoon, aiming at his chest. Suddenly, she was tossed back onto her rear, and the spoon went flying through the air. Shocked, she watched it shoot straight into Darafer's hand.

He laughed, showing her the spoon. "You were going to defeat me with this?"

She scrambled to her feet.

Darafer's smile disappeared, replaced with a cold, harsh glare. "You will be attacked. The only way to stop it is to join me."

Lord Qing pounced on her with vampire speed, pushing her back onto the ground. She struggled, but his superior strength kept her pinned down. His fangs popped out, long, lethal, and sharp.

Guang giggled. "Bite her, bite her!"

Leah shook her head, but Lord Qing pressed down on her and held her head still.

She gritted her teeth. This wouldn't kill her. *Think of it as a blood donation.* She'd donated before. It was no big deal.

"I can stop him," Darafer whispered. "You know what to do."

She bit her lip. Darafer wasn't going to let her die. He wanted her alive.

The fangs scraped her neck.

"Stop," Darafer said.

Lord Qing hissed, opening his mouth to bite.

"I said stop." Suddenly Darafer was inside her cell, and with a flick of his hand, Lord Qing fell back.

Darafer gave her an annoyed look. "You won't join me to save yourself?"

Lord Qing stood, his eyes glowing. "You promised me blood," he hissed with his fangs still protruding.

Darafer motioned to the next cell. "Feed on him. Drain him dry if you want."

Guang gasped, then screamed when Lord Qing teleported into his cell. "No! Save me, master!"

The vampire leaped on him and sank his fangs into his neck.

With a sick churning in her stomach, Leah looked away. But she could still hear the sucking noises.

"He's going to die, you know." Darafer crossed his arms. "Since you refuse to save yourself, maybe you'll save someone else. I'll stop the vampire if you ask me to. If you agree to join me."

Leah squeezed her eyes shut. How could she agree to be evil?

"It's hopeless, you know," Darafer whispered. "If

you let him die, I'll just bring in more to kill. Maybe a few children could change your mind."

"Stop."

"Hmm. It might be too late for Guang. I think he's a goner."

"Stop!" She rose to her feet.

Darafer smiled. "Are you agreeing to join me?"

"I will not let you kill anyone." She lifted her chin. "But get this straight, demon. You might force me to do evil, but I will never agree to it. I have free will, and you can't take that away from me."

Darafer's eyes narrowed. "You think so?" His face grew harsh and ugly. "You think you can outsmart me with your precious free will? I'll show you how weak and pathetic you are!"

He morphed into a large black wolf with glowing red eyes. With a snarl, he advanced toward her.

Leah ran, but there was nowhere to go. Soon he had her cornered. *God help me*, she thought just as he pounced.

She cried out when his jaws clamped down on her shoulder.

Chapter Thirty

$\mathcal{D}$ougal paced impatiently in the courtyard at Tiger Town. The were-tiger men had agreed to help them attack one of Master Han's camps, but the idea of spying didn't appeal to them. None of them wanted to be separated from their families for the months the job might require. Only Rajiv's cousin Jia had volunteered.

"Absolutely not!" Rajiv fussed at her in Chinese. "It's too dangerous."

"I'm going!" Jia ascended a step on the staircase leading to the palace so she could stand eye to eye with her cousin. "My parents were slaughtered by Master Han, so I have every right to seek revenge. Just as much as you!"

Rajiv planted his hands on his hips. "You're too young and pretty. The vampire lords will want to feed on you."

"Let them try." Jia drew a dagger from her belt.

"They're stronger than you!" Rajiv yelled. "They'll force you into being a concubine."

She turned pale.

Dougal groaned. As desperate as he was to find

Leah, he couldn't allow an innocent girl to endanger herself.

"Jia," a voice called from the palace. The Grand Tiger descended the steps. "You will not go. I will."

"Grandfather, no!" Rajiv shouted.

The Grand Tiger gave him a stern look. "I will go. They will not suspect an old man who begs to be their servant."

"But Your Eminence—," Rajiv started, but his grandfather waved him into silence.

"I grow tired of sitting on the throne all day," the Grand Tiger said. "I wish to end my days doing something useful for my people." He turned to Dougal and motioned toward Angus. "Tell your leader that I will infiltrate Master Han's camp and spy for you."

"What's going on?" Angus asked in English.

"His Eminence wants to spy for us." Dougal clenched his prosthetic hand. "This isn't going to work. It could take days to get a spy established in a camp and weeks before he could learn anything useful. We need to act now!"

"I understand yer—" Angus halted when bright lights suddenly lit up the sky. "What the hell?"

"It's a sign from the heavens!" the Grand Tiger exclaimed. He rushed down the remaining steps and knelt in the courtyard.

Rajiv rushed to his grandfather's side, and Jia took the other side, her dagger still drawn.

Dougal held a hand over his eyes as the light grew stronger and closer.

On the riverbank, were-tigers gathered, pointing at the sky.

The light divided into seven balls of fire that

zoomed down to the courtyard, then hovered just inches above the stone pavement. Each fireball took on the shape of a man. Tall men, each one holding a sword extended toward the sky. Their figures flickered in the heat of the flames, then with a whooshing sound, the flames receded, rushing up their bodies and down their extended arms, till only their swords were left ablaze.

They wore pants and sleeveless tunics of royal blue. Gold bands circled their upper arms and wrists, and their chests were armored with breastplates of gleaming gold. Each one had shoulder-length hair, held back with a slender gold circlet that crossed their foreheads.

One stood in front of the other six, and when he turned his sword of fire, pointing it down to the ground, the others followed suit. They all lowered their arms, and when the tips of their swords tapped the pavement, the fires extinguished with another swoosh.

Rajiv and Jia fell to their knees beside their grandfather, and all three bowed.

Dougal leaned close and whispered in Chinese, "Does this happen here often?"

Rajiv shook his head. "Never."

"We are blessed," the Grand Tiger whispered.

Angus cleared his throat. "Welcome."

The leader gave them a curious look. "Fear not, dear souls. The Heavenly Father loves you greatly."

Dougal exchanged a look with Angus. "They must be angels."

The leader bowed his head. "You are correct. I am Briathos, commander of the Epsilons, fifth unit of the God Warriors."

A surge of hope swelled in Dougal's chest. "Then you've come to help us?"

Briathos sheathed his sword. "Our mission concerns the demon, Darafer."

"Great!" Dougal strode toward them. "Let's go. We need to rescue Leah."

Briathos held up a hand to stop him, then turned to Angus. "You will gather your forces here so we can attack."

"Right." Angus retrieved his sat phone from his sporran. "Rajiv, go wake up the shifters."

Rajiv dashed off to the guesthouses, while Angus quickly made some calls.

The Vamps teleported in, and after listening to Angus's quick explanation, they gawked at the angelic newcomers. Dougal studied them, too. The more he stared at them, the more solid they became, and the more detailed. Briathos had blue eyes and golden brown hair. The others behind him had hair ranging from blond to black.

What Dougal found strange was that if he looked away, then glanced back, their images seemed to shimmer for a few seconds before sharpening into focus once again. It was as if they were there, but not really there. He tried to recall everything Marielle had said about them. Most likely, they wouldn't kill Darafer but send him back to hell. That was fine with Dougal, as long as Leah was safe.

Connor approached him, smiling. "We'll be able to find Leah now."

Dougal nodded, then stepped toward the angels. "How is she? How is Leah?"

Briathos hesitated. The Epsilons behind him exchanged looks, then their leader finally answered,

"Her guardian angel is in contact with us. She is . . . alive."

Dougal's heart stuttered. Something was wrong. Terribly wrong. "If you're able to get involved, then that means Darafer has broken a rule?"

"The decree of free will has been violated," Briathos said quietly. "A child of God has been forced into evil."

A chill swept down Dougal's spine. "Who?"

Briathos regarded him sadly. "Leah Chin."

"No!" Dougal roared. He clenched his hands and shouted his rage to the heavens. Blood rushed to his head till he thought he would explode. With another shout, he smashed his prosthetic hand into the tiger statue, demolishing its head.

"Dougal!" Connor pulled him back. "We need to stay strong."

He shoved Connor back. "He should have taken me!" The damned demon should have taken him. Not Leah. She hadn't even wanted to learn how to shoot, she'd been so fearful of hurting someone. How could she survive surrounded by evil? How could he have failed her so completely?

"Everyone, prepare yerselves," Angus ordered. "We're going into battle."

The Vamps and shifters rushed off to the nearby building where extra weapons and ammo had been stashed.

Dougal strode toward the God Warriors. "How can I save her from evil?"

Briathos sighed. "There is no cure for a demon bite."

Dougal's prosthetic hand snapped into a tight fist. "He bit her?"

"He took the shape of a black wolf and bit her. She has been infused with evil. The only way to save her is to return Darafer to hell. Then she will return to normal."

"Then let's do it!" Dougal drew his claymore. "Where is she? Take me to her now!"

Briathos regarded him calmly. "All will be revealed in due course."

"What? What the hell does that mean?"

Briathos arched a brow. "It means all will be revealed in due course."

"I want to go now, dammit!"

"Dougal," Connor whispered. "Be respectful to the angel."

"I'm going crazy!" Dougal shouted, then turned back to Briathos. "Where is she?"

"You will have your answer—"

"When?" Dougal yelled.

Briathos frowned. "Soon."

Dougal stalked away, shouting his frustration. What did *soon* mean to an angel? A thousand years?

The Vamps and shifters returned to the courtyard, armed to the teeth. Rajiv's cousin Jia had joined them, armed with a sword and three daggers.

Headlights glowed in the distance as a vehicle approached the village. Were-tigers gathered around the jeep as it came to a stop on the riverbank.

"Dougal, behold." Briathos motioned to the jeep. "Your answer has come. And Leah's good work has been rewarded."

The were-tigers escorted the driver of the jeep up the stairs to the courtyard.

He was dressed in black with a long, hooded robe. When he pushed the hood back, J.L. gasped.

"Wu Shen?" J.L. approached him. "What are you doing here?"

"Who is that?" Angus demanded.

"He's one of Master Han's top officers," Dougal explained.

Wu Shen gave them all a wary look. "I trust you will not kill me since I come with valuable information. I know where Dr. Leah Chin is being held."

"Why should we trust you?" J.L. asked. "You could be leading us into a trap."

Wu Shen lifted his arms. "I carry no weapons. I am at your mercy. My sister and her family were from the village that Dr. Chin saved. My niece, Yu Jie, told me how they were enslaved. I will take you to Darafer's camp."

"How many men does he have?" J.L. asked.

"Forty-five soldiers," Wu Shen replied. "Several servants. And Lord Qing is there."

Rajiv sucked in a breath. "Did you hear that, Grandfather? I will avenge my father."

"I will come with you," the Grand Tiger said.

"Me, too," Jia added.

"How far away is it?" Dougal asked in Chinese.

"About three hours by car," Wu Shen answered.

"Or three seconds if you travel with us," Briathos added, then gave Dougal a wry look. "Will that be fast enough for you?"

Leah jerked awake, her vision blurred with a red haze, and her head pounding with a constant throb of raging emotion. *Hate. Hate. Hate.*

Anger slithered through her veins. Fury scorched

her skin, hot and relentless. She wanted death. Destruction. Suffering.

She jumped to her feet and stretched. A surge of power rippled through her muscles. She was strong. Invincible. Her heart thundered in rhythm to her pounding head.

Hate. Hate. Hate.

She glanced over at the neighboring cell, where Guang lay, his throat ripped out, his clothes drenched in blood.

And she smiled.

"That's my girl." Darafer moved from the shadow, his eyes gleaming with pride.

"Master." She recognized him at once and bowed her head. Only her master could be so beautiful. "How may I serve you?"

He unlocked the prison door. "We have much to do, you and I. Together, we will create a new race."

"Yes." She strode from the cell. She would be invincible. All-powerful.

"We will rule the world."

"Yes!" How fortunate she was that the master had chosen her. "Thank you, Master. I will do anything for you."

"Will you die for me?"

"Gladly." Her mouth twisted. "But I'd rather kill for you."

With a chuckle, he led her toward the stairs. "Let me take you to your new quarters. You will be dressed in the finest silks. And have the finest weapons. In case I wish you to kill for me."

"Yes, Master." She ascended the stairs by his side, each step reiterating the pounding rhythm in her head. *Hate, hate, hate.*

* * *

Dougal studied the wooden barricade that surrounded Darafer's camp. He and twenty-six Vamps and shifters had been joined by ten more weretigers, including the Grand Tiger and his granddaughter, Jia. Briathos had brought them all here with a flick of his hand. He stood nearby with his unit of six God Warriors.

Wu Shen had said there were forty-five soldiers inside, so their forces were fairly well matched. He'd come along but had decided to remain hidden in the woods during the battle. Angus had readily agreed. This way, Wu Shen could retain his position in Master Han's army and, hopefully, help them again someday.

"We could teleport in," Angus suggested. "A surprise attack."

Dougal shook his head. "You might surprise the soldiers, but it would give Darafer and Lord Qing advance warning and they would teleport away." And maybe take Leah with them.

"Darafer must not know that we have come," Briathos said. "Once we have surrounded him with seven swords of fire, he will be trapped and unable to escape."

"Jia and I have an idea." Rajiv briefly described their plan. "J.L. said he'd do it with us."

"Your idea has merit," Briathos announced. "You may begin."

Angus gave Rajiv a wry look. "I think I've been outranked. Go ahead. We'll be ready."

Rajiv and J.L. left the cover of the trees, walking toward the camp and dragging Jia with them. She put on quite a show, cursing them and resisting, but they hauled her up to the front gate.

"What is your business here?" a soldier yelled down from the ramparts overlooking the gate.

"I wish to join Master Han's army." Rajiv motioned to J.L. "My friend wants to join, too."

The soldier snorted. "And why have you brought the girl?"

"She's a gift," J.L. explained. "So you will accept us."

Rajiv pushed Jia down onto her knees. "We heard you have a vampire lord who likes pretty young girls."

The soldier hesitated, then whispered to another soldier, who rushed off. "We will inform Lord Qing of your gift. You will wait for his reply."

"Thank you." Rajiv grabbed Jia, who attempted to scramble away.

A few minutes later, the gate opened, and Lord Qing emerged.

"No!" Jia screamed, but Rajiv and J.L. held her tight.

Lord Qing's fangs popped out, and with a hissing sound, he grabbed Jia. She kicked him hard in the groin, and as he doubled over, howling in pain, J.L. whipped a silver chain around him to prevent him from teleporting away.

"This is for killing my father!" Rajiv pulled out a dagger and stabbed Lord Qing in the heart, turning him to dust.

Soldiers ran through the gate, shouting. Jia slashed at them with her dagger. J.L. and Rajiv pulled out swords they had hidden beneath their coats. The Vamps and shifters ran forward, their swords drawn, and the battle grew loud with the clanging of metal and the screams of the wounded and dying.

Dougal and a handful of Vamps charged through the gate to fight the soldiers in the open courtyard. Briathos and his God Warriors zoomed past them toward the main building. Probably looking for Darafer, Dougal thought as he slashed his way toward the stairs that led up to the building. All he wanted was Leah. Was she inside?

He glanced up and froze. She had emerged from the building, dressed in red silk with a dagger in each hand. It wasn't the weapons that shocked him but the furious expression of hatred on her face.

Darafer stood by her side, gazing down at the battle, his mouth twisted with contempt. "These soldiers are too weak. We will create an army that is even stronger!"

Leah nodded, her eyes gleaming.

"You're going back to hell," Briathos announced, suddenly appearing at Darafer's side with his sword ablaze.

Darafer stumbled back, his face growing pale as he realized he was surrounded by God Warriors and seven swords of fire.

He pulled Leah in front of him.

"No!" Dougal ran toward the stairs. Unfortunately, he had to battle a few soldiers on the way. He quickly dispatched them to hell and reached the base of the stairs.

Darafer saw him and pushed Leah forward. "Kill him for me."

"Kill, kill," Leah repeated as she started down the stairs.

Dougal lowered his sword. Tears burned his eyes

as he saw the hatred on her face. This was his fault. He'd failed to protect her.

"Kill him!" Darafer yelled. "If I have to go back to hell, then I'll make you live in hell!"

With an angry shout, Leah rushed toward Dougal.

"No!" The Grand Tiger leaped in front just as Leah's dagger struck. He stiffened with a gasp, then collapsed against Dougal.

"No!" Dougal grabbed the elderly man and eased him to the ground. Blood poured from his wound. "Why did you . . . ?"

The Grand Tiger looked up at him, gasping for air. "For true love." His eyes flickered shut.

"No!" Rajiv ran toward them.

A long, howling screech pierced the air. Dougal looked up to see Darafer stabbed through with seven swords of fire. His body wavered, then vanished.

Leah jolted and stumbled on the stairs. Her daggers fell from her hands and clattered on the stone steps. She looked down at Dougal and the Grand Tiger, and her dagger stained with blood. Her eyes widened in horror.

"What have you done?" Rajiv yelled at her.

She fell to her knees and screamed.

Chapter Thirty-one

*D*ougal carried a tray of soup to Leah's dorm room on the Japanese island. She was sitting on her bed, her knees clasped to her chest, her eyes red and swollen from crying.

She didn't say a word as he approached. Refused to even look at him. At least she'd stopped screaming. The pain in her screams had torn at his heart. Even Rajiv's and Jia's rage had dissipated as Leah's screams of anguish had continued on and on.

With the battle over, some of the Vamps had teleported the were-tigers and their fallen leader back to Tiger Town. The rest of the Vamps and shifters had returned to the renovated school.

Briathos had stopped by, informing them that he would continue to monitor their situation. Darafer had been safely dispatched to hell, but if twelve of his disciples formed a ring and called for him, he might manage to escape. Briathos assured them, though, that Darafer's arrogance had most likely given him a false sense of invincibility, causing him to neglect training his followers on how to retrieve him from hell. Dougal could only hope that was true, and that they'd seen the last of the demon who had traumatized Leah.

"I brought you some soup." Dougal placed the tray on the bedside table and perched on the edge of the bed. "And some lemonade. Ye like lemonade, aye?" He handed her the glass.

She didn't look at him or take the glass.

"Leah, ye must stay strong so ye can recover."

No response.

With a sigh, he set the glass down. "Ye still have important work to do here. Abby says the serums are working and the mutated soldiers are changing back. With Darafer gone, he canna interfere. We can bring in lots of soldiers, and ye can save them."

She frowned, then asked with a voice hoarse from screaming, "How is Rajiv? And Jia?"

"They're . . . all right. They're staying strong. We all have to be strong."

A tear rolled down her cheek.

"Something a bit surprising happened," Dougal continued, trying to pique her interest. "It turns out the Grand Tiger left a will declaring Rajiv as his heir. It has all of Tiger Town worked up that the Grand Tiger bypassed his sons to choose Rajiv."

Leah blinked. "I think Rajiv would make a great leader."

"Me, too." Dougal smiled. "But I hear Tiger Town is divided on the issue. Some are saying Rajiv should be their leader because they need to follow the Grand Tiger's wishes, and Rajiv brought in allies to battle Master Han, and he killed Lord Qing. But others are saying he's too young and inexperienced, and they're angry that he brought in foreigners who caused—" He stopped when he realized where he was headed.

"Caused what?" Leah grimaced. "Caused the

death of their leader? Why word it so nicely when I murdered him?"

"Leah—"

"It's true!" More tears ran down her face. "I killed him! And I would have killed you if he hadn't stepped in the way."

"I wouldna have let you kill me."

"You don't understand. I wanted to kill you!" She angrily wiped away tears. "How can you stand to look at me?"

"Ye were no' yerself. Darafer bit you, Leah. He forced evil on you. Ye had no choice—"

"Oh, the devil made me do it." She scoffed. "Where have I heard that excuse before? I'm no better than any other murderer out there."

"That is no' true! Connor called Marielle to tell her what happened, and she said ye mustna blame yerself, that no one can resist the demon bite. Pure evil was unleashed into yer bloodstream. Even the toughest of angels, the God Warriors, succumb to it. If they canna resist it, how did ye ever have a chance?"

She shook her head. "That doesn't take away the result. I killed Rajiv's grandfather. That beautiful old man is dead because I killed him! How can I live with that? Whenever I look in a mirror, all I see is a murderer!" She turned away and closed her eyes. "Leave me alone. Please."

The next evening when Dougal awoke, he rushed upstairs to see Leah. She was curled on her bed, sleeping, her hand clasping the jade dragon necklace. A tray of untouched food sat on the bedside table.

He trudged into the cafeteria to warm up a bottle of breakfast blood.

Abby was sitting with her husband and waved him over. "I'm worried about Leah," she said as he sat down. "She hasn't eaten a thing all day. And she doesn't get out of bed except to go to the restroom."

Gregori patted his wife's hand. "It's natural for her to be depressed. Maybe in time—"

"If she doesn't eat or drink, she won't have much time," Abby insisted, then turned to Dougal. "If you can't get her to eat, I'm putting an IV in her."

Dougal nodded. "I understand." He understood that he'd failed her. If he had protected her, she wouldn't be suffering now. "I looked in on her, and she was sleeping."

"Good." Abby sighed. "For hours she was having nightmares, and she kept waking up screaming."

"Maybe we should bring Olivia here," Gregori suggested. "Or Marielle. Someone who can help her get through this."

Abby's eyes glistened with tears. "I'm afraid she'll never get through it."

A few hours later, when Leah had wakened, Dougal brought her a tray of food and begged her to eat.

When she ignored him, he grew angry. "How can ye give up like this? I love you, Leah. We can have centuries together, but ye must be strong."

"I was going to kill you."

"That wasna you! Leah, I know how hard it is to live with regret and shame, but ye can do it. I've been doing it for almost three hundred years. Did I ever tell you how I escaped slavery?"

"No. What happened?" She looked at him, and he took her interest as a positive sign.

"I had my tin whistle with me, and I played it every night to comfort myself and the other slaves. What I dinna realize was that the master's daughter was outside my hut every night listening. Then one night, I heard crying, and I looked out the window and saw her. I thought she was a servant girl, so I talked to her. She came every night, and we talked."

"She was your first and only love," Leah whispered.

"My first. After a few years, she figured out a way to save me. When we were running to the harbor, I told her I was afraid my brand would label me as a runaway slave and get us both into trouble. It was her idea for me to get the tattoo to cover the brand. The next morning, she paid a ship to take me on as it was leaving port. I wanted to stay with her forever, but she knew her father would never accept me. I promised to make a fortune and return for her as a man worthy of her. I told her I would find her again. No matter what. I would find her again if it took a thousand years. I spent a few years pirating and amassed some wealth, but when I went back for her, she'd been sent away, forced to marry against her will."

"So you lost her?"

Dougal shook his head. "She was being sent to her new husband on a boat going up the Yangtze River. I followed after her, and I had almost caught up with her. I could see her boat, but then a storm blew in, and her boat capsized. I dove in to save her, but I was too late." He looked away with tears in his eyes.

"I failed her. She saved me from slavery, and I failed her."

Leah frowned. "The storm killed her. Not you."

"If I had never left her, she would have lived. Or if I had returned just a day earlier, she would have lived."

"It's not the same," Leah insisted. "You didn't kill her. I did kill."

"It is the same. Darafer's evil possessed you and forced you. It was beyond yer control, just like a storm. Ye canna blame yerself."

She turned away. "Darafer told me about her, that she was your one and only love."

"I love you, Leah."

She scowled at him. "You said it yourself, that you'd waited three hundred years, that you wouldn't lose me again. I'm just a replacement. A cheap copy of the girl you loved three hundred years ago."

"Nay! Leah, ye're different. If some part of Li Lei's soul has found a way to come back to me, then it isna something ye're aware of. It doesna make you who ye are. Ye've accomplished things that Li Lei could never imagine. There's no one like you."

Her eyes narrowed. "Why would you think she's in me?"

"Her father was a merchant. The family name was Ka, which means merchant. Her name was Ka Li Lei. And ye're Galileah."

She flinched. "It's just a strange coincidence. I can't be her."

"It doesna matter to me. Ye're still Leah, and I love you as ye are. Ye're strong and brave and the most brilliant woman I've ever met. How could I no' love you?"

Her face crumpled. "But you fell for me because of her. You were waiting three hundred years for a replacement."

Dammit. He shouldn't have told her about Li Lei. He had thought sharing his story of regret and shame would comfort her and let her know she wasn't alone, but it had only made things worse.

Tears filled his eyes. "I waited three hundred years for a chance to love again, and it is you I love, Leah. How can I prove to you that I love you? Ye are the one I want for the rest of my life."

She turned away, a tear running down her face. "How can you want me? I'm a killer. I tried to kill you."

"Leah, please. Doona give up on yerself."

"Leave me alone. Please."

When she continued to ignore him, Dougal strode from the room, ready to hit something. He charged outside and saw Briathos standing on the bluff, looking at the sea.

"Why were you so slow?" Dougal demanded. "If you had dispatched Darafer to hell just a few seconds earlier, then his hold on Leah would have been broken, and she wouldna have killed!"

Briathos regarded him sadly, then turned to look at the sea once more.

"Do ye know how much she's suffering?" Dougal asked. The cold wind whipped at his face, making his eyes tear up. "She wants to die! Do ye even care?"

"Of course I care." Briathos sighed. "You may question *what if* for hours, but a truth remains that cannot be avoided." He faced Dougal. "When a child of God is consumed with evil, there is always a price to pay."

"She dinna ask for evil!"

"She was consumed nonetheless. The price must be paid." He wavered, then disappeared.

Dougal stood there, watching the waves crash on the shore. A price must be paid.

His eyes stung with tears. She was suffering so much. He couldn't bear to watch it. And now she even doubted that he loved her. How could he prove he loved her? How could he ease her suffering?

He could pay the price for her.

The idea flickered in his mind, and with desperation, he latched on to it and let it grow. It was in his power to take the pain away from her.

He strode into the school and headed for the lab. Laszlo and Gu Mina were seated together at his worktable, and Abby and Gregori were at her table.

Abby sat up. "Did you get her to eat?"

"Nay."

Abby exchanged a look with her husband. "What can we do? I'm afraid she's suicidal."

"Doona fash. I have a plan." Dougal took a deep breath. "I will erase all her memories of China. 'Twill be like she was never there. She will remember only the good progress ye're making here. But ye all must play along. Pretend she was never in China."

Gregori frowned. "That seems a bit extreme."

Abby touched his arm. "We have to do something."

"It is the only way." Dougal's heart squeezed in his chest. She wouldn't remember their night of lovemaking in Tiger Town. She wouldn't know that she'd agreed to marry him. How could he erase bits and pieces of their relationship? The holes left behind would make her suspicious.

The solution hit him like a battle-axe, and he stumbled back. The only way to protect her was to make a clean sweep. No memories of China, and no memories of him. She wouldn't suffer from the humiliation of feeling like a replacement. She would simply complete her job here, then return home to Houston, happy and proud that she'd accomplished something good.

She would be free from pain. He would take all her suffering away and heap it on himself. He would pay the price.

"I'll erase myself," he whispered.

Abby gasped.

Laszlo frowned. "Surely that is going too far."

Dougal shook his head. "It is the only way I can protect her."

He trudged down the hall and entered her dorm. She was still in bed, refusing to look at him.

He sat on the edge of her bed, his heart breaking. He would have to lose her in order to save her.

His eyes burned with tears. "I will find you again. No matter what. If it takes another three hundred years. Or a thousand years. I will find you."

She looked at him. "Are you going somewhere?"

"Aye." He placed his hand on her forehead, slipped into her mind, and began erasing.

Chapter Thirty-two

A week later

Leah finished checking her patient's blood pressure and smiled at him. "Perfect! You're one hundred percent back to normal."

"Thank you, Dr. Chin." He grinned. "Does that mean I can go home?"

She nodded, looping her stethoscope around her neck. "Tonight. We'll have one of the Vamps teleport you back."

Her patient bowed his head. "Thank you! Thank you, Dr. Chin. I can't wait to see my family again."

"And we have a parting gift for you, thanks to our benefactor, Kyo. A sack of rice for you and your family."

"Thank you!" He beamed at the other six patients, who had come out of stasis the day before. "We're free!"

They all cheered, and Leah grinned. She was so glad she'd accepted this job. At first, working with Vamps and shifters had seemed totally bizarre, but as far as she could tell, they were all a bunch of great guys who were making a difference fighting evil. They even had a resident angel, Briathos, who stopped by every day.

"Are you married, Dr. Chin?" one of the patients asked.

"You can't have her. I want her," another patient said. "Marry me, Dr. Chin. I'll give you five chickens!"

"I'll give you a pig," another boasted.

Leah laughed. "That's very sweet, but I'm married to my work."

From what she'd heard there were still close to a thousand mutated soldiers who needed to be changed back. She hoped they would all welcome the change like these guys had. They were eager to be reunited with families they hadn't seen in years. And they were angry at Master Han for turning them into mindless robots. Unpaid robots, it turned out. Most of these boys had agreed to join Master Han believing he would send their wages to their families. But once Master Han had people under his control, he no longer paid them the wage they'd been promised.

"I have more good news for you," she continued. "We're going to reimburse you for your lost wages."

Her patients clapped and cheered. "Thank you!" they shouted over and over.

Leah gave them high fives. After Angus and Roman had learned how these young men had been cheated from their earnings, they'd decided to make things right. It was a touching gesture from the Vamps, Leah thought, but also a smart move. In the future, all the cured soldiers would be on the side of the Vamps.

"I'll bring you something yummy from the cafeteria." She left the clinic as they continued to cheer.

Briathos was standing in the hallway, and he nodded at her as she passed. "You have done well. The Heavenly Father is most pleased."

"Oh. Thank you." Wow. Even God was happy with her. Did life get any better than this?

"May I be of service?" Briathos asked.

"I'm fine. Thank you." She hurried down the hall to the cafeteria, wondering why the angel asked her that every day. Maybe it was just an angelic thing.

She piled six ice cream sandwiches and six juice boxes on a tray and delivered them to her fan club in the clinic. They were still arguing over who should win her hand, though they forgot about her when they saw the ice cream.

Smiling, she strolled into the lab. "Hi, Abby. Hi, Mina."

They greeted her with smiles.

"I have serum ready for ten more patients," Abby announced. "We can have the Vamps bring more in tonight."

"Wonderful." Leah went to her worktable to finish the paperwork on the six cured ones in the clinic.

Hopefully, when the Vamps came tonight with their delivery, the good-looking one in the kilt would be with them. She'd spotted him for the first time three nights ago, and ever since then, she'd looked forward to a glimpse of him every night. Unfortunately, he always did his job quickly and left. How could she talk to him if he never looked her way?

She glanced out the window at the gray sky. It was freezing cold outside, but she enjoyed going out for a few minutes every day. She was extra careful because about a week ago, she'd slipped on an icy patch and fallen, hitting her head on a rock. She didn't remember it, but Abby said she'd suffered a concussion. That was why some of her memory was a little sketchy. She could recall Dr. Lee hiring her, and she remembered the shock of learning about Vamps and shifters at Romatech, but she couldn't recall her trip here to the school.

She dragged a hand over her head. Whatever bumps she'd incurred during her fall had gone away. She wasn't sore anywhere. It seemed like she should have had some abrasions or bruises. After all, she'd fallen on the rocky shore.

"Two hours till Laser wakes up," Gu Mina announced. She was sitting at Laszlo's table, sewing a button on his lab coat.

Leah smiled. The fox shifter and Laszlo were so cute together. It was fun watching such a sweet romance blossom. Her hand went to her chest to grasp something, but nothing was there. She frowned. It was an annoying habit, one she did several times a day, and she wasn't sure why.

"You're really serious about him, aren't you?" Abby asked.

Mina nodded. "I found out why he pulls his buttons off. Do you want to hear?" She glanced around. "But don't tell anyone."

Abby slanted a glance at Leah. "We can keep a secret."

Leah nodded. "Tell us."

"Well." Mina knotted her thread and cut it. "He grew up in a village in Hungary. Just him and his mother. Everyone thought she was a widow. And she was a—what's the word? She made fancy clothes for rich ladies."

"A seamstress?" Leah asked.

"That's it." Mina threaded her needle. "They were very poor, and she worked long hours, sewing. Laser learned as a young boy that the only way he could get attention was to pull off a button. Then she would sew it on for him and talk to him. Over the years, it became a habit."

"Oh." Abby grimaced. "He must have been lonesome."

Mina nodded. "When he was nine, he was sent away to a fancy school. A mysterious benefactor was paying for him. But the rich boys picked on Laser, and he felt so out of place that he kept pulling on his buttons."

"Poor Laszlo," Leah murmured.

Mina sewed on another button. "Then he learned that his benefactor was really his father. The man was alive, after all, and lived near the school. So every time Laser met a man, he wondered if he was meeting his father. It made him very nervous."

"No one would tell him who his father was?" Abby asked.

"No." Mina continued to sew. "After he finished college in Vienna, he set out to find his father. And then, as he traveled a dark road one night, he was attacked by vampires." She sniffed. "Poor Laser. He gave up ever finding his father. He was afraid his father would think he was a monster."

Abby sighed. "That's so sad."

Leah frowned. "Poor Laszlo." Did all the Vamps have sad stories like that? What about the gorgeous one with black hair and green eyes? He seemed so quiet and . . . intense. As if there was a huge storm of emotion carefully hidden beneath the surface. No doubt he had a fascinating story. If only she could get him to talk to her.

Was she falling for a vampire? Somehow that didn't seem strange at all. Maybe because Abby was married to one, and Gu Mina was thoroughly smitten with one. It just felt right.

She glanced at the window. "It's snowing!" She jumped to her feet, smiling. "Come on, Abby. Let's go outside."

Abby looked at the window and winced. "It looks cold."

"Just put on your coat and gloves." Leah headed for the door.

"I forgot to pack gloves," Abby muttered.

"I might have something you can use." Leah motioned for her to follow. "Come on! It'll be fun!"

She dashed down the hall, noticing that the angel was gone. He was odd that way, coming and going without warning.

In the dorm room, Leah opened her bedside table drawer and removed her hat and gloves. Her coat was hanging on a peg on the wall by the door. She pulled her suitcase out from under the bed and opened it. Her memory of packing was sketchy, but she knew she'd packed for cold weather.

She found a thick sweater and pulled it on over her long-sleeved T-shirt. Now to see if she'd packed an extra set of gloves or mittens. She dug under another sweater and spotted something red and flimsy.

A nightgown? She picked it up, and it unfolded.

"That's pretty," Abby commented as she entered the dorm room.

"I don't remember packing it." Leah dropped it back into her suitcase. Why would she pack something so flimsy and sexy for a business trip to a freezing cold island?

"Don't let it bother you," Abby murmured as she sat on her bed.

Leah searched her suitcase. "A-ha!" She pulled out a knitted mitten. "Here you go!" She tossed it back to Abby, then grabbed its twin. It snagged on something, and she winced as a thread pulled out.

"Shoot. It's caught." She pushed clothing items aside to see what had snagged the mitten. It was a half-opened chain on some kind of leather handbag.

"What is this?" She pulled it out. "A sporran?"

"Yes." Abby reached for it. "Let me see if I can unhook the mitten."

Leah passed it to her. "Where did I get a sporran?"

Abby's eyes widened. "I-I guess you must have bought it in Scotland."

"I was in Scotland?" How could she forget something like that? She'd always wanted to go to Scotland.

"You—you went with Emma and Angus." Abby worked the chain loose. "They wanted to ask Marielle about angels and demons."

"Marielle." Leah frowned, trying to remember. Flashes zipped through her mind. Inverness. A shopping trip with Marielle and her son, Gabriel. "I do remember! I bought a kilt, a blouse, and a sporran. And a red beret!"

Abby smiled sadly. "That's great that you remember. You had a wonderful time on that trip."

"I did! I met one of Marielle's angel friends. A Healer named Bunny. Isn't that crazy?"

"Yes." Abby's smile seemed strained as she placed the sporran back into the suitcase. "Let's go outside."

After fifteen minutes in the snow, Abby declared she'd had all the fun she could take and handed her mittens to Leah before going back inside.

Leah finished her miniature snowman, using small pebbles from the beach to make his eyes and smiling mouth. Half frozen, she dashed back to the dorm room. After removing her coat, hat, and gloves, she dropped the spare mittens into her suitcase.

"A sporran." She picked it up and ran her hand over the slick fur. There was something about the leather bag that made her heart expand with joy. She looked inside. It was empty except for a handful of dried heather.

Had she picked these flowers herself? She must have. Emma and Angus wouldn't have picked them for her.

She sat down on her bed, gazing at the dried flowers in her hand. Where had they come from? Somehow, it seemed terribly important that she remember. She strained her mind, but she couldn't recall Emma or Angus being with her on that trip. But who else would have teleported her to Scotland?

"*Here,*" a male voice flashed across her memory. She had a sudden vision of a man giving her the bouquet of heather. She couldn't see his face, but he wore a kilt, and his deep voice was laced with a Scottish accent. "*To remember yer first trip to Scotland.*"

"*Thank you,*" she responded, dropping the heather into her sporran. "*I'll always remember this.*"

"Agh." She leaned forward, rubbing her brow. If this moment in Scotland was so important to remember, why was she having so much trouble recalling it?

She set the heather on her bedside table. Maybe if she kept looking at it, her memories would come back.

She had a terrible feeling she was missing something important. Her hand went to her chest again, grasping at air. There should be a necklace there. So where was it?

Leah said a cheerful good-bye to the last three patients as they teleported away with Angus, J.L., and Kyo. The Vamps were returning the cured men home, and it was taking them two trips to transport all six.

The gorgeous one hadn't come. Swallowing her disappointment, she strode to the cafeteria to eat supper with Abby.

She sat at a table next to Abby and dug into her salad. Green. The color stared up at her. Green eyes. Did the man who had given her the heather have green eyes? She frowned. Angus had green eyes, but she couldn't imagine him giving her flowers. He was totally dedicated to his wife. Could it be . . . ?

"What happened to the other Vamp?"

"What other Vamp?" Abby bit into a chicken leg.

"The Scottish one with black hair and green eyes."

Abby choked, and grabbed a glass of water to

drink. "Oh. Well." She wiped her watery eyes with a napkin. "There have been a lot of Vamps coming through here in the last few weeks. Some of them are staying at Tiger Town in China."

Something skittered at the edge of Leah's memory, but she couldn't put her finger on it. "This memory loss stinks."

Abby winced. "I'm sure you'll get better with time."

Leah sighed. Why did everything seem like a clue? The broken chain on the sporran. The red nightgown. The handful of heather. The phantom necklace. Green eyes. Her lack of abrasions and bruises. She felt like she had the pieces of a jigsaw puzzle but no idea what the final picture was supposed to look like.

An hour later, when Yoshi told them the Vamps had brought in new soldiers, she rushed to the clinic, hoping to see him. Angus, J.L., and Kyo were there, dropping soldiers onto stretchers.

The gorgeous one wasn't there.

A surge of loss hit her so hard that she gasped from the pain.

"Are you all right?" Abby asked her as she put one of the new soldiers into stasis.

"I-I'm fine." But she wasn't. Something was wrong. Why would she feel such a terrible loss over someone she'd never met?

Chapter Thirty-three

 $\mathcal{F}$ ive nights later, she finally spotted him. Leah's heart leaped in her chest when she saw him in the clinic. He was with the other Vamps, delivering a new set of mutated soldiers.

She studied him from the back. He was wearing pants tonight, black pants with a black sweater and jacket. His long hair was tied at the nape of his neck with a strip of leather. Knives were strapped to his legs, and a sword was sheathed on his back. He was huge, powerful, and absolutely gorgeous.

She walked up to the stretcher where he'd deposited a soldier. "Hi. I'm Leah Chin."

He stiffened. He glanced halfway toward her. "Good evening." Then he turned and strode from the room.

"What's with him?" Leah asked Abby, who was standing by the door, a pale look on her face.

"Nothing." Abby dashed over to the stretcher to put the soldier into stasis.

The other Vamps nodded at Leah and left the room.

With a sigh, she wandered over to Abby. "Why did he leave like that? Does he dislike me? Is he married?"

Abby shook her head.

"Is he gay?"

A pained look crossed Abby's face. "No."

Leah groaned inwardly. Why did her heart sing whenever she saw that man? Why did she miss him so terribly when she didn't see him? Why was she thinking about him all the time when he was a stranger?

Or was he?

"Do I know him?"

Abby winced. "I-I'm busy right now."

"Right. Sorry." Leah quickly took the vital signs on the new soldiers, then headed to the lab with their charts.

Briathos was standing in the hall, and he bowed his head as she walked by.

"Hi." She never quite knew what to say to an angel. She wasn't even sure if he was completely there. His image tended to shimmer if she didn't stare at him, and staring seemed a bit rude.

"May I be of service?" he asked.

"I'm fine. Thank you." She walked into the lab and set the charts on her worktable. The outdoor lights were on, and she spotted movement outside. She moved closer to the window.

It was him. He was standing on the bluff, looking at the sea.

This was her chance. She ran to her room, threw on her coat, hat, and gloves, then stepped out the front door.

He was gone. *Dammit.* She walked to the bluff. Had he teleported away?

No. There he was. On the beach. Carefully, she made her way down the icy stairs and across the pebbles. She didn't want to slip and clonk her head again.

"Hi!" She glanced up and was taken aback by the stark expression on his face. Sheesh. Was her company that bad?

"I was wondering if we'd ever met before?" She winced. Wasn't that an ancient pickup line?

"Ye may have seen me before," he answered quietly. "I work for Angus."

His voice had a deep, lyrical tone that sounded familiar. Her hand went to her chest for the phantom necklace.

He was even more gorgeous close up. Strong jaw, beautiful mouth, incredibly green eyes. A wide forehead and eyebrows that seemed so expressive. Why did he look like he was in pain? "Are you all right?"

He nodded. "How are you? Are ye happy?"

"Yes." She smiled, hoping he would smile back, but the pain in his eyes only seemed to deepen.

Her eyes lowered to his chest, and she flinched. "What—" It was a jade dragon. *Her* jade dragon. She winced. Why would she think that?

He grabbed the jade pendant and stuffed it underneath his sweater.

Why was he hiding it from her? She rubbed her brow. "Are you sure we haven't met?"

"I need to go now. Good evening." He strode toward the stairs, then glanced back. "Ye shouldna stay out here in the cold."

Her heart fluttered at the way he said "*oot.*" So familiar. Why couldn't she remember?

With vampire speed, he dashed up the stairs and into the school.

She huffed, her breath vaporizing in the cold air.

For a big, tough vampire, he scared off awfully easy. She turned to gaze at the dark waves crashing on the pebbly shore.

A memory flitted by. Waves crashing on a beach of golden sand, warm beneath her bare feet. The scent of flowers and tropical plants in the air. And so much love. She was full of love. And she felt so loved. She opened a small box, and inside was a pendant. The jade dragon.

The memory dissipated like a cloud of smoke, and she reached once again to hold the phantom necklace. Only this time, she knew what it should be.

He was wearing her necklace. Why?

Who was he? And why the hell couldn't she remember him?

Twelve nights he'd survived. It felt more like twelve years. Dougal had asked Angus for a transfer, but it had been refused. Angus needed him here because he could speak Chinese. A sad, pathetic part of him had wanted to stay so he could make sure Leah was happy. But each time he saw her, it was like being stabbed through the gut.

He trudged into the cafeteria to warm up a bottle of blood. Just as he pulled it out of the microwave, Abby marched up to him, glaring at him.

"It was a mistake," she whispered angrily. "You shouldn't have done it."

He groaned inwardly. "I doona want to talk about it." Even though he questioned himself constantly. Leah had been wronged by Darafer, but had he committed a second wrong to make things right?

"We have to talk about it," Abby insisted.

"She's happy. She told me she was happy. There is nothing more to say." As long as she was happy, he could tell himself he'd done the right thing. He took a swig from his bottle. "I'm leaving as soon as I finish this meal. They're expecting me in Tiger Town."

"Wait." Abby grabbed his arm. "She-she's attracted to you."

His heart squeezed in his chest. He hadn't counted on that. But he should have. No matter where they were, their souls would reach out for each other.

"If you start courting her again, I'm going to freak out," Abby said.

"I willna court her."

"This whole thing is driving me up the wall. You get to run off and hide, but I'm stuck here having to lie to her. I had to tell her she went to Scotland with Angus and Emma. I can't do it anymore!"

"Ye agreed to my decision."

"I know!" Abby dragged a hand through her hair. "I was so worried about her."

"Aye. I was desperate, too."

"But now—" Abby grimaced. "She loved you so much. It seems criminal to take that away from her."

"I had to do something. I couldna bear to see her in pain. I should have protected her, but I failed her. 'Twas my fault she was suffering."

Abby's eyes widened. "Oh my gosh. You—you did this to punish yourself."

"Nay! I did it to save her. It was the only way to protect her. I took away her suffering."

Abby's eyes glistened with tears. "You took her suffering onto yourself."

"So? Should I no' do that when I love her?"

Abby punched his chest. "She loves you, too, you noble idiot! And you took that away from her." With a huff, she marched out the door.

Dougal finished his bottle, then teleported to Tiger Town. Already the were-tigers were starting to gather in the courtyard for the Grand Tiger's two-week memorial. Rajiv had asked him to play the tune his grandfather had loved.

Dougal's gaze wandered to the tiger statue he'd broken with his prosthesis. He'd been filled with so much rage and frustration. Now he was full of doubt and despair.

Had he made a terrible mistake? He'd been devastated by his failure to protect Leah. How many times had he sworn never to fail her? He'd failed Li Lei, and for that, he'd suffered almost three hundred years of shame and regret.

Then a miracle had happened, and he'd gotten a second chance. Li Lei had come back to forgive him, but he'd failed her again. And Leah had suffered terribly for it. How could she ever forgive him?

How could he forgive himself?

He strode down the alley to the guesthouse to get his pipes. Was that why he'd been so eager to erase Leah's memories? Not just to ease her suffering but to punish himself as well?

Because he couldn't forgive himself. He stumbled to a stop. What a fool he'd been. Why had he longed all these years for Li Lei's forgiveness? The fact that she'd come back for him meant she still loved him. Her love had spanned the centuries to find him.

She had been the one to keep the vow. She'd found

him. And she'd always forgiven him. Always loved him.

Would Leah do the same? Would she find him again? Would she cling to her love for him no matter what?

Tears burned his eyes. He didn't deserve such devotion. But he wouldn't let his shame and regret get in the way. Somehow, he would move forward. Forgive himself. And beg Leah to take him back.

With a groan, Leah gave up. She'd been trying for ten minutes to remember, but it was only giving her a headache.

She crunched across the rocky shore and climbed the steps to the school. Was the mystery man still inside? She could track him down, but he'd probably just run away. Or teleport away. And never come back.

Inside the foyer, Briathos was standing. He inclined his head. "May I be of service?"

"No, I'm fine. Thank you." She wandered back to her dorm to take off her coat, hat, and gloves. If she was going to piece together this jigsaw puzzle, she would need more pieces. More clues. Her gaze fell to her suitcase under the bed. There had been several clues there. Maybe she'd find more.

She squatted down to pull it out, when something caught her eye. A piece of paper sticking out just a tiny bit from underneath her mattress. She pulled it out, and sitting on her bed, she unfolded it to read it.

Dear Leah,

I know I frighten you, but I pray you will give me a chance. I know my chance is small, for you are so clever and beautiful. How could I ever be worthy of you?

You are a treasure to behold, a sweet melody to my ears.

You shine light into my dark nights and bring warmth to my cold heart.

You fill me with hope that all things are possible, even an eternity of love.

Dougal

Tears filled her eyes. A terrible longing welled up in her chest, and she cried out. He had loved her. And she had loved him. *Dougal.*

How could she have lost him?

It was him. The mystery man. It had to be him. *Dougal.*

She read the note again, her tears falling down on the paper.

What had happened? Why were they apart? Why couldn't she remember?

Her skin chilled with a sudden thought. Why didn't other people remember?

She stood, clasping the note to her chest. Other people had to know. Nothing was private around here.

Wiping her face dry, she marched down the hall to the lab. Abby would know. But if she knew, why was she keeping it a secret?

"May I be of service?" Briathos asked as she passed by.

"I'm fi—" She halted. Why did she keep lying to an angel? She wasn't fine. Her eyes burned with more tears.

She turned to look at him. "What kind of service can you do?"

He regarded her sadly. "Dear soul, what is it you need?"

A tear fell down her cheek. "I need to remember."

Chapter Thirty-four

*L*eah approached the angel. "Can you help me?"

"Yes." Briathos watched her intently. "But I must warn you. The good memories you seek will not come alone. There will be others that will cause you great pain. You cannot have the good without the bad."

Another tear rolled down her face, and she clutched Dougal's note tightly to her chest. "I'll do it."

A flicker of light made her blink, then she realized another angel had joined them. "Bunny."

Buniel smiled. "You remember me."

She nodded. "You healed my ankle."

"She wishes to have her memory restored," Briathos announced.

Buniel's smile faded. "Are you sure? Some of your memories will be painful."

She swallowed hard. "I understand. I'm ready."

Buniel rested a hand on her brow, then stepped back. "It is done."

She blinked. "But I don't remember anything."

"The memories are there. You must find the key to unlock them."

"The key?" She gave Buniel an exasperated look. "What key?"

"Look into your heart," Buniel replied.

She groaned. Why did the angels have to work in such mysterious ways? She glanced down at her chest, where she was still clutching the note from Dougal.

Her heart swelled with longing. She needed him. He had her heart. "Is Dougal the key?" When she found him, would she remember everything?

She dashed down the hall to the lab. "Where is Dougal?"

Abby gasped.

Gregori put a protective arm around his wife. "Do you remember him, Leah?"

"I'll remember everything if I can just see him. Where is he?"

Gregori winced. "This is not a good time."

"He's in Tiger Town," Laszlo said.

"Laszlo." Abby gave him a look of warning.

"I will not continue with this lie." Laszlo stood, pushing back his stool. "They belong together. It was meant to be."

Mina gazed up at him with wonder in her eyes. "You're so brave, Laser."

"I need one of you Vamps to take me to Tiger Town," Leah insisted.

Gregori winced again. "They're having a memorial service tonight. It would be bad form for you to show up. Given the circumstances."

What circumstances? "I need to see Dougal!"

"We will take you," Briathos said behind her.

She started. "Y-you can teleport me?"

Buniel smiled. "Put your coat on. It's cold outside."

She headed down the hall, then stopped, glancing back. Buniel was wearing a white hooded robe, and Briathos was dressed in his usual attire—pants and sleeveless tunic topped with a breastplate. "Don't you guys get cold?"

Buniel shook his head, smiling.

Briathos frowned. "We are not of this world."

"Right." Like that explained anything. She ran to her dorm, threw on her coat, hat, and gloves, then dashed back to the foyer, where the angels were waiting.

Abby was standing nearby with her husband. "Be careful." Her eyes glistened with tears. "And if you remember everything, try not to be angry. We were worried about you."

"I'll be fine." Leah gave Abby a hug. "Thank you for being a good friend."

Abby sniffed. "Go on. You're going to make me cry."

Leah's eyes misted with tears, and she faced the angels. "How do we do this?"

Buniel wrapped an arm around her shoulders. "Simple."

A flash of light blinded her for a second, and she stumbled. Buniel steadied her.

She looked around. They were in an alley between two stone walls.

"This way." Briathos motioned for her and Buniel to follow. "Remain quiet. They're having a memorial service."

He led them around a small house built in the Chinese style, then up onto a covered porch where they would remain hidden in shadow. Before them stretched a stone courtyard, filled with people sitting on mats woven from reeds.

These had to be the were-tigers, Leah thought. They were all facing the palace, their hands pressed together at their chests while they prayed. Who was the memorial service for?

Two men emerged from the palace and descended the steps to the courtyard. One she recognized as Rajiv, though he was dressed much fancier than she'd ever seen. The other was the mystery man. He was dressed in a kilt and was carrying Uilleann pipes.

And nothing happened. No memories. Wasn't he Dougal?

She turned to the angels. "What's wrong? Why don't I remember?"

"All will be revealed in due course," Briathos said.

She frowned at him. "What the heck does that mean?"

His mouth twitched. "You two are well suited."

"Patience, grasshopper." Buniel motioned for her to sit beside him.

She sat beside the Healer, while Briathos remained stiffly erect.

The mystery man sat on the steps and began to play his pipes. The plaintive sound filled the courtyard. A beautiful, sad song.

A flash shot through her mind. She'd heard that song before. Dougal had played it on the grounds at Romatech. More flashes zoomed by. Her initial attraction. Stealing into the basement at the townhouse to look at him. Their trip to the Empire State Building.

Their first kiss. His trip to the hair salon, and her confession. More kissing in the gazebo. The trip to Scotland. The heather he gave her. Their sporrans hooked
together. Their lovemaking in her apartment.

"I remember," she whispered. She remembered
everything. The teasing, the longing, the joy.

The sad song swelled, louder and more poignant,
as if Dougal was pouring all his emotion into it. And
then the bad memories poured in. The kidnapping.
The terror. The demon bite.

The murder.

With a gasp, she doubled over. *Oh God, no.* The memorial service was for the Grand Tiger. And she'd
killed him. A sob choked in her throat.

Buniel patted her on the back. "I know, dear soul.
It's bad."

"H-how do I live with this?"

"There is no cure for this kind of pain," Buniel said
sadly. "You cannot have the joy without the pain."

Tears ran down her cheeks. "Why?"

"As long as evil exists, there will be pain," Briathos muttered.

"But we can give you some comfort." Buniel
wrapped an arm around her and squeezed.

An instant wave of peace swept through her.
"Thank you." The pain was still there, but dulled
a little.

"Come on, big guy." Buniel waved Briathos over.
"Help me out."

Briathos shifted his weight. "I'm not a Healer."

"You're still an angel. Come on." Buniel motioned
for him to move closer.

Briathos inched over and awkwardly patted Leah
on the head. "There, there, dear soul."

Another wave of comfort trickled through her. "Thank you."

Briathos eased back, frowning.

Then suddenly a flood of love washed over her. Her heart stilled, stunned by the power. It gave her strength. Strength to endure. And hope. Hope that she could live with the pain. And wisdom. The assurance that the Heavenly Father still loved her and forgave her. And if the Father could forgive her, surely she should forgive herself.

She gazed at Buniel in wonder. "Did you do that?"

He smiled with tears in his eyes. "That was Josephine. She loves you greatly."

Leah smiled back, more tears running down her face. "Thank you, Josephine." She wiped her face. She could do this. She could move forward with her life. Loving Dougal and fighting evil.

The music continued, so sad and sweet. "His music was the key."

Buniel nodded. "It was his music that originally connected your souls. Close your eyes and listen. There's more to remember."

She let the music envelop her, and more flashes flitted through her mind. She was sitting outside a slave's hut, listening to him play. Night after night, she listened to his music. Then she was running with him to the harbor. The sun was bright, glistening off the waves. And Dougal was young. A bit thinner. But his eyes were the same. He looked at her with so much love.

He didn't want to leave her. He wanted her to run away with him and live with him forever.

And she refused.

The last tearful good-bye and his parting vow.

I will find you. No matter what. If it takes a thousand years, I will find you.

Leah opened her eyes. She was Li Lei. She'd always loved Dougal. And she'd found him again.

Dougal finished his music and moved quietly across the courtyard.

"Come." Briathos motioned for her to follow, and he led her back to the stone alley. "He will pass this way."

"Call me if you need me." Buniel gave her a hug, then vanished.

She turned to Briathos. "You were trying to help me for days, weren't you?"

He inclined his head.

"Why did you want me to remember? Are you a romantic at heart?"

He looked taken aback. "Of course not. I'm a God Warrior. I do not indulge in such—" He cleared his throat. "Dougal stole your memories without your permission. He violated your free will. I wanted to set things right."

"I see." Leah smiled to herself. He was a romantic. "Well, thank you." She glanced at him, but he was gone.

Dougal crossed the courtyard, his heart aching. How had he managed to make such a mess of things? How could he live without Leah? How could he live with her? How could he explain to her what he'd done?

He turned into the alley and halted with a jerk. His pipes fell to the ground and let out a mournful cry.

"Leah?" Why was she here? Why was her face wet from tears, and her eyes red and swollen? "Y-ye remember?"

She nodded. "Yes." She glanced back at the guesthouse at the end of the alley. "We made love there, didn't we?"

His heart squeezed. "How . . . ?"

"The angels helped me." She fished a piece of paper out of her coat pocket. "And then there were clues. Like this love letter from a guy named Dougal. Apparently, we were very much in love, so it totally confounds me that you would erase that!" Her voice rose to a shout.

"I-I can explain." He winced inwardly. Could he?

She stuffed the note back into her pocket. "I don't know whether to hug you or slap you. We had a beautiful affair to remember, and you made me forget? How could you erase everything we went through?"

"I failed you. I failed to protect you. And I failed to convince you that I love you. Ye thought ye were a replacement. And ye were suffering so much. I couldna bear it. I was trying to save you."

She said nothing, just continued to watch him with tears glimmering in her eyes.

"I'm sorry, Leah. I was desperate to take away yer suffering. Abby says I was a noble idiot, and she's right. I made a terrible mistake."

"I think I was the one who made a mistake." Leah walked slowly toward him. "We were there at the harbor, and you were begging me to go with you, and I refused. I didn't want to bring shame on my family." She snorted. "I guess I was a noble idiot, too."

His heart stilled. "Y-ye remember that?"

She smiled, lifting her hands in the air. "I remember everything."

"Ye remember Li Lei?"

She nodded. "I would say your kissing has vastly improved over the years."

He stiffened. "Ye were my first."

"You were my first, too."

"Can ye forgive me?"

"For what? I was the one who refused to run away with you."

"I promised to find you again, and I was too late. I saw yer boat capsize in the storm."

She sighed. "I don't think I fought very hard to survive. I had realized my mistake, and I didn't want to live without you." She wiped her eyes. "Can you forgive me?"

"For what? Ye came back to me. Ye gave me another chance."

She frowned at him. "And then you tried to erase it all. Were you going to wait another three hundred years, hoping that I would reincarnate and find you again?"

He winced.

She huffed. "That's all fine and dandy for you. But what about me? Was I supposed to miss out on this lifetime? Don't you dare mess with my head again!"

"I dinna think ye would miss me if ye couldna remember. Now I realize I was punishing myself. I couldna forgive myself for failing to protect you."

"How could you have protected me? Dougal, there was nothing you could do. And when the demon bit me, there was nothing I could do. We just have to live with it."

He nodded. "I am trying to forgive myself."

She smiled sadly. "I'm trying, too."

He stepped closer. "So . . . am I still at a hundred percent?"

"Yes."

He took her hand. "And ye still want to marry me?"

She nodded. "Yes."

"Ye agreed to have five children."

Her eyes widened. "I did? I don't remember that."

His mouth twitched. "Nay. Ye dinna. I was just testing."

She swatted his shoulder.

He pulled her into his arms. "Did ye want to molest me in my room over there?"

She splayed her hands over his chest. "Yes. And I want my dragon back."

"The one in my kilt?"

She snorted. "The one you're hiding under your sweater." She found the chain and tugged the jade dragon out. "I can't believe you stole my necklace."

"It kept me from going insane. I missed you something fierce." He kissed her brow.

She wrapped her arms around his neck. "I love you, Dougal. I have always loved you."

He hugged her tight. "I love you, too."

With a playful shove, she pushed him back, then scooped up his pipes and ran for the guesthouse.

He followed her. "Och, lass, I see ye're in a hurry to get under my kilt."

She laughed. "You wish."

"I do wish."